PENGUIN B
Retrogr

Emilee is a self-proclaimed Somerset Cowgirl, born and raised in a seaside town in Somerset, England, where she's one of few people wearing cowboy boots to the pub.

With her dad, who spent years working in Formula 1 while Emilee was growing up, she began attending World Endurance Championship races. Her love for motorsport grew rapidly, and Spa Francorchamps started to feel like home.

When she isn't writing, she is holed up in local seaside restaurants (Greek food is her fave), hanging out with her dog, Fudge, or rewatching *Grey's Anatomy* for the millionth time.

Retrograde

EMILEE CARTER

PENGUIN BOOKS

PENGUIN BOOKS

UK | USA | Canada | Ireland | Australia
India | New Zealand | South Africa

Penguin Books, Penguin Random House UK,
One Embassy Gardens, 8 Viaduct Gardens, London SW11 7BW

penguin.co.uk
global.penguinrandomhouse.com

Penguin
Random House
UK

First published by Penguin Books 2024
002

Set in 12.5/14.75pt Garamond MT
Typeset by Falcon Oast Graphic Art Ltd
Printed in Great Britain by Clays Ltd, Elcograf S.p.A.

The authorized representative in the EEA is Penguin Random House Ireland,
Morrison Chambers, 32 Nassau Street, Dublin D02 YH68

A CIP catalogue record for this book is available from the British Library

ISBN: 978–1–405–95807–3

www.greenpenguin.co.uk

To my parents for believing in me so wholeheartedly, to the Lucies of the world who have big dreams and even bigger hearts, and lastly to my girls for showing me that true love can come from friendship too.

If you ever thought it was too late to save yourself, you were wrong.

I

'Honey, I'm home!' Lucie flung the door open, expecting to be greeted with the typical chaos of the Jensen-Moretz household. Instead, she was met with silence.

Silence which lasted all of ten seconds before a grey and white ball of fur came hurtling towards her, covered in dirt. Ford. Her best friend's aptly named step-dog. He put his paws up on her shoulders and licked her face, a habit Faith had spent the entirety of her marriage so far trying to train him out of. 'Ford Moretz, get back here right now!'

Lucie encouraged him down before he could get into any more trouble as Faith rounded the corner, her denim dungarees covered in a combination of muddy pawprints and paint splatters, and her blonde hair, now a few inches past her shoulders, dripping wet. 'Did I catch you at a bad time, Jensen?'

'What kind of racing driver decides to start painting the exterior of the garage during race week? I'm about ready to strangle my husband. Anyway, why are you here early?'

'Sorry.' Lucie smiled sheepishly. 'I was trying to surprise you before I checked into the hotel. Brett and Marco aren't here yet, and I didn't want to be lonely.'

'Oh! You're welcome to join the madhouse. Jules let his second child out in the fields unattended, and he

I

burrowed. Again. Came back all proud and promptly shook his fur coat. Mud everywhere, all over our fresh paint job. Julien is in zen mode so of course he's unbothered. I get the hosepipe out, Ford thinks it's a game.'

Lucie scratched behind the husky's ears. 'He lets the dog get away with everything.'

'Same can't be said for his *actual* child who is far better behaved.'

Lucie laughed and shuffled further away from the front door, finally managing to close it behind her. Julien's daughter Jasmine was an angel of a kid, and Faith had hit the jackpot with her new family. Stepping into a maternal role had come naturally for her and the only thing Jasmine ever asked for was the chance to attend a race. Oh, and VIP tickets to see Taylor Swift which, between her dad and his teammates, she had managed to bag for her birthday.

'Where's he at? Out back?'

'Wherever there's work to be done, that's where he'll be.'

They grabbed a fruit juice on their way out, and as she stepped onto the patio, Lucie's heart skipped a beat. As a social media manager for the IEC, one of the biggest motorsport organisations in the world, she had known Julien for the majority of her career and he had owned his compact, but architecturally beautiful Malmedy farmhouse the entire time, but the view never failed to amaze her. The trees of the Ardennes Forest lined the property, but in the foreground were lush green fields which all belonged to Julien.

He even had stables, a new addition, where he let the neighbours keep their horses and taught local kids to ride. When he was here, anyway. He and Faith split their time between Belgium and Hawaii, where Jasmine lived with her grandparents while Faith and Julien were travelling for races and team events.

'Carolan!' Julien dropped his paintbrush, right back in the sage-green pot of paint, and stood up to give her a hug. 'Where's Brett?'

'Late. He detoured to Brussels to meet . . . Casey Winters? I think? I can't keep up with which drivers he hangs out with and when any more, to be honest. Anyway, he'll be here in the morning.'

'Seems strange seeing you here without him.' Julien pulled a face.

'Feels weird, too. He keeps disappearing on me for weekends with the lads. Literally left me at a resort in Marbella a couple of months back in the middle of our stay.'

'Please don't say "lads" again.' Faith curled her lip in disgust. 'You're too American.'

'I'm Italian.'

'Born and raised in America.'

'Point taken. Am I still allowed to say "shagging"?'

Faith rolled her eyes. That had been Lucie's favourite British slang word when she'd first met her two seasons ago, when Faith had joined Revolution Racing as a social media manager and the pair of them had been put in charge of the main IEC socials, and she had been relentless in using it whenever she could. 'Fine.'

'Marco still comes into town tonight?' Julien quizzed. 'I'll get him to come here. We can have a chilled couple of days before we all head to the hotel and get to work. I'm going down to the track tomorrow though, just to admire our girl.'

By 'girl', he meant this season's Revolution Racing car. His pride and joy, and the car he shared with Brett Anderson and Marco De Luca. And the mechanics, engineers and team bosses, but primarily, she belonged to the drivers. They were the ones who had to learn every part of her as they careened around the twists and turns of racetracks across the world, and they were the ones who consistently took her over the finish line in front of hundreds of thousands of spectators. Usually in a position that put them on the podium.

This season, she was called 'Lola', which was some sort of Marvel reference. It had been Marco's turn to name the car and he was two years deep into consuming anything and everything to do with the franchise. Brett liked to go for names that sounded like they belonged to someone's grandma, and Julien always went for something cheesy and cliché.

'Where are Esme and Bea? They didn't tag along either?' Faith asked.

'Bea is still in Paris, doing some last-minute shopping because, you know, the pit lane is also a catwalk when your name is Beatrix Miller.'

'Wouldn't it be hilarious if Gabriel and the other CEOs introduced an official uniform for the photographers? Something really dull like black jeans and an

IEC polo shirt.' Julien chuckled to himself as he cleaned the paintbrush.

Bea was one of their closest friends, head of photography for the IEC, and the girls' business partner for their women in motorsport campaign. The friendship part of their relationship was a new thing for Lucie, who had maintained a hatred for the woman until Faith came along.

Faith had shown everyone that Bea had a very different side to her, despite the reputation she'd gained from entertaining the drivers in the bedroom and spending their money like it was going out of fashion. Julien included. That phase of her life was the unfortunate result of a mountain of insecurity that came with being thrown into the lifestyle of the rich and famous with little time to prepare. But even Faith's influence couldn't deter her from dressing to the nines everywhere she went.

'We all know Gabriel is scared of her,' Faith laughed. 'Esme is at a team event for Eden Racing so she'll be here later in the week.'

'I miss her, it's a shame we can't have her on our team too.' Faith pouted.

Esme was the newest addition to their circle. She had always been around but on the outskirts. Because she did social media for an opposing team, she never had much reason to hang around with Revolution. That was until Faith, Bea and Lucie saw her potential and got to know her a little more over the course of last season, and decided to bring her on board as their fourth business partner for Girls Off Track.

She was softly spoken and shy when she wasn't in work mode, and she was several years younger than the rest of them who were all in their late twenties or early thirties now, but she just fit in with the group. She had the same work ethic, ethos and determination to bring more women into motorsport that they all shared. She was also willing to put up with the chaos that followed the Revolution drivers, Brett especially, and wasn't easily embarrassed by their antics.

'You saw her last week.' Lucie rolled her eyes. 'You spent hours traipsing around London, looking at wall-paper samples for the office bathrooms.'

The Girls Off Track London office was the next chapter in their growing endeavour, and decorating it had almost been more stressful than getting the programme up and running, but a nice kind of stress. Some of the hardest decisions they had to make were based on colour schemes and cushion textures and seating layouts, not 'how many podcast guests can we afford this quarter' or 'where's our next workshop going to be?' That had all fallen into place easily as the company grew.

So, when Bea had suggested a stereotypical pink colour scheme for the entire office, they had all agreed because it was a fun colour to work with. They had even bagged a pink racing car to display in the foyer. It had been a gift from one of the female-run IEC teams, who had jumped at the chance to be able to contribute to a cause so close to their heart.

They wanted women to walk into their office and be wowed by bold prints and the eclectic look of the place with lush green velvet sofas and brass lamps, to feel less like they'd stepped into a formal meeting space and more like they were having coffee and cake in their living room. It allowed for creative freedom and frankly, Lucie thought the men of the motorsport industry should take notes. How did anyone come up with ground-breaking ideas while staring at blank, white walls? Where was the inspiration? Well, clearly they managed, but she liked their way of doing things far better.

The podcast now had a designated studio space, with equipment that had made Lucie's eyes almost fall out of her head when she saw the price. Faith, the expert on sound recording and new technology, had insisted this was what they needed, but Lucie had struggled to grasp why they couldn't just use the portable equipment they'd been working with up until now.

It certainly softened the blow when they'd posted photos of the new studio on the business's social media accounts. In an age where podcasts were the in-thing, and with Faith and Bea's history with *Across The Line*, their engagement from that post alone had been astronomical. It had been the first post they'd made about the new office, and weeks before the opening, their follower count was sitting at a million.

The paddock was excited. There was a buzz about it; drivers were spreading the word, begging to be on the podcast, signing their daughters and sisters up for workshops. Girls Off Track was working, and they had barely got started. You couldn't walk ten feet through any race paddock now without seeing a young girl wearing their merchandise. They were still struggling to keep up with stock demands, having only *just* signed a contract with a new manufacturer, and they were working on building a merchandise shop in the office's reception area. A new collection was high on their agenda for this season.

'So, tell me, how was Sri Lanka?' Faith confiscated the hosepipe from Ford's mouth in an unbelievably calm manner considering water was still dribbling out of the end as he flung it around, soaking her.

'Incredible. You two need to go!' Lucie gushed. 'The hotel was probably the best I have ever stayed in, and the *food*. Wow.'

'We're so sorry we couldn't make it! Jasmine was stressed about exams so we wanted to be in Hawaii with her. We figured by your lack of updates that you were having a fab time! Brett made your birthday special?'

'We hiked to watch the sunrise at Ella Rock and he presented me with a picnic breakfast. I think he paid someone at the hotel to do it, but still. It's the thought that counts.' Lucie laughed as she remembered wondering where Brett could possibly have managed to get all the ingredients together for the picnic. He'd even got a wicker basket.

Sri Lanka had originally been a group trip planned for Lucie's birthday week, but as each of their friends had to drop out for various, very valid reasons, she had wanted to cancel the whole thing and visit her family instead. Brett had refused to let that happen because he knew Lucie was desperate to tick Sri Lanka off her bucket list, so he had bought the non-refundable tickets and hotel rooms from everyone and paid for Lucie's parents and siblings to go with them. Lucie rarely saw her siblings, who lived in Los Angeles, and had been slacking on visiting her parents in Tuscany. She'd ended up with the best of both worlds and the only person out of pocket was Brett.

But that was Brett. He did that a lot. Threw his money around like it was nothing, bought Lucie anything she wanted and refused to take things back to the store when she told him it was too much. Fancy dinners, trips away with all the luxuries when she had originally planned something more budget friendly, more in keeping with her salary and lifestyle.

His world had exploded in line with the IEC's new approach to social media, and he had more followers and brand deals than he knew what to do with. She knew he had boatloads of money, and an actual boat. Or two. All the Revolution Racing drivers did, as did most of the grid. Yachts in Monaco were the norm. But it made her uncomfortable when he spoiled her like a husband would spoil a wife when Brett and Lucie were just . . . Brett and Lucie. They were co-workers, best friends. But that was where they drew the line.

'I cannot *wait* for Vegas.' Julien was practically buzzing as he snapped Lucie out of her thoughts. Now that his daughter was a couple of years older than when he had first met Faith, he was able to travel a lot more freely with the team in between races, and it meant he could finally come on their annual Vegas trip for Brett's birthday in a couple of weeks.

'You,' Faith pointed a finger at him, 'need to focus. Put the paintbrush down, stop gassing, and get your ass inside. Your racing sim awaits.'

'I'm a master at what I do, babe. I have time for another coat.' He pouted like a child being told off.

'Julien, you haven't been on it at all today. You won't be one of the best racing drivers in the world if you don't work at it.'

'My mind needs to keep busy with other things.' He waved his paintbrush for effect.

'Your hands need to keep busy, too.'

Lucie watched them bicker back and forth like she was watching a tennis match.

'My hands will be plenty busy later on tonight.' He gazed at her with a disgustingly lovey-dovey look on his face.

'Oh, *ew*! Not in front of the children.' Lucie covered her ears.

'Inside.' Faith gestured for him to leave, not taking any of his shit.

Wrangling Julien, Brett and Marco was much like running a crèche, but nobody was better suited to the job than Lucie and Faith. Although they were only their social media managers, they were trusted to keep the team in line because they had the whole close relationship thing working in their favour. People often came to them and asked them to talk sense into them or push them into the right headspace before or even after a race. After all, Revolution Racing were a team, and that went beyond the three drivers.

'I'll tell you what, Jensen.' Lucie breathed in the fresh air, the scent of pine and earth filling her nostrils and making her feel relaxed. 'It feels good to be back.'

'Here's to one hell of a season.'

'Mars!' Lucie jumped into Marco's arms the second he walked into the garage.

'Hey, Lucie!' He spun her round, his small frame not much bigger than hers but certainly a lot sturdier. 'I'm sorry I never made it to Julien's. When my flight got diverted via Switzerland, I figured I may as well go and visit my brother and nieces. It's been a while since I saw them.'

'Oh, that's fine. It's good to see you.'

'You, too. How's my favourite fake Italian doing?'

'I am not a fake! Both of my parents are Italian born and bred. It is not my fault I was raised in Hell on Earth.' She scowled.

'LA is nice! It has . . . beaches, uh, Hollywood?' He ran a hand through his curls, trying to find the words. Marco hated pretty much anywhere outside of Europe. He said he thought Hawaii was okay, but who could ever hate a paradise like that?

'It's no Italy though, right?'

'Exactly. Have you seen Brett, yet?'

They were down at the track while the team set up, being nosy and overseeing the inner workings. Lucie and Faith had got some content for socials already and held meetings with the social media personnel who were here early for other teams.

They were able to take more of a back seat this season because there were only one or two new staff, and everyone else was well-versed on how the IEC, and Lucie and Faith, wanted things done and what their team principals liked and didn't like. The only things they were stricter on were longer videos as they would lose engagement rate, and short-form video trends which had sexual undertones. The fans may love those, but the sponsors not so much.

'There she is!' an Australian accent boomed, answering Marco's question.

'Found him.'

Lucie turned but before she could take a step towards him, Brett was sweeping her up into his arms. 'Hey, my sunshine girl.' He placed one hand on the back of her head and inhaled in an exaggerated manner. 'Mm, your hair smells like coconuts.'

'Hello to you too, Anderson.' Marco threw his arms up in exasperation and Brett instantly dropped Lucie, repeating the bear hug with his teammate. 'Jesus, okay,' he choked out as he was squeezed tightly. 'Let me go, man.'

'What a day for it, eh?' Brett looked out at the pit lane, where the sun was shining down on them.

Spa was known for complex weather conditions which flip-flopped between snow, sun and rain with little warning or sense, but somehow, year after year, the IEC were graced with the big yellow thing in the sky. Brett always told Lucie it was her that brought the sunshine, in both a metaphorical sense and a literal one. She liked to think it was all him.

'It's due to rain for an hour or two tomorrow.' Lucie bit her lip.

'Why are you still stood here, then?' Brett stared at her blankly.

'What?' She hated when she couldn't sense sarcasm. Being friends with this idiot for ten years should have strengthened her sarcasm radar, but she was still a bit hopeless unless said sarcasm was leaving her own mouth.

'Get your little self out there and do a sun dance.'

'I don't think that's a thing, sweetheart. You're getting mixed up with a rain dance.'

'Oh.' He looked genuinely confused. 'Definitely don't do that. Mind you, we all know Moretz would put in a hell of a lap in the wet. Maybe it wouldn't be such a bad thing.'

'Did I hear my name?' Julien rounded the corner in his race suit.

'Moretz, buddy. How are the wife and kid?' He slapped him on the back.

Faith chose that moment to appear with Ford on a lead. It was an odd sight to behold, a husky in the Revolution Racing garage, on a workday, surrounded by all the people. But he looked happy as a clam despite the noises of the pit lane being too much sometimes even for the human ear.

'How the hell did you get him past security?' Lucie gestured at the husky, whose tongue was now lolling out the side of his mouth.

'Lucie, my furry friend and I are the power couple of the grid.' Julien said it with such a straight face that she wished she had caught it on camera for the sake of the fans, who were almost as invested in Julien's love story with his dog as they were in the one with Faith.

Marco held his hand out for the lead. 'Can I take him for a walk?'

'Not too far.' Faith handed it to him and immediately took her phone out of her pocket to snap a shot, showing Lucie her lightning-fast editing work before posting it online.

'Morning, kids.' Jasper Kotosovski, the principal for Revolution, appeared behind them, coffee in hand. He had about a gazillion cups a day to fuel him through the stress of managing the team, but he enjoyed his racing family.

'You're only *just* old enough to be my dad, Jasper. I'm no kid.'

'Moretz, you brought your dog to work. You're a big kid at heart, admit it.'

Julien scowled, shoving his hands in his pockets. 'He's my baby. I'd like to point out I do bring my human baby, too. You know, the teenager I raised.'

Faith tucked herself into his side and smiled up at him. 'You can still be a big kid, babe. I think it's a good thing.'

'Right, enough of the lovey-dovey shit. It's too early in the day.' Brett rolled his eyes.

'It's two o'clock in the afternoon, Anderson,' Julien defended.

'Exactly.'

'You guys all set for quali tomorrow? Heads in the

game?' Jasper asked the group. 'Got to keep Kahan Racing off our tail. Their rookie driver is really something else.'

'He's got nothing on us. One drop of rain and that team falls to pieces. They don't have our secret weapon.' Brett nodded in Julien's direction, hyping up his teammate's impeccable driving skills in the awful weather.

It didn't matter if rain was pelting his helmet and blurring his vision through the visor, Julien Moretz wasn't going to let up for anything or anyone. Cars would spin left, right and centre and he would just keep driving like there was nobody else on the track. Unless the safety car came out and the race was yellow flagged, of course. Each of them brought something different to the team, which made them almost unstoppable. Marco was an expert at keeping the pace steady in longer stints and Brett at fighting their rivals off at high speeds.

'We'll have another strategy meeting at four. Until then, get comfortable with her.' He gestured at the car, sitting proudly before them in all her ruby-red glory.

'I meant to say earlier, Jasper, the new livery looks so good! Imagine how much it's going to stand out on the feed! Plus, it'll be super easy to spot on the TV footage amongst the more minimalist liveries,' Faith commented.

Revolution Racing had been known for their subtlety in the design of their car. They had always opted for red and kept the zebra stripe pattern strictly for the drivers' race suits, but this season they had gone all out. The stripes were *on* the car. It looked bold, and it stood out on the track amongst more than sixty other cars from thirty-plus teams.

Most teams stuck to one or two colours, with the occasional one opting for an artistic design if they had a collaboration in the works. But none looked as impressive as the work of art that Revolution had presented this season. They would change it for Le Mans, of course, they always did. Teams typically came up with a one-off livery for that particular race due to its grandeur. But for the rest of the season, this was what they were working with.

'We're the best of the best, Lucie. Got to have a design to match,' Jasper grinned.

This was the worst part; waiting around for the race to start. Autograph sessions were done, fans had all had a nose at the car and the garage and tracked the drivers down in the paddock, and now Brett stood silently watching them in the grandstands from his spot in the garage. They were cheering as IEC staff used T-shirt cannons to launch merchandise in the air for them to catch from their seats.

'Nervous?' Lucie sidled up to Brett, who was in full racing gear. They'd spent the last couple of days holed up at the track, barely spending any time at the hotel in favour of working until the sun went down and returning before it rose.

'Nah, you know me. Cool as a cucumber, Sunny.'

'You know you don't have to play that game with me,' Lucie murmured so the mechanics and engineers wouldn't hear.

Brett turned to look down at her, his gaze burning into hers. 'I know. But I'm feeling particularly confident today. Don't know why. Must be because my lucky charm is here.'

'You know I'm always by your side at a race, nothing different there.'

'Yep, which is why I don't get nervous.' He tapped her nose fondly, but she knew he was lying. She'd seen the panic attacks and the fear in the past, particularly in his early days in the championship when he'd had less confidence, experience and a smaller fan base, but she'd let it slide. If he needed to convince himself there was nothing wrong then that was fine.

'Did you have a good few days in Brussels?'

'Mm,' he mumbled absentmindedly, a sure-fire sign his nerves were getting the better of him. 'Exactly what I needed. Managed to blow off some steam, have some drinks with the lads. Feeling refreshed.'

'Drinking before a race?' She eyed him, hoping he couldn't see the judgement written across her face. The drivers rarely drank in the lead-up to a race, they needed to be at peak fitness before they got in the car. They were all about health and nutrition and Jasper wouldn't be impressed if he knew one of his drivers wasn't taking good care of himself.

'Don't give me that look, Sunny, it wasn't a heavy sesh. Oh, I got you something.' He beckoned her to the back of the garage, where his rental car was parked. A Ferrari, of course. Bright red, so in-your-face one would only assume it belonged to a driver. Brett didn't know how to keep things low-key. Then again, any driver who didn't rock up in an SUV typically rented a sports car. It wasn't just a Brett thing, he was just far less subtle than most.

'Is the something a puppy?'

'Oh yeah, got you a chihuahua. She's sitting in here with the windows up, suffocating in the heat,' Brett teased as he opened the door and leaned across to the passenger seat.

'If you knew me at all, you wouldn't even joke about that. Do I look like a chihuahua kind of girl?' She raised a brow as he turned around, a small gift bag in his hands.

'You've got the attitude.' He thrust the bag into her hands. 'Open it.'

Lucie tossed the tissue paper out and let it float towards Brett, who caught it effortlessly. There were two things inside, one being a small box of Belgian chocolates. She studied the card which described each one. Champagne-filled truffles, pineapple and passion-fruit pralines. These wouldn't last the day. Once she and Faith had done most of their social media duties for the six-hour race, she would likely demolish the entire lot and blame it on stress. Lucie relied on rushing up and down the pit lane and all around the circuit during race week to keep her fitness levels and body in check. There was no personal trainer and gym time in her schedule.

But that wasn't the gift Brett was urging her to open as he took the chocolates from her so her hands were free. At the bottom of the bag was a ring box. Lucie could feel her face flushing from the moment she spotted it. 'Anderson?'

'Just open it, Luce! We haven't got all bloody day.'

She lifted the lid to reveal a yellow sapphire oval-cut star ring staring back at her. It looked like an engagement ring. Anyone who didn't know their relationship would think it was an engagement ring, only Lucie knew that wasn't the intention behind it. 'Brett, it's beautiful.'

'I know it's a bit of a weird gift to buy your best friend of the opposite sex, but I couldn't help myself. I always say you're like sunshine in a bottle, and that's what it reminded me of. And I might have ordered the matching earrings . . . drop earrings, I think they're called? They'll be waiting at our hotel in Vegas in a couple of weeks, so you can wear them out.' He was grinning from ear to ear, clearly so thrilled with his find.

'Thank you.' She did all she could not to tear up, and instead buried her head in his chest and tried not to sniffle too loudly. Thank the heavens for the car that started up in the garage next door, muffling the sound. She was quite a sentimental person, and this gift was personal. It showed her friend really understood her.

'Of course. Maybe . . . don't put it on *that* finger. We don't want anyone to get the wrong idea about us, do we? I got it in the same size as that opal one I got you for your birthday years ago, so it should fit on your index finger. We can't have the fans running wild again, that was overwhelming to say the least.' He grimaced, remembering when a photo had gone out with his hand on her ass last season and the fans lost their minds on social media.

Without much to go on, the fans rocked up to multiple races over the course of the season with actual signs and flags in the grandstands, all of them 'shipping' Lucie and Brett. Lucett. There were still fan edits floating around to this day, and as more fans found them, more of these videos popped up online. Their bosses found it hilarious, as did Brett, but Lucie was embarrassed every time and still hadn't learned to brush over it.

'Fits perfectly,' she beamed. 'Right, you'd better hurry up. Race starts soon.'

'Yes, ma'am.' He saluted and walked off to find his teammates with a spring in his step.

Lucie wandered back in, tracking down Faith and trying to hide her hand so she didn't blind her friend with the massive, shiny gemstone that now adorned it. Her plan failed when she realised that to do her job, she needed to put the chocolates down.

'What the hell is that?!' Bea got to her before Faith did, dropping her DSLR camera on sight and letting it swing from the sparkly strap around her neck. 'Lucie, that's gigantic! Who gave you that?' she gushed, tugging on Lucie's hand.

'Brett.'

'We keep telling you, that man adores you,' Faith interrupted, eyes nearly falling out of her skull when she saw it. 'Jesus, how much did that cost?'

'I know he adores me, he makes that very clear pretty much every single day. That's why he's one of my closest friends.'

'No, but like . . . Lucie. Come on. No guy buys a ring like that for a *friend*.'

'He always goes on a little bit of a spending spree before and after a race. Plus he was on holiday when he saw it so he got it on a whim.' Lucie shrugged it off, thinking nothing of it. Gifts were his thing, and she wasn't the only woman he had purchased jewellery for. He'd got his sisters necklaces, Faith earrings, Bea a bracelet. 'Stop acting like he got down on one knee. It's just a sweet gesture.'

'Uh-huh. You know, you still haven't told me if he's ever got down on *both* knees for a very different reason.'

'Goodbye, Beatrix. The race is starting.'

Lucie's cheeks were practically crimson by the time she about-turned out of there. Her mind couldn't help but take her back to a night that neither she nor Brett spoke about with their friends. Ever. And yet with how vividly the memories were replaying in her head right now, she would be surprised if Faith, who was stood next to her filming the commotion in the garage, hadn't caught on.

'Earth to Lucie?'

'Huh?' She blinked twice, forcing herself out of her daydream.

'I said, can you get closer to Brett and Marco and film their reactions to Julien's race start? We can use it on stories and in the recap vlog. They're already waiting at the monitors.'

Lucie headed towards them to do exactly that, but despite trying her best to get into work mode, she couldn't deny that the yellow sapphire glistening in the sunlight wasn't almost as big a distraction as Brett himself winking directly at the camera when he noticed her coming up beside him. This was going to be a long six hours.

3

'What kind of idiots decide to travel across two countries the *day* of an event?' Lucie scoffed, fiddling with the string attached to the gold balloon she had just filled with helium.

She was in London with Faith, Bea and Esme not even forty-eight hours after the first race of the IEC season had finished at Spa. They had abandoned the post-race celebrations at Julien and Faith's house in Malmedy, having celebrated enough Revolution race wins in the last few years to last a lifetime. The drivers, however, had insisted they could squeeze it all in as long as De Luca, the most sensible of the three, stayed sober.

So now the girls were at their brand-new London office, stringing up balloons and decorating the foyer for their launch party without their promised help, and berating their friends' lack of time management when it came to anything except their careers.

'I should have confiscated Julien's house key,' Faith laughed. 'They wouldn't have gotten very far without it.'

'Of course they would.' Lucie handed her the finished balloon. 'Your property sits on acres of land. They'd have climbed the fences, taken their beers and sat in the grass until the sun came up. Honestly, I don't know who's the worst influence, Jules or Brett.'

'Ha, that's easy! It's Brett. No doubt,' Bea chimed in, shuffling the custom cocktail menus in her hands.

'Yeah, I've got to back her up there,' Esme shrugged. 'He's a bit of a wild card.'

Lucie sighed, annoyed that their event hadn't taken priority with the guys. Then again, they were the ones who had scheduled the launch for tonight of all nights. They had to choose a day when most female team principals across the industry could make it, and that meant inconveniencing a handful of people in the IEC for the sake of a hundred-plus key guests they'd been desperate to snag for the launch.

Still, Brett and the guys could have celebrated in London rather than staying in Belgium for 'tradition'. They didn't need every male driver on the grid in attendance. Most of the female drivers were here, supporting them, but their best friends had opted to nurse their hangovers on the Calais-to-Dover ferry with six hours until they cut the ribbon. A very big, very pink sparkly ribbon – Bea's choice, of course. It may not have been the obvious choice for women in a motorsport company, but damn Beatrix Miller and her stereotypes. She even had a matching one in her hair.

'Jada Scott has confirmed she can make it last minute!' Faith waved her phone around, showing them the email she had received from a sports journalist. 'Things are shaping up very nicely, ladies,' she grinned.

It was mostly thanks to Faith's career prior to joining the IEC. They had been slowly working on building the business up and doing the occasional workshop over the last season, but it was joining forces with Faith's motorsport podcast that had been the final factor and given them the boost they needed to take things to the next level.

Girls Off Track had taken over the podcast and its merchandise business and rebranded accordingly, and they were starting to get huge numbers of women involved. Female drivers, team principals, engineers, mechanics, journalists, social media crews. The sky was the limit, but it had all happened so fast that they needed this London office as a base. It was a capital city which made it easy for people to travel to from all over the place, and a lot of racing teams had offices here, too. Or at least were based in the UK, a short drive away. Silverstone was a mere couple of hours from them.

Pop-up workshops across the globe were still going to be a key goal, but the UK was their starting point and their waiting list was already a mile long. The days of motorsport being known as a 'man's sport' were numbered.

Having said that, the men of Revolution Racing played a huge part in this, too. They were silent partners and had helped the girls financially, emotionally, verbally, you name it. Daily social media shoutouts were Brett's favourite thing and there wasn't a single post of theirs that the guys hadn't hyped up, but the daily running of Girls Off Track was all them.

Bringing Esme on board had been a risk, given they didn't know her too well outside of work, but she had slotted into the team perfectly and splitting the work between four instead of three had been a big positive, allowing them to work more efficiently and maintain this alongside their commitments to the IEC.

'My darling husband has just sent me a selfie and I have to say, he doesn't look too hung-over. Maybe he'll be able to handle "Faith's Jungle Juice"?' she snorted.

'Excuse me!' Lucie turned her nose up. 'We don't need to bring your bedroom antics into this conversation. Not again.'

'It's the name of one of the cocktails!' Faith gestured at the menu.

'Oh dear, I knew we should've asked to approve that list.' Esme grimaced in Lucie's direction, peering over Faith's shoulder at the names.

'We've also got the "Lucie Sunrise", "Long Island Iced Bea", and the "Esme Fizz".' Bea smiled proudly, fanning herself with one of the menus.

'Of course you get the best name.'

'Jealousy is an ugly trait, Luce!' Bea placed the final menu on the top of the bar and flounced off across the room, heels clacking across the floor.

The four of them carried on with the finishing touches to the décor and let the caterers in before they scarpered off to the bathrooms to change into their outfits for the night. They hadn't stopped working since they had arrived in London, which had resulted in each of them looking a state, and Bea would never allow them to look anything but their best on such a big night. She had made calls to get a last-minute makeup artist, but even with all her connections, the plan had fallen through. So, when

Brett video-called Lucie right in the middle of her using her phone camera to do her mascara, she cursed.

'Fu— Hey, Anderson!'

'Sunny! Whatcha doing?'

'Making myself look pretty.'

He replied with, 'You always look pretty,' at the same time as Julien said, 'Should we notify your guests that you need another six hours, then?'

'Julien Moretz, marrying my best friend is the worst thing you've ever done.'

'What?!' Faith gaped at her, lip gloss in hand.

'The sass! Since meeting you, he has become *so* sarcastic.'

'I taught him well.'

'At least they're not at loggerheads any more,' Esme added.

Lucie laughed, remembering the screaming matches the couple had once regularly engaged in at races. She was surprised they hadn't shattered windows in the trailer or broken the door from slamming it so forcefully mid-argument.

'Hello!' Brett shouted, bringing the attention back to them. 'Let us in, we've just pulled up. Can't believe you have parking spaces outside your office.'

'Welcome to London,' Lucie laughed, abandoning her almost-finished makeup to go and buzz them up to the top floor. Another perk of the guys' financial backing; a top-floor office with incredible views of the city.

'I'm starving,' Brett announced as they stepped out of the lift, all three of them in full suits. They all looked

29

incredibly handsome, but it was Brett who stood out in Lucie's eyes.

His dark-brown hair was perfectly styled in a fresh cut: short back and sides. He'd definitely done it himself while still hungover at Julien's, because there was no way he'd have had the time since she last saw him. A naïve part of her wondered if he'd done it for her. Brett usually wore his hair slightly longer, more grown out, but she had never shied away from telling him she liked his hair like this. It was a silly thought and she pushed it away just as fast as it had blossomed in her mind.

'Go get something from the caterers. Ask for Leanne and say we said you're allowed something from the secret stash. She'll know I sent you.'

'All right. You look stunning, babe.' He leaned down to kiss her on the cheek before heading off in the direction of who knew where, but he'd find his way. 'Babe' was new. It was also incredibly odd hearing it from his lips.

'Babe?' Marco whispered, but Lucie simply shrugged. The key thing she had learned in ten years was that sometimes it was best not to question the mystery that was Brett Anderson. He was a natural flirt, and there were few lines he wouldn't cross. He'd earned himself a wallop round the head when he'd accidentally said something mildly suggestive to Faith last season, but despite that, his filter was non-existent.

Lucie gave Julien and Marco a sweeping tour and allowed them early access to the bar, giving herself and the girls time to finish up. They'd spent all day in sweatpants and oversized hoodies, and now it was time to hit the reset button.

When they finally emerged from the bathroom and graced their guests with their presence, they felt brand new.

'I feel like I'm in that scene in *Miss Congeniality* except I have two days' worth of dry shampoo in my hair,' Esme groaned.

'You look fit, Ez,' Faith reassured her. 'Oh, look! Danika Beacham is here. I can't believe she actually found the time in her schedule and showed up. She's probably one of the busiest women on the planet.'

They circled the room for twenty minutes before Brett appeared with a full plate of food in one hand and a cocktail in the other. 'That buffet is next level,' he said, taking a bite of a samosa and chasing it down with a sip of Lucie Sunrise. Interesting combination, but his palate wasn't exactly known for being refined. He was still, despite his years of fine-dining experience and love of expensive whisky, a burger and fries kinda guy. He did love to play a self-titled foodie in new places, though. He was always hunting for the best restaurants.

'I think Faith is talking Danika's ear off over there,' Julien grimaced as they watched Faith flailing her arms around and talking animatedly with a renowned Dakar Rally driver. To give the driver credit, she was leaning in and listening intently.

All four women had been trying to keep calm, but the reality was, they couldn't contain their excitement. Everyone in this room was here for them, for everything they were building and everything Girls Off Track stood for.

'I think it's time for the welcome speech!' Faith clasped her hands together, looking ready to get up on their makeshift stage. But it was Lucie who received a shove in that direction. 'Go on, Luce. You've been in the industry longest out of all of us.'

'Me?! I don't know what to say!' She had assumed all four of them would go up there and it would be Faith leading them, since she'd spearheaded the whole idea. She always planned the podcast scripts and interviews.

'Just . . . thanks for supporting our campaign? You're all badass women, superheroes, all that stuff. Empower them! And then tell them if they don't help us out with hosting workshops, they're anti-feminist.' Faith shrugged.

'Jensen!' Lucie scolded. 'They're incredibly busy women.'

'Yes, but if they're here tonight, it means they should care. This event isn't for show, is it? We want them all to actively be involved going forward.'

'Okay, well, I'm not going to make them feel bad if they can't do things,' Lucie sighed, resigning herself to the fact she was going to have to go up there with zero preparation. 'Hold my mini charcuterie board.'

'Go on, Lucie!' Brett yelled loud enough for the crowd to hear, garnering her some attention as she walked up to the mic, legs shaking in her heels. She could handle public speaking, but this business was her baby. There was a lot of pressure.

'Hi everyone, can I have your attention, please?' She looked out at hundreds of faces staring back at her, and suddenly she felt confident. Their guests weren't the only ones in the room who had achieved incredible things in their sport. Lucie herself had worked her way up to the top and made a name for herself, and now she was helping put others on that same path.

Brett led the shushing of murmurs, the music was turned down, and suddenly there was silence. The floor was hers.

'The Girls Off Track team and I would like to thank each of you for making the time to be here. When we set out on this journey, we wanted to create a space where young women and girls could get an insight into what the motorsport industry is like. When I first started out, and when a lot of the women here tonight embarked on their own careers, our sport looked very different. You would walk through the paddock of any championship and see maybe one or two women passing you, and the rest of us were working behind closed doors. The front-facing roles weren't there for us. But things are changing.' She glanced at her friends, all stood at the front of the crowd, bursting with pride.

'We plan to transform motorsport one workshop, podcast or brand deal at a time. We want to show these girls that they belong here, too. The growth of the company has been monumental, and we're so proud to finally have a home base and be able to provide jobs for people who are passionate about the sport. To those who have helped us on our endeavours so far, and to those who are lined up to help. The future women in motorsport owe it all to you.'

The room erupted in cheers, the loudest ones by the Revolution Racing drivers, and Lucie took a step back, admiring the scene. She felt proud of her friends, and lucky to be in a position to make a difference.

'My turn!' Brett rushed up, shooing her back off the stage. 'Hey, guys. Just wanted to toast Lucie, Faith, Bea and Esme, the wonderful ladies behind tonight's set-up, and Girls Off Track. I knew Luce was a firecracker when I met her, and watching her grow into a confident, powerful businesswoman has been an honour. All four women have done a fucki——, oops! Language, sorry.'

'Is he drunk?' Julien murmured to the group.

'He's had a fair bit, yeah,' Marco replied.

'As I was saying,' Brett continued, his drink slosh-ing over the side of the glass, 'all four girls have done a stellar job at figuring out ways of getting more young women interested in the sport, giving them opportun-ities and ensuring the longevity of their mission. I for one am glad we're no longer letting the sport be dictated by old dinosaurs who have a one-track mind and only care about money and power. It's about time we made changes, and made our industry a place of acceptance, empowerment and community. Cheers to the girls.' He held his glass up, a quarter of the liquid now in a puddle at his feet which would have to be blue-rolled away in a moment. But regardless of his tipsiness, Lucie beamed up at him.

He breezed off the stage as the music continued and

chatter filled the room once again, Bea being dragged away by a herd of team principals and Esme gravitating towards a rookie Formula One driver.

'Thanks, Anderson.' Lucie gave him a quick hug, only managing to sneak one arm around his waist before he was pulling her out to the rooftop garden.

'I'm so proud of you, Sunny,' he gushed, the door not even closed behind them before he let the enthusiasm take control of his body, arms flailing wildly.

'I know. I'm feeling proud of myself, too,' she smiled.

'Nah, Luce. You're fucking incredible. You've blossomed over the last few years, and I'm so grateful I got to witness it happen right before my eyes.'

'Don't make me cry, I look really good tonight.' Her bottom lip quivered, watching her best friend gaze down at her with the London sunset behind him.

'You do, and you feel good, and I'm so glad you do. You're gonna have one hell of a season this year, Sunny. You know that? Girls Off Track is going to skyrocket.'

'I hope so.' She leaned on the railing, playing with her ring as Brett came up behind her, wrapping her up in his arms. She felt safe here, and she knew if she didn't have people like him lifting her up all the time, reminding her what she was capable of and pushing her, she might not be where she was in her career. Might not have had the gall to go after what she wanted.

'Love ya, Sunny.'

'Love you, too.'

4

The Las Vegas Strip was magical. There was so much happening at any given moment, every time Lucie came to the city of sin it put her in a daze for a solid week. The lights, the constant buzz of excitement in the air as people gambled their life's savings away. Lucie didn't gamble, but she enjoyed watching Brett and Marco dabble. Julien was on a very strict budget now he had Faith looking over his shoulder, but in previous years, he had been just as bad as his teammates.

She tugged her dress down for the third time that night, feeling a little unsure of herself in the gold, sparkly ensemble she had borrowed from Bea. The zip had broken on Lucie's original dress, and her friends had insisted she couldn't outfit-repeat in a place like this, so wearing tomorrow evening's dress twice was off the cards. But Lucie rarely wore short, fitted dresses, and her curves filled it out more than Bea's petite figure, which meant that the hem sat a little too high on her leg for her liking. The yellow sapphire drop earrings Brett had presented her with on arrival weren't helping to ease her anxiety, either. They were just as flashy and over-the-top, even more so when paired with her ring.

'Will you stop fussing? The amount of second looks you've had walking down the Strip is insane. I watched one girl trip over her own feet,' Bea scowled at her disapprovingly.

'I just sort of wish I was in my cowboy boots.'

'You should've said! I had another dress they'd have worked perfectly with!'

'Well, I didn't know if Vegas was the place for them. Plus, you and the girls are all in heels so I'd have been the odd one out.'

'No, Luce. You'd have been yourself.' Bea shrugged like it was a simple answer, like Lucie was fully comfortable being herself in an industry where models swarmed the paddock.

They rushed ahead to join the rest of the group, who seemed to be on a mission to get to dinner. That was another thing she still wasn't used to when travelling with the guys; they never reserved tables. Julien in particular could just walk into almost any restaurant and the staff would go to extreme lengths to make space. Brett's influence had grown over the last couple of seasons too, but he and Marco didn't like to use their power to feed their empty stomachs. Which was a surprise given how much they ate when they were bulking.

'Are they going to make us eat sushi again?' Esme whined. 'We always have sushi. I want burgers, fries, shakes. Anything my body hates.'

'You want burgers?' Brett's head whipped around like a dog hearing the word 'walkies'.

'Please. I am begging.'

'Well, it's my birthday trip, so burgers it is.' Brett flung an arm around Esme's shoulders playfully and steered

38

her in the direction of an upscale restaurant, famous for its vegan burgers which would keep Marco happy, and Lucie felt that unwelcome pang of jealousy.

'I take it he's paying for this,' Bea whispered, 'because I sure as hell can't afford to drop ninety-plus dollars on a piece of meat sandwiched between two slices of bread. I've got a tiny budget for the casino later.'

'You know what the guys are like, someone's card will be waved around. If not, I can go halves with you,' Lucie reassured.

She could count on one hand the number of times over the years that their friends had allowed them to pay for meals when they went out as a group, and while it meant they could save up for flights and hotels on their non-work-related travels, it still felt wrong. It was hard to process just how much money the guys had to spend from their Revolution contracts alone, let alone personal sponsorships and brand deals and all the investments they'd made.

'How fucking much?' Faith's eyes nearly fell out of her head the second she sat down and opened the menu. That seemed to be her favourite phrase.

'Shhh!' Julien put a hand over mouth. 'Babe, not so loud.'

'Jules, this is ridiculous money for food! Nearly eight hundred dollars? We have a kid to put through college. *Medical* school, if that's what she settles on.'

'Ah, don't worry, Jensen. I've got this.' Brett shrugged nonchalantly, finding it somewhat amusing that his teammate's wife still couldn't grasp that the money in her and Julien's bank account was shared, and in seven figures at least. She still bought cheap wine, and meal deals at British supermarkets.

'We'll split it three ways,' Marco suggested, and Lucie gave Bea a look that said, 'I told you so.' They would have happily gone to a fast-food place.

'Sorry, and thank you for offering, guys. Still not used to this!' Faith glanced around nervously like she feared she looked out of place, but actually, she looked right at home in her red silk dress, blonde hair in soft waves around her face. She and Julien were one hell of a power couple, and the jealousy hit Lucie again.

She wasn't sure when she started wanting more for herself, but all she did know was that it was a difficult thought to process and she had no idea where to start. She hadn't dated seriously for years, and she had such high standards. If Lucie was going to share her life with someone, she wanted the fairy-tale romance her best friend had got. Only she wasn't certain that option existed in her world, because the only fairy tale her imagination could muster up included Brett.

'You all right, Sunny?' Brett's hand grazed her knee under the table and she jumped before placing her hand over his and giving it a squeeze. 'You look a little lost over there.'

'I'm fine, sweetheart.' She smiled, flipping Marco off when he pretended to gag. 'Oops, sorry, forgot we're meant to be classy in here, aren't we?'

'Yeah, we'd better behave, Dad might tell us off.' Marco grinned at Julien, who was shooting the pair of them a look that could kill.

'So, guys.' Esme put her menu down having been told she had to have the most expensive option because it was the best. 'Do you ever get tired of winning?'

The table laughed at her joke, but really it wasn't a joke. Esme was on socials for an opposing team, and the drivers at Eden Racing had been a little standoffish when she had begun hanging out with the Revolution crew. They were close-knit, and in theory, Esme shouldn't have fitted in as well as she did, but having Bea there most of the time balanced out the dynamics. Bea was Switzerland. Not that they ever divulged team tactics with either of them around, and neither did they gossip about the Eden drivers. When they weren't at the track, they were friends first.

'To be fair, we *almost* didn't win at Spa!' Marco defended.

'Yeah, it was your team who almost took us out. If Jules wasn't so good in the wet, they might've got past him on that one turn.'

'I'm just too good.' He sat back in his chair and crossed his arms, looking smug.

'Oh my God, Jules! Your head is expanding!' Bea gasped.

'Shut up, Beatrix. I'd like to see you get behind the wheel of a race car. You can't even handle the traffic coming off the Dover ferry.'

'No, but I can steer my way through a crowd of people with a ten-thousand-dollar camera round my neck. You require a security guard to get through crowds,' she shot back.

'That's because the people love me and they're always trying to rip my shirt off.'

'And? Half the drivers on the grid *have* ripped my shirt off.'

The rest of the group lost their minds laughing at that. As Bea had grown into herself more, she had started making light of her previous behaviour rather than letting anyone else try to use it against her. Lucie was just glad she hadn't mentioned the fact Julien had once been one of those drivers, because as close as she and Faith were, it was still a bit weird to think about.

'I never thought you'd be one of my favourite people on the planet, Bea Miller, but I have to say you are really something else.' Brett chuckled but stopped when he felt Lucie tense up. This green-eyed monster lurking around her was pathetic and she didn't know where it had come from. She only hoped nobody could detect it.

'You all right, Lucie?' Marco asked, meaning she was doing a poor job at hiding her sour mood from her friends.

'Yeah! Sorry, Vegas just takes me out of my comfort zone a little.'

'Can we get this woman a drink?' Brett held his hand up in the air as a waiter passed, only adding to the ruckus they had been causing since they walked in. 'What do you want, babe?'

'Uhhh,' she stuttered as her brain processed this new nickname he'd given her. 'Vodka cranberry?' It was less of a request and more of a question. What was going to get her drunk the fastest? She didn't want to be sober

42

and in her feelings for much longer, not while everyone else was having fun and she was feeling like an outsider for no logical reason.

'Vodka cran please, mate. Make it a double. Actually, bring two.'

'Two?'

'You don't seem yourself. This'll take the edge off.' And then his hand was skating up her thigh again, and Lucie knew she risked ending the night crying in the bathroom.

'Fuck yeah, De Luca!' The rowdiness continued into the night as everyone surrounded Marco at a roulette table, waiting impatiently. Time after time, the guys bet on red. The signature colour of Revolution Racing, regardless of whether they found much success with it or not.

Everyone was well beyond tipsy by now, but the best thing was watching Faith and Julien truly letting their hair down for once. They were always semi-switched on and in parent mode even when Jasmine was miles away at home in Hawaii, but birthday trips were different. They often missed them, but Brett had begged and pleaded with everyone to come this year on the basis that it was Esme's first time joining them.

Esme was having the time of her life and egging them on every step of the way. She'd only toned it down briefly when she'd been about to text her driver friend at Eden for a five-thousand-dollar loan and Marco had caught her, insisting she could use his money like it was her own. Of course, drunk Esme had taken full advantage but Marco was loving showing off his gambling skills so he wasn't likely to care in the morning when the hangover hit and he realised how much he'd lost. He liked to think he was good at gambling, but he was a bit hopeless.

'Did I actually win?' Marco's jaw dropped.

'Ten grand, my son!' Brett slapped him on the back and Julien jumped up and down like a little kid. They shouldn't be let loose in a place like this.

'Poker next. Come on, Sunny. Be my good luck charm?' Brett gave her puppy eyes, but she always thought he looked more like Wall-E, that Disney robot.

'What exactly does that entail?' She raised an eyebrow, placing a hand on her hip and almost stumbling in those stupid stilettos.

'A kiss?' He snaked an arm around her waist.

'In your dreams.'

'It's my birthday.'

'Tomorrow.'

'I get a kiss tomorrow?'

'No, I meant it's not your birthday until tomorrow,' she stood her ground.

'Shit best friend, you are.' He pouted but squeezed her hip gently to signify he was just messing around. Except this messing around was becoming a common occurrence.

'I'll give you a kiss, Anderson.' Julien grabbed both sides of Brett's face and planted one on his lips, grinning like the Cheshire Cat. He was without a doubt way over the line of just being tipsy, and was veering into drunk and disorderly territory, but he was highly entertaining. Lucie loved seeing Julien letting loose after he'd spent so long in parent mode twenty-four-seven.

They headed over to the poker table where Brett stole a pink feather boa from an old lady and looped it around Lucie's neck. 'I'm so sorry!'

The lady just gave her a sloppy smile. 'You go for it, sunshine.'

'Nice to know other people see what I see, my sunshine girl.' Brett snuck a cheeky peck on her cheek, proud of the nickname he'd selected for her so long ago, and got to work.

Lucie watched in awe as he worked his magic, and before she knew it they'd been there for an hour. Brett lost and won repeatedly against an elderly man who clearly also had more money than sense, and now he was about to bet his Sydney apartment.

'Anderson, no. Too far.'

'Nah, it's chill. I know what I'm doing, Sunny.' He smirked as he did another shot of tequila.

Lucie looked to Julien for help, knowing he was the only one who stood a chance at asserting some authority here. If Lucie tried again, Brett truly would shut her up with a kiss. Which she wasn't entirely sure she minded, but she couldn't let either of these things happen.

'Come on, Anderson. Esme is throwing up, she needs us,' Julien called out, furiously typing on his phone.

'Oh, shit! Apologies, sir. Good game.' His last remaining opponent simply laughed it off. He looked to be a seasoned regular, so he was probably used to people getting carried away and their friends saving them from making mistakes.

'She is actually okay, isn't she?' Lucie whispered to Julien.

'Yeah, I told her to fake it.'

By the time they reached Marco and the girls, Esme had slightly smudged eye makeup and was pulling a face that suggested she felt unwell.

'Oh, Ez! Are you good?' Brett patted her on the back gently.

'Better now,' she mumbled, but as soon as Brett looked away she winked at Lucie.

'Right, where to next? The bar?' He was already walking away.

Lucie tugged on Julien's arm to slow him down. She didn't want the rest of the group to hear and make a big deal out of it.

'Jules, I think he's had too much to drink. The amount he had while he and I were stood at the poker table was enough to last one person all night.'

'Should we convince everyone to call it a night?' Julien glanced up at his teammate, who was giving Marco a piggyback and running down the street.

'I think it's for the best. We've got to do it all over again tomorrow, and I don't want him to embarrass himself or do something he'll regret on night one. Besides, I think Marco could do with getting himself to bed, too.'

'Hey! Guys!' Julien shouted ahead. 'Gather round.'

'Brett! Get back here!' Bea put on an angry tone and beckoned him over.

46

'I think we should call it a night,' Julien said. 'It's already nearly three in the morning, and we wanted to go for pancakes for breakfast, remember?'

'We're in Vegas, Moretz. We can go for afternoon breakfast pancakes.'

'Yeah, but Brett, you might not be tired but everyone else is.'

'Yeah, we are.' Faith faked a yawn.

'Guys, come on! It's my birthday.' He used that as an excuse to get his way for about the eighth time tonight, except this time it was technically true.

'Why don't you and I go get some fried chicken, *then* go back to the hotel,' Lucie suggested.

'Fine. Let's go, Sunny, let these boring fuckers go to bed.' He tugged her along hand in hand, leaving Lucie to give them a grateful wave. 'Night, losers!'

She knew he would make her sit and eat half the menu, including fries dipped in milkshake, and they would be out for another two hours, but at least the drinking would stop. She would eat all the fried chicken in the world in one sitting if it kept Brett safe from his own stupidity.

5

Lucie had the taste of champagne on her tongue, and she still despised it. Pretending to like it was a full-time job at this point. She still couldn't fathom how the drivers didn't physically gag on camera during podium celebrations, because she still failed to hide her distaste most of the time. *Surely* they didn't like it. She was a wine, fruity cocktail or beer girl; preferably local to wherever she was visiting at the time. Anything else was for rich people.

So really, it made sense that racing drivers didn't complain; they fell into the rich people category. Not that it was a bad thing. That circle of rich people consisted of her friends and co-workers, and she loved them all dearly, but she still had every right to judge their questionable taste in alcohol.

She swatted Brett's hand away in disgust as he lifted the three-litre bottle to her lips again. The birthday boy wasn't getting away with it this time, she'd had enough. In a sweaty, overpriced club on their second night in Las Vegas, she was desperate for a decent glass of red. Was a wine glass the most practical thing to take onto a dance floor? Perhaps not. Was she past the point of caring? Yes.

'Live a little!' Brett yelled in her ear.

'I am living a *lot*, sweetheart. Who was dancing on the bar an hour ago? Me or you?'

'Don't *sweetheart* me, Luce.'

'I always *sweetheart* you. It's our thing,' Lucie scowled up at him. She'd known this man since they were eighteen years old and not a single day had gone by where they didn't call each other by a nickname. Admittedly, she'd used his a lot less in the last couple of years.

'Yeah, and our thing cannot be a thing when I have alcohol in my system and there's a hundred thousand dollars a night hotel room with my name on it.' He looked at her with a fire in his eyes that she had seen a million times.

'Oh, calm down, you think I'd let anything happen?'

'You gave in two years ago.' Brett nudged her arm gently, reminding her that as much as she had tried to extinguish the fire, it was always there. Burning slowly, waiting to be stoked. But Lucie would never be the one to stoke it, not again.

'That was two years ago, Brett. We should move on!' she shouted, as if to emphasise that she was done with the topic, and almost collapsed with relief when she saw their friends making a beeline for them through the crowd. Friends who were oblivious to their secret little rendezvous and found their flirting adorable.

Marco, puppy-like as he was, clung to Bea's arm like he feared he would get swallowed up by the socialites and cougars of Las Vegas. To be fair to him, it was highly likely. The entire club knew who the boys were. Brett Anderson, Julien Moretz and Marco De Luca, three of the most famous racing drivers in the world, the men who made up Revolution Racing.

They had placed on the podium for every race since the team was formed eight years ago. For context, that was fifty-six races. Even their rivals couldn't help but admire the talent coming from their garage, and women threw themselves at them. Like the leggy blonde gazing longingly at Brett from across the room, who Lucie knew more than likely had a shot if she timed her approach right.

Despite Lucie being aware of the woman, Brett was not. He was crossing into Lucie's personal space, pulling her in close like he was protecting her from something. The only thing she needed protecting from was hormones: his and hers. She knew when Brett was after something, and as his lip hovered closer to her ear, she somehow knew what was coming.

'You're getting dangerously close, Anderson, and we promised we wouldn't go there.'

'I'm just fantasising.' He was so nonchalant, so calm and collected. How could he act like there wouldn't be consequences? He may not have been affected last time, but Lucie had been battling confusion from the very moment she had woken up next to his naked, albeit perfectly sculpted body.

'Dare I ask?'

'I'm just thinking about how I want to take you up to the penthouse suite and give you the kind of experience that requires you to sign an NDA in the morning. Relive our night in the Alps.' Brett spoke in a murmured tone, but she heard him loud and clear, even amongst the noise. Of course, it helped that he had pulled her into a quieter corner of the club, where there was a little less attention on them.

As she stepped away from him and caught the way his eyes raked over her body like she was a five-course Michelin-star meal, something inside her screamed to give him what he desired. *No.* God, where had their friends disappeared to? Faith could talk sense into her. Not Bea. Bea was the devil incarnate and would encourage every intrusive thought Lucie had when it came to this six-foot-two, tanned, beautiful man.

Faith may be all happy and shacked up with the Belgian god of racing, but Lucie didn't *want* his Australian counterpart. Their slip-up two years ago gave her a taste but that was all she could ever allow herself. She had seen enough before – and after – that night in Italy to know that she was better off without the drama that would ensue if they crossed the line again. Brett was hers; he had always made that evident. Just not in the one way she truly wanted him if they were to ever go all the way down that path.

'Jensen, where have you been?' she cried out when Faith finally appeared behind her at the perfect moment, one pina colada in each hand.

'Getting you this.' Her friend held up a coconut with a pineapple wedge, a blue cocktail umbrella and a neon-pink plastic swirly straw.

'They do cheap umbrellas and swirly straws in a club like this?' Lucie raised an eyebrow.

'No, but they'll go to extreme lengths for the birth-day boy.'

'This isn't for the birthday boy.'

'No, it's for his Lucie-bear.' Lucie scowled at her least favourite nickname, the one everyone around them had given her to wind her up. Brett, thankfully, had only used it once, but of course the others had overheard it and it stuck. 'And what Lucie-bear wants, Lucie-bear gets. I'm getting quite good at making demands, you know. Comes with the trophy-wife territory,' Faith stated proudly.

'First of all, being attractive and being married to a man like Jules does not automatically label you a trophy wife. You don't exactly fit the stereotype.'

'Luuuuuucie!' Julien flung an arm over Lucie's shoul-der, weighing down her tiny frame and resulting in her nearly losing her footing.

'Jules, please take it easy. I do not want to deal with your hangover.' Faith gently coaxed his glass of bourbon out of his hand and set it down on the bar.

'Me? You were the one dancing on the bar!' Julien feigned outrage. What he hadn't noticed was that his wife was actually still sober.

'Don't you think they should get back up there, Moretz?' Brett chimed in, holding Lucie's gaze as he spoke. He was testing her, and she'd never been good at tests of any kind. Tests that involved avoiding a spe-cific part of Brett's anatomy, however? She usually aced those.

'Oh look, Brett! That girl who was eyeballing you is

making her approach! Enjoy.' Lucie grabbed her coconut cup, Faith's hand and her clutch bag and made a swift exit in the direction of the ladies' bathroom.

She hadn't even taken two steps before an entire group of women swarmed around the boys. Julien, as drunk as he was, waved a cheerful goodbye and turned back to the bartender for another whiskey. Marco and Esme stayed by Bea's side, looking lost as ever, and Brett? Well, Brett was Brett. He mingled and flirted and all thoughts of Lucie were forgotten.

Lucie leaned on the counter and stared at her reflection in the mirror. She somehow still looked relatively put together despite how hot it was in there. Her lipstick was slightly smudged, her skin was dewy and her hair could do with some detangling, but it could be worse. Her dress was a backless silver cowl-neck ensemble that Bea had got her for her birthday a few months ago, and it was her first time wearing it.

While her friends had body confidence to be envious of, Lucie sadly couldn't muster it. In all her years of working in social media and content creation, she was yet to post a bikini photo, and if it wasn't so hot every time her friends did a resort trip or beach holiday, she would happily lounge by the pool in an oversized tee.

'Faith, are you ready to head back out?' she called out to the cubicles. Silence. 'Faith?'

A quick sweep revealed that every cubicle was empty. With an eye roll and a sigh, Lucie ventured back into the depths of the club alone.

She glanced at the bar to see that everyone had left Brett to the wolves. Sorry, a group of attractive women. Not wolves. Though they behaved like it. Why did this always happen to her? Leave her alone at a racetrack and she could handle herself no problem. In clubs and social settings? Forget it.

She felt the anxiety set in right as Brett looked up and found her, then a split second later the bartender was tapping his shoulder and she'd lost him again. But it wasn't until she saw what the bartender was passing him that she realised she was in luck. Two shots of tequila, meant to kill her nerves. She leaned against the wall, waiting for him to reach her. If anyone could calm her down, it was Brett. She never felt out of place when his attention was on her.

'You all right, my sunshine girl?' He passed her a shot.

'I will be.' She downed it and grimaced.

'Everyone disappeared, huh?'

'As always. Esme and Marco probably went to find food, I'm sure they'll be back.'

'Mars did mention something about fries.'

'Uh-huh.' Lucie took a deep breath and scanned the room. The dance floor was more crowded, fewer people were observing from the sidelines and more of those scary, gorgeous women she'd taken note of before were flinging their limbs around in an effort to dance and embarrassing themselves in the name of fun. Now *that*, Lucie could relate to.

'Do you want to leave? If you're uncomfortable, we'll go.'

'Do *you* want to leave?'

'I mean . . .' He shrugged, trying to pretend that he didn't care either way, but Lucie knew him better than that. This was his night. A night he looked forward to every year. Besides, the others would probably come back soon, the night was still young. And if they didn't? Brett and Lucie had been a duo for years. They took trips together, spent months at a time in Australia with his family, spent their working weeks together. They were used to hanging out one-on-one. What difference did it make if the rest of tonight was just the two of them?

'Just answer the question, Brett.'

'I'd like to stay. But only if it's with you.'

'Then we'll stay.' She offered him a small smile and he took that as his cue. A wicked grin spread across his features as he placed the empty shot glasses on the table beside her and took her hand in his, enticing her into the mass of people. Lucie rolled her eyes playfully when she realised the DJ's latest song choice. Only Brett Anderson could get away with dancing to 'Get Busy' in this day and age and look good doing it. Sean Paul would be proud.

'You know you want to dance with me, Sunny,' Brett smirked as she gave in. He was right, she did want to dance with him. She wanted every other woman in here to know that Brett had chosen Lucie over and above them. Because their friendship topped anything they could offer him. Call her possessive, she didn't care. That green-eyed monster was even more prominent when she'd had a few to drink, whether it should be there or not.

Before she could start stressing about what anyone else thought of her dancing or her outfit, she was letting Brett turn her around so her back was against his chest, his hand on her hip. One look at them and you would think there was more to it, but this was just how they were. There were no boundaries between them, and yet no lines would be crossed. Whether it was a hand squeezing the curve of her waist, his breath on her neck, or their bodies touching where no platonic friends' bodies ever should, Brett and Lucie didn't know how to *not* act like this. This was their normal.

How they had only crossed the line once in those ten years, when they had behaved like this since day one, was a miracle. Or maybe it was Lucie's stubbornness. Regardless, on nights like this with everyone watching, her confidence rocketing and her skin tingling from his touch, her head was scrambled.

'You are truly,' Brett said, spinning her round to face him, 'the most perfect woman on the planet, Miss Carolan. Anyone ever told you that?'

'Ha! You're funny. Also, you tell me that regularly. And every time you do, I laugh in your face.' Lucie looped her arms around his neck, pulling him down closer so they didn't have to shout above the music.

'Yeah, why do you do that? You don't believe me?' Brett maintained his signature cheeky grin, and she wanted to wipe it off his face. He was still in that teasing mood he'd been in earlier, and she didn't doubt that he'd stay true to his word and throw her over his shoulder.

'You could have anyone, Anderson.'

'That's true. And yet it's always you that I want to wake up to.'

'You wake up to me frequently, fully clothed.' She shrugged, pretending that when they shared a bed she didn't consider herself extremely fortunate to be greeted by the sight of a shirtless Brett in nothing but his boxers.

'Yes, but I know, thanks to our night in Italy, that you *unclothed* is a real treat.'

'Do you ever behave yourself? Like, even for two seconds of your life?' She tried to brush away the comment, the mention of Italy.

'If I did, would I do this?' He ran his hand along her jaw and even though she knew what he was doing, she allowed him to close the gap and capture her lips with his, their tongues dancing in a way that was far more magical than the way their bodies had been moving mere seconds before.

This was only the second time they had ever kissed, and it felt just as right this time as it had the first. Lucie didn't want it to. She wanted it to feel wrong, for them to both want to pull away and go back to dancing like nothing had happened. But they had chemistry that they, or rather she, had been pushing aside for their entire friendship.

Maybe they were supposed to be friends who kissed on dance floors and in hotel rooms in the Italian Alps. Friends who took one look at each other and forgot the rest of the world existed.

'Brett –' She took his pause for breath as an opportunity. For what? She wasn't quite sure. All she knew was that whatever she had been about to say went out the window once she saw the desire written in his expression, ten times more intense than it had been all night. It was just them. Their friends were gone, they weren't at a work event, nobody would know. So, when Brett glanced over her shoulder at the exit to the club, a silent invitation, she took it.

6

The sun *hurt*. Every time Lucie drank alcohol, she woke up the next morning wishing she lived in Alaska where they could go two months without seeing any sunlight. What a bloody dream. Why had she chosen a life of travel? And a life with so much free-flowing alcohol?

She was meant to be on a plane to London tonight with Faith, but she failed to see how she was going to pull herself together in time, let alone actually look presentable enough to walk through the hotel lobby. Brett already had the hotel room for one extra night . . . she could crash here. Her finances could take the hit if she paid for a new flight, right? She could stay right here in this very spot and rely on room-service burgers and nachos to get her through the hangover from hell. She squeezed her eyes tight shut again, willing her headache to go away.

Lucie wished they'd been smart enough to close the blackout blinds last night, and that she had the energy to get up and search for the remote. All this money, and they didn't have blinds that operated on clapping or clicking or mumbling 'For the love of God'.

Then she remembered the specific reason the blinds had been left open. The gorgeous man lying next to her had led her to the window and come up behind her. The view from the Bellagio was stunning, and they'd been fortunate enough to have a room facing the fountain, but it seemed to act as a reset button. Brett had removed the straps of her dress from her shoulders, letting it drop to the floor, and then Lucie had let reality get the better of her poor, bruised heart and ruined it all.

'Stop.' She'd blushed under his touch, but it was out of embarrassment more than anything. 'I'm sorry, I can't do this, Brett.'

'What's wrong?' He'd brushed her hair behind her ear.

'I just . . . I don't want to ruin us.'

'Nothing could ruin us, Sunny. We're grown adults, what's a night of fun, no-strings-attached sex between friends?' He'd shrugged like it was no big deal.

'It's not that simple, Brett. You're my best friend.'

'Yeah, and I respect you. Isn't that enough?'

'No, it isn't. You know I don't do casual sex. I need more from a partner.'

'That didn't seem to stop you two years ago in Italy, Sunny.'

'That was a mistake.'

And that was Lucie's problem. She had so desperately wanted to allow herself to get lost in the moment, to get carried away and recreate that one perfect night they'd spent together, but Lucie could never have casual, no-strings-attached sex with a man like Brett Anderson. She'd learned that the hard way. There were far too many emotions involved.

Relationships came and went and people betrayed her when the next best thing came along. He had just told her in not-so-many words that he would do the same thing to her that all the men of her early twenties had. If something happened between them again and he broke

62

her heart, she would lose everything. A romantic entanglement just wasn't on the cards.

So instead, they'd ordered every type of cheesecake from room service and sat in front of that very same window, her in his shirt, talking into the early hours of the morning with a bottle of Lucie's favourite red wine. Nothing had changed, and the only regret Lucie had woken up with was the kind that she could live with. The regret of a what if . . . and a killer hangover.

'Anderson, wake up. I need breakfast,' Lucie mumbled into her pillow. *Nothing.* 'Brett, come on. They have blueberry pancakes. It's our last day, we can't waste the breakfast menu. It's blasphemy.' But the Aussie giant didn't move a muscle. If the mention of blueberry pancakes couldn't coax him out of his slumber, nothing would.

Wet washcloth in hand, she stomped back over to him and prayed he woke up before she reached him because once she did this, he was going to be in a horrendous mood until the pancakes saved her reputation.

Brett, despite getting up before dawn for training or race-week prep, was not a morning person. It was a struggle they shared, and they were the worst on the team for it. He would be in a bad mood all day if she approached this wrong. Maybe she should set an alarm and leave her phone right next to his head? There was that default ringtone society universally hated, and that was the one thing that could get *her* up. But she remembered she had tried that before, and Brett had slept through it. He could probably sleep through an earthquake. Maybe even an ice age.

Since he had fallen asleep with his whole face shoved into the fluffy white pillows, she had no choice but to slap the washcloth onto the back of his neck. She braced herself for a temper tantrum, but it never came. 'Brett?' She shoved him. 'Brett.' She shoved him again, harder this time. Silence. Positioning her small frame so she could use all her strength, which wasn't much, she rolled him over to her side of the bed. His arm flopped out and his head lolled to one side, but he didn't even flinch. This was far worse than his usual deep sleep and Lucie was trying to quell the part of her brain that was telling her something could be wrong. She gave it one final shot. 'Wake up, Anderson.' She slapped him right across the face this time.

'What the fuck, Sunny?' Brett startled awake, glaring at Lucie.

'About time! Jesus, Brett, how much did you drink last night?'

'Not as much as I would've if you hadn't been on my ass about it.' There was a venom to his tone that surpassed tired disgruntlement.

Lucie had been half-joking, but his tone put her back up. He'd never spoken to her like this, even when he was stressed.

'Brett, I almost couldn't wake you.'

'But you did.' He rolled his eyes at her, like she was being dramatic.

Perhaps she was. Or perhaps she was starting to put the pieces together. Their night in the casino had been one thing, when he hadn't wanted to stop. This? This was unnerving. He usually had control and knew when to rein it in, he didn't lie motionless in bed and not wake up to the racket she'd been making.

'Don't you think you took it a bit far last night?' She softened her tone, hoping she didn't come across as accusatory.

'Nope.'

'Brett, come on . . . this isn't like you. You've been partying a lot lately, I mean, you were in Brussels just recently for a weekend fuelled by alcohol. You never used to do that.'

'I'm fine, Lucie.' He gritted his teeth so hard she was certain they'd shatter, but she wasn't quite done with this conversation.

'Brett . . .' she put her hand on his leg over the duvet, 'are you sure everything is okay, sweetheart?'

'Don't fucking call me that while you're being a pat-ronising little bitch.' His words, still slurred like he was just as drunk as he'd been the night before, struck her through the heart and she blinked back tears, recoiling from him.

Scrambling for her phone, she found it on the floor next to the bed. She had ten per cent battery, just enough for one phone call. As she hit the call button, she prayed her knight in shining armour would pick up. 'Julien?'

'Finally, you guys are awake!' Julien answered on the second ring. 'Do you want to go and get breakfast? Faith has just gone to wash her hair, then we can head down and find somewhere.'

'Jules, can you come in here? Bring Marco.' Lucie

knew she didn't need to expand. The tears were un-usual for her.

'Why do you need them?' Brett scoffed, throwing his arms up in disbelief.

'Because you're not acting like yourself, Brett.'

'Lucie!' There was a knock on the door a mere sixty seconds after she'd put the phone to one side, and she jumped up to let the boys in.

'He's being fucking horrible.' Her voice wobbled. 'I almost couldn't wake him, it took me ages and he woke up raging at me. I have this sinking feeling there's more to it, with the drinking.'

Julien gently pushed past her and went straight to where Brett lay in the middle of the king-sized mattress, pretending to have gone back to sleep. Regardless of how obvious it was that he was faking, Julien spoke like he wasn't in the room. It would no doubt anger Brett more, but at least the guys could handle it.

'You left early last night, right? Around eleven? Did you both keep drinking after you got back to the room?' Julien asked, his eyes on his teammate.

'We didn't even finish the bottle of wine, and I had a glass more than he did.'

'Brett, get your ass up.' Jules began pulling the covers back, and it was then that Lucie realised she was still wearing Brett's shirt and nothing else. They probably thought that last night she had become just another one of Brett's sexual conquests. That they'd partied together and had meaningless sex until the sun came up. That she was a bad influence.

66

'Luce, don't cry. It's okay. He's just got an attitude and a hangover from hell. He'll be all right.' Marco spoke softer than Jules did, but that was because Julien was in full dad mode.

'Lucie, go to my room, okay? Faith will let you in. Get Bea and Esme, hang out with them for a bit.' Julien may have been in dad mode, but he was pissed off. Whether it was at the situation in general or at Brett himself, she couldn't be sure, but as she grabbed a robe from the bathroom and made her escape, Lucie finally caught sight of two empty JD bottles on the coffee table. Those hadn't been there when they'd gone to sleep.

'There's your culprit.' She gestured at them.

'Why the hell would you drink *that* much whiskey alone?' Marco scolded Brett but Lucie had already closed the door on them. She was certain she knew why.

Brett didn't handle rejection well, and although they'd had a great night, she had done just that. He'd tried to take her to bed, and she'd turned him down. When she had told him they couldn't take things further, she could see the hurt in his eyes and knew at that moment something had shifted between them.

Even though they had stayed up most of the night and talked, their previous antics not mentioned again, she'd made him think she didn't want him in the way that he wanted her, and because he was human, that must have stung. He was probably embarrassed, maybe he thought there was something wrong with him. Or maybe he thought he'd offended her by even trying. She recalled the moment he had flinched when she'd put her hand over his as he passed her his shirt, and a wave of regret hit her.

Despite Julien's reassurance, and despite knowing Brett would be fine when he'd fully sobered up, as Lucie padded down the hotel corridor with bare feet, she felt awful. This was her fault. She should've explained herself better. Poured her heart out, told him the only reason she didn't want to sleep with him last night was because she wanted more than that from him.

If she was going to have Brett Anderson, she wanted all of him. The good and the bad and yes, looking at the state he was in now, the ugly. But Brett was not the kind of man who could commit to her, and Lucie was in so deep with him that anything less would break her into pieces.

'Lucie, love?' Faith opened the door, a mug of coffee in her hand. 'Take this, drink it and then go shower and wash your hair. I've left spare sweatpants, underwear, socks and all that in the bathroom for you. Sweatpants are Julien's so you might have to roll them up, but they should be okay for now. Bea and Esme are on their way. I'll call room service, too. Blueberry pancakes?'

Lucie looked at her friend and burst into tears. 'Thank you.' She pulled her into a tight hug and let her mascara-saturated tears fall onto the soft white cotton of Faith's top. Stain remover and dry-cleaning existed for situations like this. Well, maybe not the *best friend may have a drinking problem* part, but the *crying in last night's makeup* part.

'Nothing to thank me for. Off you go, you'll feel clearer-headed after.' Faith shooed her into the bathroom, coffee mug and all. If there was anything Faith could do well, it was nursing other people's hangovers and heartbreaks. She'd used the tough-love approach on Bea when she'd almost broken up with Ricardo De La Rosa over a tiny blip, and on Julien's daughter, Jasmine, when her first-ever school crush rejected her. This situation was potentially a little more serious, but Lucie still appreciated it.

If Faith wasn't there to look after her, she'd have sat in Julien's hotel room and stared out at the Las Vegas Strip, letting her thoughts run wild. It wasn't healthy. But Faith knew exactly what Lucie needed. She knew her almost as well as Brett did. Their friendship had blossomed quickly, and although they didn't have ten years behind them, they did have an instant bond that had grown over the last two race seasons.

Stepping into the shower, Lucie's mind was still clinging to guilt. Analysing his recent behaviour, Lucie came to the realisation that Brett had indeed been drinking more. A few extra beers at dinner, whiskey before bed. They had spent more vacations in cities and popular tourist spots than in quaint European villages or at luxury spas. There had been more trips to bars and clubs than trips up mountains.

They'd spent four days at a ski resort in the summer; it was meant to be a hiking trip and he'd only hiked once, which seemed strange for Brett. He instead opted to drink and admire the view from the restaurant's balcony.

Alone. He'd called it 'taking a break' and she hadn't paid any mind. How had she *missed* this? She should have seen the signs. This definitely wasn't just a reaction to her rejection.

She sat on the floor of the shower, letting the water wash over her and ignoring the girls' knocks for what felt like hours. Her eyes stung and her skin burned with the heat, but she couldn't bring herself to get up for the longest time. Only the knock from room service and the subsequent waft of pancakes brought her out of her spell, and she finally turned the water off.

Faith was right, Julien's sweatpants did drown her, but she didn't have the energy to care right now. If Marco and Julien came to the same conclusion and they mutually agreed Brett needed help, she'd be the one to do it. Get to the bottom of whatever this was. He would do the same for her if she was in his position.

That was one of the things she loved about the IEC. They were a family, and nobody had to struggle alone. She had heard about the drama in other racing championships and could count on one hand the number of scandals she'd heard of within the IEC. Once drivers were involved with the organisation, it took a lot for them to leave, which gave everyone the chance to build genuine, long-lasting friendships – of course there were always going to be hiccups along the way, but this wasn't a toxic place. If Brett needed more help than they could provide, they'd rally around him.

'Hey, there you are.' Esme spoke softly as Lucie stumbled out of the bathroom in a daze, the cool air awakening her senses more than the shower had managed. 'We ordered you granola and fresh orange juice, too. It's all on Julien's credit card, take full advantage.'

'I will.' Lucie let out a gentle laugh.

'So, what happened?'

'I couldn't wake him up. He was completely unresponsive for far too long, I was close to checking his breathing. And then when I finally got him to surface, he just wasn't Brett. He was so . . . so cruel.'

'You guys didn't go *that* wild last night, did you?' Faith frowned.

'You were gone when we came back from our hunt for food,' Bea added.

'Spotted two empty bottles of JD on my way out. He must have stayed up after I crashed.'

'Oh . . . that's so strange,' Bea pondered.

'I'm worried I might have sent him over the edge, or at least rocked the boat. We almost slept together last night.' She grimaced, waiting for the dramatics.

'I bloody knew it!' Faith shouted.

'That stays between us.'

'Of course,' Esme added. 'But why only almost? You two are *so* right for each other.'

'I freaked out, I want more than just sex with a person, so I pushed him away.'

'Oh . . .' Faith trailed off. 'Lucie Carolan, you'd better not be blaming yourself.'

'A smidge,' Lucie shrugged.

'That's ridiculous and you know it. This whole drinking thing has clearly been brewing for a while, we've all been questioning just how wild he's been partying. Especially at the launch, it was so unlike him and you didn't do anything then. Here, have some yoghurt.' Faith thrust a bowl at her. 'Enough with those thoughts.'

The three of them sat there for another forty-five minutes, stuffing their faces with food and scrolling through Bea's social media, engaging in mindless gossip about the latest influencer dramas. The distraction was welcome, but not entirely effective. Lucie spent most of that time silent, pretending to listen. She had to keep talking herself out of going back into Brett's room.

'I've got a text.' Faith reach for her phone. She looked up with a smile on her face. 'He's perked up a bit, they've got him drinking some water and he seems to be sobering up quite fast. Apparently, he's cracking jokes now and insists he's fine and had tipped most of the JD down the sink, which makes no sense. Julien thinks he's putting on a front, and just doesn't want to talk emotions. He also said for you to let Brett sulk for an hour or so before you go in. He feels really bad and keeps asking for you.' Faith continued reading out the key parts of the message, but Lucie was focused on one thing and one thing only.

For the first time in their entire friendship, she was scared of what would come next.

7

'There she is, my sunshine girl.' Brett sat propped up in bed four hours later, surrounded by room-service food with a superhero film playing on the flat-screen TV at the foot of the bed. He looked like he hadn't slept for days, his hair sticking out at odd angles. In all honesty, he looked adorable. She had always loved how he looked in the mornings: innocent, naïve.

He didn't look like he was recovering from a wild drinking binge, he just looked like Brett. Lucie's façade almost crumbled, but she couldn't let his treatment of her this morning slide. She wanted to come in here with a tough-love approach, because it was exactly what she would want Brett to do if she was in his position.

It was also the nature of the sport Brett loved. Jasper and the team at Revolution Racing approached things the same way. They yelled at each other over the radio, they had blazing rows in conference rooms, but it was because they cared. They had passion. They were a team. Just like she and Brett were and had been for a decade. This was a blip.

'Uh huh. Good to see you're feeling chipper.' Lucie raised an eyebrow as mayonnaise fell out of his chicken burger and landed on his bare chest. 'You need a bib. You're like a big baby.' She willed herself not to laugh as he wiped it off.

'Do you hate me?' He looked up at her with big, round eyes. He looked just like that GIF of the cat from *Shrek* and it almost succeeded in making Lucie melt.

'I'm certainly not impressed.' She crossed her arms and leaned against the doorframe.

'I woke up on the wrong side of the bed and my head was pounding.'

'That's no excuse for that kind of behaviour, Brett.'

'I know.' He looked nauseous, and she didn't think it was just the result of alcohol.

'You scared me. I've never seen you in that state before. And for you to speak to me the way you did?'

'I'm so sorry, Luce. Seriously. I shouldn't have let myself get that drunk.'

'You hurt me.' She felt her eyes sting again.

'Oh, Sunny. Come here.' Brett put his food aside and held his arms out.

When she settled into him, like he was made for her, and laid her head on his mayo-free chest, she felt him breathe a sigh of relief. It was the same relief she felt the second he embraced her, and it was then that she knew if she had to lie here for the next twenty-four hours, flight to London be damned, watching crappy action movies and gorging out on greasy food until he felt human again, she would.

'You deserve better, Sunny,' he muttered into her hair, running his fingers through it in an effort to soothe her.

'You owe me big time, Anderson. I want a lifetime of unlimited blueberry pancakes. Might as well just hand your credit card over now.'

'How about we go out tonight? There's a really cool bar on the Strip that we didn't get to last night. I know the owner; I can get us a booth. Just me and you, fuck everyone else. I've got the room until tomorrow anyway.' She felt the low rumble of his voice as he spoke, felt his chest rise and fall. But surely she had heard wrong? Surely those words had not just come out of his mouth.

'Brett, are you serious?' She sat up and stared at him in bewilderment.

'What?' He looked at her blankly.

'What do you mean, *what*?'

He shrugged nonchalantly. 'It's just a hangover, Luce. I'm fine.'

'You're not fine, Brett. You are *so* far from fine. Do you not see it?'

'Lucie.' He attempted to silence her.

'Brett.' She was firm, staring him down and ensuring he knew just how serious her tone was.

'Lucie . . .' Brett trailed off upon realising this had the potential to be a huge blowout.

'This is not just a hangover. You know that. You know deep down that this is so much more than just a hangover, Brett. Please. You drank two bottles of JD on your own!' She got up from the bed and stood with her arms crossed. Brett never took her seriously when she was mad, but this time was an exception. He looked guiltier than she'd ever seen him. But the guilt didn't mean he was going to admit to having a problem.

'It's not a big deal, Lucie,' he shrugged. 'We're in Las Vegas. Loosen up a bit, you're supposed to take it too far

75

in a place like this. I mean, look out the window. What do you see? Bars, casinos and nightclubs everywhere. Was I meant to be on my best behaviour and go to bed after two beers? Set my alarm for six a.m. and go for a run? We're on holiday, we're away from a race weekend and we're allowed to let our hair down and have some fun.'

'Have you lost all sense of control? It's not just a weekend here and there any more, it's *all the time*. You just seem to no longer give a fuck about your health. Mental or physical. We make these kind of mistakes at college, when we're younger, we don't do this now. You're damn lucky you have people who care about you, Anderson. If you value your career and if you value us, if you value *me*, you'll stop drinking so heavily. Get some help for whatever it is that makes you need the alcohol.'

'Sunny. We've all done things we regret; we've all drunk too much before. It was my fault for not realising my limits last night.' He looked at her with pleading eyes.

'No. Don't *Sunny* me. Don't try to manipulate me into letting this go. What if you embarrass yourself publicly? Do something while intoxicated that paints you in a bad light? Hell, what if one day you drink so much that you *don't* wake up?'

'I drive fast cars for a living, Luce. My fans worship the ground I walk on. They're not gonna go anywhere.'

'Your fans might not, but the sponsors will. You lose them, and you lose your seat. Revolution will take a massive hit, and then Jules and Marco might lose their jobs, too. Are you really willing to risk it? You used to avoid excessive amounts of alcohol because you don't like not being in control, you said it made your brain fuzzy and you needed to stay sharp to be the best driver the IEC has ever seen. This is so unlike you. What changed? Am I that terrible of a friend that I didn't notice something?'

'You're not a bad friend, Luce, but damn I wish you'd stop making such a fucking fuss.' He gritted his teeth, his eyes burning with anger. 'I liked you better when you just shut up and let me get on with my own life and you got on with yours. Except that has never been the case, really, has it? Because you just can't leave me alone.'

If his voice hadn't cracked as he said it, she might have thought he meant it. If she hadn't witnessed the anger dissipate from his expression and morph into regret the second a tear rolled down her cheek, she might've believed every word. Lucie had never been one for heartbreak; never let anyone get that close. Her walls were always up. But Brett might just end up being the person to shatter her into a million pieces.

'Screw you, Anderson.'

Lucie wasn't even halfway down the corridor before Brett was chasing after her, but as tears blurred her vision and she slammed her fist against the call button for the lift, she ignored him calling out to her. If she looked back at him, she knew she would cave.

'Sunny, wait,' he pleaded. 'I didn't mean it.'

She let the door close on his guilt-ridden face and took a deep breath, half-wishing she'd heard him out and half-grateful to have a moment to gather her thoughts. She walked through the hotel lobby in her oversized sweatpants and slippers, bypassing the Bellagio's upper-class clientele and for once paying zero attention to whether or not she was out of place.

The Nevada sun had disappeared behind the clouds and as she headed to the nearest coffee shop round the corner, she thought about how they never should have come on this trip. But then, if they hadn't, Brett's declining mental health might have gone on unnoticed.

Maybe she and Julien were being dramatic. Maybe Brett was right, it was Vegas, this was classic Las Vegas behaviour. It wasn't like he was recreating *The Hangover*, but the change in his behaviour was scary. It was the anger towards her that had been the giveaway. Perhaps if he had been his usual cheery self, she could have overlooked it.

Lucie hadn't even taken a sip of her iced latte before Brett was walking through the door, pulling out a chair and making himself comfortable at her table in the back corner. There was no point in stopping him and causing a scene.

'Knew I'd find you in here.'

'I don't want to talk, Brett.' Lucie sniffled then sighed.

'Well, tough shit. You made me listen to you, now you're going to listen to me.'

'I don't owe you anything. I don't have to have this conversation if I don't want to, regardless of your needs.'

'Come on, Sunny. We're a team, remember? I can't do this without you,' he pleaded.

'Brett –' She clenched her jaw, torn between letting rip again, storming out or giving in.

'Luce, put the coffee down. Look at me.' He gestured at her cup, which she was clutching tightly with both hands. She didn't want to look at him, not while they were *both* hurting.

'For Christ's sake.' She heaved an almighty sigh, rolling her eyes at herself as she let him win the battle. She should've walked out of the café.

'I'm sorry.' Brett almost whispered it to her.

'I know.'

'No, you don't know. You'll never understand how awful I feel about what I said. For drinking too much and scaring you. You're my best friend, Sunny. My right-hand woman. There is nothing on this earth I wouldn't do for you. You know that, right? You're my number one, always.'

'I shouldn't be your number one, Brett. *You* should be. You have to deal with whatever this is for yourself, not just for me.' She shook her cup, the ice cubes rattling. Anything to distract from just how serious this conversation was getting.

'I think you might be right, there's more to it.'

'Really?'

'Yeah.' He looked out of the window. 'I'll reel it in.'

'I love you to pieces, Brett. Please, don't let this get any worse. And *never* speak to me that way again, or trust me, Brett, I will consider walking out of your life.'

'I'm scared,' he admitted. 'I don't feel like myself any more.'

79

'The Brett I know doesn't let fear win.'

'The Brett you know has been slowly disappearing for a while.' He couldn't even hide the sadness in his voice, and it broke her heart.

'Hey.' She reached for his hand. 'He's still in there.'

'I want to go home, Sunny. I need to go back to Sydney. I think it's about time I started facing my demons.'

'I wish you'd told me you had demons in the first place.'

'Yeah, well. I'm Brett Anderson, world-class racing driver. I can't show weakness.' He gave her a shaky smile, and the look of pain on his face made her want to wrap him up in her arms and never let go.

'You can show weakness with me, Brett. You know you can. Nothing has changed from the beginning of our friendship.'

Lucie remembered the first time they met at Monza. It was her first week on the job, and she'd been so nervous to meet him. She could still recall the tremble of her voice. Brett had been a pretty big name in motorsport for two years, ever since he was sixteen and racing in a junior championship, and Lucie had celebrated her eighteenth birthday a mere two weeks before she started on the catering team. She had a baby face, and she was dinky to match.

She'd bumped into him outside his trailer before a race and he'd been flustered, and blurted out to her, a complete stranger, that he was nervous about the race, verging on a panic attack. His usual pre-race ritual wasn't working for him. She'd offered him her headphones and played her favourite song and they had sat on the step of his trailer listening to it for three minutes and twenty-nine seconds. It was in those three minutes and twenty-nine seconds that they had formed an unbreakable bond.

Brett confessed to her a year later that he had never admitted to being nervous about a race before, ever, but there was something about Lucie that made him feel instantly at home. He had been listening to that song before every race for the whole season, and now, ten years later, it was still part of his ritual. She just *got* him.

'I think . . . and please don't take this the wrong way, but I think I need to go back to Sydney alone. Take a few weeks to figure myself out and get my head back in the game.'

'Are you sure, Brett? What about the next race of the season?'

'I think part of my problem is that I've finally allowed myself to get caught up in the whirlwind lifestyle of the rich and famous. You and Faith have done too good a job at making us so well-known and in demand, I've let myself get carried away with it. If I said that sentence to anyone else, they'd laugh at me. They'd tell me to stop being ridiculous, to enjoy the life I've got and stop worrying, that it's just a phase. And maybe it is, but what if it isn't? I'm sure Jasper can find a replacement for me. Just for one race.'

'Okay. I'll help you pack, and I'll be there when you call Jasper. If you want, that is.'

'Lucie?' He took her hand in his.

'Yeah?' She turned to look at him and for a split second, he felt like that same vulnerable, eighteen-year-old Brett she'd met outside the trailer.

'Thank you.'

'You can thank me by just being your old self again.'

8

'You did not seriously bring *Versace* slippers.' Lucie removed them from Brett's suitcase and held them up with a frown.

They were packing for Brett's flight home to Sydney and her flight to London to visit the Girls Off Track HQ. She was scared to be away from him at a time like this, but he was a fully grown adult. She had to let him go. Even if she did want to install a tracker on his phone to be sure he was behaving.

'They're my babies, Luce.'

'They're *slippers*. Honestly, I don't know which is worse. The fact you have designer slippers in the first place, or the fact you brought them to a hotel.'

'Hey, I have to look my best to feel my best.'

'In a hotel room where nobody can see you? Crying because you got a speck of dirt on your designer sneakers was bad enough.'

'Sneakers,' Brett snorted. 'You and your Americanisms.'

'Stop changing the subject.' Lucie launched a balled-up pair of socks at him which he dodged, chuckling softly as he stuffed them in his case.

'Okay, okay. Are all Italian women as scary as you? Do they all fling socks at their husbands when they're not behaving?'

'You're lucky you're not my husband, Anderson.' Lucie walked off on the hunt for his aftershave and toothbrush, making sure she didn't forget a single product from his skincare routine. She would never hear the end of it.

'Don't you wish we were driving to the airport together?' he asked.

'Not today. I'll let your cab driver suffer alone.' Brett was a terrible traveller, no matter the distance. He talked incessantly, as if he wasn't enough of a chatterbox as it was. He requested the radio station be changed the second a song came on that he didn't absolutely love, never settled between having the window down or the air con on and insisted on stopping at 'cool-looking diners' throughout every journey. Ninety-five per cent of the time, their exteriors were wildly misleading.

'If we were travelling together while I am *also* recovering from a hangover, I would have purchased a muzzle.'

'What is that supposed to mean?!' He pressed a hand to his chest. 'You don't like it when I sing "Halo" at the top of my lungs?'

'I don't think Beyoncé herself likes that, and she can't even hear you.' Lucie stared at him with a blank expression.

'Luce . . .' Brett's entire demeanour softened, and his voice lowered. 'Are you sure you're not offended that I haven't asked you to come?'

'Why would I be offended?' Lucie frowned up at him.

'We go everywhere together. Most of the time, anyway.' He toyed with the string of the hoodie he was holding; one he'd been struggling to fold.

84

'I've got plenty to keep me busy, Brett. I was already meant to be going back to London for work, we've got a bunch of podcast episodes to film along with a variety of other tasks for the business to tackle.'

'Still, I'll miss having you around,' he mumbled.

'You know as well as I do that you'll be busy with your family and catching up with old friends. Let's not forget the skating! I can't skate to save my life.'

'It just feels strange to be heading home alone. You always come to Sydney with me, you're part of the family.' Brett shrugged, and Lucie put down the T-shirt she'd just picked up to walk around the bed and stand in front of him.

'Brett, you've got to do this yourself.' She gazed up at him through thick lashes, craning her neck so she could study his face. He looked so confused.

'What did I do to deserve you?' A slight smile played on his lips.

'It's me and you against the world, remember?'

'Always.' Brett pulled her into one of his classic bear hugs, except this time there was no ruffling of her hair or a tight squeeze. He just held her, until she could feel him relaxing into some sort of realisation. Brett had to trust himself.

'Right, you shower and finish packing while I run out to get you pre-flight snacks. Any special requests?'

'Oysters to go?'

'Not a chance.'

'A BLT?'

'That's more like it.'

Brett winked at her. It was so like him, so carefree and charming. But it didn't stop the horrible feeling in her stomach that this wasn't the end of his troubles. Sydney wasn't enough to fix whatever was going on inside his head, whatever had led to him being so reckless for so long.

But Lucie couldn't give him all her focus. The workload for Girls Off Track had more than doubled since their launch. They'd cut back on so many travel plans for the upcoming year, and even after doing that they still had a packed schedule. It was an exciting time for them, and Lucie felt a rush whenever she thought about how far they'd come. She was happy to forgo the trips to build the business; after all, it was something that she could be proud of. It was her legacy.

As it stood, Jasper, their team principal, was fully aware that Brett needed some time to be with his family and get himself back in the game. Julien and Lucie had highlighted to him that there was more than meets the eye here, that Brett's mental health needed a reset. They had reserve drivers for a reason. Drivers got sick, had family emergencies. As far as Jasper knew, they were knocking the alcohol thing on the head before it became a real problem, but Lucie wasn't sure how true that was.

If Brett didn't feel ready to return for Monza, though? He could be out for the rest of the season. The team couldn't afford to take the risk. They needed a driver they could rely on. Everyone at Revolution was adamant that was still him, but what if it wasn't? Lucie shook the thought away, she wouldn't catastrophise, not yet.

She ambled back up to the room an hour later. Brett's

suitcase was packed and waiting by the door, his kanga-roo luggage tag on the handle.

'Do you think Mum will appreciate a lodger?' Brett appeared in his towel, water dripping from his golden, toned abs. Lucie tried not to stare.

'You're not staying at your place?' Lucie arched an eyebrow.

'I left it in a mess . . .'

'Well . . . clean it up?'

'There's alcohol bottles everywhere. And potentially some other substances left behind, which are one hun-dred per cent not mine,' Brett quickly added as Lucie went to scold him, and he caught his bottom lip in his teeth, his face a picture of worry. 'Not exactly the best welcome home gift at the minute.'

She glared at him but knew now wasn't the time for a lecture. 'You know she'd love to have you, Anderson, but it might do you good to clear your place out. Start fresh. I got you some thriller novels to read, by the way. I imagine you'll have quite a lot of downtime even with your sisters hassling you non-stop.'

'Lucie Carolan, did you check my Goodreads account?' He gasped as he pulled out a new release that he'd added to his wish list. 'This came out literally two days ago.' Lucie smirked. She checked it every birthday and Christmas and played it off like she'd just randomly selected whatever was on the shelf, but now he knew her secret.

'Damn it, Brett, now you know. I do the same for your sisters. Speaking of, Cleo is far too young to be reading the things I've seen on her list. I have half a mind to screenshot it and send it to your mum.'

'Who do you think bought her half the books on her shelf?' Brett grinned.

'Oh my *God*. She's fifteen!' Lucie's mouth hung open.

'She's got an older sister and nobody in my family has a filter.'

'I'm surprised Piper hasn't put a stop to that.' Brett's twin was too sensible for her own good. 'Speaking of . . . have you spoken to her? Told her why you're coming home?'

'No, and I'm not going to.'

'Brett.' She gave him a disapproving look, suddenly aware it was the same look Piper would give him if she were in Lucie's shoes.

'I have to protect my family. This would devastate them, they don't need to know.'

'It would devastate them more if they knew you were struggling. Think about –'

'Do not say my dad. This is different. I'm not dead.'

'I-I –' she stuttered when she saw the way he clenched his jaw.

'Lucie.' He used his warning tone. He may think he was the opposite of Piper, but he was just like her in more ways than one. They must have got their stubbornness from their dad, because Maggie could *always* see reason.

'I just don't want to lie to your family.'

'I'm not asking you to, Luce.' Brett gave her a tight hug, but it did nothing to settle the feeling of dread settling in her stomach.

9

Six hours into his flight home, Brett was trying and failing to fall asleep. He'd got to the airport, demolished his BLT, boarded the plane, listened to some bullshit podcast about sobriety and meditation until he'd heard enough to put his own playlist on, completely unintentionally sung some old-school Justin Bieber out loud, then grabbed the pillow he had swiped from the hotel and leaned up against the window. It must have had duck feathers or something in it, because it was like having a portable cloud. But he couldn't switch his brain off.

He needed rest. He was emotionally exhausted, and he was scared. Scared of his own brain, of being unable to save himself, of letting people down. Brett was the oldest of his siblings and he had to play the role of protector, he was the man of the house after his father's passing, he couldn't let them down.

He didn't get to where he was in his career by letting fear win, but he'd bottled up his emotions for too long and now Lucie and their friends were the ones having to pick up the pieces.

Brett couldn't deny it any more, he needed help. This wasn't something that some R&R and his friends could fix.

He had been going back and forth in his mind for

months now about checking into rehab, but there was always something stopping him. He'd been screwed over so many times by people he considered friends, how could he be sure that someone at the rehab facility wouldn't sell his secrets? He had limited his circle to co-workers, his childhood best friend and his immediate family.

He thought back to the mindset Julien had been in before he met Faith, that everyone wanted a piece of him to either sell to a tabloid or exploit for themselves; it had prevented Jules from letting Faith in at first, and it was more damaging than any driver realised. Trusting *anyone* was a risk. Lucie had been there the day Brett discovered his ex, Sienna, had cheated on him. If you couldn't trust the person you had chosen to spend for-ever with, who you had given your heart to, who *could* you trust? Lucie had seen what that had done to Brett, how his walls firmly came back up.

Brett was as fun as he always was, but ever since Sienna, he had let that fun take over. He was known to have a woman in every city, never one to settle down, not willing to commit, and it was only since the Alps that he'd toned it down. When they had finally given in to whatever it was that was simmering between them in the Alps, Brett knew that no other woman could reach him like Lucie could. Having her in his arms and tangled up in his sheets just for one night had opened up a whole new world for him. It was like someone had flipped a switch, and suddenly all he wanted was her. But Lucie had made it clear in the months that followed, he just wasn't enough for her.

Brett knew that he couldn't give her everything she deserved, she needed stability and safety. Someone who had their shit together and thought about the future. He lived a life with zero responsibility off the track, and Brett didn't know how to change that.

He caved and connected his phone to the plane's wifi. Lucie had gone to meet the rest of the group for lunch before flying back to the UK, and he had done a runner, too embarrassed to face them after the way he'd behaved this week. Julien and Marco had texted him, but he had ignored them.

He messaged Lucie a sleepy emoji.

She replied immediately. She must be waiting to board by now. *Tired, bud?*

Bud? He scowled.

You don't like that one?

Don't ever call me that again.

Why not?

It's insulting, he typed, wishing he could tell her the real reason he didn't want her to call him *bud*.

He wanted to tell her they were more than just *buddies*. He wanted to tell her that there was more to their relationship, there had been since they'd slept together. But what good would it do? She had been deflecting his advances ever since.

Okay, okay. Won't happen again. She sent a winking face, but he wasn't done.

Bud is what I call Mars and Jules.

Are they not also your best friends?

Yeah, but you're, you know . . . He couldn't believe he

was about to send this over text. If any of their friends looked over her shoulder, he'd never hear the end of it.

I'm what? Lucie quizzed.

You have boobs.

What?

I'm just saying that I've literally been inside you and we've crossed lines, so I can't consider you just a friend. Anyway, this is weird.

So, I'm not allowed to call you sweetheart or bud?

You can call me sweetheart. I just told you not to the other night because when I'm drunk it does things to me. Things that you don't want from me.

I guess from this day forward we won't have that problem.

She skirted over what he was trying to pull out of her, but he wasn't going to give up easily, he knew there was something here.

Oh, we'll still have that problem, Luce.

There was a truth in that statement that Brett had never expressed while sober. There had been plenty of moments when they could have crossed the line with no alcohol in their system, could have thrown caution to the wind and explored their attraction without the haze of toxicity clouding their judgement. He just thanked the heavens she always put a stop to it before one of them regretted it.

'I'm a bit miffed he didn't say goodbye.' Faith was huffing and puffing her way around the office, stocking the staffroom with teabags and pods for the new coffee machine.

'He was just worried what you'd all think of him.'

'Seriously? We're all proud of him! I think it's incredibly brave of him to do what he's doing, to take a temporary step back from racing. He must really be going through it.'

'I really hope he's okay.' Lucie trailed after her with a mug in each hand.

'What did you say to his mum in the end?' Faith asked, reminding Lucie that she had an unread message from Maggie. She was concerned. Brett had been cagey about why he was home earlier than planned, but Lucie didn't know how to respond.

'Nothing. I'll just reply later, tell her I've been busy all day. Suggest she speaks to her son as it's not my place. Then he can decide how much or how little to tell her.'

'Good idea,' Faith nodded. 'Are *you* okay?'

'Not really, but I can't do much about it.'

'We can fly out there, if you want? Jules will loan us the money.'

'No, no. I don't want to smother him. I need to respect that he asked for space.' She knew this was the right decision but she couldn't deny she'd thought about getting on a plane at least three times an hour since he'd landed.

'I don't think you would be, but I hear you.'

'I'm just emotional, and I know it's not going to be easy for him.'

'Brett's a tough cookie, Luce. He'll be okay. Plus, he knows he's got all of us to help keep him on the right path when he's back.'

'That sort of makes it sound like he's in prison.'

'I don't think they'd let him keep that pillow he stole if he was in prison.'

'The bloody pillow. Honestly, who does that?'

Faith snorted, 'Rich people.'

'Says the girl who is married to one.'

'Jules isn't that crazy.'

'Yeah, *right*. The man spent all those euros to win you a stuffed shark at the funfair.'

'That was in the name of love. So, that's fine.'

'How *is* your beloved Mustang?'

'Jasmine stole him. He's back in Hawaii with her.' Faith pretended to be sad about it, but realistically she'd probably willingly given him to her stepdaughter so she wouldn't feel obligated to keep dragging a giant stuffed shark around the world with her.

'I know this is probably inappropriate, all things considered, but can we go to a fancy bar and get very, very drunk.'

'Oh, one hundred per cent. And it isn't inappropriate at all. Brett is the one with a drinking problem, not you. You're still entitled to let your hair down, Luce.' She nudged Lucie's hip in encouragement.

'Okay, thank you. Look, I'm going to head back to the hotel. I've given myself a headache and I think I need to sleep it off and just shut my brain down for a bit.'

'All right, I'm just going to finish up here then I'll be back. God, I wish I still had my flat! Love you, Carolan.'

'Love you, Jensen.' Lucie offered a weary smile and headed out to the nearest tube station.

As she stood behind the yellow line amongst a sea

of office workers desperate to get home, she wondered what Brett was doing right now.

Lucie wanted to know he had the support he needed back home, but she'd promised not to say anything, so for now, she should rely on Brett telling her the truth about how he was feeling. Something about lying to Maggie Anderson felt very wrong. She treated Lucie like her own daughter, and Lucie had *never* lied to her. If she told his mum and sisters what was really going on, beat him to it, yes, they would be worried, but at least both Brett and Lucie could lean on them for support throughout this journey.

She realised how ridiculous that sounded, even in her own head. She and Brett weren't together. They never had been. Lucie shouldn't be leaning on his family; she should be leaning on her own. *Damn it.* She had to tell Maggie the truth.

10

Of all the places he could have bumped into someone. Of all the people he could have bumped into. Why did she have to appear here, outside his *favourite* hidden gem café? Alone, too, so she would have no hesitation in stopping for a chat. And he let her, because he was weak and his ex-girlfriend had always had a hold over him.

'Hey, Brett!' she gushed, and it was so over the top but even the fake enthusiasm tugged at his heartstrings. There was so much unfinished business here.

'Sienna?' He blinked at her, feeling a little lost. Should he be friendly? Passive-aggressive? Bitter? Instead, he just felt confused. 'I didn't realise you were back in Sydney.'

'Likewise. I'm surprised you're not still gallivanting around somewhere in Europe.'

'Don't like to stay in one place too long.'

'I know.' She looked down at her Birkenstocks, playing with her keychain.

'So,' he cleared his throat, 'how did ya find out about this place?'

'Zara's sister owns it, didn't you realise?' Her brow furrowed. Zara was an old school friend of theirs, and funnily enough the friend who had re-introduced them years ago at a party. Cheers, Zara.

'No way is that Zara's kid sister!' Brett gasped, peering

through the door to where she stood at the till. He suddenly felt very old.

'Yeah,' Sienna laughed. 'You don't pay much attention to what goes on around here any more, do you?'

'Nah. Moved on with my life.' He shrugged.

'Have you?' Sienna eyed him wearily.

'Um . . .' he hesitated. The truth was, he hadn't moved on at all, had he? What Sienna had done to him had sent him into a spiral. But maybe seeing her here now was a sign from the universe. A sign of what, he wasn't quite sure.

'How have you been, then?'

His crush on Sienna had begun way back in school, and transitioned into more when they met again as adults. There was something about her that always drew him in. She was fiery, feisty, independent. She reminded him of Lucie, except he didn't feel the same pressure to provide stability for her. She'd been a party animal, it was her nature. Just like him. But he couldn't deny that cracks had started to show, he'd been spending more time travelling and less time back in Sydney with her, and she wouldn't come with him. Then he found out about the cheating, and the trust was gone.

'I've been all right. You?' He shifted uncomfortably.

'Yeah, good. Look, I'm gonna go. I get the vibe you don't feel like catching up.'

Before she could walk away, he grabbed her hand. 'Sienna, wait. I'm sorry. Do you want to sit down and have a coffee with me?'

'Really?' Her blue eyes went wide and as he looked at

her, he saw a childlike innocence. Childhood memories came back to haunt him, and it made it hard to hold a grudge.

'Yeah, come on. My treat.'

As they sat down together, Sienna having come back inside for her second iced latte of the day, it felt surprisingly normal. Brett wasn't sure how that made him feel, or whether he actually wanted to be sitting here.

'How's the family?' She sipped her drink slowly, cautiously. It couldn't be more obvious that she didn't know how to act around him either.

'Yeah, great. How's your mum?' He bit into his croissant. 'Oh my god, this is unreal!' He looked at her, guilty for the interruption. 'Sorry, continue.'

'That's fine,' she laughed. 'Same old Brett, eh? Mum is good. Married again.'

'Again?!' Brett gawked. 'That's . . . what? Husband number six?'

'Yep. I like this one, though. Hopefully he sticks around. So, when's your next race?'

'Uhh, about two weeks' time.' He swallowed roughly. Could he trust her? Jasper wasn't releasing a statement about his absence from Monza for another week, but did he really want to tell her while he wasn't even sure where they stood?

'Oh, Monza?' she smiled.

'That's the one.' Brett grinned back at her.

'I'm glad you're still enjoying racing. It's hard to imagine you doing anything else.'

There was something odd about her tone; did she

wish she had gone around the world with him? Or did she just regret making herself the enemy in the end?

'Neither can I.' And it was true. It was just another reason he needed to pull his socks up and stop drinking. 'What have you been doing with yourself the last few years, then? Still causing trouble in the clubs and bars?'

She practically burst with pride when she nodded in response. 'That side of me hasn't gone anywhere, I still like to have fun with the girls. But I have the day job of my dreams! I've finally taken the plunge and started my own fashion brand. Got a store in Darlinghurst.'

'Sienna, are you serious? That's what you always wanted, right?'

'Yeah. I used my money from influencing to do it. So, you know, it wasn't all a waste.'

'Hey, I never said it was a waste.'

'No, but you didn't exactly approve.'

'Just sometimes it felt like you were using me. But if it worked out . . . I'm happy for you.'

She sighed and leaned back in her chair, looking defeated. 'I never used you, Brett. It was a confusing time for us both, but I realised my mistakes after you and I broke up. I pined for you for months, praying that you'd call and come back to me. I wished I could undo it all. I'll always have a soft spot for you.'

'You really fucked me up, Sienna.' He let out a shaky laugh.

If only he could tell her just how much. Tell her she'd ripped his heart to shreds, put his walls up, driven him to drink his feelings away behind closed doors and eventually, in the open, too. Not a whisky bottle was devoured without his mind going back to her. Remembering the good and the bad. His sunshine girl took up one half of his brain, and Sienna the other.

'I fucked myself up too, Brett. If only you knew how much.'

'Fuck, I'm going to regret asking this, I'm sure of it, but do you wanna go out tonight?' The words hadn't even left his mouth before he knew he was making a mistake, but he couldn't help it. His poison was right in front of him, and he was confused and tired and just wanted to feel like his old self again. Maybe rekindling *something* with Sienna would help him.

'I'm going to regret saying yes, but I don't want to say no.' She tucked her hair behind her ear, and he smiled softly. He used to love lying on the sofa and playing with her hair while a television show of her choosing played in the background. He'd never watch it, he always watched her. He knew he loved her more than she loved him, but he'd been willing to accept it in order to keep her in his life. Now he was in the same boat with Lucie.

'You still living in the same apartment?'

'Uh-huh.' She nodded.

'I'll meet you at your place at six thirty.' He stood up abruptly.

'Oh, are we done here?' She gathered up her things in a hurry.

'Sen, it's gone three o'clock. You haven't even fake-tanned.'

'Shit!' She immediately went into panic mode.

'I still know you, Sienna.' He laughed, and after a few seconds of hesitation, kissed her on the cheek. 'I'll see you tonight.'

'Brett, I don't like this.' Maggie frowned and he regretted coming over.

'You don't have to like it, Mum. I love you, but this is my life.'

'I just don't want you getting tangled up in that woman's bullshit again, honey. She's a right little witch.' Maggie stood in the hallway with him, trying to pull his shoe out of his hand while he was putting it on.

'A witch.' Brett laughed. 'Mum, chill. People change, you know?'

'This is bizarre, Brett. Even for you. You hated her guts the past few years, and now you're home unannounced, getting ready to go hang out with her. Why isn't Lucie with you? Have you had a falling-out? Do I need to set Piper on her?' She cast a look back towards the living room where his twin was watching a crime documentary.

'We talked about this yesterday, Maggs. Sunny and I are all groovy, I just need a break from cameras and journalists and all that crap. I need to relax, hang out with my faves.'

'And Sienna is suddenly your "fave"?' She pulled a face, her frown lines prominent. It was all the stress of worrying about her beloved only son that had aged her, according to her.

'No, you are.' He squeezed his mum tight.

'Don't be sweet. I expect I'm supposed to keep this part of your visit a secret from Lucie, aren't I? She'd be straight on a plane if she knew!'

'I have skeletons in my closet. Luce knows that better than most, so I'm sure she would understand my need to do this, but yeah, keep it hush hush. She's got too much to think about right now. I'll tell her eventually.' He did partially mean that. Lucie was incredibly busy at the minute, but he also knew she would chew him out far harsher than his own mum.

'How is our Lucie?' Maggie passed him his other shoe, giving in to the fact he was about to make a potential mistake.

'She's fine. She's got meetings galore this week. That's why she isn't here.'

'Hmm. I'm glad she's garnering so much success.' Maggie pursed her lips like she didn't quite believe him. 'Anyway, be off with you. And please, Brett, end the night in your *own* bed.'

What in the hell are you doing, Anderson? He mentally cursed himself as he stood outside Sienna's apartment. He was stone-cold sober, and in an ideal world he would be staying that way. But God, he could use a drink. He had half a mind to turn around and go home, or better yet, get on a plane to the UK. But tonight was about closure. Or at least, that was what he had been telling himself for the last hour or two.

'Hey!' Sienna opened the door looking flustered, but also extremely put-together. Her blonde hair was in waves with a large black bow on the back of her head, keeping some of it pinned back. She had tanned, and she was wearing a black mini dress that revealed so much thigh she may as well have not worn anything at all. It was hurting his head.

'You look nice,' he complimented, unsure if that was a thing they were still doing.

'Thanks, B! You want a drink?' She led him into the kitchen, and it was at that moment he wished he'd just met her at the bar.

Somehow, being in an establishment dedicated to serving alcohol seemed less tempting than standing in front of a counter where she had laid out every type of alcohol she owned. Whisky, beer, vodka. You name it, she had it. He shouldn't have been surprised; Sienna was always known for hosting before they went out.

'Uhh, thanks, but I've already had a fair few. Got to pace myself.' Now, how was he going to keep *that* lie up? He could have taken her to dinner. The cinema. Rented a boat. A helicopter tour over the harbour. Anything except clubbing. He was a monumental idiot, but he didn't want to upset her and he couldn't tell her the truth.

'Fair enough!' She necked the last of her gin and shook herself out. She was nervous. Brett wasn't sure what to do with that. She had been nothing but apologetic, and he had been nothing but confused all day.

Ever the gentleman, Brett reached his hand out for her as she descended the steps, and held the door as she got into the taxi. Was he giving off signals? Did he want to give off signals?

By the time they made it to the first bar, his head was utterly scrambled. Sienna had talked his ear off, and he had barely said a word. She must have noticed. She would coax more out of him, and he would oblige, but the conversation depended on her fighting his sudden lack of a personality and pushing through the awkwardness.

It was probably why the second they sat down on those bar stools, Brett found himself ordering a drink. A double JD, his favourite vice.

'What's going on?' Sienna leaned on the counter and gazed at him. He couldn't even look her in the eye.

'This just feels a bit weird, right?'

'We haven't seen each other for years, Brett. And we didn't exactly end on good terms. It's bound to take a minute to find our rhythm and feel comfortable around each other again, but isn't that what tonight is about? Navigating a friendship? Well, as close as we can get in a short space of time.' She was so calm about it, her nervousness seeming to have disappeared, not by choice but to save them from an awkward lull.

'You're right. I'll loosen up after a few drinks.' So there it was. His admission that he wasn't stopping at one, and he'd already screwed up. He'd been home two days.

'So, how long are you home for?' She asked the one question he didn't want to answer.

'I'm not so sure. You might see me around more often going forward.'

He hadn't even figured out if home was where he wanted to be. He already missed his friends, his team, and if he stayed here too long, he risked growing detached from them. His life for the last ten-plus years had involved going wherever the wind took him, wherever his friends were, wherever there was an event to race. He didn't know how to stay in one place.

'I'd like that.'

Brett watched her, paying little attention when his drink was placed on the bar. Was this woman, his childhood friend, previously suspected to be the love of his life, truly the reason for his downfall? Did she hold that much power? Because as she gazed at him softly, he realised all the things he could have done to salvage their relationship. He didn't give her enough of his time, because he had been busy giving it all to Lucie. Travelling with Lucie, texting Lucie. How had he expected Sienna to compete? Brett should have been doing those things with her.

'Do you think I was a shit boyfriend?' He winced both in anticipation of her answer, and at the burn in the back of his throat when he took his first sip.

'I just think you weren't ready to be someone's boyfriend, Brett.'

'Oh, right. Probably.'

'I wasn't the best girlfriend, either. I didn't respect your lifestyle, and whether that's because I didn't understand your world or because I was feeling a little bitter, I'm still not sure.'

'Thanks for being honest, Sen. Think I needed that.' He clinked his glass against hers, and although her words should have provided closure, he could still feel a downward spiral pending.

'I really did care for you, Brett. I still do. Just think you and I are better off keeping things casual, maybe? I've accepted I'm not the girl for you, but I do hope you get your shit together and admit what you've always wanted.'

He frowned into the amber liquid in silence, too shy to ask what she meant. But as the night wore on, and his phone buzzed a few times with Lucie's texts and he caught Sienna looking, he figured it out. She meant he should get his shit together and claim Lucie.

But the more he thought about it, and the more he let the consequences weigh on his mind, the further his body shifted towards his ex. A few drinks later and he was practically on top of her, and right as the world came into focus and he was about to take a step back, Sienna made her move. It was the alcohol. It was definitely the alcohol. But hey, she had suggested they keep things casual, and she may have just meant as friends but she hadn't verbally ruled out sleeping together. Or kissing. His mind was running wild.

The cold, hard truth was, he missed Lucie. And the drink wasn't enough to make him forget her, but Sienna might just do the trick.

The history-filled streets of Monza passed by in a blur, and Brett let the cool spring air hit him through the open window. He liked to make an entrance to every team event or race in a fancy sports car, acting as though it was written into his contract. It wasn't, it was just written into his personality. Unlike Julien, who hated showing up in a car like this and preferred to keep things discreet, only ever showing off his car collection when his ancient Range Rover broke down. Brett had always played into the fame that came with his career, and Faith and Lucie's social media revamp two seasons ago had been a dream for him.

He liked his privacy, especially where his family was concerned, but he wasn't afraid to give the fans what they wanted. If he didn't show up today, he'd be letting them down.

Was Lucie going to murder him when he rocked up at the race he wasn't supposed to be at? Most likely. Should he have come back to work so soon? Well, that was debatable. In Lucie's eyes it would be a flat-out 'no', he shouldn't have. But racing was in his blood, he couldn't miss this, and he definitely wouldn't miss it for something he deemed unnecessary. His drinking problem wasn't life or death at this stage, not in his opinion, and he wouldn't let it get that far.

To him, every race was equally as important as the twenty-four-hour race at Le Mans. All eyes were on Revolution Racing this season. They had started the season with high-tech upgrades, a new livery, they were straight off the back of a championship win, and everyone wanted to see what they could deliver. Brett *needed* to be part of it.

Jasper had been over the moon when Brett had called a few days ago from the airport and told him he felt well enough to return, but he had made him promise not to tell anyone. Not because he wanted to surprise the team, but because he didn't want to get off the plane to a flood of disapproving text messages. His early return wasn't a group discussion, it was between him and his boss.

Thanks to his friendship with Marco, who had spent the last few years showing off his home country any chance he got, Brett had begun to consider Italy as his second home. Belgium was his third. He would love to build a life of his own in rural Europe one day, with mini goats and three, maybe even five dogs. A horse, if Lucie was still stuck on that dream.

Not that he imagined she would spend the rest of her days there, with him. By the time he was ready to buy some land, settle down and let his career take the back seat, she would probably be married to some Italian guy with ten kids. Brett would be left in the dust.

Brett was a city boy by circumstance but not by choice, so every time one of his friends offered up a trip to their respective hometown to spend time with them and their families and be out in the fresh air, Brett couldn't say no.

This week was different, though. This week, he wasn't on uncle duties to Julien's teenage daughter, Jasmine. He wasn't here to bake bread with Marco's nonna or fix Lucie's dad's classic cars. He was strictly here on racing driver duties. He had a job to get done, a car to take over the finish line in first position.

Except he had an obstacle in the form of Lucie, who was likely going to verbally destroy him when she saw him in the garage. Not quite the warm welcome he wanted, but he would suck it up if it meant he still got to play a part in making history with his team. There were other drivers who deserved a shot, but their time would come. It just wouldn't be him making the sacrifice. Not until he was old and grey and didn't have the energy any more.

Brett had been with Revolution Racing since the team was founded, and before that he had led smaller teams to victory. He had raced alongside Julien and Marco since they joined Revolution as a trio ten years ago. Lucie had always been right there in his pocket, the pair of them attached at the hip from day one.

That was another reason Monza was so special to him. It was where he'd met Lucie when they were eighteen, where he'd opened up to someone outside his family for the first time about his anxiety, and it was where he'd formed bonds that had guided him through some of the rockiest periods of his life.

At the start of every season, he vowed to bring the

trophy home not just for the team, but for his dad. Because every time he spun out on track or crashed and got out of the car unharmed, he was convinced his dad was responsible. His guardian angel looking down on him.

He breathed a sigh of relief when he saw the sign for the Autodromo Nazionale Monza and bypassed the hotel, knowing full well that there was no room reserved for him there. Even Gabriel had failed in all his CEO glory to find an extra bed for one of their star drivers; there were just too many people to cater for and Brett's room belonged to someone else.

It looked like Lucie was getting a roommate for the week. If she was too angry to even look at him, he'd have to spoon Marco every night. Just as well he and the guys were close.

The circuit was buzzing with activity despite it being days until fans were allowed through the gates. Brett flashed his ID at security, and they waved him through. Jasper might be willing to let him drive, but he had to earn back the trust of his team. The reserve driver had already been let go, which had cost the team an undisclosed amount of money, and Jasper had made it clear he wouldn't be easily forgiven if he let them down.

On the drive through the paddock towards Revolution's garage, he swallowed the nerves and listened to Lucie's favourite song. It was the one she'd played to calm him down during their first conversation. He needed that sense of calm again now. There was real potential here that Marco and Julien could kick up a fuss and refuse to race with him. He didn't want to go home. He didn't want to admit defeat. He was exactly where he should be, although he wasn't sure how he was supposed to prove to the guys that he was fit to race in the two days until free practice began.

Marco was standing next to the trailer on his phone when Brett pulled up, his mass of brunette curls a familiar sight that immediately put him at ease. After his teammate's initial shock dissipated, he flashed him a genuine smile, like he was happy to see him. Thank heavens for his beloved De Luca. 'Man, you're in deep shit.'

'Good to see you too, Mars,' Brett grinned at him.

'She's going to go full Rottweiler on you, if Jules doesn't beat her to it.' Marco hugged him once he was out of the car, clapping him on the back. 'Jasper pulled me aside this morning. Told me you were coming. Julien is being notified now, so . . . good luck with that one. And Carolan.' He gestured at Lucie.

He didn't know where he stood with his friends, but if Marco could forgive him for his behaviour then he figured everyone else eventually would too. Having said that, De Luca had always found it impossible to hold a grudge.

'Guess I'd better get this out of the way quick. See you later.' Brett headed into the garage to meet his fate.

There was something about Lucie standing next to his race car in his favourite lavender floral dress that sent Brett's pulse skyrocketing. His two greatest gifts from the universe, side by side.

She immediately tensed up when she felt his presence

behind her and she whipped round to face him, her jaw slack. 'What the –'

'Surprise?' Even Brett noticed the way his voice shook.

'What are you doing here?' Her brown eyes gazed up at him through thick lashes.

'Came to see you.' Brett placed one hand on the small of her back and he could've sworn he watched her physically melt under his touch.

'I'm flattered, but seriously, Brett. Why aren't you at home? Sorting yourself out?' She looked around the garage. Nobody was listening, but still, his deteriorating mental state wasn't exactly something Brett wanted to shout from the rooftops.

'I don't need it, Luce. I caught up with old friends, did some sightseeing. I'm okay. I know my triggers; I know what to do when I feel tempted to drink. I don't need to sacrifice a race.'

'Are you sure? It's only been two weeks, you were supposed to have six weeks off.' She looked at him hesitantly, not sure whether to trust him. She shouldn't, considering he was doing something he had never done before, he was lying straight to her face.

'One hundred and ten per cent. You're not mad?' He had braced himself for a major freak-out and a whole lot of hostility, but instead she just looked kind of broken.

'No. Not right at this second, anyway.' She was still eyeing him cautiously.

'Can you stop being so scared I might break and put your arms around me? I missed you.'

She nodded slowly and wrapped her arms around his waist. Brett had forgotten how to live a life without Lucie Carolan, and he didn't ever want to remember.

She was going to murder him. Verbally. Actually, no, she wasn't. She was going to stay cool, calm and collected. She was just going to run this week like a military operation and keep a very close eye on his behaviour. If he slipped up even once, or showed any minor indication that he wasn't okay, she was taking charge of the private jet and sending him back to Sydney. Verbally assaulting him and voicing her frustrations would do nothing except push him away.

Brett wasn't the kind of person who took well to criticism, and if he knew how furious she was, he might act out and turn to alcohol. Because let's face it, two weeks was nowhere near enough time to kick an addiction issue and treat ten-plus years' worth of deep, emotional trauma.

'Lucie!' Faith ran after her, an iced coffee in each hand. 'Take this.' She held out the creamy brown liquid, ice cubes rattling against each other.

'Oh, thank God.' Lucie heaved a sigh of relief, her eyes practically rolling back in her head as she took a long sip. Caffeine was her guilty pleasure, and it always calmed her down on particularly stressful days.

'Tell me I didn't just see Brett?' Faith's blue eyes were wide, Lucie's own concern reflected in them.

'If I told you that, I'd be lying.'

'Is he okay?'

'That's the thing, I don't know. I'm not going to know until something happens, and then it will be too late. I know Brett like the back of my own hand, but even I can't work out if he genuinely believes he doesn't need more time and more help, or if he's lying to me so I let him stay without ratting him out.'

'Is Jasper annoyed, do you think?' Faith glanced at the team's mobile HQ where Jasper was having a lunch meeting with Julien.

'Well, he did have a reserve on standby . . . but he said weeks ago that if Brett wanted to race and he showed up sober and with his head in the game, the seat was his. Brett is an idiot sometimes, but he's not that stupid. He would never put lives at risk on the track.'

'No, of course not. If there was even the slightest doubt in Jasper's mind that Brett was incapable of keeping himself, the car, and everyone else safe, he would be cut from the team. Immediately. Any of the boys would be.'

'Yep. So, I guess we just have to believe that Brett knows what he's doing.'

'So, here's what we do know. Let's talk it out. He's sober right now, there have been no stories in the press of him out drinking in Sydney, and he's told you he feels fine. So as far as he's concerned, and as far as we are concerned, he's fit to race. At least this week. We'll monitor the situation for each race going forward.'

'I guess.' Lucie bit her lip.

'He's got this, Luce.' Faith placed a reassuring hand on her arm. 'Just don't yell at him.'

'Ha!' Lucie heaved out a laugh. 'Trust me, I want to. He's lucky all I could do was stand and gawk at him.'

'He does have that effect on women.' Faith shrugged and was immediately met with narrowed eyes. 'Okay, okay. Not you, obviously.' She raised an eyebrow, knowing full well that Lucie definitely *did* fall into that category.

'How likely do you think it is that I could convince him to speak to the team psychologist?' Lucie bit her lip, already knowing it wouldn't go down well.

'I say we leave that to Jasper.'

When they rounded the corner, Jasper was embracing Brett in a tight hug. Their boss didn't dish out hugs often, and he tended to save them for when a member of his team was going through a hard time. He was always there when you really needed him. 'Ladies! Can we make sure we shoot some content with Anderson, today? Maybe copy some video trends or something, keep it light.'

'Oh, sure,' Faith agreed.

'We haven't announced Woods as the reserve yet, so we won't have to clarify anything on social media. He's here at the track, hovering in the background, but he won't be featured in any content. We need to write Anderson into the schedule for the rest of the week. Now we've got our guy back, I also want a vlog of him and the boys. Second race of the season, team! Let's get on it!' Jasper clapped his hand on Brett's back and smiled at them.

So that was it, then? It was business as usual at Revolution Racing.

I 2

The team's trailer had been upgraded this year. It was now a full-blown motorhome and had gained a whole extra floor, which was no doubt Julien's doing. Lucie distinctly remembered a team dinner last season when he'd been moping about Jasmine not being able to come to many races because she needed somewhere quiet to do her schoolwork. The whole second floor of this trailer was designated to Julien, Jasmine and Faith. She'd joked earlier that they should have a welcome mat outside with 'The Jensen-Moretz's' written in a fancy font, but of course Jules had taken it seriously and started scouring the internet.

She wondered how much of his own money Julien had offered the team, or how many extra networking events he'd agreed to attend throughout the year, because no other team on the grid had anything remotely like this. It was extravagant, and the other drivers were loving ripping into Revolution for being so over the top.

They may be the laughing stock of the paddock but drivers had been knocking on their door for 'tours' which turned into them asking to use the coffee machine or the gaming consoles. Eden Racing had spent an entire hour in here at Spa, playing *Call of Duty* before Esme and her co-worker had to hunt them down to fulfil their press duties.

Lucie was busy looking for her favourite cookies when the door opened. Despite the trailer being huge, it still shook like it was a fragile little caravan when the door opened and closed. Brett appeared behind her, his frame filling the doorway. She turned to see him with his arms crossed, she couldn't get a read on him at all based on his expression. He was just studying her in silence and her guilty heart started to pound ferociously.

'Hi?' She breathed out.

'Hey. What ya doing, Sunny?' He nodded at the open cupboard above her head.

'Looking for those pistachio cookies I love. I know Jules brought some with him from home, but I can't see if they're up there. I'm too short.' She jutted her bottom lip out.

'Ah, so you need your knight in shining armour, huh?' He uncrossed his arms and broke into a smile, discreetly mocking her for her lack of height.

'You know I'm the last person who needs one of those.' She rolled her eyes. 'However, if you're offering . . .' She stepped aside to give him access.

Brett didn't even have to stretch. He reached up, did a sweep of the cupboard and within seconds, there was the beautiful sound of packaging being rustled. He held them above his head, taunting Lucie until her mouth was practically watering.

'I know they know.' He lowered his arm and watched her reaction carefully, but she didn't give him one. If he was mad about it, she was going to have to stand her ground. She had acted with his best interest at heart, just like she always did.

'Who knows what?' she challenged.

'Mum and Pipes.' He narrowed his eyes at her, but he wasn't coming off as angry. Just mildly disappointed. 'I had a sickeningly sweet message from Piper, asking me to come over for dinner. She doesn't do cute messages, she's all bitching and moaning and memes. So, I figured she was on to me, texted her to ask if she'd spoken to you, and Mum called me crying.'

'Brett, I'm so—'

'Sorry? Yeah, I should think so. It put me in a really tough position, Luce. They staged a bloody intervention, tried to therapise me. It was extremely awkward and uncomfortable for all three of us, and it wasn't a conversation I was ready to have. I need to know I can trust you with my deepest, darkest secrets, you know?' He tried to hold her gaze but she looked away.

'I know nothing I say will make it okay. But just know, I thought I was doing the right thing. For you, that is.' She swallowed the lump in her throat, hating being called out.

'I thought about it a lot after they interrogated me. I never should've asked you to keep something like this from them. I'm sorry, too. Mum said she debated murdering me when she first got the news, and do you know what I thought?'

'What?' Lucie teared up.

'I thought, *sounds like my Luce*. You two have always taken care of me in the best way you know how. I don't want to let either of you down again, or myself, for that matter.' Brett took Lucie's hand in his, giving it a tight squeeze. 'God forbid my little sister ever found out about this. She's young, I don't want her growing up with a big brother who threw his life away for a temporary fix. Who uses drink to numb his emotions instead of facing them head on. She deserves more from me.'

'She's fifteen. She doesn't need you to be perfect, both she and Piper just need you to be their brother. Neither of them would think any less of you, they would understand that you have experienced the same loss they have, and you have a lot of stress on your shoulders. You basically replaced your dad as the breadwinner when you were eighteen, and as the male role model of the family.'

'Exactly, so I should've known better. I should've been more like him, but I was so busy doing my own thing. I haven't been present in the way they needed me. I haven't been there to help with homework, uni decisions, *life* decisions. I show up to visit and we have a great time, but my head is always somewhere else.'

'You've been working damn hard for ten years straight, Brett. Even longer than that. You've never taken a substantial break from the intensity of training, dieting, racing, travelling. You've never sought emotional relief, either. Not from a professional. How many times did you turn down your team psychologists in the early days?' She hadn't intended on mentioning it, but it had slipped out.

'Like, twelve. They all told me I might regret it, and here we are. I just don't know why Julien handled his dad's death so well, and I've somehow handled mine worse as the years have passed. It's embarrassing.'

'You can't compare yourself to Jules. Everyone tackles situations differently, and there's no shame in the way you went about it. It's so easy to fall into the habits you did, it could've been any of your siblings in your shoes. *Nobody* is immune to the risk, in fact. You pass by anyone on the street, and it could easily be them. Hell, it could be *me*. Sometimes it doesn't even take a traumatic event. Sometimes it just takes a few bad days, of which you have had *many*, or a certain type of personality, and that's enough to fall into a cycle. It doesn't make you weak. It makes you human.'

'You've got a lot of sense in that tiny head of yours.' He tapped the side of her head gently, then finally opened the cookies and helped himself to half the packet.

'And apparently you've got an almighty appetite in that tiny body,' she smirked.

'You did *not* just call my body tiny.'

'Mm,' she mumbled through a mouthful. 'Could be better.'

'Are you being serious right now? Look at these.' He flexed his biceps. 'Moretz and De Luca could only ever dream of having muscles like this. I'm basically Arnold Schwarzenegger.'

'Oh, come on. You and Jules look almost identical from the neck down. You just have the whole Aussie tan thing going on, which I guess accentuates your muscles a bit.'

'You've been admiring Jules, huh? What would Faith think about that?' He narrowed his eyes at her in fake suspicion.

'I'm simply stating facts. And Faith isn't blind. She knows her husband is nice to look at.'

'Okay, but *this* body is the one that absolutely ruined you for all other men. Have you slept with anyone else since Italy? Or do you lie awake at night, reliving every single second like I do?' Brett spoke with so much confidence that it stunned her into silence.

'I –' Lucie stuttered because no, she hadn't slept with anyone else. He knew that. She had been with him almost every day since. She hadn't necessarily been avoiding all other men, but she hadn't exactly been putting herself out there. She'd been too busy dodging Brett's advances, both the subtle ones and the not-so-subtle ones and pretending she didn't desperately want a repeat.

'Exactly what I thought.'

'It's hot in here.' Lucie's throat was dry.

Brett snorted at her statement. 'Smooth, Sunny.'

She wasn't naïve, she knew he'd been with other women. Snuck them into his hotel room, disappeared at parties. She'd even caught him in a bathroom at a restaurant once during a team night out. That was just who Brett was. Did it bother her? Yes, but at the same time she didn't *want* him. Well, she did. Just not like – you know what? Never mind. Lucie had to admit she had been growing more and more confused by her feelings for Brett every year. Being so close probably didn't help, but they were attached at the hip. Living their lives any differently just wouldn't make sense to them.

This whole situation would be a million times easier if he wasn't Brett. If she didn't know him as well as she did. She knew everything there was to know. The way his mind worked, how he approached conflict and the problems life threw at him. Well, aside from indulging in excessive drinking. She'd missed that one.

But most of all, Lucie knew that Brett loved everything about his life. He lived the kind of lifestyle no man in his right mind would want to give up, and she would never dream of asking him to, but their two wants and needs around a relationship just didn't match. Especially not after he'd tried to settle down with Sienna, and that went up in flames. Nothing would sway him into commitment.

'I'm going to make a banana smoothie, you want one?' Brett rifled through the refrigerator, oblivious to her inner turmoil.

'I'm good, got to go and shoot some content. See you later.' Lucie scurried through the door, forgetting she had a half-eaten cookie in her hand. The only thing she did have an appetite for was Brett Anderson.

'I think we have to accept there's a strong chance he's bullshitting us and that he's not actually okay,' Julien mumbled to Lucie.

They were in the garage on the morning of qualifying, watching Brett do yoga in the middle of the garage. Yoga mat, workout gear, the lot. He even had the sunrise behind him, making the scene look like one of those social media photos with motivational quotes on. Lucie thought how funny it would be if he were doing this when fans were in the pit lane, viewing the cars. They would give anything to witness a racing driver in downward dog.

But instead, it was barely dawn and Lucie and Jules

were concerned. Brett had done this three days in a row in various places; the garage, the trailer, and in his and Lucie's now-shared hotel room. Her room had a double bed, but Brett was naturally a touchy-feely person even in his sleep. He was making her life hell with their night-time spooning and 'cuddle time'.

He'd been making smoothies multiple times a day, eating healthily aside from stealing her pistachio cookies, turning down alcohol at dinner and going for runs twice a day around the circuit, either alone or with his trainer. He'd even had a couple of chats with the team psychologist.

Those were all normal things for a racing driver, but they weren't normal for Brett. He had always been able to get away with half-assing those things on race week because he was so overly-prepared the rest of the year.

'It's like he's going over the top in an attempt to prove himself, right?' she whispered.

'Yeah, and all it's doing is making us think he's worse than he's letting on,' Julien frowned.

'We have to trust him until he gives us a reason not to, though. We can't baby him otherwise he'll start shutting down and hiding his emotions. I got him to open up a bit yesterday, I think he's on the right path.'

'I don't know, Luce. I'm just worried that this complete one-eighty he's done is too good to be true. I've seen this before, my very first teammate completely let himself go. Lost everything. We thought he was okay, but he wasn't.' Julien's jaw tensed.

Before she could answer and ease Julien's concerns, Brett's voice reached them from his spot on the floor.

'Are you guys just going to stand there and stare at my ass all day? I know the view is impressive, but please, have some self-control. You're embarrassing yourselves.' Brett looked at them upside down from between his legs. 'Anyone joining me?'

'Screw it, I will.' Lucie whipped her Revolution Racing hoodie off, revealing her purple sports bra, and left it in a heap on the floor.

'You two are ridiculous.' Julien laughed while they got into the lotus position, shaking his head as he left them to it.

'We could try these yoga positions in the bedroom instead, if you want?' Brett winked at her with a low laugh.

'Anderson!' Lucie's arm shot out and smacked him in the chest, disrupting the peace. He had joked about it before the Alps, but back then she had believed it was just that: a joke. Now that lines were slightly more blurred, she could never be sure if his teasing held more meaning. Given that they had almost slept together again in Vegas, before her freak-out, she feared it might be the latter.

He shrugged. 'Offer's there.'

'I thought you were swearing off women for a few months, anyway?' Lucie asked. He'd made a passing comment before he went back to Australia about not getting mixed up with anyone, and her stupid brain had clung to that with what she unfortunately believed might be an inkling of hope that he was waiting for her. But these comments showed he was the same old Brett, he only wanted one thing and that wasn't a relationship.

'You're not *women*, Lúcie. You're you. The trust is there, the sexual chemistry is there. What if it's just as magical as it was two years ago?' Brett's tone was softer than usual, like he knew this was a sensitive subject. His usual cocky confidence was nowhere to be seen, and when Lucie's eyes flew open in shock, his were still closed. *Magical*? Did Brett ever think that about other women he'd been with?

'Brett, you don't mean that.'

'What makes you think I don't mean it?'

'Have you ever looked at the type of women you go for?'

'What?!' His own eyes shot open, and he gawked at her in disbelief. 'The women that I – Lucie, do you not remember that I *went for* you? I *go for* you almost every day that I'm with you. I know you're worried about boundaries, but that's my whole point. I respect you, Sunny.'

'I know, but I'm nothing like your ex or any of the girls you meet at parties.'

'You're right, you're worlds apart from them, especially from Sienna, but not in the ways that you think. Your differences don't equate to how beautiful you are, Luce. For a *start*,' he emphasised, holding his hand up to signify a number one, 'your eyes have gold flecks in them. When you insist on sleeping with the curtains open, those gold flecks are the first thing I see when the sunlight streams in and our alarm goes off. Don't get me started on your body. Do you know how hard it is not to touch you? To not place my hand on the curve of your waist, touch your neck in the way I *know* makes

128

you shiver, and take you back to that night in the Alps? That night has been on replay in my mind ever since, and watching your face when you reached your climax? Yeah, I'm telling you now, I've slept with plenty of other women and nobody came *close*.'

'I –' Lucie stuttered.

'Wasn't finished,' Brett interrupted. 'I don't want you to think I'm trying to use you for sex. I just think that you and I both need a healthy release, and we trust and respect each other enough to be able to find that release in each other.'

'I just don't know if it's wise, Brett. What if it changes how we are? Our dynamic?'

'It's risky, but we don't know unless we try. I won't ask you again, okay? But think about it, and just know that if the answer is yes, I'm open to it. But don't think I'm expecting a yes, this is your choice.'

'I'll consider it,' she agreed, already knowing her answer was a flat-out no. Her head was scrambled enough without throwing frequent casual sex into the mix of their relationship. She knew that she would always want more, and she knew that it would destroy them when Brett couldn't give it to her. One night together was enough to mess her up. But he wasn't going to ask again, which meant she could just never give him an answer, and they could brush it under the rug.

'On another note, you want to come back to Sydney with me next week?'

'To see your family?'

'No shit. That's where they live, Carolan.' He rolled

129

his eyes as he uncrossed his legs and stood up, rolling up his pink yoga mat.

'Yeah, I'll come. I've missed them.' It had been months since she'd seen his sisters outside of a video call, and she was long overdue a coffee catch-up with his mum.

Lucie had been planning on going back to Los Angeles to see her own siblings, or to Tuscany where her parents were renovating their farmhouse, but if Brett wanted her at home with him, then that was where she'd be. At least this way she could keep a close eye on him and still have a great time during the break between races.

Her siblings didn't care either way, they were used to Lucie being a wild card. She'd never missed a holiday and she always video called and sent gifts on their birthdays, and that was all that mattered to them. There had been multiple times over the years when her family had flown to Australia or Brett's family had flown to America so they could all hang out together. Their families meshed together in a way that just made sense. It wasn't like she was ditching her family; she was just spending time with the other half of it.

She just had one concern about Sydney. They were in Brett's apartment instead of a hotel room, and she knew from all her years of trying, and succeeding, that Brett was exceedingly hard to resist when he was standing in his kitchen shirtless, cooking her a fried breakfast and telling her how good she looked despite her bed hair. She was a glutton for punishment.

13

Lucie *lived* for race day. Much like Brett, racing was in her blood. Neither of them had racing in their family history, but they had grown into adults within the motorsport industry and spent years trackside as children. Brett had been karting from a young age, and Lucie had been taken to other championships with her dad and siblings.

Her dad knew the owner of one of the major catering companies for the IEC, and they had taken Lucie on board as a waitress when she'd announced she didn't want to go to college. Being young, enthusiastic and passionate, Gabriel Lopez had taken notice of her. She served him food three times a day during race week, striking up conversation each time, and two seasons in, he had told her he could see she was itching to get involved in the action.

He'd invited her into one of the garages and let her shadow an existing social media team. She'd learned the ropes from Louise Beacham, her predecessor in the IEC, offering to help her edit late into the night and following her round with a spare camera on her breaks from waitressing. She had taught herself how to use the necessary software, earned a marketing degree from the Open University, and a few months later, Jasper had handed her a contract to be Revolution Racing's social media assistant.

From that day forward, she had worked to prove that she belonged there. Early on, it often felt like she didn't. Some of the interns tried to push her out, but Lucie fought back. She had forged working relationships with drivers, engineers and mechanics, showed off her portfolio and showered teams with content ideas, and invited herself to be part of their world, parties and casual drinks included. Her determination had resulted in her being able to get up close and personal and earn their trust.

These days, the team of interns had been carefully curated by her and Faith, and any behaviour like her fellow co-workers had exhibited back then would be firmly dealt with.

Adding Faith into the mix was like adding that last missing puzzle piece, and the entire organisation relied on them to maintain their stellar social media content. Sure, it was stressful. It meant holding meetings at every given opportunity, strict scheduling and constantly running around the paddock to check in with the other teams, but if it meant getting to share their beloved championship with the world, they'd do anything it took. The IEC deserved a chance to shine like some of the bigger championships did.

She and Faith had their entire filming schedule for today planned out down to the hour. It was based on the team's race strategy, and which driver was in the car and when. They had spent the last few days getting the drivers involved in various fun challenges with each other and with other teams, another part of their wider plan. Although there was competition between different teams and manufacturers, Gabriel and the other CEOs were committed to fans seeing and believing that the grid was a family.

'Marco! Can you check this edit for me, tell me if you're happy with it?' Lucie passed him her headphones and pressed play on her laptop. She was huddled at the back of the garage in a camping chair, rushing to get a video uploaded onto the Revolution Racing channel.

She didn't have to get the green light from the drivers when she posted, just Jasper or his assistant and a member of the PR team, but if there was time, she still liked to out of respect. She had spent years tiptoeing around Julien, who had been anti-social media until Faith came along.

Now, she left his social media presence entirely to his wife, who was slowly introducing the world to his daughter. He'd kept her hidden since she was born at the very start of his career with the IEC, but she was old enough to use social media herself now so there was little point in hiding her for her own protection. Jasmine wanted to get involved in her dad's world.

'Love it. You made me look like less of a stuttering idiot, and for that I thank you.' He passed the headphones back. They had filmed a challenge video with Eden Racing, and because Esme had wanted a video for Eden's channel too, she had been there. Marco had blushed. A lot.

'You're not a stuttering idiot, Mars. You've had plenty of media training.'

'Yeah, but Esme makes me nervous, and it was super obvious in the original footage.' He shrugged nonchalantly, like he hadn't just admitted to his feelings for Esme.

'Esme's cute, huh?' Lucie teased.

'Oh, don't start. She's always wearing bright yellow with a massive smile on her face. It's hard not to be drawn to her.'

'Would you like me to put a good word in?'

'No, I would not.' Marco's cheeks turned an adorable shade of pink. 'Besides, I don't need advice from *you*, thank you.' He picked up a bunch of grapes and a cube of cheese from Lucie's heaped buffet plate.

'What is that supposed to mean?'

'It means, I know your secret.' He winked and turned on his heel, leaving Lucie sitting there in silence.

She pressed the export button on her editing software and abandoned her laptop under the watchful eye of Jasper's wife, who was attending this race as his guest, while she scuttled away to find Faith, who may be about to deal with Lucie's unleashed hell.

'Jensen.' Lucie flung the door to the trailer open, expecting to find Faith working away. Instead, she found her and Julien in a compromising position on the sofa. 'Oh, God.' She was never sitting on that sofa again. They were mostly clothed, but that was beside the point. It was like walking in on her brother.

'Oops, sorry!' Faith stuttered, having the decency to look embarrassed.

'It's Jensen-Moretz now,' Julien stated.

'I don't care. My eyes are burning.' Lucie covered them with her hands to emphasise her point. 'I think I'm actually blind.'

'Don't be dramatic, Luce. I am just loving on my wife.'

'I think I might throw up.'

'Jules, play nice,' Faith scolded her husband. 'Time for a chat?'

'Please.' Lucie peeked through her fingers to check all their clothes were back on.

'Julien, out.' Faith shooed him out of the trailer.

'If I need to yell at anyone, you just let me know!' he called out over his shoulder.

Once Julien had shut the door, Lucie eyed Faith suspiciously. She sat on the sofa, eyes wide, looking totally innocent. 'Wait, am *I* being yelled at? Did I do something?'

'I don't know, did you?'

'Stop talking in code, Luce. What's up?'

'Did you tell De Luca that I almost slept with Brett in Vegas?'

'Absolutely not! Lucie, I haven't even told my husband. He has his suspicions, of course, but my lips remain firmly sealed. Your secrets will always be safe with me.'

'Okay.' Lucie blew out a breath, feeling guilty for semi-accusing her. 'He said he knew my secret, and I panicked. Sorry.'

'I think Marco just has eyeballs. Don't you read the comments on the team account?'

'Well, as long as Brett doesn't know people are talking about it, I don't care. He's got too much on his plate to be worrying about his love life being in the media again.'

'You really are a wonderful friend to him, Luce. To all of us. You're a proper mother hen in all the best ways.' Faith jumped up to give Lucie a hug. 'Right, come on. I let Jules distract me for too long, let's go shoot some vlog footage.'

'Sunny, can you help me?' Brett popped his head out of the trailer's bedroom a couple of hours before the race, a round pair of designer sunglasses perched on his nose. The irony of her nickname being used in that moment made her laugh.

'What do you need?' Lucie joined him to see multiple PR boxes on the bed, where Brett had spread out an array of sunglasses and was studying them.

'I've been sent these by our new sponsor, but I have too many options. My sunglasses collection now beats Julien's. They've sent *so* many.'

'Well, you are all official brand ambassadors. But I'm not sure the ones you've got on suit you. They're much more Marco's vibe. Try these.' She held up a gunmetal pair which were slightly more hexagonal, and he switched them out.

'Better?' He checked himself out in the mirror, touching up his hair.

'Absolutely. I think that should be the first pair you wear.'

'I feel guilty,' Brett sighed, removing the sunglasses and catching her gaze in the reflection. *Vulnerable Brett incoming.*

'About what?' She stepped forward, turning him round by his torso and wrapping her arms around his waist to give him a comforting hug.

'The reserve driver not getting his big moment. I was so happy to be back, so determined, that I didn't really think about the fact I was taking a monumental opportunity away from some kid who's been dreaming of this moment. Of racing with a top team, or even just racing in the IEC at all. It was his time to shine.'

'Woods will get his shot. Just like you did, just like every other driver in the history of motorsport did. Remember how many times Sarah Ridings thought she was going to get a seat and then they chose someone else over her? And now look, she's one of the best drivers in her class. Garrett Woods will be no different to anyone else. We all know he's talented, he just has to wait for the right time, and this wasn't it.'

'I just can't help but think that he deserves to be here more than I do right now.'

'Anderson, no. That's just the guilt talking. You're talented as hell, you've got the grit and the determination. Jasper wouldn't let you behind the wheel if he didn't think the same thing.'

'I'm so scared I'm going to fuck this up.'

'You can't think like that. You have to learn to trust yourself more. You may not always have complete control, and that's okay. But don't let the fear of relapsing dictate your career. You worked hard for this, Brett. You deserve to be with your team.'

'And what if I *do* fuck it all up?'

'Then you're honest with yourself. With your fans. You use your voice. You do something good with this, because I *know* you'll be okay in the long run. You're made of strong stuff, and you've got the team, and me, and your family behind you. If you fall, you'll get back up. Taking care of your mental health is a lifelong journey, and you've got the resilience for it.'

'I can't believe I let myself get to this point, Luce.' He rested his chin on the top of her head, running his hands up and down her back. He clearly knew she was hurting, too. Even though *he* was struggling, it was having a direct impact on Lucie. She had always been an empath, but because it was Brett who was broken, her heart was being ripped in two.

'I've got you. I'll remind you every single day if I have to, okay?'

'I've got you, too. Even without Revolution, we're a team in our own right.' He kissed her hair and let her go, physically shaking himself off. 'Okay, I'm over it. For now.'

'Come on, let's go get a shot of you in action. I can do a promo video, get a shot of the brand's logo on the livery, some shots of you and the guys wearing different styles. I'll edit it together quickly and post it mid-race when all the attention is on the team. Bring those ones for Mars!' She was halfway out the door before he could even get his race suit on, afraid that if she stayed

in there for a second longer, she would give in to temptation.

'Make sure you zoom in close on the logo for Sundaize,'
Faith reminded Lucie. It was vital to meet the sponsors'
requirements. After all, they had invested a lot of money
into the team's development, the least the team could
do in return was include a quick shot in a social media
video.

Lucie studied the contracts closely at the start of each
season so she and Faith could incorporate any social
media requirements into the schedule, for the team
accounts and for the drivers' personal ones. Sometimes
sponsors just required the team to attend their events
and post about it, sometimes they wanted more of a
feature.

Sundaize and other fashion and lifestyle brands were
the easy ones. A sprinkling of driver photos where
they wore the sunglasses – or watches or jewellery –
was enough, but they could get creative if they wanted
to. Lucie loved working with them. Loved coming up
with content ideas. Energy companies, financial companies and other corporate sponsors were the boring
ones. They couldn't have any fun with that content, and
frankly, the fans didn't care. They wanted products they
could buy themselves, not business opportunities.

'Which one of you is filming the hot lap?' Jasper
asked. These were fan experiences which were usually
won in competitions run by the organisation. A driver
would take them around the circuit for a lap or two,

hitting the high speeds. For this race, Revolution were being asked to do it with a driver of their choice behind the wheel of a Porsche 911. In an ideal world, the fan would get to go round in Revolution's car, but it was a one-seater.

'Luce? You want to do it? I'll get this edited.' Faith waved her phone.

'Absolutely. Is the fan here yet?' Lucie peered around the garage, then spotted Brett with his new helmet tucked under his arm, a custom black and white one with his parents' and siblings' zodiac constellations across the top. He was talking to a young boy, no older than eleven or twelve.

'That's him over there.' Jasper pointed to where she'd been looking. 'I thought I'd let Anderson do the driving; he's got the personality for things like this. Plus, I figured he could use the boost,' he added, and Lucie smiled knowingly.

Heading over to them, she noted that this kid was fully decked out in Revolution Racing merchandise. Someone at the team had clearly got to him the second he'd stepped foot in the garage, because some of it wasn't on sale to the public. He was bouncing on his heels, and the way his eyes lit up when Lucie walked towards them with the camera told her all she needed to know. He was going to battle Brett as the star of the show and give the organisation some great content to work with. The GoPro reaction clips would be gold.

'Hi! I'm Lucie, I'm part of the social media crew for Revolution Racing.'

'Hey! I'm Theo. Are we ready?' He beamed at her, cutting straight to the point.

'Have you done all your health and safety checks, signed the consent forms?'

'We've taken care of that, haven't we, mate?' Brett nudged him, equally as excited.

'Yeah. Basically signed my life away to one of the best racing drivers the IEC has ever seen. No big deal. My friends are going to be so jealous.'

'Well, you're in safe hands. You cool if I just keep the camera rolling while we get you set up, and then again when you get out? We've got in-car cameras too, to the left, right and in the middle of the dash. And as you know, the footage will be posted on YouTube, Instagram, TikTok and Facebook by both the IEC and by us.'

'As long as you make me look good. I've got to impress the ladies.'

Brett roared with laughter. 'I love this kid.'

They led Theo out of the garage and down to the far end of the pit lane, where a representative for the IEC was waiting along with someone from the main media crew who was in charge of the GoPro, a health and safety official and the medical car. It made this whole situation seem very daunting, but Theo was totally unfazed. He looked like he was about to burst. This car went fast, but still not as fast as Revolution's car. It was from a different class within the competition, and it was also a winner.

As Theo was briefed, again, this time by the health

and safety woman, Lucie walked around to the driver's side of the car where Brett was getting himself situated and leaned in the window.

'I love doing this. I reckon this Theo kid is going to be an absolute blast.' He pulled his helmet on over his head.

'Make sure you get me my content.' Lucie patted his chest.

'Of course.'

'I'm in! Let's *go*!' Theo cheered as he got strapped into his seat.

Lucie stepped back, camera aimed at the car. She was definitely going to keep the wink Brett shot in her direction in the final edit. The fans would go wild for that, but she knew he hadn't done it for their benefit. That wink was for her. That wink was him telling her he was about to kick ass and be the Brett she knew and loved. The one who had got his fire back.

She waited for them to complete the standard two laps, laughing when Brett took Theo for a third and a fourth, interrupted only by the IEC rep telling him over the radio that the marshals needed to clear the track of the gravel he had just flung everywhere, in preparation for the race. Brett always liked to push the limits and give the fans an experience they'd never forget, but he was always skating on thin ice with health and safety. Still, everyone knew Theo was in safe hands. And they knew Brett would simply give his signature cheeky grin and all would be forgiven and forgotten.

'That was amazing!' Theo was still yelling when they pulled up next to her in the pit lane again, competing with the idling noise of the engine. Lucie had a feeling the in-car microphones would have struggled with the volume of his screams.

'Glad you enjoyed it,' she smiled.

'Thank you for today. It was the best day of my *life*. I'm going to get me one of these one day.' Theo patted the side of the car in appreciation.

'No worries, mate. I had fun.' Brett shook his hand. 'Let's take a quick photo before you head back into the paddock. Luce?'

'It was so cool meeting you, Mr Anderson,' Theo gushed after they'd posed for the camera, and Lucie tried not to snicker at the formality. She didn't think she'd ever heard anyone refer to Brett as a Mr. It was just Anderson.

With Theo whisked away in the direction of the hospitality area for his next adventure, Lucie sidled up to Brett. 'How do you feel?'

'Unstoppable.' He breathed out a laugh.

'That's because you are. I've been telling you.' She rolled her eyes playfully.

'I have never felt so mentally prepared for a race. I'm going to go get ready.' Brett kissed her on the cheek and ran off to find his team, leaving Lucie standing there in a daze, unable to wipe the pride from her expression.

The tension in the Revolution Racing garage was palpable. Not one member of the team was looking anywhere other than at the screens as Brett tailed Kahan Racing's number eight car. He'd been trying to overtake for three laps, and they were only two away from the finish. If he couldn't catch them, Revolution would lose at Monza for the first time since the team was formed. Brett obviously wasn't going to let them lose in Marco's home country. Not without one hell of a fight.

Lucie and Faith always left Marco and Julien alone in moments like this, choosing to stick together at the back of the garage and shoot their content from a distance. Until their car was over the finish line, the drivers couldn't be spoken to. It was like they tuned out the rest of the world and their only focus was the race win, and somehow the garage was deafeningly loud and silent all at the same time. You could hear the cars out on the track, the engines roaring as they passed the pits, none of them coming down the pit lane so late in the race. The smell of burning rubber lingered in the air, and Lucie's palms were sweating.

He needed to win this. Not just for his team, but for himself. And she needed him to. To prove that leaving Sydney prematurely hadn't been a waste, that it had done him some good. If he lost, he would enter his usual downward spiral, only this time it was likely to be far more intense and have bigger consequences.

But right as she was starting to worry, to lose hope, ruby red shot past metallic blue and with one lap to go, Brett was ahead. Way ahead, in fact, as the Kahan Racing driver momentarily lost control of his car and those precious seconds allowed for a gap that there was no coming back from.

'No way.' Faith breathed out a laugh, in disbelief. That

was the difference; Lucie wasn't surprised he'd done it. This was what Brett was known for.

'Let's go.' Lucie pulled her out to the pit wall, her co-worker still not used to this moment of the race. They always did this, every team who placed on the podium.

Julien helped Faith up onto the wall, then Lucie, and before long the majority of Revolution were hanging on to the metal fence that separated the pits from the track.

The chequered flag waved, the crowds went wild, and their beloved Aussie driver crossed the line in first position, seconds ahead of anyone else. Brett was back.

14

The sun was setting as race day came to a close, and Brett was starving. The team had been awake since five o'clock in the morning, gone straight to the circuit and only left forty-five minutes ago. The whole day had been jam-packed, and he just wanted some pasta. And a drink. Some white wine or something, just to help release the stress that still hadn't left his body since he got out of the car. But he couldn't be seen drinking, and nobody else was either. He knew it was a show of solidarity for his drinking problem. Brett still wasn't convinced he needed to be babied like this. He also didn't need heart-felt speeches from Lucie that made him feel belittled.

He was going to hell for lying to Lucie. And his team-mates and his bosses and his family. But Lucie most of all. He didn't know what had come over him when he'd suggested to Lucie that they enter some sort of friends-with-benefits situation, considering he'd been in Sienna's bed mere days ago. Those women often made his head fuzzier than alcohol. And he'd lied about his sobriety, too. A sure-fire sign of addiction that he was going to continue to push aside.

As the waiter came round and mistakenly offered him alcohol, he felt all eyes on him. He was sick of it. They didn't need to walk on eggshells around him. 'I'm okay, but how about a round of tequila shots for everyone else?'

'We're all right, mate,' Julien rejected his suggestion, which irked Brett even more.

'The hotel's walking distance, go on. We're here to celebrate, aren't we?' He was challenging him, Julien continuing to say no would cause a scene.

'I'll take his shot, so one for each of us.' Marco thanked the waiter and nodded at Brett, signalling that he had his back.

'Sorry I'm late!' Bea burst in right as the shots were delivered and helped herself to one, saving Marco, world's biggest lightweight, from giggling into his pasta when the main courses came out.

'You okay?' Lucie leaned into his side.

'Fine.' He hastily turned to talk to Gabriel and Jasper so she couldn't make a drama out of nothing. His plan worked and she chatted away with the girls, but it didn't stop her from resting her hand on his knee like he was about to crumble. Which, in fairness, he was.

He should tell her about Sienna, or at least tell someone. Julien would get it, he would understand. Instead, he excused himself from the table and took his phone with him.

'Hello?' She sounded happy to hear his voice, and it broke him even further.

'Hey, Sen. What you up to?' He didn't quite know what to say to her, considering he hadn't seen her since that night at the bar, and they'd barely texted.

'Uh, I just woke up . . . is everything all right?'

'Oh, shit! I forgot it's early morning there. I'm so sorry.'

'No worries. So . . .' She trailed off. Right, he should speak. He called her.

'I don't really know why I called . . . I guess I just wanted to check in.'

'You don't have to, Brett. If you wanted the other night to be a one-time thing, for old times' sake, then that's what it is. Don't stress about it.' She didn't sound sure, and he *wasn't* sure.

'Um . . . can I get back to you on that?' He grimaced. He sounded like such a tool and he hated himself for it.

'Sure. I'm going back to sleep, Brett. Take care of yourself, okay?'

'You too.'

He slunk back to the table, his cheeks flushed with embarrassment for who he was becoming. He was turning into a stereotypical bloke who played with women's feelings and the horrible feeling in the pit of his stomach only grew as he watched Lucie laughing with their friends. How could a man like him ever be ready for a woman like her?

'Would you like a glass of wine?' Lucie nearly jumped out of her skin when the flight attendant appeared at her side, looming over her in the dim lighting of the cabin.

'I'm good, thank you.' She nodded at the gigantic bottle of water on the table beside her, her third since they'd boarded the flight to Sydney five hours ago. She and the airplane toilets were becoming fast friends. Since

Brett was equally as dehydrated, they'd raced each other twice and fought their way into the tiny cubicle. Brett might be fast, but Lucie had elbows she wasn't afraid to use.

'Excuse me, ma'am? Do you happen to have any milkshakes? Chocolate, strawberry? I'll take banana as a last resort.' Brett spoke loud enough that anyone in the surrounding seats could hear him, and Lucie tried to hold in her laughter. She failed when she caught his eye.

'A milkshake? Sophistication truly is not your strong suit, is it?'

'What? I need some sugar. Don't mock me, Sunny. Do you think *he's* mocking me?' He gestured at the older gentleman in his suit in the seat next to him. 'No, he's minding his own business, like you should.' He fake huffed at her.

'Hello, Mr Anderson. Nice to have you flying with us again. But as I told you last time, we don't do milkshakes. Can I get you something else?' The flight attended raised an eyebrow.

'What if I had type one diabetes and was having low blood sugar?' Brett blinked at her.

'We have Coca-Cola.' She waved a menu at him.

'Fine, that'll have to do. Two, please.' He tapped his card on the machine. 'So, how's your flight, Susie?' he grinned up at her.

'Susan. My flight would be better if I didn't have to deal with your mischief.'

'Come on! Admit I brighten your day.'

'It's like having my grandchildren at work with me.

By the way, they loved the signed caps you sent them. Haven't taken them off.' All the sarcasm dropped from the woman's tone and she lit up.

'Any time.' He took the drinks from her and she ambled her way back down the aisle, pushing her cart as Brett passed a cup to Lucie. 'Want to watch a movie with me?' he asked.

'Which movie?' They never agreed, they just sucked it up, but it did mean that Lucie had managed to slowly convert Brett into a romcom fanatic, and she bet she could convince him to watch *How to Lose A Guy In Ten Days* if she said yes.

As if he'd read her mind, he said, 'I'm in a Matthew McConaughey mood.'

'Make room, I'm coming over.' They had established this routine years ago. On a long-haul flight, rather than trying to sync up the on-board entertainment systems, Lucie would sit in Brett's lap for the duration of whatever they were watching. They even had a headphone splitter especially for these situations. The only period of friendship when they hadn't done this was when Brett was dating Sienna; even Lucie knew it would be inappropriate. She wouldn't want a girl curled up on her boyfriend's lap, no matter how innocent it seems.

Lucie took the blanket with her, which may have given the elderly man next to Brett a heart attack if he looked over and got the wrong idea, but she didn't care. She needed warmth and Brett was her human radiator.

She snuggled into him while he set about organising cables and navigating through the romcom category, ultimately settling on the exact one she wanted without her having to ask.

Laying her head back on his chest and letting Brett wrap his arms around her, chin resting on top of her head, Lucie was fast asleep before Andie and Ben had even met.

'I'm so happy you came back here instead of going to LA.' Brett's mum squeezed her arm as they walked along Palm Beach. They had left Brett to take his sisters to the aquarium, much to his disgust, but the girls hadn't wanted a beach day. They lived here, it was nothing special to them. But Lucie and Maggie loved getting away from the chaos and having a gossip.

Lucie was too embarrassed to admit to them all that the main reason she'd been grateful when Maggie offered her an escape route was because this was where they filmed one of her favourite Aussie soaps, and if Brett could see the way her eyes lit up when she spotted the film crew, he would never let her live it down. His mum, on the other hand, was just as much of a fan.

'Well, you know, LA has plenty of celebs, but it isn't home to the River Boys.'

'Brett told me off once for gawking at them so openly when they were filming a surf scene years ago. Apparently, they noticed, but it's not like I was ushered away from the set, so clearly it wasn't a problem. They're probably so used to it. He acted like I'd thrown myself at them.'

'Ah, sounds like jealousy to me!' Maggie chirped.

'Brett, jealous of a couple of actors? Maggie, have you ever noticed your son's massive ego? I don't think he was jealous; I think he was embarrassed by me literally drooling over a bunch of shirtless men.'

'You two are the biggest idiots I have ever known.' Maggie rolled her eyes playfully, and Lucie felt no need to push her further. She knew exactly what she meant.

'But you love us.' She nudged her.

'You have no idea how much.'

'I'm sorry, Maggie,' Lucie's voice softened, 'for not taking better care of him.'

'What are you talking about? You take better care of him than *anyone*.' Maggie looked genuinely shocked, her greying hair pulled back off her face. Her eyes looked exactly like her son's. Maybe that was one of the reasons Lucie felt so at home around her.

'I feel like I let him down, and you.'

'Of course you didn't! He's a big boy, Lucie. He makes his own choices. All that matters is that you were there when he realised his mistakes, and you were there to guide him back on the right path. You could so easily have abandoned him and left him to screw up his life, but you stuck by him. That's not letting him down, Lucie, that's lifting him up.'

'I don't know if Piper will see it that way. She still scares me.'

'They've got that whole twin thing going on, and I think it's just hard for her to accept that maybe she didn't know him as well as she thought she did. Pipes loves you, too. When we got the text that you two were coming to Sydney, she was almost bouncing off the walls. Cleo said it was like she'd been possessed. That girl never gets excited unless she knows she's seeing you.'

'Really? I genuinely thought she hated me for taking Brett away from you guys so often.'

'You're not taking him away, Lucie. He was in this long before you came along, it was in his blood. We wouldn't have you in our lives without the IEC. You two have incredibly exciting lives, and yes, we envy you both and we miss you *both*, but we're so proud of you. Brett could've let his dad's death get in the way of all this success, but because he had you by his side and he wanted to make Jack proud, he prospered.'

'He had a very strong woman behind him.'

'He has two.'

'Luce, you want a sparkling water?' Brett shouted through from the kitchen, his voice echoing, the only sound in the whole apartment.

'No, I do not want TV static! Stop with the stupid questions, Anderson! You know me better than that!' she shouted back.

They were in his penthouse, which overlooked Sydney Harbour. Lucie remembered the first time she'd come here and been too scared to touch anything. She'd watched as Marco and Julien had flung themselves down on the sofa, thrown a football around and put their beers on the coffee table without a mat, while she stood by the front door and stayed away from the pristine white walls, sandy shoes placed firmly on the doormat.

Now, she was tucked up in Brett's king-sized bed in a pair of old Christmas pyjamas from three years ago, waiting for him to return with a DIY chocolate fondue buffet which posed a risk to the crisp white bedsheets, replaced by Maggie two days prior to their visit.

Despite this place being ridiculously big, there was only one bedroom. The others had been converted into an office, a walk-in closet for Brett's obscene trainer collection, a personal gym and a gaming room. It was the view that over time had made it feel like home to Lucie.

There weren't many personal touches in the apartment because Brett still had his childhood bedroom at Maggie's and that's where most of his things lived, but every time Lucie looked out the floor-to-ceiling windows, she was looking out at Brett's home. It didn't matter where in the world he went; Sydney was where his roots were. It was where his memories of his dad had been formed, and one of Lucie's favourite things about being around his family was hearing stories about Jack.

'Your majesty, supper awaits.' He walked in wearing his pyjama bottoms and a frilly apron, no doubt stolen from his mum, holding a tray of grapes, strawberries, sliced apples and bowls of melted chocolate. It looked like heaven, but her mouth wasn't watering over the food.

'Do a twirl,' she gestured with her hand, to which he spun around and wiggled his hips.

'You like?' He looked over his shoulder.

'Pastel pink is your colour.'

'Cheers, Sunny,' he winked.

They settled in to watch a motorsport documentary of one of Brett's idols, only stopping when he paused mid bite to comment on something and chocolate dripped from his strawberry, sending the pair of them into a blind panic. Lucie was currently in the utility room, loading the duvet cover into the washer with stain remover.

If Brett didn't have such a sweet tooth, maybe he wouldn't have loaded the strawberry up with quite so much chocolate. Also, if he hadn't paid hotels extra to do his laundry for the last ten or so years, maybe he would be the one trying to figure out the buttons on the washer instead of leaving Lucie to wing it and hope that whatever button she was pressing was the right one.

'Those tatty reindeer PJs have no right looking that good.' Brett's voice was soft, and alarm bells were ringing in Lucie's head as she turned around and saw him staring at her with those gooey, loving eyes.

'It's probably because they're too small,' she shrugged. 'Come on, let's go to bed. It's been a long week; I need to be horizontal for at least nine hours.'

Even as she said it, she knew she should've volunteered to sleep on the sofa. But then he'd know she was weak to his charm today, and if he realised that then he'd go the extra mile to push her over the edge. She'd just have to face the other way, look out at the city instead of at him as she tried to drift off into a peaceful slumber which wasn't filled with dreams about the way he had touched her the last time.

They crawled back into a clean bed, yet another white duvet cover on. Why he hadn't chosen a darker colour this time, she had no idea. He was very fussy about the way things looked, and she had never known him to use anything other than white bedsheets.

'Luce,' Brett mumbled into the darkness of the bedroom a few minutes after they'd said goodnight and both pretended to go to sleep. 'I know you're awake, you're breathing funny.'

'Yeah?' She sighed, eventually rolling over and ending up in his arms after he'd sneakily shuffled closer to her side of the bed. He smelled of vanilla and it killed her. She still had no idea which product made him smell like that, and she had done her investigations, but it was her favourite scent in the world.

'I'm glad you're here with me.'

'I wouldn't want to be anywhere else, Anderson.'

Brett wrapped an arm round Lucie's waist, pulling her to him and placing a gentle kiss on the side of her head. She sighed with contentment, and he smiled sleepily.

There was no denying that every time he held her in his arms, it felt like the whole world made sense. Like she was the perfect fit. She was so small against his broad, muscular frame, he felt like he was able to protect her from anything. He just knew that despite how hard he tried, one day they were going to reach a point where he couldn't protect her from him.

His sisters had been bugging him all day about Lucie. Their cute little sibling trip to the aquarium had turned into an interrogation. The three of them had sat in front of the shark tank, surrounded by blue hues and reflections of the shimmering water where the sunlight above was hitting it. Brett had thought at the time that it would make a beautiful photo, and nobody seeing that photo would have known that both of his sisters were attacking him, right there in the middle of the aquarium, for sleeping in the same bed as Lucie. He might as well throw himself into the tank and let himself be eaten alive by Kaya the Zebra Shark before Piper and Cleo murdered him instead.

He wasn't quite sure how he had let that one slip, but they'd eventually got it out of him that they had been sharing beds for pretty much their entire friendship. To them, it was normal. But that answer wasn't good enough, especially for Piper who now seemed to be the leader of the Lucie Protection Squad. They told him it was unfair to lead a girl on like that. Except Brett wasn't leading her on, because Lucie didn't want him in that way. If anyone was being led on, it was Brett. By himself.

They didn't cuddle often. Almost as if they knew that if it became a habit, everything *else* would become a habit. Brett wasn't sure if he minded that. Kissing Lucie every day would be a privilege that nobody else had ever had. She'd never been in a serious relationship because she'd never had the time or the desire, or found some-one who would treat her right, and Brett hated that in her mind, he was probably just a one-night stand. Well, he knew he was also her best friend, but knowing he wouldn't ever be more than those two things hurt. It made him want to go out to a bar, get drunk and find the first girl who gave him the right signals. But none of them were Lucie. Even when he'd slept with Sienna, he'd thought of Lucie.

So, he just lay there next to her, reliving his one night with her for the billionth time, wishing she would wake up from her peaceful sleep and tell him that she wanted him. Because being wanted by a woman like Lucie Carolan was like wearing a badge of honour. She was particular. She knew what she wanted. And Brett loved that about her. He knew that when his girl settled down, she would have made the right choice. She just wouldn't be his girl any more.

15

Twenty minutes into an episode of *Black Mirror*, Lucie paused the TV and glanced over at Brett. He was sat on the opposite end of the sofa, arms crossed, eyes glued to the screen. It was like she'd hit the pause button on *him*. He hadn't even noticed that the show was no longer playing, and he hadn't touched the warm, buttery popcorn sitting on the white oak coffee table in front of him.

'Do you want to go and see her?' Lucie asked.

'What are you talking about?' His head turned.

'I'm not stupid, Anderson.'

'Correct, you're not.' He faced the TV again, swivelling his LA baseball cap around so the brim covered his eyes and he didn't have to look at her.

'You don't need to hide from me.'

Brett had been quiet since they'd returned from lunch with his family. He'd mumbled his way through painful small talk, but he'd been overly affectionate with Lucie while they cooked dinner. A kiss on the forehead, a hand on the waist. It was like he was trying to apologise for something. It wasn't until Sienna's name had appeared on Brett's phone while his back was turned and Lucie had seen it that she'd worked it out.

'I don't want to let you down.' He removed the cap, looking right at her.

'This isn't about me, Brett. This is about you doing what you need to do. I can't stop you from doing this, all I can do is be here if you need me.' She swallowed the lump in her throat because it wasn't an 'if', it was a 'when'.

She had no idea how long they'd been back in touch, but she feared something had happened last time he was home. It wouldn't surprise her. Sienna always knew how to get her claws into him, and this time would be no different.

He didn't have the capacity to handle this right now. But she couldn't just keep him here and confiscate his phone. She had to let him go even if there was a risk of losing him again.

Lucie had so much unwarranted hatred for Sienna. Yes, the woman had betrayed Brett but he was no angel. Rather than fixing his relationship, he had let the physical distance interfere with the emotional and neglected her. But that wasn't what bothered Lucie the most. It was the way Sienna had pulled Brett away from Lucie, too. Demanded it. Lucie understood how hard it must be for your partner to have a best friend of the opposite sex who he did *everything* with, but Brett had pushed her away in more than a physical sense. He stopped coming to her for heart-to-hearts, put an end to their movie nights. He hadn't even defended her when Sienna had made snide comments about her appearance, her financial status or the outfits she wore on shared nights out. But of course, because Brett was Brett and Lucie was his sunshine girl, as soon as his relationship had fallen apart, she had been there to pick up the pieces.

His ex had always felt like Lucie's biggest competition, an obstacle in their friendship. That feeling had stayed years after they'd broken up, and right now she felt like more of a threat than ever before.

'You should go, Brett.' Lucie fiddled with the buttons on the TV remote. Now she was the one who couldn't look at him.

'Will you be all right on your own?' He sat forward, already raring to go. That hurt her the most. The fact he seemed genuinely eager to go and see her.

'I'll video call the girls. Bea has a lot to catch us up on.'

'Okay. I guess I'll go pay her a visit then. If you're sure?' He hesitated, waiting for her to stop him. But she wouldn't.

'Yup.' Lucie did her best to conceal her shaky voice as he reached over and squeezed her hand in appreciation.

This was why she couldn't cross the line with him. Tonight, her gut feeling had been proven right. No matter how much Brett adored her, how much he claimed she was his favourite person and he'd be lost without her, he could never give her his heart in the way she needed him to. The way she'd given him hers in the Alps, unbeknown to him.

Who was she kidding? She'd belonged to him far longer than that. It was just that he had never belonged to her in return. Lucie had read stories of unrequited love, but none compared to her own. None of them were as heartbreaking as actually living it.

As the door clicked shut behind him, Lucie let out a deep sigh. Now she got to sit here for hours and wonder when he was coming home. Starting a group video call with Faith and Bea, she wasn't surprised to see Julien on her screen before anyone else.

'Hi! How's Oz?' He grinned at her, holding the camera right up to his face.

'Jules, move the phone back,' Lucie laughed, fighting the sniffles that threatened to turn into full-blown waterworks if she wasn't cheered up ASAP. She ignored his question.

'Oh, my bad. Faith was getting dressed in the background, so I thought I'd use my big head to block the view. She'll take over in a couple of minutes.'

'Hi, ladies! Oh, hello, Julien.' Bea appeared, giving Julien her usual prim and proper greeting to wind him up.

'Bea, what's the tea?' Julien asked, happy with himself for learning slang from his teenage daughter no matter how wrong it sounded coming from his mouth.

'I'm here!' Faith launched herself onto the bed and into frame, taking the phone from her husband but keeping him in shot.

'Right, so you know how Ricardo has ignored me for nearly a *year*? Even at races? Does anyone want to take a wild guess as to why that arsehole called me this afternoon? He told me he loves me. I mean, what the *hell*? Is it just me, or is that slightly unhinged?'

'So basically, he's matching your energy and it's freaking you out.' Julien shrugged; his insult mildly disguised with what could be considered advice.

'I *was* unhinged, Moretz. *Was*. I love him, but this is a lot to take in. How do I trust that this is what he wants?

Oh my God, he's calling me *again*,' Bea yelled in exasperation. 'I'm going to give him a piece of my mind. Will update you tomorrow.'

'You avoided my question. Don't think I didn't notice.' Julien raised an eyebrow at Lucie.

'Australia is fine. Brett is fine. I'm fine. How's Jasmine? I saw she posted that she was at a go-kart track today.'

'Yeah!' The pair of them lit up. 'She's fast, just like her dad.' Faith beamed.

Following a long catch-up, with a large hot chocolate with extra whipped cream and marshmallows in her hand and her favourite hoodie, Lucie settled down in bed to watch a film. She was supposed to watch this one with Brett, but he owed her this. Go out with your ex-fiancée and sacrifice watching *Anyone But You*.

By the time the credits rolled, Lucie couldn't have told anyone what the film was about even if she'd been held at gunpoint. For the whole two hours, her mind had been on nothing and nobody except Brett and Sienna.

She was starting to realise that Brett could be her person, and she might be about to lose him all over again. And yet, she couldn't possibly tell him this. He had vowed to never commit again after Sienna, so why would Lucie's confession change his mind?

Was he going to bring her back here? Should Lucie extricate herself from Brett's luxury cotton bedsheets and check into a nearby hotel? Camp out in his childhood bedroom and cry to Maggie and his sisters? No, she belonged here. Brett always made sure she knew that, so why should she start doubting it now?

Still, it didn't stop Lucie feeling like she should go home to Los Angeles or visit her parents in Europe. Leave Brett to his own devices for a while. Then she remembered the man she'd be leaving behind had a drinking problem. She had to take care of him, even if that meant her own heart had to ache for a while. She'd take her space when she knew he was okay.

Brett sat in a booth at Sydney's newest bar. It was opening night, and Sienna had told him that if he wanted to see her, this was where she'd be. She wasn't willing to change her plans to suit him, which made sense considering how wishy-washy he'd been with her.

She looked stunning. Platinum blonde hair down to her waist, piercing blue eyes and heels that made her almost the same height as him. She was a knockout. And yet as she begged him once again to have a vodka coke and loosen up a little, he wished he was at home watching a film with Lucie. He felt sick to his stomach as he sipped his cranberry juice.

'How's Lucie?' Sienna smiled but he knew it was fake. Why was she bringing her up?

'She's great.' Brett's jaw ticked.

'Is she in Sydney with you?' The small talk was beyond painful, but now Brett was here, he didn't quite know what to say. It felt different to when he'd seen her a few weeks ago.

'Yeah.' Lucie was a topic he didn't want to discuss with her.

'Why didn't she come here with you?' Sienna challenged. She knew why.

'I wonder,' he scoffed, recalling how she had treated Lucie in the past.

He had never been Sienna's best friend, and she had never been his. Their relationship, in truth, had always been surface level. His *real* best friend, the one who he loved unconditionally and who he knew with utter confidence would always be by his side, was Lucie.

And he'd fucked up. He'd left her sitting at home by herself in a city she wasn't overly familiar with while he was out here trying to make amends with someone who should be left in the past.

'I can't do this, Sen.' He shuffled out of the booth.

'What? B, please. I don't want you to go. I know you haven't forgiven me yet, but you will. We can work through it. What we had was special, I realise that now. Breaking your trust is my biggest regret. If I could take it back, I would.'

'I'm not convinced what we had was even real. I know my lifestyle wasn't right for you, but you should have just ended it when you knew I wasn't the one. But no, you got chatting to a random guy on a night out, when you should've been at home with *me*, and next thing I know my whole world is falling apart. You cheated on me, what was it? Eight times? Your friend over there told me all about those other guys.' He pointed directly at her redheaded friend, who was looking at them in fear. *Sorry, Amelia.*

'Just give me one more chance. I won't hurt you again,' she pleaded.

'I'm going to go home to Lucie.' He held her gaze.

'It's always going to be Lucie, isn't it?' Sienna sighed.

'Yeah, it's always going to be her.'

Lucie woke hours later to the front door opening and closing softly, followed by only one set of footsteps coming down the hallway. Thank *God*. Brett appeared, his frame filling the doorway. He looked as exhausted as she felt.

'Nice night?' She peered out from the blankets.

'No.' Brett disappeared into the bathroom to clean his teeth.

'Oh, really? I'm surprised,' she called through.

'Don't act all smug, Carolan.' He walked back into the bedroom, sans clothing, and climbed into bed in his boxers. Although they covered everything, they left very little to the imagination and she wished he'd wear sweatpants to bed when they were sharing.

'I'm an idiot.' He let out a bitter laugh.

'No, you're hurting and you needed to see her in order to move forward.' Lucie sat up.

'It was a waste of time.'

'I'm sorry, Brett.'

She turned to face him, smiling at the sight of his face buried in the pillow. He didn't seem utterly heartbroken, which was good. Sienna may still hold some power over him, but at least he wasn't going to cry about it and drown his sorrows.

'So, what have we learned today?' She prodded his arm.

'Lucie is always right,' he mumbled into his pillow.

'Sorry, what was that?' She smiled into the darkness.

'I said,' he lifted his head and propped himself up on his elbow, 'you're always right, and you're the only woman I'll ever need, Sunny.' Brett's lips hovered above hers, and as soon as she realised he smelled like peppermint rather than alcohol, she pulled him to her.

16

Lucie hadn't taken a solo trip in years. She used to love exploring alone, and she had been feeling suffocated lately. Being cooped up in Brett's apartment, high up in the clouds of Sydney, was no good for her soul. So she had left him safe in the company of his family, and fled to Italy for a couple of days away from reality.

It wasn't in her budget for the season, but she cut into what few savings she had for the sake of her *own* mental health. She'd been so focused on Brett's that she hadn't stopped to think about what she needed. And what she needed was to play tourist in one of her favourite cities.

She navigated through the crowds at the station in Rome with ease. She was used to travelling with a minimum number of belongings, but she always went over the top when the team paid extra for hold luggage or provided use of the private plane. Today, though, she'd hopped on a cheap, last-minute flight with everything she needed for approximately three days. Her sunshine keychain hung from her rucksack, reminding her of a group trip to Paris where Brett had spotted it and insisted she must have it.

It felt strange being here without him. Or without Marco, Julien, Faith or Bea. She sort of wished she'd invited her mum, but it would defeat the purpose of a solo trip. She was good at making new friends, anyway.

As she checked into her aunt's apartment, at the top of a three-storey building, the memories of her teen years came flooding back and almost knocked the wind out of her. Or maybe that was a result of climbing all those stairs, with a rucksack so heavy she'd felt as though she might topple backwards and fall to her death.

She'd spent a lot of time here from the ages of thirteen to eighteen. She had always been forced to bring her sisters with her, but this city had always felt like somewhere she could just *be*.

The apartment was old, but it was beautiful. The floors were all wood, not a single carpet in sight. There were scuff marks in the hall, burn marks in the kitchen. The living room had an open staircase that led up to an upstairs bedroom, a double bed filling the space. There was a second bedroom downstairs, opposite the bathroom, which had huge windows that opened out over the street. The kitchen had every utensil you could possibly need, cupboards filled to the brim with ingredients. Every woman in this family was an excellent cook except for Lucie. And it was fifteen minutes from the Trevi Fountain, which she would be avoiding like the plague during peak hours.

It wasn't quite tourist season, which would have been the worst possible time for her to have come. In a capital city in Europe, there were always tourists swarming the streets and crowding the landmarks, but in the height of summer? It would've been awful. Even without the tourists, she preferred to head all the way to the river Tiber, near Vatican City, and wander round, sit in cafés and just relax. It was quite far from the apartment, but she remembered it being much calmer. More up her street.

Sitting in an outdoor bar with her aunt's old photo albums, which she had brought out to keep her occupied while she sipped on an Aperol spritz, Lucie realised her aunt was a lot like her. She didn't have firm roots so it wasn't worth making a house a home. She was in her fifties, single, didn't have kids, travelled all the time, went on month-long cruises with her friends. While Lucie had loved living her twenties the way she had been, she was starting to think she might want something different for herself. It scared her. She was so used to her life, so well adjusted to her routine, or rather lack thereof, that she had no idea how she would ever transition into a new chapter.

Her peaceful Lucie-time was rudely interrupted by a man sitting two tables over from her, smacking his fist against the table as he scowled at his phone. He looked like a stereotypical Italian guy in his late twenties, early thirties. Dark hair, olive skin, gold-rimmed sunglasses and a fashion sense most men wished they could pull off.

On the third '*Cazzo!*', she decided to intervene. Not only in an attempt to restore peace and quiet, but also to help the poor guy.

Lucie couldn't help but admire his muscles as he clenched his fist again. Until she realised she was being creepy and if he caught her, it would be incredibly awkward considering she was now hovering at the edge of his table.

'Excuse me?' she called out, hoping he could hear her over his headphones.

The man looked up, scared for his life. 'Oh!'

'I'm sorry! I didn't mean to startle you.'

'It's okay!' he laughed, his accent thick. 'Was I disturbing you?'

'Uh . . . I just wanted to check you're okay. You seem quite stressed.'

'Oh, I'm fine. I just lost out on a work contract I'd been wanting. I was supposed to head out to Palma de Majorca today and join a charter yacht. They hired some other guy last minute. I'm Davide, by the way.'

'Lucie. That sucks, sorry to hear that. What do you do for work?' Lucie was always chatty around strangers, it was part of her job to be a social butterfly. To steer the conversation. It came naturally to her.

'I'm a private chef. But looks like I'm staying here another few days, until I find a job elsewhere. And what do you do?'

'I'm a social media manager,' Lucie said, then realised she should be hyping herself up. This guy had a cool, interesting job and so did she. 'For a motorsport championship. I also run an academy for women in motorsport, we do workshops and podcasts, et cetera.'

'Seriously? That's amazing. Take a seat, tell me more about yourself!' He gestured to the wicker chair opposite him and she hesitated. She didn't know why she was so nervous, maybe it was the piercing blue eyes

174

burning a hole through her skin. 'Unless you don't want to! Apologies, I always like conversations with strangers on my travels.'

'Me too,' Lucie laughed. 'I'll sit! Let me just grab my things.' She picked up her drink along with the photos and her bag, making herself comfortable at his table.

'So what brings you to Roma?' He looked her up and down, so subtly she nearly missed it. She couldn't quite figure out how she felt about it, but she was going to roll with it.

'Umm, I don't really know what I'm doing here except . . . being spontaneous, I guess? I'm staying in my aunt's apartment. Been a while since I travelled solo.'

'When's the last time you had a sightseeing tour of Roma?'

'Forever ago.'

'Well then, once you finish your drink and I finish my beer,' he raised his glass, 'would you like to come and explore with the best tour guide the city has to offer? For free, of course. I only ask for your company. And maybe someone to indulge my love of coconut gelato.'

Lucie grinned at him, grateful to have someone new to traipse around with. This was half the fun of travelling. 'You're on.'

Climbing the Spanish Steps was not the best time for Davide to be asking her questions, but he was insistent on knowing the ins and outs of her job. He was excited when she started her story with the fact she'd begun working for a catering business. Of course, that was only the start, and when she told him all the details, like which team she worked with and the places she got to visit for work, he looked like his head might explode.

'So, you get to travel around the world with this racing team? And film them?'

Lucie laughed at his wide-eyed expression. 'You make it sound so easy.'

'I don't mean to! You seem to have a lot going on.'

'Let's put it this way, my laptop comes everywhere with me. I left it in Sydney once and had to edit a week's worth of daily vlogs on my phone. Way harder than you think.'

'So, you're in charge of the entire race organisation's social media?'

'Yep.' Lucie nodded. 'Faith, Bea, Esme and I all create content and post on the IEC's main accounts and manage the socials team, and Faith and I are responsible for Revolution Racing, too. Each team has allocated social media people, but we have to make sure everything they post is up to a certain standard and ensure nothing inappropriate is put out on the internet.'

'Have you ever had a big scandal? Where one of them has posted something bad?'

Lucie thought about it, taking pride in her ability to do her job. 'No, not really. We once had someone convince their drivers to do a dance challenge which was trending at the time, but the song wasn't really family friendly. We want the content to be suitable for everyone. It was never posted because it came to me first.'

'I've thought about taking my talents online, creating

a brand for myself as a chef. Could probably get more work that way.'

'Have you seen that reality show?'

'Oh, *Below Deck*? Yes, that's what gave me the idea to go into the private charter business. I just think, why would anyone want to be stuck in one place? I've travelled a little bit the last few years, since my divorce, and it gave me a taste of what I've been missing. I've done three charter seasons already.'

'You were married?'

'Yes, which is crazy considering I once vowed I would never go down that road. But, for the right person, a man will do anything. As it turns out, she was not the right person for me. We were both miserable. Got married on a whim. You know how we Italians are, hopeless romantics.'

'Uh, yeah. I have to say, that trait didn't really insert itself into my DNA. So why did it all fall apart? Other than being miserable. There had to be a reason.'

'She wanted to settle down, have eight billion children the second we tied the knot, stay here in Roma. I wasn't opposed to children, just didn't want them yet, and she was insistent. I wanted to leave the city, definitely wouldn't raise children here. It's too dangerous, there's too much going on, too many people. We ultimately realised that as much as we loved each other, we wanted very different things and there was no way to compromise. We were at different stages in our lives.'

'I get that. I have a . . . well, a Brett.'

'What is "a Brett".' He raised an eyebrow.

'He's my best friend. One of the drivers I do social media for.'

'Oh, and you have feelings for him?'

Lucie bit her lip. She'd never admitted it to a stranger. 'Yes.'

'And you've crossed the line . . .' Davide looked like he was enjoying getting the gossip.

'Quit looking at me like that!' She elbowed him jokingly, feeling at ease after spending a number of hours getting to know him already. 'It's a very recent thing. Well, two years ago. Then nothing until we kissed a week or so ago. But he isn't . . . I don't know, *right* for me? Well, he is. He's perfect. We know each other inside out. I just mean he sleeps with all these different girls, as any single racing driver would, and he likes to be a free bird. I can't see him ever giving that up.'

'He might, for you.'

'But he shouldn't have to give anything up.'

'No, perhaps not, but you should allow him to choose.' Davide shrugged, like it was obvious. And she knew it should be as uncomplicated as that, but it couldn't be.

'And if he chooses anything other than me?' She squinted in the sunlight.

'Now I see your problem. There's no going back from that.' His face was full of sympathy.

'Exactly. It would change our dynamic forever, and he's all I know.'

'He's all you know?' Davide frowned, the confusion making him look adorable.

'I haven't slept with anyone else since him, and I've

never been in a long-term relationship. I've dated, but never seriously.' Her cheeks were tinged pink. It was embarrassing, saying it out loud. It wasn't that she had been waiting for her best friend to fill the gap, she just hadn't felt the inclination to sleep with anyone else. She'd been too busy fighting the chemistry between them.

'Woah, Lucie. I think you need to explore the world a little in terms of *men*.'

Her whole body felt like it was on fire, both with embarrassment and sexual attraction. She wasn't blind to the appeal of other men, and Davide was incredibly handsome. She imagined his charter guests ate him up. Tipped him *unbelievable* amounts of money.

She cleared her throat. 'Where's next on your list?'

The Trevi Fountain was unusually quiet considering the time of day and the weather. The sun was blazing, and Lucie's shoulders were burning. It had been winter in Sydney, and she welcomed the change.

'You know, I've never made a wish in this fountain.' Lucie peered into the water, seeing all the coins at the bottom. She'd watched countless films where the characters tossed coins into it, but she'd never bothered. Her sisters had thought it was laughable, and she'd been too embarrassed to do it.

'Never?' Davide put his hand on his chest. 'You must do it.' He rooted through his wallet for some euros, coming up triumphant with a coin.

'Isn't there a specific way?' She turned the coin over in her hand.

179

He turned her round so she was facing him and positioned her. 'What you want to do, is keep your back to the fountain –'

'So, you don't toss it in like it's a frisbee?'

'Never. How dare you suggest such a thing,' he teased. 'You have to use your right hand and throw it over your left shoulder. You throw one coin; you will return to Roma. You throw a second, you will fall in love with an Italian.'

'Oh . . .' Now she felt shy.

'Don't worry, I only have one coin. Your racing driver beau is safe.'

'He's not my –'

'I am just playing.' He laughed, his smile reaching his eyes. He was a natural flirt and a great conversationalist, which was confusing, but only because one half of her wanted to flirt back and the other half felt like she was betraying Brett.

As they walked through the streets on the way to Altare della Patria, his hand on the small of her back to guide her through the crowds, her lack of a filter got the better of her. 'You make me nervous, and I don't like it.'

Davide breathed out a laugh, his hand squeezing her waist. That felt weird too, but not in the way she'd expected. It felt kind of exhilarating. 'You make me nervous too.'

She hadn't thought about anyone but Brett for so long, but he hadn't given her the same treatment. And now Davide was here. In front of her. She just had to figure out if it was worth clinging to the past or trusting the present.

17

Her aunt needed to invest in better mattresses. She'd tried both bedrooms, and both were horrendous. Her back pain was worse than it was after napping in camping chairs at the back of the Revolution Racing garage, and she was hunting for painkillers in the bathroom cabinet when everything that had happened yesterday started to sink in.

Davide had taken her on a forty-five-minute walk across the city to a gelato shop, where they'd held up the queue while deciding on which flavours they wanted. They'd settled on a scoop of Nutella, one mango and one coconut and Lucie had decided Ben & Jerry's and a film in bed had nothing on traditional Italian gelato in a little wooden tub, enjoyed on a cobbled side street in one of the few capital cities she liked.

Opposite the gelato shop was an Irish pub, which the city had a lot of. They all poured a double rum like it was a quadruple. She'd taken one look at the tourists drinking beers and cocktails on the side of the street, tables wobbling on the uneven ground and music blasting from inside, and decided she needed to be amongst it all.

She had expected Davide to complain or to tell her he was going home for the night, but he had entertained her request, indulging in the happy hour offer on cocktails and presenting her with four pina coladas to herself. They had spent a solid two hours discussing their favourite travel memories, including Lucie's visit to an Italian restaurant in Milan where the American-hating owner had slammed her Coca-Cola down on the table in front of her, and Davide's first Métro ride in Paris when he had gone the wrong way across the city.

They were on their sixth cocktails when a group of tourists joined them outside, mid smoking break. They were from Eindhoven, Manchester, Melbourne, New York. All over the place. And they had all shared travel stories up until the bar staff had to turf them out to close up, then wandered through the city to find fast food, and continued drunkenly chatting as they scoffed their fries and burgers.

Davide had walked her to her door and placed a gentle kiss on her cheek, and Lucie had fought not to make a move. She knew she'd regret it when she was sober. Except now she was sober, and still debating if she should've bitten the bullet and just done it. She was going home tomorrow, and then she could almost guarantee she wouldn't see Davide again. But Lucie had let the sensible side of her take over and closed her door behind her, leaving Davide to go home alone.

Her phone buzzed in her room, and she rushed to answer it. Until she saw the name on the screen. She had been in a Brett Anderson bubble for so long, she was supposed to be having some time in the real world.

'Lucie, you up?' Davide hammered on the door of

her apartment. It was ten in the morning already; she'd treated herself to a lie-in after a late night with her new-found, temporary friends. Although she was pretty sure she'd drunkenly promised them VIP race tickets so she was bound to hear from some of them again.

She headed into the hall and opened the door to a beautiful smirk on his beautiful face, and one glance up and down her body, his gaze lingering on her bare legs, ignited a spark. Fuck it, this trip was for her. Why shouldn't she be reckless for once?

His hands were in her hair in an instant as his lips crashed down on hers. She jumped up, wrapping her legs around his waist as he gripped on to her thighs, holding her up. They hadn't even made it through the front door, and she was ready to rip his clothes off. As her hands roamed his body she could feel every ridge and curve of his.

'Lucie.' He pulled away and rested his forehead against hers, his fingers stroking her skin. He was dangerously close to her inner thigh, and she found herself adjusting so he got the hint. This was what she wanted. 'What about the racing driver?'

And there it was. That reality she had been craving. A reality where she realised there *was* no escaping the Brett Anderson bubble.

'I'm sorry.' She slipped out of his grasp, suddenly feeling vulnerable.

'You have nothing to be sorry for. I only came to ask if you wanted to go exploring again, after breakfast of course. I know it's your last day.'

'Yes, I'd love to! Um, want to wait inside while I get ready? Won't be long.'

'Take all the time you need.' He smiled and she almost laughed. She may only need twenty minutes to be physically ready, but she needed a hell of a lot more time to process her thoughts.

'You've never been to the Colosseum?' Davide stared at her in disbelief while they queued to see one of the most iconic pieces of history on planet earth up close. Somehow, this was a new experience for Lucie.

'My sisters always preferred shopping.'

'Well, I'm glad you didn't ask me to do that with you.'

'I can't believe I've waited so long to see this. You know, I aced history back in high school?' She rubbed her hands together, ready to wow him with her knowledge of the Romans. All things he already knew, no doubt.

'I thought you had a creative brain, judging by your job.'

'What can I say? I'm a woman of many talents.'

'I don't doubt it,' he smirked.

She felt that funny feeling wash over her again as they shuffled closer to the entrance. That strange sensation of being attracted to a man other than Brett. She was still battling her head and her heart, only now, her heart was equally as confused. She wondered if she should just go home and pretend this trip hadn't happened, that she hadn't almost slept with Davide, but she knew it was serving a purpose. It was waking her up. What to? She wasn't sure. But it would become clear sooner or later.

'This isn't what I expected.' Lucie scrunched her nose up in annoyance as she was shoved into again. '*Lizzie McGuire* set my expectations too high.'

'Would you like me to start singing?' Davide grinned. 'Hey now, hey now . . .' He sang quietly so nobody else could hear.

'It's okay,' she laughed, hoping he wouldn't continue.

He glanced at her, a twinkle in his eye, before projecting his voice above the chatter of tourists. 'This is what dreams are made of!'

'Davide!' She slapped her hand over his mouth, mortified as multiple tour groups looked at them in confusion. A few girls in their twenties carried on singing the rest of the song to themselves, the only people around them who seemed to understand the reference.

'Am I embarrassing you?'

'Just a smidge.'

'I'm sorry,' he shrugged. 'Don't you think it's so cool that we're standing here right now? Where actual gladiators were. There's so much history in these walls.'

'Or lack of walls,' she noted. 'It's amazing that it's still standing.'

'I bet you've seen some amazing things thanks to your job, no? All those racetracks, just as a starting point. But you must have been all over the place.'

'I'm super lucky, yeah. I don't think I've stayed in one place longer than two weeks since I joined the IEC.'

'Still, it's always good to have somewhere you can call home.'

*

After lunch, Lucie made her excuses and left Davide to wander round alone. It felt different today, the more she stewed over their kiss, and she had regrets. She needed to get back into the comfort of her own company and her own space.

She hadn't spoken to Brett for two days and she was starting to feel something in the pit of her stomach. A sense of emptiness. Longing. She had attachment issues, but who wouldn't in her shoes? If it hadn't been for the fact he was battling an alcohol dependency problem and resolving his trauma without her help, maybe she would be able to go about her day in peace. But the unfortunate truth was, Lucie would never stop worrying about him. Or missing him.

Back at the apartment, she made herself a herbal tea and curled up in a tattered old armchair, ready for a catch-up. What would she say? Would she tell him about Davide? *Should* she? Not necessarily the kiss part, but just his general existence and the fact she'd spent the last couple of days with her own personal tour guide, and she'd had a great time exploring with a Rome native.

She didn't know why she was so nervous about it when Brett knew she made friends everywhere she went. It was the guilt of that kiss talking. Guilt that wasn't even warranted. Her head was a mess.

It became even more of a mess when his phone went straight to voicemail. The feeling in the pit of her stomach somehow shifted into something else. A fear that somehow he knew. Or worse, he'd screwed up.

'Maggie?' Lucie's voice came out panicked when his mum answered on the third ring.

She heard chatter in the background, heard Brett and Piper cheering, and suddenly all was right in her world. 'Hi, Lucie! How's Rome?'

'Hey, Sunny!' Brett yelled out. 'We miss you! I'm thrashing Cleo at pool!'

'Pool?' Lucie asked.

'Yes,' she muttered. 'Brett got us a pool table for the house. They had it purchased and set up by this time last night, and today, they got a diving board fitted in the swimming pool. Honestly, Lucie. They're a nightmare.'

'I bet. Rome isn't exactly relaxing, but I'm pretty sure it's more peaceful than your house right now.' Lucie laughed as another cheer erupted, this time from Piper.

'Hang on, I'm taking this call outside,' Maggie sighed, and after a few moments of shuffling, heaved a sigh of relief. 'That's better. I can hear properly now. So I'll ask again, how is Rome?'

'It's great. I made friends!' She decided to mention it, because she realised she wanted to share the photos and Davide was in some of them. As well as the group from the bar, of course.

'Oh, I'm so glad you did! I bet it was so freeing just being able to do whatever you wanted for a couple of days.'

'Absolutely. And yet here I am worrying about your son.'

'Oh, don't worry about him! I'm keeping an eye on him. You have to focus on your own mental well-being,

Lucie. You've done so much for Brett, but you also can't support him if you're not putting yourself first. I strongly suggest you stay in Italy for another week. Go see Marco or something. You have that charity event in Monaco next week anyway, right? Brett can just fly out and meet you there, you don't need to come all the way back to Sydney for him.'

'Yeah . . . you're right. But promise me something, Maggie.'

'Get in touch the second I think he's up to no good? Consider it a deal. If you keep me updated with your travels so I can live vicariously through you. I think I'll have to visit your parents in Tuscany this year, Australia is feeling claustrophobic!'

'They'd love to have you, Maggs. Right, I'm going to call Mars, see if he wants a house guest. Tell Brett I'll text him tomorrow or something.'

Lucie hung up, and felt a strange sense of peace wash over her. It was like she was starting to find her feet again after all her recent stress. Brett was fine. He didn't need her around all the time, which meant she could travel and work and not feel guilty about leaving him behind. But she knew it was still a rocky path he was on, and he might not be okay forever.

18

Revolution Racing were at an event in Monaco for their sponsors, and they were all dressed up to the nines. It was a fashion show for a luxury formalwear brand, and they had provided everyone's outfits. Lucie had chosen a strapless satin maxi dress in red which clung to her curves in all the right places, and the slit in the thigh was giving her an air of confidence that she hadn't felt in a long time.

Or maybe that was down to the way Brett had slipped his arm around her waist, leaned in close and told her she looked phenomenal before they left the hotel room. It had sent a shiver down her spine in a way that almost made her pull him back towards the king-sized bed by his tie. Which was also red, because that was their team colour, but it made her heart flutter that they matched.

This dress, and her hormones, had her acting out of control. They hadn't kissed again since their second night in Sydney, hadn't even talked about it, but Lucie had been physically turning her head or her body so neither of them were tempted. She had even started wearing an eye mask to bed and claiming she was exhausted, so they didn't lay awake talking. A pillow wall between them had been briefly discussed.

Lucie was one more intense moment of chemistry

away from giving in to his suggestion of a friends-with-benefits situation. She was craving another taste of him regardless of the consequences.

Tonight was a big night for the team, and it was up to Lucie and Faith to hype it up across socials. The sponsors wanted them to film everything they got up to and the team were thoroughly enjoying a chance to play fashion influencer for the evening. The drivers had gone up on stage and modelled their suits themselves, much to Julien's disgust. He hated attention unless it was for his efforts on the track. Faith was yapping in Lucie's ear about Jasmine's school project and how she had created an exact replica of Jupiter with paint and papier mâché.

'That sounds cool,' Lucie mumbled absentmindedly, pretending to be paying attention to every word she said. Brett eyed her from his table, and she thanked the heavens she was standing at the bar at the opposite end of the room. She turned away quickly, looking back at her friend.

Faith narrowed her eyes suspiciously. 'Something's changed between you two.'

'Don't be ridiculous. We're the same as we've always been.'

'No, you keep looking at each other like you're the only two people in the room. The energy feels different. Have you slept together or something?'

'No!' Lucie's voice rose several octaves and her cheeks reddened.

'*Nothing* has happened? Nothing that would cause a shift in your behaviour now?'

'Okay, so obviously there was the drunken almost-sex in Vegas . . . maybe we kissed in Sydney. Stone-cold sober.'

'You've what? You've kissed? Just, a casual peck or like, a full-on, clothes thrown across the room, hard to resist taking it further kind of kiss?'

'Uhhh . . . tipped my entire world on its axis. I laid awake for hours.'

'Oh lord, those are the best kind.'

'I *know*. But it's Brett. This can't be a thing.'

'Why not? You two are soulmates, it's frustrating watching you two not realise it.'

'He's a wild card. I don't think anything could make him settle down.'

Faith frowned. 'Hmm.'

'What?'

'I hate to admit it, but I think you have a point.'

'Exactly. So, we need to rein it in.'

'I don't think you should completely close the door on it.'

'Well, I can't *talk* to him about it.' Lucie widened her eyes as if the idea was ludicrous.

'Of course you can.'

'No way. That will make things awkward.' She fidgeted with her bracelet, one that Brett had got her when her grandma passed away. It had her nonna's birthstone, amethyst, in it.

'Lucie, are you for real? If a one-night stand two years ago hasn't made things awkward, neither will addressing said one-night stand.'

'He did also offer a friends-with-benefits arrange-ment . . . I'm still not sure if he was joking. I laughed it off, anyway.'

'He what? Girl, take it!' Faith's drink sloshed as she lurched forward and gripped Lucie's arm. This was the most they'd gossiped about the guys since the IEC trip to Hawaii two seasons ago, when Faith had told her she and Julien had been secretly sort-of dating.

'I can't do that!' She was already dangerously close, but right now, in this moment, logic was in control of her emotions.

'Why not?'

Lucie chewed on her bottom lip, ruining her recent gloss application. 'Because . . .'

'Oh, shit! You're in love with him!' Faith whisper-yelled and caused the bartender to look their way. It was just as well nobody else was at the bar, because this would be all over social media before long if they weren't careful.

'Congrats, you worked it out.'

Faith's jaw dropped, and Lucie became hyper-aware that Brett was likely still looking in their direction. If they didn't move this conversation elsewhere, or tone it down a notch, he'd be over here in a millisecond, trying to get in on the gossip. What excuse would Lucie possibly give him if he did catch on to their top-secret exchange?

'I can't believe it's taken me this long to figure it out.' Faith sat there dumbfounded, like she had just uncover-ed the world's greatest love story.

'I'm not too sure when *I* figured it out, to be honest. It was almost like I didn't have to.'

'You've just kind of always felt it?' she said, dreamily.

'For as long as I can remember. But it's like that night we spent together reignited the spark, and I can't push it down any more.'

Faith's entire demeanour softened as she took on the role of a concerned friend. 'Luce, don't you think you should tell him? Get it out in the open?'

'Maybe. Even if it blows up in my face, I probably need to spit it out eventually. But not yet. He's got too much going on in his head, I have to time it right. When I tell him, it could ruin our friendship for good. He needs me too much for me to be selfish at the moment.'

'God, this is going to be painful.'

'Oh, I'll be fine. I've been doing this for years.'

'Not for you, for me.' Faith placed her hand over her heart. 'I just want to know if he feels the same way. I've always thought he does, but that doesn't mean he wants a happily ever after.'

'I don't even know if I do. I don't know if we would work if we stepped over the line. It's one thing to love a person, but it's another to actually be compatible or share the same hopes and dreams. Anyway, you're being super unhelpful right now, Jensen,' Lucie deadpanned. 'Let's head back over to the table. We're starting to draw attention to ourselves and I do *not* want to deal with an interrogation . . .'

Sitting back down with the team, Lucie's attention was on glassware. Each glass on the white tablecloth was filled with water. Just plain old aqua. None of the team were drinking alcohol at the table, they would instead head to the bar and stand there until their drinks were finished, leaving Brett to mingle. Even then, she didn't think any of them had drunk more than two and they were already a few hours into their evening.

So far, Brett had kept quiet, not touched a drop of alcohol and accepted the situation for what it was, but slipped Lucie his credit card and insisted she let him treat her to something other than room temperature water. His only complaint of the entire evening had been that an event catering to such high-class clientele should up their ice game.

As she leaned back in her chair, her dress seriously restricting her movements, she observed Brett while he turned to speak to Ricardo De La Rosa at the table behind. The same De La Rosa they were supposed to hate since he'd broken up with Bea via a break-up announcement on social media instead of communicating with her directly. The same De La Rosa who was making a poor effort at winning her back. Nonetheless, Brett was happily chatting away. As loud as ever.

It wasn't until he turned back around and knocked his drink over that doubt started to crawl up Lucie's spine. Water spilled everywhere. On Brett's phone and Marco's, all over Brett's suit trousers and on the silky material of Faith's dress.

'Anderson!' Faith rolled her eyes and stood up, dabbing at the material with a napkin before sighing and hurrying away to the bathrooms.

Her dress belonged to the brand that was sponsoring them and if it was ruined, Faith would have to pay the costs. Lucie knew based on her own dress that her gorgeous floor-length gown was upwards of four grand.

'Aw shit, sorry man, is your phone all right, De Luca?' Brett frowned as Marco inspected the damage. Julien watched on in silence, concern etched across his features. His gaze didn't even follow his wife out of the room like it usually would.

'All good. Yours?' Marco was typically unbothered.

'Yeah, think I need to go get the hand dryer on my trousers though.' Brett excused himself and left his friends sitting there in an awkward silence. Someone needed to say it, but who?

'Luce, what's in that glass? Give it a quick check before he comes back.' Julien pointed at the half-empty glass of water that Brett had been drinking from.

Lucie picked it up, lifting it to her nose and inhaling before taking a hesitant sip for good measure. It was plain water, no doubt about it. She felt guilty for them all accusing him of breaking his sobriety so soon, but she had a feeling that for now, this would be a regular thing. They would constantly be suspicious of his every move. At least for tonight, they could just put it down to Brett being clumsy. He would no doubt receive a dry-cleaning bill from Julien's wife, however. Or Julien himself, who still looked monumentally pissed off.

'Will we ever be able to trust him?' Marco said exactly what she'd been thinking. He usually liked to sugar-coat things, but it seemed that he was equally as worried about his teammate. After all, if Brett messed up and lost his seat or if it got out to the press, Jules and Marco would have to deal with the fallout.

'Probably not. But it doesn't mean we love him any less.' Julien looked pointedly at Lucie. Could he see right through her? Did he know how she felt about their best friend? Or was he just clarifying that they would be there to support him, too? That she didn't have to do it alone.

She observed the room. It was packed with business-people, higher-ups from the team. Not just the sponsor they were here for tonight, but other sponsors, too. The *owner* of Revolution Racing, who was a step above Jasper. Every single one of these people would have a negative reaction if news of Brett's issues surfaced. They would cut donations, end contracts. It could run the team into the ground.

How was she supposed to monitor Brett's every waking move without him getting angry? Would he get angry, or would he thank her for holding him account-able and saving his ass from losing the career he'd fought so hard for? Jasper hadn't said it, but he was counting on Lucie. So was Gabriel. So was *everyone*. She could feel the pressure mounting, suffocating her.

Lucie needed to get out of this room. Faith was taking a while in the bathroom, so she used that as her get-out clause. 'I'm going to go help your wifey with her dress.'

'Sure. If you see Anderson, tell him us three drivers need to start making the rounds again. There's loads of people we haven't greeted yet and I can feel the PR team breathing down our necks. You know how Chelsea gets when things aren't done her way.'

'Faith?' Lucie hovered in the long, dimly lit corridor leading to the bathrooms. Both were engaged, and she assumed Brett was in the second one. She knocked on the first.

'Luce, is that you? I'll be out in a minute! My dress is almost dry. Brett is saved from my dry-cleaning bill!' Faith's voice called out over the noise of the hand dryer.

'Hi, Sunny.' Brett flung the door to the second rest-room open, swaying slightly as he smirked at Lucie, his eyes glazed over. 'Fancy seeing you here.'

'Get back in there, right now.' Lucie shoved him backwards and slammed the door, angry tears threatening to blur her vision. 'Show me your pockets.'

'If you wanted to get in my pants so bad, why didn't you just say that weeks ago?' he snorted. Actually *snorted*, as he laughed at his own bad joke.

'You're drunk,' she stated. It was clear as day. How had he changed so much in fifteen minutes? Was it because now she was looking harder for the signs? Because she was already suspicious? Yet again, she hadn't paid enough attention. She'd been too busy vlogging.

'No, Sunny. I'm Brett.' He grinned at her.

The swaying had raised her suspicions once again, but the snort had done it. Brett never laughed quite like that. His glass may have been vodka-free, but he must have something on him.

'Pockets, Brett. I'm not fucking around.' Her jaw ticked.

'Okay! Jesus.' He put his hands in his trouser pockets and pulled the lining out, showing her that they were totally empty. 'I don't have anything.'

'Did you somehow manage to snag an alcoholic drink at the bar? I thought one of the guys had been up with you every time.' She eyed him cautiously.

'Sunny, I'm sober. Not a drop.'

'Not even a shot? That guy from the tequila company didn't persuade you?' One of their potential new sponsors was a big tequila brand who had been invited along tonight, and their CEO had been pushing everyone at the event to try it out tonight. Maybe he'd got to Brett.

'One.' Brett bit his lip, having the decency to look embarrassed.

'Okay, so you lied to me then,' she scoffed. 'You're too drunk for it to have been just one shot. What else?' Lucie crossed her arms, and for once, Brett looked scared of her.

'Nothing.'

'Stop lying.'

'Fine.' He let out an exaggerated sigh like a child having a tantrum and flashed the inside pocket of his tux. That's when she saw it. The unmistakable flash of silver. How had he possibly managed to sneak a flask into his jacket when she had been helping him get ready in *her* room?

'Show it to me.'

Brett took it out and handed it to her, wincing harder than she did when she smelled the whisky. She shook it. There was barely any left.

'It's not mine.'

'Oh! Well, that's fine then!'

'I swiped it from Jasper. I know he likes the strong, expensive stuff.'

'You swiped it from your *team principal*? Have you lost your fucking mind? Do you want to lose your entire career?'

'Stop swearing. It doesn't suit you.'

'It doesn't suit me? Alcoholism doesn't suit you, Brett. But here we are.'

'Maybe you just fuck off out of my life, then. Leave me to it.' His words were like knives. He had never, in all their years of friendship, said anything like that. If anything, he'd only ever begged her to stay. For him to be risking *her*? This was worse than Lucie had thought. He wasn't miraculously healed after spending time at home, he was merely masking whatever pain he was in, in order to get back behind the wheel of his beloved race car. And the worst part? She couldn't blame him.

'Don't move. Julien can deal with you for tonight. I'll give you space.' She wrenched the door open and was greeted by Faith's panicked expression.

'Are you okay? I heard yell—'

'Fuck your *space*, Lucie. You might be able to control your little social media interns but are you *fuck* going to keep controlling me.' Brett's voice echoed into the corridor before she could shut the door on him, right as Jasper rounded the corner. Lucie stared at her boss, eyes wide, and she knew in that moment that Brett was screwed.

199

'Don't you dare speak to her like that, Anderson.' He kept his voice low, but his tone said it all. If Brett reacted, he could blow his entire career.

'It's Lucie, I'll speak to her however the fuck I want.' And that was it.

Jasper clenched his jaw and his fist simultaneously, and herded Lucie and Faith behind him as he got in the face of one of his star drivers. 'No, you won't. If it wasn't for her, your career would be done, Brett. Over. For good. But you're a damn good driver, and I love you like a son. You're not throwing this away. Understood?'

'Mmhmm.' Brett stared at the swirls on the carpet, refusing to make eye contact.

'You're taking the rest of the season off. You can take a few months to do what you need to do, and then we'll ease you back into team responsibilities over the winter. But you are not getting back into that car this season. You're not to show up at the track, either. I don't want to see you anywhere that has any ties to the motorsport industry unless I specifically invite you.'

'So, am I done?' Brett mumbled.

'No, you idiot. If you can sort your shit out, if you do therapy and prove to me that you're doing it, you can come back next season. But not before. I don't want to lose you, Anderson. You're part of the team, and the fans and sponsors love what you bring to the table. But man, you've got issues. Deal with them.'

'I'm off the team?'

'No, you're taking a step back.'

'But I'm not racing at Le Mans?'

'No.'

'Shit.' Brett's eyes welled up with tears, and despite the way he'd just spoken to her, Lucie squeezed past Jasper and wrapped her arms around her best friend.

He wasn't himself. That much was clear. Brett liked to think he could put on a brave face and just get on with life, but tonight had unveiled the truth. He still had a long way to go and a lot of trauma to work through, and he couldn't do it alone. Whatever he did next, he needed to hit the reset button. And Lucie knew exactly the place to take him.

19

After he'd literally got on his knees and begged for her forgiveness, Lucie and Brett had been snuck out of the back entrance of the event in Monaco, still in their formalwear, and Jasper's driver had taken them to the airport, where their suitcases had been delivered from the hotel and there was a small flight crew waiting to take them away.

'I'm sorry, Sunny,' he mumbled again, close to a full-scale breakdown in the bedroom at the back of Revolution's private plane.

'I'm at my breaking point too, and I'm not trying to guilt trip you, but you have to understand that your choices don't just impact you. But I don't need verbal apologies, I need action. I need you to focus on getting to the root of your problems.'

'You don't have to be here with me, Luce. I understand if you want some space.'

'No, I told you, we're a team. But don't think you're going to be easily forgiven.' She swallowed the lump in her throat as she watched sobs wrack his body.

'I want to get better, Luce. I don't want to keep hurting myself, or you, or my family. My fucking *teammates*. I've let so many people down just because I couldn't hold it together. I was stupid to think I had it all figured out. I just wanted so badly to believe that I was fine, that I was healed.' Brett fiddled with his watch, a Rolex gifted to him by the organisation on his first race win. 'I was spiralling when I flew home to Sydney without you.'

'I think tonight was a bit of a giveaway, Anderson. But you can't use me as a crutch, you've got to learn to cope on your own.'

'I slept with Sienna.' He sobbed again, a fresh wave of tears hitting him.

'You did *what*? Was it just the once? The first time you went home?' Lucie couldn't hide her anger at his stupidity, it was like he was actively trying to hurt himself at this point.

'Yeah.' He looked as sick as Lucie felt. 'Nothing happened the night I came home to you. The night I kissed you.' As if that made it any better.

'Why didn't you just walk away?'

'I wasn't thinking straight. It was a *lot*, all the emotional upheaval from the last couple of months. My head was a mess. I wanted answers, closure, to feel like the old me again and forget everything else I was feeling. We'd bumped into each other that morning, and it felt normal. Comfortable. That second night I went to see her, I was just reminded of the way she betrayed me and I realised I shut the door on her for a reason.'

'That door is now deadbolted, right?' She took a deep breath.

'Thrown away the key.'

'I hate to ask, but she doesn't know about the drinking, does she?'

'No, but . . . maybe I should speak out about my situation, let my fans know why I've just disappeared off the face of the planet. They're going to be confused about why I'm not racing all of a sudden. Especially because I raced at Spa and Monza. I started the season, but I'm not going to finish it. That's not usual.'

'You know it's risky, Brett. Sponsors might not like the truth.'

'No, but they might like the honesty. The opportunity to bring awareness to mental health and the effects of alcoholism,' Brett mumbled, proving he wasn't confident in his words.

'But first, you need to focus on getting yourself into a position that allows you to use your voice in the way you want. Right now, you're in the thick of it. Barely in the first step of recovery.' Lucie spoke gently, hoping she didn't offend him.

'Yeah, speaking of. Where the bloody hell are you taking me, Carolan? I'm being held hostage on my own team's plane. We're about to be thirty-five thousand feet in the air. It's unnerving. For all I know, you're going to drop me over some deserted island and make me live out the rest of the season catching my own food and shredding coconuts.'

'Do you trust me?' she laughed. Now the hard stuff was out of the way, jokester Brett was allowed to make his return. Anything to make this feel a little more normal.

'Always,' he nodded.

'We're going to spend the summer with my parents.'

'In Tuscany?' Brett's face lit up.

'Yep. We're going to help them renovate their farmhouse in Capannori.' Lucie stood up, leading him out of the bedroom so they could get seated for their meal. Brett still needed to sober up.

'You mean to tell me I get to spend the summer indulging in Rosa's cooking, working on your dad's classic cars and lounging around in the sun?'

'And journalling, therapy, painting walls, fixing the roof . . .'

'Yeah, yeah. I'll be a busy boy. Still, I can't think of anywhere better to get myself on the straight and narrow. Do you think your mum will make me her famous tiramisu?' he asked, and he wasn't exaggerating. It was literally famous; she had a bestselling cookbook published many moons ago.

'I'm pretty sure she's planning on bringing some to the airport so you can eat it in the car.' Lucie's mum had been making her 'adopted son' a tiramisu every single time she saw him for years.

'I think I'm going to have to ask your dad for his wife's hand in marriage.'

'Brett, my darling!' Rosa Carolan's voice rang through the arrival terminal of Florence's airport and just as Lucie had suspected, she stood there with her flip flops, summer dress, straw hat and a dish of tiramisu while Lucie's dad, Mateo, waved an Australian flag on a stick. Never mind the fact their own daughter was there, too. Where was the American flag? Brett always got the fanfare, not just at the racetrack.

'God, I love them,' Brett laughed, causing Lucie to scowl and yank her suitcase out of his hand. She would carry it her damn self.

'Hi, Mum. Dad.' Lucie hugged them both before stepping aside so they could fawn over her best friend, pinching his cheeks.

'Rosa, you made this for me?!' Brett pretended to be shocked, and Rosa played up to it. She was born to be a perfect hostess.

'Of course! We couldn't welcome you without it.'

'She already had it in the fridge,' Mateo chuckled. 'We're so happy to have you both with us, we're going to have such a good summer!' Mateo flung an arm around his daughter as they walked to the car, unable to do the same to Brett due to their height difference. Lucie and her siblings were never going to inherit good height genes from her parents.

'Brett, honey, you look like you need a couple of days lounging by the pool before we put you to work.' Rosa spoke so fast, Lucie almost missed the insult.

'Mum!' Lucie whisper-yelled at her, but Brett looked nothing but amused. He was used to the lack of filter that all the Carolan women had been cursed with.

'Goodness, I'm so sorry. That was insensitive.'

'No worries, Mrs C. I can't wait to see the farm. Did all your cars make it over in one piece, sir?' Brett asked Mateo.

Her dad had inherited a car from her grandpa ten years ago, right when Lucie had started with the IEC and made a friend in Brett. Since then, he and Brett had travelled all over the world to find more for his collection. Mateo called them 'investments'. Brett had gifted him a few; one for his fiftieth, one just because, and one when Mateo and Rosa had retired.

'Oh, yes! I'm converting the barns to keep them all safe. Rosa is sacrificing her precious horses, at least until we figure out an alternative. Maybe another barn . . . custom built.'

'Dad! You promised Mum she could have animals,' Lucie tutted.

'I don't mind. If he's out there converting the barns, then he's out of my kitchen. You know how he always gets in my way. Drives me up the wall.'

'Yeah, and she can have chickens instead. There is a lovely chicken coop out back.'

Lucie glanced at her mum as Brett and Mateo hurled the luggage into the car and was met with a look of pure disgust. Rosa may not want chickens, but she'd accept the apologetic gesture from her husband without complaint to save him feeling guilty.

Lucie couldn't wait to see the kitchen in all its glory, almost certain that the photos she'd been sent didn't do it justice. Her parents had begun renovating when they'd moved here a few years ago, and her Mum's dream kitchen was a mammoth task that they'd been working on for the last eight months. It had terracotta accents, an island in the middle with wicker bar stools, two stoves because one would never be enough for Rosa, and an emerald-green tile splashback.

It reminded Lucie of her grandparents' apartment in

Rome, it was where her parents had got their inspiration from, and Mateo had worked day and night when they'd first moved to give his wife a place that felt like home. Their house in Los Angeles had been *way* too modern, and not to their taste at all. That house had been all about making a good impression to their upper-class social circles.

They had both been born and raised in Italy. Rosa was an Italian film star, Mateo a budding director. They had moved to Los Angeles for bigger and brighter opportunities and hit the jackpot. Her parents may have been famous, *especially* in their home country, but the world had no idea Lucie and her sisters were connected to them. Sure, people knew they had children, but their identities were kept hidden much like Julien's daughter had been until recently. Mateo had adopted the use of Rosa's maiden name, Clemente, and they had both built their reputations on that. Their children used Mateo's actual last name, Carolan, and lived a life out of the public eye.

The motorsport world didn't know they had the heir of Hollywood cinema working for them, and Lucie preferred it that way. Only her closest friends knew.

She had overheard Jasper and Gabriel freaking out over her mother's retirement from acting a few years ago in the back of the garage, and thanked the heavens she'd never told them. She was there to do a job she loved, not take the spotlight away from the drivers and the sport by journalists fishing for stories about her parents.

Rosa and Mateo had put so much money into their

kids' futures, and so much *time* into ensuring their family was supported and cared for, that their own careers had fallen by the wayside. Opportunities dried up, their money dwindled and despite still getting attention from the media, they had to accept that Los Angeles wasn't the place for them any more. They loved Italy, and they were excited to spend their retirement relaxing, and watching their lineage continue the family legacy in new and exciting ways.

Lucie's oldest sister was a neurosurgeon, her middle sister a trauma surgeon and the youngest a pastry chef. Lucie was closest to the spotlight, but even she was so focused on the IEC's social media presence that she often let her own slip through the cracks.

There would be months when she stayed logged into the team accounts and barely even checked her own, leaving her own followers to know she was still alive by the content Faith tagged her in. Faith was the true influencer on the team, not her.

'Now, don't comment on the exterior. It still needs work,' Mateo said to them as they pulled up to the farmhouse, through wrought-iron gates with a sign that read 'Villa Clemente' hanging above them.

He was right, it still needed a *lot* doing to it. It had always reminded Lucie of the shambles of the hotel in *Mamma Mia!* when Donna had first arrived, except this was Italian, not Greek. Still, despite it being run-down and in need of some TLC, she knew this place would stay in the Carolan family for generations.

There was an orange tree in a large, round brick

planter. It sat in the middle of the driveway and was one of the many sources of the smoothies and juices her mum had been making for breakfast every morning. The plan was to eventually have a proper orangery somewhere in the grounds. The stone exterior, despite being damaged, was beautiful and Lucie didn't doubt that her parents would seek out a local stonemason to do the repair work to restore it to its former glory.

The sage-green shutters over the windows were rotting, but they just needed to be replaced and they would help bring the outside of the property back to life. One of the upstairs rooms, the master suite, had a small balcony, not big enough to step onto but so that the big, oak doors could be opened and let the light and the air in. There were plants everywhere you looked. Not just flowers, but hedges, trees and vines that filled the empty spaces. The place was huge, and Lucie couldn't wait to see the finished gardens and the terrace out the back.

'Damn, that view,' Brett commented, peering out the windscreen at the rolling Tuscan hills that stretched out ahead of them. The farmhouse was sat atop one of these hills, and every key room in the house had a perfect view of the landscape.

'That was the main reason Mateo's family bought it all those years ago. It's just a shame we've got to pour so much time and money into renovations,' Rosa smiled sadly. It was bittersweet, knowing they still had such a long road ahead before they could enjoy it to the fullest.

Rosa hadn't had any big acting roles since their youngest, Isabella, had been in high school and she'd graduated seven and a half years ago. Mateo's last two films had flopped, too, despite having big names attached. They were lucky they had been left their dream house in a will. The sale of their LA home still wasn't quite enough to cover all the work that needed doing, and they were relying on royalties to help them live.

'I'm sorry about the state of everything.'

'Mum, stop worrying. We're here to help you, remember?'

'Okay.' Rosa took a deep breath. 'I just want you to have a nice break.'

'Mrs C, being here is exactly what I need to sort myself out. I could have a sleeping bag in the barn for all I care.' Brett reached into the back of the car to squeeze her hand in appreciation.

Rosa looked at him with the kind of love his own mother looked at him with. It made Lucie's heart melt. 'I think this is the perfect environment to help you heal.'

'I think your cooking alone could do the trick.'

'Especially your focaccia,' Mateo chimed in. Focaccia had been a staple food in their household growing up. It was one of the only ways Lucie would consume bread.

'But seriously, thank you both for letting us come. I have a long way to go, but I know I'm in safe hands and I'm so glad I can help you out in the process. I love you guys like you're my own family.' Brett abandoned his signature cheeky grin for a genuine, heartfelt smile aimed at all three of them. It caused Rosa to dab at her eyes with her handkerchief.

'That's because we *are* your family.'

20

'Luce, I can't sleep in here. I was serious about the sleeping bag in the barn, I don't need a nicely decorated room to be happy.' Brett gestured around the guest room he'd been assigned to. It was the only bedroom that was fully decorated, and he was point-blank refusing to sleep in it. Lucie was tired, but not *too* tired to argue.

'Yes, you can. And you will,' she insisted, hauling his suitcase onto the bed and unzipping it for him, opening it to reveal an array of designer clothing. To his credit, it wasn't like a summer doing farmhouse renovations had been on the cards when he'd been packing for a quick trip to Monaco.

'You or your parents should have it until your rooms are done. Then we can swap.'

'My parents wanted *you* to have it. You're a guest, it's only right. And my room is fine, too. Just needs a lick of paint and a better mattress.'

'A better mattress? At least sleep in here with me, then.' He was equally as exasperated as she felt. How had two of the most stubborn people in the world ended up being such good friends?

'No, you need space. It's fine, Brett. The mattress will be here in a few days.'

When Lucie had contacted her parents not even six

hours ago about bringing Brett here for the summer, she knew it was a huge ask. There would be instances where Lucie had to jet off for work commitments and leave him there under their watchful eye, but she was lucky that they loved Brett as much as she did. They didn't treat him any differently than they would treat their own kids, and that meant they were equally as willing to prioritise his health. They'd even volunteered to sign an NDA.

Brett needed a sanctuary. He was going to have a lot to do to keep him busy and distracted, but this trip wasn't going to be without its challenges. Therapy was going to take a *lot* out of him. The Carolans mutually agreed that he needed somewhere to escape to at the end of the day, somewhere to relax. It didn't feel right to expect him to do that surrounded by storage boxes, peeling paint and broken floorboards. Lucie was still worrying about falling through the floorboard right next to her bed.

'I love being an honorary Carolan.' Brett pulled Lucie in for a hug, his broad frame encompassing her petite one. She wasn't sure who needed the comfort more, but either way, she felt safe in his arms. She just hoped he felt the same way.

'If it makes you feel better, we can start on Mum and Dad's room as soon as the living area is done. The furniture and décor for both rooms are all in storage in one of the barns already, I just need to take a few road trips to find some artwork and paint the walls. After I've argued with Mum about what colour paint she wants.' She pulled back, removing his Gucci loafers from the case and holding them out for him to slip on.

'Road trips?' Brett's face lit up.

'Yeah.'

'Does that mean . . .'

'That you can drive one of Dad's classics? Yes. At a *reasonable* speed.'

'Aw, Luce, come on! There are some quiet roads out here, surely. Those cars are just crying out for the open road. They *need* me. They need my talent.'

'The cars *need* you, do they?'

'Well, maybe I need them more. But hey, racing is my one true love, and I'm not allowed in my beauty of a race car until next April. That's . . .' he counted on his fingers, 'ten months. *Ten months*, Luce. I've never been away from a racetrack for more than two. I can't be expected to stick to the speed limit all the time. I'll use my common sense. Have I ever got a speeding ticket or been pulled over on the roads surrounding Julien's property in Malmedy?'

'No,' she sighed, defeated.

'Exactly! I'll still be sensible, promise.'

'Just think, when you do finally get back in the Revolution car, it will have had a load of upgrades. It won't be the same car you tested in for this season.' The team was constantly working to improve the car, making sure they stayed at the top or at least in line with their competitors.

'Fuck, yeah, of course. I'm going to hold on to that.' Brett swallowed an invisible lump in his throat, but Lucie caught the falter in his expression.

'This will be worth it, you know. I know it's hard and it's not how you wanted things to play out, but Jasper

215

didn't just do this for the sake of the team. He did it for the sake of you and your future in motorsport. We all want to support you in the best way we know how, and that means giving you some tough love. Work on yourself and you'll be able to return next season, better than you've ever been.'

'I'm going to blow Jules and Marco out of the water. You watch,' Brett smirked.

Lucie laughed at his confidence and made a mental note to check in with the team on the progress of their big surprise. The trouble with Brett missing a whole race season was that he still needed to keep up with the other drivers, and if he wasn't training somehow, he risked falling behind. He needed to remember circuit layouts, different approaches for different parts of the tracks. The feel of the car. It would be so easy to get caught up in farmhouse renovations and therapy, and the team didn't want to risk his career taking a back seat during this healing process. His head had to stay in the game, and the Revolution crew would do everything they could.

'So, what do you think of this room?' Lucie gestured at it.

There was an exposed brick wall behind the bed, and the rest of the walls were white. Most rooms in the house had the same feature wall, but holes needed to be filled and the plain walls needed to be replastered or transformed from terracotta to white. Rosa had thrown an orange and red patterned throw across the bed in the classic way interior design magazines did, and that along with the beige cushions and the rug under the bed provided a perfect balance of textures. There was an archway leading to the ensuite bathroom which featured not only a walk-in shower, but a gigantic bathtub. The room was a combination of the kind of luxury Brett was accustomed to, and the classic Italian architecture that fit the Carolans down to the ground.

'It's beautiful. I love your mum's little touches.' He referenced the plant on the dresser, the ceramic trinket tray for his watch, chain and bracelet. The photo on the wall of the racetrack in Monaco. Although Brett had never raced there because it wasn't on the IEC's schedule, he had taken Mateo years ago to watch another championship, and it had been cemented in her dad's heart as one of his favourite racetracks in the world.

'After we've been for a walk around the property, do you want to come and help me pick the tomatoes for dinner?'

'What? Your parents are growing tomatoes?'

'They're growing all kinds of fruit and veg. That's part of the reason they moved out of LA. I'm sure Mum would love it if you did some gardening with her, too.'

'Absolutely. My grandparents had a greenhouse and I loved it. I keep bugging Jules to start one at his place in Malmedy so I can get my hands dirty when I visit.'

'Do we need to schedule your days down to the minute? They're starting to get packed,' Lucie laughed.

'Nah, but I think I need some new clothes. Everything I've brought is designer . . .' Brett looked at the shirt he was holding. He was right, he needed basics. Things that could get destroyed with mud and paint and plaster.

'We'll go shopping. Oh, hey, do you want blackout curtains in here?' Lucie gestured to the curtains that were currently in place. They were beautiful, and the view was out of this world, but they let in a lot of light. With Brett's emotional exhaustion that came with the territory of therapy, he might want naps in the daytime, or he might need lie-ins.

'That might be a good idea. I'll buy them, then if your parents don't want to keep them once I leave, they haven't wasted their money.'

'Don't be silly, we'll buy them.'

'Lucie. You have seen my bank statements.'

'It's the principle.' She crossed her arms.

'Well, if your parents do want to keep them, they can consider the curtains a gift.'

'Fine,' she frowned. Lucie had been raised in a very traditional family, and that meant that when you were playing host, you went above and beyond. She knew Rosa wouldn't like Brett buying the curtains, either.

'How long do you have until you need to leave?'

'I've got to attend the reveal of the livery for Le Mans in a few days. That's in Emilia-Romagna so it's just a short drive. I've got two weeks until I go to Le Mans itself. I've got a lot of work to be doing while you and Dad are doing renovations, too. Girls Off Track has an entire photoshoot waiting to be edited, and I have a video interview with a sports magazine. It's the one Faith used to write for.'

'That's pretty cool. Proud of you.' He smiled fondly at her. 'Hey, can I post renovation updates on my social media?'

'You can, but you have got to ignore comments about why you're missing from the grid. The team are going to put out a statement, saying you're taking a break for mental health purposes. But Brett, you cannot talk about it. Any press enquiries will go through myself or straight to the PR team. You showing yourself here, exploring Tuscany, working on the farmhouse, that's enough. Fans and sponsors will just think, "Oh, he's taking an actual break." It's too soon to go preaching about alcoholism and therapy. Save that for when you're back in that seat and you've done the hard work. Then we can talk about your journey.'

'Noted. So, show me living life as normal, and nobody will think anything is up.'

'Exactly. And like Jasper said, we'll get you to attend some events in a few months' time. We'll also keep posting content on the team accounts that shows you haven't been permanently replaced. Throwbacks, that kind of thing. I'll make sure to give you a couple of shoutouts here and there, share your posts.'

'I can't tell anyone else, can I? Not the guys at Havelin or Odesza?'

'Jasper has made the entire crew at Revolution sign NDAs, although not everyone knows the real reason. If you want to tell Elliot or Casey or anyone, I suppose you can if we make them sign one too, although we would advise against it. Just think about whether you feel you need their support, or if the support you've got is enough for you.'

'You're right. And to be perfectly honest, Luce, the

only support I need is yours. And a therapist's. And, I guess, Jasper's so I get to keep my job when this is all over.'

'You'll keep your job, Anderson.'

'Mmhmm. Anyway, enough of the emotional shit. Can we go tomato hunting?'

'I mean, I don't think "hunting" is the right word, but yes.'

'Do we need to take a basket or something?'

'Mum should have a couple of tin buckets we can use.'

'Tour first though! I got so excited about the tomatoes, I almost forgot there's still so much to see. Your dad was saying something about the water fountain they restored and how it's got the most hideous gargoyle thing he's ever seen.'

'Oh, yeah. Mum won't let him get rid of it. She said it adds character.'

'We'll see about that. We might have to start a petition to get it thrown in a skip.'

There was a long corridor just outside Brett's room with big, beautiful, rounded archways that connected all the guest bedrooms and bathrooms, and as they walked through it, every footstep echoed. It was bound to drive Lucie mad by the end of the first week. You had to walk through the living area to get to the dining area and then the kitchen. The lounge had cloudlike white sofas, which would be destroyed when the grandkids came to stay. Rosa didn't care about things like that. She wanted a house that looked lived in, for once.

Lucie showed Brett the family photos on the wall, all in black and white with black metal frames. There were photos of every Carolan, from grandkid to pet, and even a group shot of the Anderson family. In the middle was Lucie's favourite: a family portrait of all of them, in front of the Carolan Christmas tree back at their home in California. That was five years ago, and every face had changed so much. She barely recognised Brett's younger sister.

To the left, where the television hung and there was a huge dark oak coffee table on the cream rug, Lucie admired the stone fireplace and the built-in bookshelves. Between an array of crystal bookends, candles and film and television awards, was a perfect mix of motorsport history books, cookbooks, thrillers and romance novels. It summed up her parents perfectly.

When they reached the kitchen, Lucie gushed over the new addition to the house. The terrace. Glass doors ran along the entire length of the room, opening up to the outdoor space. Under a ceiling of vines and fairy lights sat a twelve-seater table with wooden chairs. It was already set with beige cloth placemats, plates, wine glasses and cutlery, ready for Rosa and Mateo to host at any given moment. There were candles in hurricane vases and more vine-type leaves covering the middle of the table, making it look incredibly inviting. Lucie couldn't wait to sit down for dinner tonight and spend the evening sipping on alcohol-free rosé under the cool evening breeze.

'Let's go take a walk. We didn't explore properly the last couple of times we came.' Brett gestured towards the fields. The existing barns where Mateo was housing his cars were all close to the house, but if they were to build more for Rosa's equestrian dreams, they'd be further out.

After spending an hour trekking around in borrowed work boots, Lucie and Brett stumbled across a field of wild horses. She assumed they were wild, anyway, unless they belonged to her parents' neighbours, although she wasn't sure how close they lived. The two of them had gone way beyond the lines of the property. They were probably trespassing, but Brett was like an excited child, and she didn't want to deny him the adventure.

'You ever ridden a horse?' Lucie asked him.

Brett eyed her cautiously. 'You're not suggesting we ride these ones, are you?'

Lucie shrugged, letting what appeared to be a Maremmano nuzzle her hand, its chestnut-brown coat glistening in the sun. 'Hmm. Maybe not. This one seems friendly but if they're wild, I don't think they're going to be keen.'

'You're also not much of a cowgirl,' Brett snorted.

'Hey! I grew up going to the stables every weekend!' she defended.

'Okay, but just because you rode horses *with a saddle and reins*,' he emphasised, 'doesn't mean you can just giddy up and go with any old horse.'

'I guess,' she mumbled.

'You'd look sexy as hell in a hat and cowboy boots, though.'

Lucie's skin tingled with his compliment, and despite her keeping her attention on the horse, she could feel his gaze burning into her. 'Correct, I would.'

'With lingerie, too. Would complete the look.' She could hear the smirk in his voice.

Lucie's entire body heated up. 'Will you behave?'

'Ahh, it's so beautiful here.' Brett changed the topic fast, unaware of the effect his words had on her hormones. 'Can we just live here?' he sighed wistfully.

'It would be nice, wouldn't it?' she agreed.

'Not that I want them to go anywhere yet, but you tell your parents they'd better keep this place in the family. I want to be visiting here when I'm old and grey. Mateo can leave his car collection behind too, if he wants.'

'That's very morbid, you know.'

'Just saying. Doesn't get much better than this.'

'How the hell do I know if a tomato is ripe?' Brett stared at the plants in awe. 'I cannot let Rosa down with this. She's depending on me to save the salad *and* the lasagne.'

He had taken his tomato-picking duties seriously and told Lucie to let him take charge, right up until they'd arrived at Rosa's vegetable patch, and he'd realised he didn't have a clue what he was doing.

Lucie had done farm work in Australia for a month during her first season with the IEC, so she smugly came to the rescue. 'Look for the colour first. They should be quite a rich, deep red. They should also be firm, but they should have a little give when you squeeze them. They should also separate from the plant quite easily when you give them a tug, but you can just use the pruners if you want.'

'Awesome. Thanks, Gardener Luce. You're basically the modern-day Alan Titchmarsh.'

'Who?' Lucie watched as he picked his first tomato, admiring it and gently placing it into the bucket like it was made of fine China.

'He's a famous British gardener.' He raised an eyebrow, as if she should know who that was.

'You're clued up on British gardeners now, are you?'

'Nah, met him at a fundraising event in Oz about eight years ago. Nice bloke. I aspire to be just like him one day. Going to rival the Garden of Eden.'

As Brett continued to add to his impressive collection of round, red fruits, Lucie studied him. He was completely in his element. Maybe he wasn't going to live the playboy lifestyle forever . . . Eventually he'd settle down, buy a house with some land and spend his days doing exactly this. He just said this was what he wanted one day. Was Lucie really that delusional if she thought she might get to be a part of it?

'Which fruits are ready to harvest? I want to make smoothies for everyone.' His voice pulled her out of her thoughts.

'Strawberries, peaches, apricots. You'll have to wait a bit longer for anything else. We were lucky to get this many tomatoes so early on, I thought we'd have to wait another few weeks, at least.'

'How do you know so much about everything, ever?'

'I've learned a lot on my travels.'

'Yeah, like the fact I am *amazing* in bed.'

Lucie felt her cheeks immediately flush at his remark and turned away. 'Could your head get any bigger?'

'Probably, if I tried. Oh, look! That one looks perfect!'

Brett pointed at a tomato he'd spotted, hidden away. He reached over the plants on his side of the planter, almost falling face first into a mass of leaves and soil.

'Go round the other side, idiot,' she sighed.

'Got it!' He leapt up, victoriously holding the tomato in the air before losing his footing and stumbling backwards. Right into the bucket full of fresh, ripe tomatoes.

Lucie keeled over, her body trembling with laughter. 'Oh, my God.'

'My babies!' he cried out, his devastation distracting him from Lucie whipping her phone out and capturing the moment for the world to see. 'Don't just stand there!' He held his hands out for her to help him up. It was a big bucket, which meant he'd sunk into it.

'Have any escaped unscathed?' She peered into the bucket, studying the aftermath.

'I hope so, but I haven't.' He twisted to look at the back of his shorts, which were covered in wet, juicy tomatoes. 'These were expensive,' he whined.

'I knew we shouldn't have tried to do any form of work until we'd been shopping. You're worse than Gabriel, sometimes. The pair of you are so clumsy.'

'Hey, that's cold.' He feigned hurt. 'I've never run over plant pots in a golf cart.'

'No, but you've just destroyed dinner.'

'Shit! Have I really?'

Lucie reached into the bucket and pulled out the remnants of a tomato, promptly launching it at Brett. His T-shirt wasn't expensive. She would know, because she'd bought it. And the shorts were beyond saving. When it made contact with his shoulder, Brett's face lit up with the challenge. Then Lucie remembered what she was wearing. A white dress. 'Oh, no.'

'You started it, Sunny.' With a wicked smile, he shot a tomato at her. She tried her best to dodge it, but Brett was trained to have good hand–eye coordination. It was part of being a racing driver. She had no hope.

The tomato splatted right in the middle of her chest, almost winding her. What had he used, a catapult? 'Ow!'

'Did that actually hurt? Luce, I'm so—' She cut him off by firing one back. 'You *snake*!'

They spent the next few minutes hiding behind various plants and trees throughout Rosa's garden, neither one surrendering. Lucie's dress was more red and orange than it was white, and she had already said her mental goodbyes to it.

Brett stripped off his T-shirt, attempting to use it as a shield. It caused a momentary pause in their battle, during which Lucie shamelessly admired him. She couldn't help herself. His hair was clinging to his forehead with sweat, his body glistened from the heat, and he had that look on his face. The look she tried to avoid, to shut down at any opportunity.

But the Tuscan sun must be getting to her, because when Brett made advances towards her side of the battle zone, she didn't stop him. She didn't step back, didn't launch another tomato in his direction. She just waited for him to close the gap across the garden and take her in his arms.

He tastes like tomato. That was her first thought when

his lips met hers. His hand tugged at her claw clip, setting her hair free from its grip and replacing it with his own. Once the shock wore off, Lucie let him pick her up, wrapping her legs around his waist while he held her with one arm. It was so much easier to kiss him like this, when they were a similar height and she could focus on the way his tongue parted her lips and danced with her own.

It was magical. But she didn't want it to be magical. She wished she could hate kissing him. She wished he would just let her down, and they could go about their day as if it hadn't happened. Except they had a family dinner to get through. A family dinner where she was going to take one bite of a tomato and be taken right back to this moment. Every time she tasted a tomato for the rest of her life, all she was going to taste was Brett.

21

Brett watched the way Lucie's face flushed when her Mum handed her the tomato salad across the table. He felt a sense of pride within him, knowing that the reason her cheeks were red was because of him. She was remembering every moment vividly, just as he was. The way she'd sighed and collapsed under his touch. The way he'd held her tight to him so she wouldn't fall, and because he knew it was as close as she would ever let him get.

He wasn't stupid, he knew she would never let things go as far as they had in the Alps. But there was something about them being in Italy that had him reminiscing in ways he tended to avoid. Usually, he could turn it off. Think about something else. Right now, though? He was remembering her in a compromising position that he knew was implanted on his brain for the rest of time.

He couldn't deny that he loved pushing her boundaries. In those moments that she let him get close, he believed that she craved him just as much as he craved her. But as much as he wanted to raise the friends-with-benefits topic again, he respected her enough not to push her *too* far. If anything further happened between them, it would be on Lucie's terms and Lucie's terms only.

The reputation he had created for himself did more

229

harm than good these days. Maybe if he hadn't been so wild, such a party animal and a flirt, he'd have a shot with a woman like Lucie. Well, not a woman *like* Lucie. Just Lucie herself.

The only person he would ever even *consider* getting down on one knee for, if the stars and planets ever aligned and put them on the same path, was Lucie.

The same Lucie who couldn't even look him in the eye right now. They'd only stopped kissing when they'd heard Mateo starting up the tractor, and Lucie had slipped from his grasp, her dress bunching up in the process. If Mateo hadn't been right around the corner, Brett might have taken her into the greenhouse right then and there.

He didn't know how she had so much willpower around him. He had made so many moves, ninety per cent of them rejected. But that ten per cent? He clung to that ten per cent. He could feel it in the way she looked at him. Her eyes full of desire, her cheeks rosy. She wanted to cross that line again. It was written all over her face.

It was those *almost* moments shared between them that he lay in bed and fantasised about every night. That he woke up thinking of. He spent countless mornings staring out the window of wherever he was, remembering the way his best friend felt beneath him. Lucie was always the first and last thing on his mind each day.

Brett didn't think she would ever understand the hold she had on him. Nor did he think he would ever be able to express it. Brett held on to his emotions. He released them on the track for the most part, but he also, in recent years, sought other vices. Alcohol was the winner. He would never say this to her, but sleeping with Lucie on that hiking trip may have been his downfall, not Sienna's betrayal. The whole fiancé-cheating-on-him thing was old news. He'd got over that with a string of women, until that night with Lucie. Since then, there had been nobody except her. Well, apart from his attempt to forget Lucie with Sienna.

Lucie thought there had been other women, and he'd let her believe it. If she thought he was waiting for her, and she didn't want the same thing, he'd be embarrassed. Vulnerable. He hated being vulnerable. Usually, Lucie brought it out in him, but when she was the cause, how was he supposed to let her know without damaging their friendship?

So, he let her catch him in what she thought was 'the act', let her think he'd taken women back to his hotel room. But instead, he ended things after a kiss and sent them on their way. Nobody would ever compare to his sunshine girl.

'Luce, your mum and I were talking about a family camping trip next summer,' Mateo chirped, serving himself a hearty slice of lasagne and sprinkling it with extra parmesan.

'When you say family . . .' Lucie's face paled.

'He means everyone,' Rosa added, already looking tired at the mere thought.

'We could fly back over to the US, and we could go somewhere like Utah, or Virginia.'

231

'Dad, that's a lot of people. We might as well hire a whole campsite.'

'Hey, maybe that's not such a bad idea!' His eyes lit up.

'Slow down. There's what, nine adults including partners? That's already pushing it. But there's also six kids between them. Bianca and I are the only ones who are kid-free. Can't you just take us? We know we're your favourites, anyway.'

'I do not have favourites!' Mateo scolded. 'Besides, it would be nice to have everyone in one place for once. Perhaps the Andersons would like to come, too.'

'Mateo, darling, you're going to give yourself a heart attack if you attempt this.'

'But we had so much fun when the kids were growing up,' he frowned. 'Remember when Lucie fell in the river and Bianca had to jump in and save her?' Mateo roared with laughter.

'Dad, that wasn't funny! I could've drowned!'

'Oh, we wouldn't have let that happen. I was holding a stick out to you, remember?' He wiped a tear from the corner of his eye.

'I only fell in because Elena pushed me. You never punished her.'

'You guys were just having fun! It's what siblings do.'

'When she left Isabella alone in the shower block, you were ready to murder her.'

'She was only three and I didn't know where she was. That was different. I had eyes on you the whole time you were in the water, I knew you were fine.'

'I literally hit my head on a rock before Bianca got to

me. And I'm pretty sure a fish nibbled my foot.' Lucie scowled at him, looking ready to launch her bread at her dad.

'At least it wasn't a crocodile,' Mateo chuckled.

Brett laughed along with him, but he couldn't ignore the stabbing pain in his chest that resurfaced whenever he spent time with the Carolans. He adored Lucie's dad, and Mateo had been one of his biggest supporters for the last ten years. He treated him like his own, and Brett appreciated him. But it just reminded him of the cold hard truth. His dad was gone.

Jack used to take him and Piper camping in Darwin. He would claim he was just giving the twins time to bond, surrounded by nature with no gaming devices or a young, screaming Cleo, but Brett always knew it was really because he liked the peace and quiet. Although Piper had always been the fieriest of the family, when it was just them and their dad in a tiny little tent next to the lake, she was calm. She thrived.

Those trips were where Brett and Piper had built a strong relationship, and eventually, they'd managed to make it hold up the rest of the year when they were back home in Sydney, and years since the camping trips stopped, it was stronger than ever as adults. When Jack had died, they'd leaned on each other. They had held on to those memories of summer with every fibre of their being, and although Piper had processed her grief and moved on, Brett hadn't. He hadn't been camping since.

One part of him wanted to help Mateo fulfil his

fantasy, but the other part of him couldn't imagine pitching a tent, barbequing and playing badminton or football with anyone who wasn't his dad. It felt like he was disrespecting his memory. He knew that was stupid, but it scared him. It would be too much like replacing him, and oftentimes he already felt that he had.

It was like when Mateo had come to support the team at a race a few years ago. Mateo had been so excited to be there with his hospitality pass and his official team uniform. Cap and sunglasses on, of course, so he wasn't recognised as Mateo Clemente. He'd been proud, and he'd expressed that. To Lucie *and* to Brett. But when Brett had seen him standing in the garage, waving his Revolution Racing flag, that same fear struck.

It should be *his* dad standing there. Jack Anderson had taken Brett karting for thirteen years. Every weekend. It was because of *his* dad's support and encouragement, his determination for his only son, that Brett had successfully got into his first racing championship at the age of sixteen, before he'd made it to the big leagues. They had spent those two years attending every race as father and son, travelling together and soaking up every moment.

But the IEC was their end goal. Winning Le Mans was a dream, to be compared to the likes of Tom Kristensen and Jacky Ickx, and while Jack had been there for the first phone call from Brett's original team, the contract-signing and the first race, he hadn't been there for the first championship win.

Brett had wanted to get out of the car and see him, and it crushed him to see Mateo instead. And then

Mateo had clapped him on the back in congratulations, and Brett felt sick to his stomach for feeling that way.

'Brett, would you like tiramisu for dessert? We have plenty left.' Rosa began clearing plates, shoving him back down in his chair when he tried to help.

He had tuned out the rest of dinner, oblivious to the conversation. He liked that nobody had bothered him, forced him to interact. Lucie's parents were just like her in that sense. They respected when people needed space, and they had an acute understanding of his emotions.

'Just a small serving, please.' He smiled at Lucie's mum, her dark hair up in a bun, apron stained with flour and tomato. He tried to think about his kiss with Lucie again, but the only thing that ever stopped him from spiralling about her was spiralling about his dad instead. It was a double-edged sword.

'You okay?' Lucie mouthed across the table. Instead of responding verbally, Brett nodded and gave her a half-smile, silently thanking her for her concern.

He wished he was sitting next to her so he could hold her hand in a death grip. He did that a lot when he was lost in his thoughts or anxious; she was an anchor to keep him in reality. But lately, reality hadn't been that much better. It had just gone downhill until he'd hit rock bottom.

Lucie awoke that night to the muffled sound of shouting. She lay amongst her terracotta cotton sheets, trying to get a sense of her surroundings. As she forced her eyes open, greeted by darkness, she realised where it was coming from. Brett.

Launching herself out of bed, not bothering to slip into a robe, she made a beeline for his room across the hall. The door opened to Brett, sitting bolt upright, eyes wide as he yelled out for help. Thank God her parents were way on the other side of the farmhouse. Even in the moonlight, she could see the fear across his face, the way his hair stuck up at odd angles as if he had been tossing and turning.

Lucie didn't know if the rule of not waking someone up only applied to sleepwalking. Did it apply to night terrors? She could wake him, and he could be confused and disorientated, and he could hurt her. But seeing him like this was breaking her heart. She felt like screaming *with* him.

'Anderson!' Lucie yelled. She shook him, snapping him out of it.

It was as if she had flipped a switch and reality was coming into focus again, his eyes finding hers in the dim lighting. Lucie studied his expression, silently pleading with him to stay with her. Letting him know he was safe. He looked as broken as he had on the day he'd got the phone call about his dad. Was that where he'd been? Transported back to that moment? He had suffered night terrors and panic attacks for years when Jack had first passed.

'Fuck,' he breathed out. 'Sorry.'

'Don't apologise. Are you okay?'

'I think so.' His breathing was still heavy.

Lucie got him a cold flannel from his en-suite and perched on the edge of the bed handing it to him. 'You want to talk about it?'

'Do I have much choice?'

'Well, I'm not leaving this room either way.'

'Okay.' He swallowed harshly, preparing himself. 'I've been having dreams about my dad's death again. Like the ones I had at the very beginning. Of the exact moment he took his life. I see it. Every detail. And I know it's not real, I know it's my imagination because I wasn't there, I didn't witness it, but I found him. I saw the aftermath, and it was gruesome. And every time I wake up . . . fuck, I –'

When he took a while to speak again, chest still heaving as he struggled to find the words, Lucie gently coaxed it out of him. 'I promise whatever you say, I won't judge.'

Brett kept his gaze fixed on his bedsheets, but he squeezed her hand in response.

'I hate him. I hate him for leaving us, and I know that's shitty. He wasn't well, he needed help he wasn't getting. But I needed *him*. We all did.'

'It's not shitty. He took something from you, Brett. You're allowed to feel angry, and hurt. You're also allowed to miss him and remember what an incredible dad he was to you.'

'Not only do I feel like I'm becoming him the more I spiral, but I also feel like I'm replacing him.'

Lucie knew what he was getting at without him needing to expand. She had seen the way he'd acted at dinner, the way he'd shut down. She had seen him watching her interactions with Mateo. She'd heard the panic in his voice when he'd turned down the invitation to a game of Monopoly. She wasn't stupid.

'You're not. At all. Nobody will ever replace your dad, and nobody wants to. Mateo loves you like a son, but he would never dream of trying to replace him. He just wants to support you, be your friend and make sure you have someone you can rely on. He's raised four children of his own, it's in his blood.'

'I guess I hadn't thought of it like that. Mateo probably would've treated me the same even if my dad was still around. It's just who he is.'

'Exactly. And as for your dad? I bet he'd be over the moon to know you have someone like that in your life, supporting you in the ways he can't. Family comes in different forms; we both know that better than most.'

Even though he looked slightly relieved and less at war with himself, nothing she said could make this any better for him. She couldn't take the pain away. All she could do, all she knew how to do, was just be there. So, she crawled into bed next to him and held him all night, wishing she had the ability to heal his broken heart.

22

Things were supposed to be different now. Now that there was a spare bedroom, Lucie was supposed to be sleeping in her own bed, and waking up alone. And yet here she was on the very first morning, waking up in Brett's arms. Or rather, he was waking up in hers. She genuinely hadn't meant to fall asleep in here, and she was annoyed with herself for doing so.

Lucie knew she needed to re-establish boundaries. Brett would tell her there was no need, but if she was going to stay sane and he was going to stay focused, they needed to learn to keep their distance and not give in to old temptations.

She stretched out across her side of the bed. This was by far one of the most comfortable beds she'd slept in for years and it made her long for a future where she'd return to the same comfortable bed every day.

Lucie had been travelling for ten years now; when she wasn't travelling for work, it was for pleasure. She must have slept in over a thousand beds by now, and none of them quite measured up to this one. Being here felt right. It felt like home.

She looked over at Brett. He looked like he had the weight of the world on his shoulders even in his sleep, and she was reminded that she would go to the ends of the earth for him. It was like she and Brett sleeping together that one time had meant she'd automatically signed herself up for a lifetime of loneliness.

Most men she'd tried to date had seen the way she interacted with him, and immediately backed off. Even other drivers steered clear. The ones who had stuck around, who hadn't ditched her for the next best thing, she'd ended things with before they reached a third or fourth date. She found something wrong with each of them, even the tiniest things. The silliest reasons it could never work. It was as if she was just looking for excuses to stay single, and to continue pining after someone she couldn't have.

Fighting the stinging in her eyes, Lucie threw her legs over the side of the bed and let her feet sink into the rug. If there was one thing her mum was good at, it was finding luxurious rugs that felt like clouds to bare feet.

Lucie sometimes worried she'd been reckless by going down this path. She had no security, nothing to fall back on, very few savings and no permanent roof over her head. It was part of the reason she had been so keen to help launch Girls Off Track: a second source of income was always going to be beneficial. She felt like something was missing, but she wasn't quite sure what, until now.

The morning sun was shining through the bathroom window, her *own* bathroom, as she showered, attempting to wash away her intrusive thoughts. Her parents were already heading to Florence to choose tiles for the master bathroom, and she wanted to crack on with some work before Brett woke up.

It was his first full day here, and while she knew it was important for him to keep busy and have a focus, she also wanted him to ease into it. Lucie's mission today was to paint the living room walls, she didn't need help for that. For all she cared, he could stay in the vegetable garden all day and help Rosa with dinner. Lucie, in all honesty, could do with being left to her own devices without Brett hanging around her, shirtless, getting in her personal space.

Brett looked at his reflection in the mirror, wincing when he saw how puffy his face was. There were pillow creases embedded on his cheek and he vaguely remembered that he'd cried himself to sleep. He felt so defeated that he didn't even have the energy to be embarrassed about it.

By the time he'd returned from his morning run around the perimeter of the property and showered off the sweat that would just build up again throughout the day, he was ready to tackle whatever job Lucie was doing. He fired off a text to Jasper, assuring him that he had scheduled his first therapy session. He'd decided to decline the offer of the team psychologist because he wanted a fresh start with someone who didn't already know him personally.

He stopped in the doorway to the living room, knocked for six as he watched Lucie tie her hair up. She was wearing denim dungarees and a white cropped top, her feet bare. She looked like she should be in a home makeover show.

She pulled her brunette hair off her face, exposing her

neck and the dainty gold chain he'd got her for her twenty-first birthday. Every time he saw her wearing any of his gifts, it felt like for a split second, she belonged to him.

'Woah! What you doing, Carolan?' He made his presence known as she went to move the sofa. It was huge and there was not a chance on this earth she was strong enough to move it on her own without pulling a muscle.

'It's in the way and I need to paint.' She tugged on one end of it.

'Luce, stop!' Brett yelled. 'Let me help you.' He picked up the other end and together, they moved it to the middle of the room and covered it with a dust sheet.

She stood upright and scowled at him, but he could tell it wasn't her serious scowl. It was merely frustration at herself, and as her eyes scanned his body, he couldn't help the smirk that made its way onto his face. 'Where's your shirt?'

'It's eighty-one degrees outside.' He defended his outfit choice, or rather lack of, using Fahrenheit to suit her American upbringing.

'*Signore, abbi pietà,*' she muttered. Brett didn't know any Italian, despite Lucie trying to teach him for years. She had grown up fluent, but her siblings hadn't quite got the hang of it so the Carolans spoke English at home. Lucie just liked to use it when she didn't want him to know what she was saying, except she'd said that phrase so many times that he'd looked it up.

'Mmhmm, and why do you need the Lord to have mercy, Carolan? Can't handle the view?' He put his hands on his hips, standing tall before her.

'I'm just saying,' she mumbled as she struggled to peel the lid off the paint, 'I would probably get more work done if you were fully clothed. I'm just a girl. I get distracted by pretty things. Not that I'm saying you're pretty, but you know . . .' She gestured to his body.

'It's just as well you need a strong, physically fit athlete around to help, isn't it?' He took the paint pot from her and removed the lid with ease, revealing the milky off-white liquid that had been carefully selected by Rosa. 'I've got to put all my gym training to good use this season since I'm not behind the wheel.'

That was the wrong thing to say. He'd been in a decent mood when he'd stepped into the room and seen her, but one sentence and she was looking at him with pity. He couldn't stand it. So, ignoring her expression, he picked up a paintbrush and got to work.

'Brett —' Lucie spoke, and he could practically hear her swallow the lump in her throat.

'Don't. If I'm going to get through this, I need you to be strict with me. Yell at me, fight me on everything. I can't afford for you to be soft on me, Luce.'

'I was just going to say you're painting wrong.'

With his back to her, he let himself smile. That was the Lucie he wanted. 'How can there be a wrong way to paint?'

'Like that.' She laughed as she came up beside him, showing him the correct way to do it. As far as he was concerned, their methods were identical. He looked at her, puzzled, then flung the paintbrush around the wall in haphazard movements, making a mess of their work.

'Brett!'

'What?! It's white, it'll blend easily.' He went back to the paint and dipped the brush in, his eyes sparkling with childlike delight when an idea struck.

'You'd better hope it does, Anderson.' Lucie carried on painting, oblivious to what he was plotting. 'What the hell?' she screeched.

Brett stood there, grinning like the Cheshire Cat as he admired his handiwork. Paint was splashed all up the wall. 'Oops.'

'Why would you do that? Do you know how much paint you just wasted?!'

He shrugged, the picture of nonchalance, as Lucie tried to roller away some of the excess and blend it out. And then, in an act of karma, Brett's foot caught on a dust sheet. He grasped at thin air, but soon realised the only thing stopping him from falling as he slid on the wooden floor was the wall. The freshly painted wall.

He body-slammed it. Full on, arms splayed out, chest sticking to it. He knew his Stone Island shorts were goners, but when he heard Lucie's laugh, he lost the ability to care. Brett rarely got to experience moments like this. Moments of pure, unadulterated fun with no responsibilities, no judgement, nobody telling him to grow up.

'Anderson!' Lucie squealed as he darted towards her and grabbed her around the waist from behind, covering her with paint. He picked her up and hauled her over his shoulder, taking her back to the paint pot and pretending to dip her in it like she was a paintbrush. 'Okay,

okay!' He put her down and stepped back to admire the finished product. Her dungarees would have to join his shorts as official farmhouse reno uniform.

He had tried to be spontaneous like this with Sienna, but there was always something stopping them. She was tired, she wasn't in the mood, people were watching, he should act his age, he was never 'cool' enough for her. He was too goofy, too immature. But he just wanted them to seize the moment and have a little fun every now and then. Lucie, though, *encouraged* him. Yet, he still wasn't enough for her.

'The state of the wall!' Some time later, Mateo stopped in the doorway and gawked at the scene in front of him.

'I'm so sorry, sir. It was my fault, I started it.' Brett grimaced. The floors still needed to be replaced, and the furniture was covered up, but he still felt bad for the mess they'd created.

'Oh, I don't care about the mess!' Mateo laughed a hearty laugh and shook his head good-naturedly. 'As long as the painting is finished by the end of the day, it doesn't bother me. I'll be ripping up the old tiles in the master bathroom if you need me. But I suggest when you're done, you wash yourselves down outside. There's a hosepipe out by one of the barns.'

'Thanks, Dad.' Lucie screeched again as she slipped on a puddle of paint.

'It's like having all the kids back at home with you two around.'

*

Having completed the first even coat on all four walls, Lucie and Brett headed outside to the barns in search of the hosepipe. Paint had dried on their bodies, and it felt gross. As they walked out of the house, Lucie patted the top of her head and grimaced, feeling the paint stuck there.

'I'll wash it out for you, don't worry.' Brett threw an arm over her shoulder.

'So generous of you, Anderson. Thank you.' Her tone dripped with sarcasm.

'Anything for you, Sunny.'

When Mateo had said hosepipe, Brett had thought it would likely be a basic one with crap water pressure, and they'd still have to shower it off properly later. He was so wrong. He pulled the trigger on the attachment and water blasted the ground, startling them both.

'Well, that should do the trick,' Lucie commented as she started to undo the buttons on her dungarees, letting the straps fall.

'What are you doing?' Brett's eyes went wide. They were outside, and although there were no neighbours within view of the property, Lucie was usually way more reserved.

'I don't want to be weighed down by soaking wet denim, it's a horrible feeling.' She stepped out of the overalls, leaving her in a white T-shirt and underwear. His heart was beating rapidly, and his imagination ran wild as she stood there, arms out, letting the material of her T-shirt stretch across her chest. 'Hit me.'

So he did as requested, knowing that this was about to

kill him. Within moments of the spray hitting her body, her T-shirt was clinging to her. Unable to hide his body's natural reaction, Brett watched in awe as she spun, the paint washing away under the pressure of the water. She caught his gaze, and the second she recognised the desire that he was positive was written all over his face, she cast her eyes downward. But for once, Lucie's cheeks didn't flush, she didn't shy away. He watched her chest rise and fall as her gaze travelled back up his body to meet his eyes again, and she stood still, facing him.

'Luce –' he started. Lucie didn't even hesitate. She took two big steps towards him and he let go of the hosepipe, catching her in his arms as she wrapped her legs around his waist, crashing her lips down on his.

The few times they'd done this before, it had always been Brett in charge. Always him pushing the boundaries. But this time? This time it was all Lucie. This wasn't her giving in, or caving to his advances, this was Lucie finally taking everything she needed from him. Her tongue found its way to his as she deepened the kiss, hands in his hair, and Brett held her tighter, walking her backwards.

He kept going until they were at the back of the barn, away from potential prying eyes. Pushing her against the wall, she tugged on his hair, earning a moan from him. Brett wasn't usually so vocal. But with Lucie, he was never able to hold back. How she found it so easy to deny him, he had no idea. Because right now, with her leading this, there was no way he was going to be able to stop unless she was the one who called time on it.

Lucie arched her back into him, silently begging for more. This didn't feel anything like their other kisses. Those were lazy, slow, intimate. Brett had kissed her then knowing that it would end, and they would roll over and go to sleep, putting their chemistry to bed until next time. But as his fingers dared to trace her skin, skimming the hem of her underwear, he knew they were about to relive Italy.

Maybe it was being in this country that made them unable to resist temptation, or maybe it was the fact that they'd spent two years dancing around the inevitable, and without the pressures of the outside world knocking at their door, they were tired of fighting it.

Brett broke the kiss, smirking when Lucie whimpered and pulled him back in for another one, but he pulled away again. Holding her up with one arm, he rubbed his thumb over her clit and watched her eyelids flutter closed as the pleasure built. He'd missed this. Missed being able to watch and feel how her body gave in to him. Her face was angelic as her mouth fell open and she moaned under his touch. He wanted to take his time with her, but they didn't have time. They were out in the open, risking it all, and he was struggling to contain himself already.

'Brett, please,' she breathed out.

The green light. The one thing he'd been waiting for. He unbuttoned his shorts with one hand, refusing to let her feet hit the ground as if contact with the earth would be like hitting the reset button. He couldn't lose this moment to the fear of consequences. Brett freed himself, grabbed the material that sat on her perfect hips and pulled those lucky red boxers down just enough so that he had access to what he constantly craved. An intimate part of her he'd been denied for so long.

'Ready?' His hand dipped between them once again, feeling how ready she was for him.

'Just hurry up before someone walks in. I need you, Brett.'

He entered her slowly and they both gasped in unison as he thrust in and out of her at an agonising pace. Within moments, she was lifting her hips to meet his, their bodies finally moving as one. Brett had stamina. He had years of experience with women, and he'd used his title as a racing driver to his advantage. But because this was Lucie, his sunshine girl, he had no control over his own body.

'Oh my God,' she cried out as their movements became quicker and more desperate. Their hips slammed into each other again, and Brett could feel her tightening around him as her eyes rolled back in her head. This was it. There was no holding back. 'Brett.' Lucie clawed at his back, pulling him as close as humanly possible.

With one final, deep thrust, Brett released himself inside her with a strangled cry. She was so tight around him as she came, he swore he could see stars. 'Fuck, Sunny.' He stayed there for a minute, his forehead resting against hers, her body trembling as he clung to her.

'I don't think I've ever finished so fast,' she laughed.

'Makes two of us.' He pulled out reluctantly and gently set her down, watching as she tried to catch her breath. 'You all right?' he asked.

As he stepped back and she muttered, 'I think so,' Brett studied her face, committing every part to memory because this was sure as hell a moment he never wanted to forget.

23

'You've slept with him *twice*?' Bea screeched down the phone.

Lucie was in the car on her way to Revolution's Le Mans livery reveal in Emilia-Romagna, and twenty minutes into the journey she had made the decision to fill Bea in on her situation with Brett. Which she was now regretting as her friend's voice came through the speakers, deafening her.

'The first time was years ago now, on a hiking trip and then . . . two days ago.'

'What do you mean a couple of years back? *And* two days ago? Does Faith know? Does anyone know? Oh my God, *and* you almost slept with him in Vegas!'

'Bea!' Lucie scolded playfully. She could rely on Bea to make light of situations, and it made everything feel a little less heavy.

'Sorry, sensitive subject!'

'But anyway, nobody else knows yet. I'll be telling Faith when I get to the hotel.'

'She knows about the hiking trip rendezvous though, right? I mean, she was there.'

'Apparently we weren't as subtle as we thought.' Lucie cringed. The whole paddock probably thought something was going on with them, but then again, they'd always been touchy-feely. Surely people would know that was just how they were?

Bea snorted, which was very unlike her. 'You and Brett have never been subtle. When I first joined the IEC, I thought you'd been dating for years. I even had a theory that his and Sienna's relationship was a publicity stunt for you two to hide behind. Anyway, care to share the details? I bet Faith won't want them.'

'What kind of details?' Lucie blushed. Her sex life so far had been pretty non-existent, and she'd never had anyone asking for information on it.

'Well, how did it start? We'll save the Alps scenario for another time but tell me about the other day! Was it romantic? Who initiated it? I want to know everything!'

'Fine. So, we'd kissed the day before, but we also kissed in Sydney. I kind of thought we were just going to keep doing that, kissing, but then we were hosing down outside and I just, I don't know . . . He gave me *that* look and I lost it.'

'Oh, I know the look. I've seen him give you that look countless times before.'

'Exactly. But anyway, I just froze. And I stared at him for maybe not even a millisecond before I closed the gap. Jumped into his arms and everything.'

'That's so romantic!' Bea gushed.

'What's not romantic is what happened next. He pinned me up against the garage wall, Bea. Like, literally held me up against it while we went at it.'

'That is *absolutely* romantic! The fact you were so

attracted to one another in that moment that you were willing to risk being caught!'

'Is it romance or just a lot of sexual tension?' Lucie wasn't so sure, she'd always expected romance to be more candles, champagne and chocolates. Not hot and heavy primal sex.

'I reckon if it was *just* sexual tension, one of your kisses would've led to more before now. Especially in Vegas when you were under the influence of alcohol. But also, Luce, you *ran* to him. I have never run into the arms of a man in my entire life. That's straight out of a film. He literally swept you off your feet.'

'Hmm.' Lucie went quiet, pretending she was focusing on driving. 'So, Ricardo?'

'We're changing the subject? Noted,' Bea laughed. 'Well, he came to Paris to see me. And he stood on my doorstep, told me he loved me and I gave in. Life's too short, you know? I love him.'

Bea was a hopeless romantic, and she'd waited years for her fairy tale. But Lucie wasn't so sure that she should be getting back with De La Rosa, not after he'd broken her heart last summer. Who was to say he wouldn't decide to walk away from her again? Lucie felt De La Rosa had a lot more making up to do, but the heart wants what it wants and Bea wanted Ricardo.

'You know, you've left me speechless many times, Beatrix Miller, but this takes the cake. I know you love him, but are you ready?'

'He makes me feel like me again. He keeps me grounded, more in touch with myself. I don't have to put on an act around him, or pretend to be someone I'm not, which isn't something I've ever had before. We all deserve to be with someone who loves us for us, not the idea of who we should be.'

'If he freaks out again, can I roast him on social media?' If she had to witness broken-hearted Bea again it might tip her over the edge.

'If you and Brett don't confess your feelings to one another by the end of the season, can I run a story in the press calling you both out for your idiocy?' Bea challenged.

'No!' Lucie wouldn't put it past her. Faith would get involved too, re-post fan edits on social media. The fans went wild for her friendship with Brett, but she certainly wasn't going to let her friends feed into it.

'Don't tell Faith about Ric yet. I'm going to tell her at Le Mans, I want to give us some time to settle back into it.'

'I have to keep this to myself for a *week*?'

'You're making me keep quiet about you sleeping with Brett . . . again!'

'For two hours! I'm literally going straight to her hotel room when I get there!'

'Can I call Brett and get the gossip from his perspective?'

'I'm going to hang up now.'

'Fine. Goodbye. Good luck with the work thing.'

'Bye!' Lucie laughed.

As Bea's voice was replaced with the babble of an Italian radio presenter, Lucie allowed her mind to wander. She had seen Brett briefly this morning, and she'd had to fight to convince him to stay with her parents for the day. He wanted so badly to be involved in the livery reveal, and she knew he felt awful about being banished from work events as well as races. She tried to reason with him and tell him that ignoring Jasper's wishes would only anger his boss, but that didn't stop Brett from moping.

It didn't help that yesterday, Revolution's PR team had released a statement announcing that Brett wouldn't be racing for them for the rest of the season. They said it was due to personal reasons, and Lucie had confiscated Brett's phone so he couldn't see responses. Fans were angry and confused, and she couldn't blame them, it was unusual for a driver to step away for so long without more reasoning but they had to trust the process.

Lucie knew Brett would risk revealing the truth one day, because nobody in the industry was open about their mental health. He had a platform, and he was going to use it. Eventually. When he was strong enough to tackle the criticism and judgement head on.

She had asked her dad to keep an eye on him and suggested maybe they could work on one of his classic cars together.

Lucie knew she couldn't wrap him up in cotton wool, but it didn't stop her wishing she could be with him today instead of travelling a couple of hours away to spend time with the people Brett wanted to be around, in the environment he was temporarily not allowed to be in. How was she supposed to document today and plaster on a fake smile when her heart was elsewhere?

As she pulled up to the hotel in her tiny Fiat, parking next to a row of black SUVs, a wave of nausea hit her. Everyone knew she was close with the team's drivers, Brett most of all, and she was no doubt going to be bombarded with questions about his welfare. The wider team didn't know what was going on with him, so they were going to push her for information out of curiosity and concern, and their friends were going to want updates.

She was supposed to be here as part of the team, to work. To do her social media magic. But in reality, she was here as Brett's spokesperson. She was going to have to put on a brave face and lie to her co-workers, to sponsors and people who cared about their teammate and friend, and she hated it. She wanted to hide. But instead, she would be there next to the stage to get those perfect shots of the car and the team, doing her colleagues proud and keeping her best friend's dignity intact.

Lucie grabbed her bag from the passenger seat and jumped out of the car, locking it over her shoulder as she hurried inside to find Faith. Maybe she shouldn't be telling her without Brett's permission, but Brett openly flirted with her all the time, so did it really matter?

Checking in at reception, Lucie turned to her left and saw Revolution Racing's reserve driver, the one replacing Brett this season. 'Oh! Hey, Lucie.'

'Hi, Garrett!' Lucie went straight into work mode, hoping she was as welcoming as possible. None of this was Garrett's fault, but it felt alien to see him standing there in team uniform. Brett's uniform. He was even wearing an ID badge with 'Driver' written underneath his name. It all just felt wrong.

'I'm sorry to hear about Anderson, I hope he's doing all right.' To give Woods credit, he did look genuinely apologetic.

'Thank you, it's appreciated and I'll make sure to pass that on.'

'I was going to drop him a message, but since I don't know the situation, I didn't want to overstep and make him feel shit about the whole thing.' Woods' cheeks flushed and he rubbed the back of his neck, shifting uncomfortably.

'It might be better to leave it for now, but I'll make sure he knows you're thinking of him. I'll let you know when he's ready though.'

'I'll be sure to do his team proud, keep his car in one piece.'

'You're part of the team too, Garrett. You know that, right?' Lucie smiled at him, trying to ease his nerves. It warmed her heart to hear how much he respected Brett, and to know that he was so grateful to be racing for a top team. At least he didn't have a massive ego.

'I know, but it's not forever. I will happily step aside again when Brett is ready to get back behind the wheel. Oh, I wanted to ask you, do I have to, sort of, match his energy on camera? Because I'm not sure I have the right personality . . .'

Lucie laughed as she took her room key from the receptionist. 'Not at all. You just be yourself, and I'll make you look good. Fans might complain a little at first, especially the die-hard Anderson fans, but they'll just have to get used to it.'

'Awesome, thank you. Anyway, I've got a meeting with my manager so I'd better dash, see you later!'

He departed and Lucie's heart sank a little. There was no denying that Brett played a huge role in the success of the team's social media content, and doing things without him was going to take a lot of adjustment. From what she knew of Garrett so far, he was friendly enough, but the humour just wasn't there. It wasn't fair to rely on Marco and Julien to carry the content, and she and Faith had to make sure that even though he was only here temporarily, Garrett was given an equal platform and shown in a good light. If sponsors and other teams liked what they saw both on and off the track, and he had fans behind him, it would give him a better chance at being signed by another team next season.

She wished that Jasper had chosen a woman to fill the position. It would make perfect sense; to have a female driver on a team where the social media content was run by a two-woman team who had an entire campaign and academy dedicated to women in motorsport. She was certain that if a permanent position on the team ever came up, she could convince Jasper to approach someone like Savi Hart or Océane Clair. Not that she *wanted* to say goodbye to her beloved Revolution Racing boys, but change always came eventually.

Knocking on Faith's hotel room door before she'd even got to her own, desperate to get to her before Bea opened her mouth, Lucie groaned when she heard

Marco's voice on the other side. She was going to have to kick the guys out.

'Luce!' Marco hugged her and gave her a little squeeze.

'Hey, Mars.'

'How have you been?' He pulled back, holding her at arm's length and staring into her soul with his piercing puppy-dog eyes; she was so close to breaking down to him.

'Okay.' She smiled weakly, her eyes welling up with tears.

'Hey, Luce!' Julien appeared next, bucket hat on.

'What the hell is that?' she sniffled.

'I got trapped into buying it from one of those stalls on the street. Faith and I were doing some exploring, taking a walk through a park nearby and I spotted this.' He pointed to his head. 'The guy saw me take one look and then gave me his whole life story and I felt rude walking away, so I bought it. Tipped him, too,' Julien shrugged.

'That's not an excuse to walk around wearing it, Jules. Cow print doesn't suit you.' Faith glanced at it in disgust as she came out of the bathroom. 'What's wrong, Luce?' She looked at her friend, whose bottom lip was now trembling.

'Guys, can I have a second with Faith? I need a woman-to-woman chat.'

'Sure!' Jules grabbed his key card and ushered Marco out, leaving them to it.

Faith led her over to the balcony, pouring her a glass of water. They sat down on the sun loungers, and while

Lucie stared out at the park opposite, her best friend studied her. 'Spill.'

'I slept with Brett.'

'Oh my God,' Faith whispered. 'When?'

'Two days ago. At the farmhouse.'

Faith beamed, looking like she'd just won the lottery, but Lucie couldn't match the excitement. She needed someone to tell her it was a mistake. 'So, now what?'

'Now I retreat back to my corner and avoid any physical touch like the plague?'

Faith frowned. 'Why would you do that?'

'I don't want to add to the long list of things weighing on his mind. He's finding his feet in a world outside of racing, and this could get messy.'

'Lucie, get real. That man is your soulmate.' Faith let out a laugh, almost in disbelief at what she was hearing.

'Well, now isn't the right time.'

'Is there ever a right time to confess your feelings to your best friend of ten years, though? Surely, at some point, you just have to rip the Band-Aid off and hope for the best. Win or lose.'

The livery reveal had gone off without a hitch, Lucie and Faith had captured some great behind-the-scenes footage of the set-up, plus clips of people's reactions. They had strayed from the red for this race and instead opted for pinks and purples, which you didn't often see out on the track. Each driver had been dressed in brand new pink and purple race suits, and sponsors were already voicing positive feedback. The consensus was that Revolution Racing should have a total rebrand next season.

Some of the sponsors and members of the team had been pushing for updates on Brett, clearly irritated when Lucie refused to give details. Jasper and the owner of Revolution Racing were the only people who knew. Lucie felt terrible, she didn't know how to tackle the questions coming from everyone. She just knew she had to try to convince people that Brett had plenty of support and he just needed some space and time away from everything.

'You don't think the whole boy-next-door thing is too similar to Marco's vibe?' Lucie questioned their approach to Garrett Woods' social media portrayal.

'Not at all. We need him to be likeable, not too cocky, he needs to be the new guy in an innocent and sweet way. Just show how grateful he is to be here, push the stats of his career prior to the IEC. Don't forget we're trying to get him a seat with another team next season so he can stay in the championship once Brett comes back.'

'Okay, got it. Friendly, not too in-your-face.' Lucie mentally took note of some ideas, like short-form videos where Garrett listed fun facts about himself or talked about his favourite racetrack and the reasons behind it.

'Precisely! Oh, you won't believe who I was talking to this morning.' Faith suddenly changed the subject, almost bursting with excitement.

When she didn't continue speaking, Lucie urged her to spit it out. 'Who?'

'Jennifer Lockhart, co-owner of Jaehn Sport, one of the top Formula Voltz teams,' she gushed.

'I know who she is, Jensen,' Lucie laughed as Faith tried to contain herself. 'What were you talking about?'

'She wants to join forces with Girls Off Track!'

'Really?!' Lucie was shocked. Their academy had only just started out, really, and yet they were already garnering interest on a wider scale.

'Yes! Our two championships can work together, and we can provide way more opportunities for girls and get twice as many people involved. This is about bringing together all of the motorsport industry, breaking down the barriers between the different championships and divisions.'

'This is *huge*!'

'I know! She wants to have a meeting in London in a few months, come to HQ and see what it's all about for herself. She even said she'll bring some other people along! While I have a second, I'm going to go and get Bea and Esme on a group call while I know they're available. You keep working. Be back in a few minutes.'

As Faith disappeared into the crowd, Lucie let out a deep breath. Whilst this was all so exciting, she had a lot on her plate this season. Between work, her career and now Brett, she felt pulled in so many different directions but this was everything she'd ever wanted. So why was she beginning to feel overwhelmed with the plates she was juggling.

'Hello, Lucie.' Jasper appeared behind her, hands clasped together as if he was nervous.

'Hi, Jasper. That went well!' She gestured at the car

in front of them, the spotlights hitting it in all the right places as it sat proudly on the stage.

'It did, didn't it? I'm feeling rather proud of the direction we've been headed in the last couple of years. How is Anderson doing? I know he's scheduled his first therapy appointment, so that's great.'

'He's doing fine, I think. He's working on my dad's classic cars today. He had a rough start to the week, but he seems to be settling in nicely.' She didn't want to tell their boss that Brett had been struggling with night terrors. He could choose what to tell Jasper and when, it wasn't for Lucie to give that detailed an update, she wasn't his nurse or his keeper, she was his friend.

'That's good. He was okay after the statement was released yesterday?' Jasper frowned.

Lucie thought back to how he'd been. Although he'd been quiet and a little shy around her, she had put that down to their antics the day before. He had formed a habit of hovering near her, starting and stopping sentences and then disappearing into the kitchen to help Rosa with baking and cooking. They were already on their second tiramisu of the week.

'He was a bit quiet, but I didn't let him on his phone or tell him what people were saying online. Obviously, he's probably had a sneaky look today since I'm not there, but I guess I'll find out how he really is when I get home. I'll keep you updated.'

'That's brilliant. Thanks for looking after our boy.' Jasper patted her on the shoulder as he moved on to find one of his clients.

This team was Brett's home. He truly was *their* boy. He would always have a place here, if he stayed committed to facing his demons.

24

Lucie had suffered a tumultuous night's sleep. The sudden shift between her and Brett made spending last night alone, without him next to her or at least across the hall, feel heavy on her heart, and she knew without a shadow of a doubt that if he let her, she would be back in his arms tonight whether it remained platonic or not. Her willpower was at its lowest point, and she didn't have the energy to pretend she didn't want him any more.

She yawned as she crossed the border into Capannori. Faith had sat in her room with her until long past midnight so they could start planning the schedule for Le Mans content.

They'd almost nailed the schedule, but knowing how particular they were, they would be emailing and texting back and forth with changes over the next few days. Their next mammoth task was rounding up the social media staff for every other team on the grid, double-checking the nature of their content plans, and finalising the social media schedule for the organisation's main accounts. Thankfully with Esme's promotion and the recent introduction of an experienced social media manager from another championship, they could keep up.

As she turned into the road leading up to the farm, Lucie could see a car she didn't recognise on the driveway.

Her parents hadn't had much of an opportunity to make friends yet, only with neighbours who all lived within walking distance.

She parked next to it and made a beeline for the voices she could hear round the back of the house. There seemed to be quite a few higher-pitched tones, and then she heard it. Cleo Anderson's cackle of a laugh. Brett's family were here.

'Do I hear my *favourite* Anderson siblings?' she called out, rounding the corner. Two heads of rich, brunette hair looked up at her and she was met with screams.

'You're back!' Cleo ran to her and jumped into her arms, her tall frame nearly knocking Lucie to the ground, while Piper held back with a grin on her usually sullen face. Maybe Maggie was right, Piper *was* actually a fan of hers.

'What are you guys doing here?' She hugged them tight, so thrilled they were there, especially when she saw the smile on Brett's face, and Maggie over at the table with Rosa, fussing over something but stopping briefly to wave at Lucie.

'We wanted to come and hang out with Brett while you're at Le Mans. Booked the flights with Mum's savings when we heard you guys were coming. It's winter break and Piper had leave to use at work, so we figured why not come and annoy our brother.' Cleo pulled Lucie over to the table, where there was fresh fruit juice, salad, charcuterie boards and pastries. It was a spread that rivalled the five-star service those in the motorsport industry were accustomed to. All Rosa's doing, no doubt.

'Are you doing the whole Euro Summer trend thing?'
Lucie glanced down at their outfits. They each wore
summer dresses; Cleo in a white one with a lemon print
all over it, and Piper in a sage-green satin midi dress.
They looked like they had been plucked straight from
a travel blog.

'Yes! We've already cycled to the market in town. We
got new tote bags, silk scarves, and Rosa recommended
the *best* fresh pasta and truffle oil which we're going to
use for dinner tonight.' Piper listed off their purchases,
her eyes alight with excitement. It was the most animated Lucie had ever seen her.

'You girls are so funny,' Rosa teased. 'I didn't even
know what the term Euro Summer meant until you
arrived! The only social media content I consume is what
my Lucie posts.'

'What *does* it mean?' Mateo mumbled, confused.

'It just means spending your summer in Europe,
embracing the culture and the fashion, Mr Carolan,' Cleo
informed him.

'Oh.' He looked down at his shorts and shoes. 'Do
crocs count?'

Everyone laughed as he wiggled his Lightning
McQueen crocs in the air, the light-up ones that were
near-impossible to find. They had been a gift from the
Andersons last Christmas, and he never took them off.

Brett poured some juice into Lucie's glass and leaned
in close. It sent shivers down her spine as she felt the
warmth of his breath on her neck. 'How was your trip?'

'It was good. Lots of positive media coverage,' she

murmured back. She didn't want to open this conversation up to the whole table and have Brett made to feel awkward about his absence. 'Woods passes on his best wishes.'

'Really? That's nice.' He smiled back at her. 'Did you all go out last night?'

'No, I worked until I couldn't keep my eyes open.'

'Sunny . . .' he tutted. 'You need to stop working so hard all the time and do something for you. The world can wait sometimes, you know. Look around you.' He gestured at the landscape. 'Enjoy this. I know the main reason we're here isn't so great, and that's entirely my fault, but it doesn't all have to be bad. We're lucky to be here, of all places. Relax, soak it all in.'

'I know, but my work barely feels like work. You know I love what I do,' she insisted.

'I just don't want the stress building up too much.' Brett's hand found her thigh and she shifted. Not uncomfortably, but cautiously. He always did that. It was a friendly gesture. Except now she wasn't so sure if there was a new meaning behind it.

Lucie helped herself to food, piling her plate high. She had skipped breakfast this morning, opting for an extra hour of sleep before setting off on her journey back home. She'd barely had time to say goodbye to the team before departing, leaving them to enjoy the city without her until it was time for their flights.

Marco had decided to head to Hawaii with Faith and Julien. If Brett caught wind of that, would it make him feel worse about everything? Maybe if he saw them posting about it, he wouldn't care. His family was here. Lucie and her parents were here. He seemed comfortable, relaxed and, most importantly, happy.

But Lucie knew it was early days and he had a long road ahead, and the feeling of being isolated was going to reside in the back of his mind until Jasper invited him back to the team. They had a Christmas fundraiser in December which Lucie imagined would be his first trial run, but that was months away. He had plenty of time to go downhill again first.

'Does anyone want more orange juice?' Lucie held up the empty pitcher.

'Yes, please!' Cleo yelled above the noise.

They were so loud and animated; it was like being at a trackside autograph session all the time. Having been raised in a big, boisterous family herself, Lucie didn't know the meaning of peace and quiet. She *liked* the noise. She especially liked that every time Brett's eyes raked over her, or his hand went back to her thigh, or his arm rested across the back of her chair, she didn't have time to let her mind wander to the consequences because next thing she knew, someone was breaking the tension with a wild story.

But still, it was getting harder not to respond and she didn't want to make it obvious to their families that something was different, so she used the juice as an escape route and hurried into the kitchen in search of the oranges.

'Lucie?' She turned to see Piper in the entryway. It was easy to forget that she and Brett were twins because they were so different; opposite in everything except their looks. None of the Anderson siblings had inherited Maggie's blonde locks, they were all dark haired and the spitting image of their dad, but Piper and Brett had olive complexions, sharper jawlines and fuller lips.

'Hey, Pipes.' Lucie worked on slicing the oranges in half. She often found herself getting shy around her in recent years, and she knew it was only because she wanted the validation of Brett's twin that she was a good friend to him. If she ever put a foot wrong and hurt him, it wouldn't be Brett's mum who came after her, it would be Piper.

'He seems happy here.'

'I think he is.'

Piper took a second knife out of the drawer and helped her, grabbing a second pitcher while she was at it. They had already been through an entire jug, and it was hot out today. 'He's happy with *you*.'

'What can I say? I'm a delight to hang out with.'

Piper smirked and took the hint. Lucie didn't want to discuss their relationship right now. It was bad enough telling her friends, but they at least shut up when asked. If Brett's family knew what was going on, they would never hear the end of it. They knew Lucie had brewing feelings, but that was all. The levels of excitement and the badgering would be unbearable if they knew the rest. Of course, they wanted Brett to be happy and they wanted the same for Lucie, but they would fail to see the negatives. All the reasons it may not work long term.

'Lucie, seriously, I haven't seen him this relaxed in

years. He hasn't mentioned missing work once. When I asked him about it, he just shrugged and said he'd get back to it eventually.' Piper put the knife down. 'I'm worried that racing isn't right for him any more.'

'Not to overstep –' Lucie started.

'No, please. Overstep all you like, if anyone's entitled to disagree, it's you.'

'Okay, well, I think you're wrong. You know your brother as well as I do, so you know that racing is what fuels him. He's content now, but it won't last beyond the summer, he'll be itching to get back to the team and behind the wheel. Right now, he just doesn't want everyone to worry about him any more. He feels guilty, and he's scared to tell your sister what's been happening, but he knows she's not stupid. Cleo is fifteen, she sees and hears things.'

'You have no idea. She's been coming out with all sorts of wild theories. My personal favourite was that you're pregnant, it's Brett's baby, and he's on paternity leave.' Piper grinned mischievously when Lucie coughed to cover up her embarrassment.

'Anyway,' Lucie emphasised, 'I know Brett is starting to realise there's more to life, and he's loving his time here, but he can't be forced out of his career, and Revolution aren't doing that. If he ever chooses a different path, that needs to be a decision he's made himself.'

'You're right,' Piper nodded. 'Changing the topic drastically . . . I can't ever imagine my brother settling down with anyone except you, Luce. You just *work*.'

Lucie cut her off by jokingly waving the knife in her

general direction. 'Nope! We are not having this conversation, Pipes. This is about Brett. Not *me* and Brett.'

'You're basically the same person at this point.' Piper's eyes widened in mock horror when Lucie waved the knife again. 'Okay, fine. No more playing Cupid.'

It was at that moment that a water balloon came hurtling past the kitchen window, saving Lucie from Piper. Abandoning their juicing task, they cautiously headed back outside where they were immediately pelted and drenched in cold water. 'Brett Anderson, you little –'

Lucie was left stranded by Piper, who had run to join Cleo and serve as her protector, and now she was stuck with nowhere to go. Even Maggie and Rosa were joining in, handing out more balloons at the refilling station. How long had the girls been in the kitchen? Things had escalated fast. She remembered childhood summers when her dad had gone crazy, taking no prisoners and insisting on being a one-man team versus his kids. A water balloon fight was a staple activity for them, and her dad considered himself an expert.

Brett came towards her empty-handed and picked her up, spinning her round and using her as a human shield against Mateo, who had found his own bucket and filled it. 'Put me down, he's brutal!' Lucie screamed as another balloon came flying at her, hitting her right in the chest.

'Not a chance, Sunny. I need you.'

'Why?! Defend yourself, Anderson! Fight back!'

'No way! I need you to cover me while I get more ammunition.' Brett began moving across the courtyard towards Rosa and Maggie with Lucie still in his arms, squirming to get out of his grip. She was making it more difficult for anyone aiming for Brett, but Mateo was relentless in his attack.

'Dad! Ease up!' She grimaced as water seeped down the front of her shirt and her wet hair clung to her forehead, droplets falling into her eyes.

'You may be my daughter, Lucie, but I have no morals when it comes to this. Brett is going down, and I don't care if I have to take you down in the process.'

With the girls all giving up in fits of laughter near the flower beds, and the pile of balloons diminishing, Brett and Mateo were down to the final two balloons. Lucie had finally been put back on her own two feet, although Brett was still guiding her around in front of him as a defence. She was pretty sure he was still bone-dry.

Lucie heard a '*psst*' and glanced over to the refilling station, where Rosa stood proudly with a secret, final balloon in her hand and with no hesitation, launched it right at her husband, who promptly dropped the one he'd been holding and surrendered the game, leaving Brett free to throw his last one at him too, striking him in the chest.

Her mum cheered. 'He lost! He finally lost!' She high-fived Maggie.

Mateo lay on the ground, pretending to be wounded. 'This isn't over.'

'Just admit it, Mr Carolan. I'm the King.'

Lucie scoffed at his smugness. 'If it wasn't for my mum, you would be in his position right now. She saved your ass.'

'That's true!' Brett gave Rosa his famous bear hug, and before either of them could stop them, Cleo and Piper, in their soaking wet clothes, joined in.

It took everything Lucie had not to burst into tears at the sight of her big, loud, extended family. Then the reality of the last couple of years came flooding back to her, bringing the butterflies in her stomach to a screeching halt. The partying, the constant flood of women. Looks could be deceiving, but this was never going to be Brett's normal.

Brett and his mum were sitting out in the garden, soaking in the last of the Tuscan sun. He hadn't had much one-on-one time with her in recent years, partly because he was always on the go and didn't get to stay in Sydney for long, but also because she'd been so busy raising Cleo and ferrying her to and from extracurricular activities, long after Brett and Piper flew the nest.

He studied her as she sipped on her drink, and for the first time he realised just how fast the years were flying by. Maggie was getting older and he didn't feel like he really knew her any more. Or rather, he didn't know who she was outside of being a parent. It was the same with his dad; who had Jack Anderson been at his core?

'Mum, what was Dad like when you met?' His words startled her, bringing her out of whatever daydream she had been so invested in.

'A riot,' she laughed. 'He was the life of the party, had a wicked sense of humour. He was the focal point of every room he was in.'

'So *that's* who I get it from.'

'All three of you kids take after him in every way.'

'No wonder he started taking me karting, he liked the adrenaline.'

'Yeah, he couldn't exactly take you to a nightclub.' Maggie chuckled.

'And yet look how I ended up.' Brett grimaced, not liking his own comparison.

'You're still young, Brett. Just like he was. But it's about how you grow, and the work you put in to be a better you.' She said it so nonchalantly, like she had so much faith in his potential.

'I guess. I just can't help but feel like a colossal fuck-up.'

'You're not, Brett. You're just on a slightly rockier path than some of us go on.'

'You're telling me.' He sighed and leaned back on the sun lounger, pulling his shades over his eyes. Typically, that signified he was done with a conversation, but his mum wasn't one to back down once she got going.

'It took us five whole years to get together after high school, because your dad was always off doing his own thing. I didn't think he'd ever settle down, but then I went on one singular date with another man, your dad saw us walking along the street hand in hand, and it's like something clicked. The exact moment I stopped waiting around for him to realise what he was missing.'

'He stole you away from someone else?' Brett's jaw dropped. He had always been told it was love at first sight for his parents, and while it may be true, he hadn't known that it had taken them so long to find their way to each other.

'I was always Jack's, in my heart. There was never going to be anybody else who could compare. He was my best friend. But my God, he was a party animal until you and Piper graced us with your presence!'

'And you weren't?' Brett raised an eyebrow, remembering seeing old photos.

'I did my fair share, staying out until dawn, ended up in the back of a cop car a couple times when I was much younger.'

'Mum!' he scolded. 'I never knew that about you.'

'Well, it's part of my history with your dad. And the trouble is, until very recently I couldn't stand to talk about the good times we shared because it only made me miss him more.'

'I get it. I don't talk about him much, either. Think about him a lot though.'

'Oh, I think about him every day. I look at you kids, and all the memories come flooding back. He loved you all so much, his family was his world. He loved spending time with you, watching you excel in your career, taking you and Piper camping, going to soft play with Cleo. You were all the apple of his eye.'

'And then he left us.' He felt guilty as soon as the words left his mouth. It was one thing to let Lucie know he was bitter about his dad's death, but to tell his wife? The love of his life, mother of his kids? He didn't want to be selfish. But at the same time, he needed her to hear it.

'Your dad had a lot of demons, honey. He wasn't well for a long time, and he fought it as long as he could. I was so angry with him for leaving us like that, but I also understood why he did it. Eventually I was able to feel relieved. For him. Relieved that he wasn't suffering any more, that he could be at peace. It was so hard seeing him in pain, shutting himself away all day when you kids were at school and trying to pull himself together by the time you got home. He was a shell of himself in his final days. He did the therapy, he took the medication, he tried to be strong for us.'

'We just weren't enough.'

'Brett.' Maggie put her drink down and sat up, scooting across to sit on Brett's chair next to him. 'He loved you so much. It would break his heart to know you felt like that, and I can guarantee you that he didn't take his decision lightly when he did what he did.'

'I'm scared I'll turn out to be just like him. I don't want to lose sight of myself, I don't want to drown in my own sorrow.' He choked back a sob.

'Sweetheart, you're here in Italy. Taking a break. You're getting the help, doing all the right things. You've got the support system. But most importantly, you're your own person. You're not your dad. Yes, you're struggling. But this is just part of your journey, not the whole journey.'

'I love you, Mum.'

'I love you, too. And I think your dad would be incredibly proud of the man you're becoming.'

*

On his way to his and Lucie's side of the house, Brett stopped in the kitchen to grab a bag of her favourite sweet and salted popcorn with a packet of peanut M&Ms to pour into it. He fully intended on cuddling up and watching a film, but he wasn't going to complain if they continued where they'd left off the other day, only this time in a more comfortable location. He wasn't sure what all of this meant to her, but to him, it was everything.

He was playing a dangerous game and he was going to get burnt in the end, but right now, he would take whatever she was willing to give. It would be worth it in the end just to be able to say he knew what it was like to have even half of her.

He knocked on the door. 'Sunny?'

'Hey!' Lucie shot up from her cosy spot under the covers and immediately came to him, wrapping her arms around him. They ignored the fact that she almost got walloped in the head by the bags of sweets and revelled in the warmth of their hug.

'It went well, it was needed and I feel like a weight has been lifted from my shoulders.'

She pulled back and her gaze softened. Every time she looked at him like that, it made him weak. Something about Lucie seemed to heal his inner child. In fact, everything about today had done exactly that.

'She told me Dad would be proud.'

Lucie smiled up at him, capturing his face in her hands. 'She's right. And *I'm* proud. This was a huge step in the healing process, Brett.'

Brett hesitated only for a moment before leaning down and placing his lips on hers, in a kiss so gentle that he hoped she felt the meaning behind it. He had an incredibly supportive family around him, but Lucie had always been different. Because Lucie didn't *have* to stick by him, she had no obligation. She had chosen him, and she continued to choose him every day.

'I got ya something,' he murmured against her lips and rustled the packaging.

'My favourite,' she smiled. 'Thank you. I've shortlisted a selection of musicals for you to choose from, but I figured *Mamma Mia!* would be the winner, so it's ready to go.'

'Am I allowed to sing?'

'Yes.'

'Stick it on, then.'

He smiled to himself as she rushed to put her phone on 'do not disturb' so she didn't have to deal with any work calls or notifications for the evening. As she pulled the covers back for him to get in, his eyes darted from the lock on the door to her, in her oversized tee and underwear. 'You can lock it.'

As they settled in to watch the film, legs intertwined under the sheets, the popcorn was discarded by the time Bill rocked up on his boat.

25

Lucie and Brett had settled into a routine over the last few days. They would wake up, have breakfast outside, Brett would start work on whichever renovation task needed his immediate attention or attend an online therapy session, Lucie would get her laptop out and type and plan away, they'd break for lunch either with or without the Andersons, go back to work, shower, help Rosa and Maggie cook dinner and then escape to Brett's room as early as possible and lock the door. Not once did they discuss what it meant, and not once did they hesitate when one of them went in for a kiss which always turned into more.

Lucie was addicted, and when Brett had been helping her pack her suitcase for Le Mans and teased that she'd better stay away from other drivers' hotel rooms, she hadn't commented. She'd leaned in for another kiss and the packing had been temporarily forgotten.

Still lost in her feelings in the boarding lounge, she came face to face with a photo of Brett on the front page of an Italian newspaper. The headline read '*Disgraced IEC Star Cut From Team Permanently.*' Lucie was seething. She knew that newspaper had a reputation for misleading stories and smearing reputations of athletes, but this one was personal. She snapped a quick, sneaky photo and emailed it to the relevant team representatives.

Brett wasn't disgraced at all. In fact, fans, sponsors and drivers had only expressed their concern, love and respect for Brett and whatever he was going through. Nobody had theorised or sent the rumour mill wild, and the team had made it abundantly clear that his absence was temporary, and he would be welcomed back when he was ready. Only Brett and the team bosses knew the timeline, so this speculation by some stupid journalist was nonsense.

She huffed and puffed while she pulled her laptop out of her cabin bag, wishing she'd had the privilege of using the team's plane today. She had a short flight from Florence to Paris and they were sending a car to the airport for her, which would stop to get Bea on the way as per Lucie's request, so at least she didn't have to sit alone with her anger for too long.

The social media crews had a busy week ahead as it was, but the Girls Off Track team had a jam-packed schedule and Lucie's head was about to explode. She was just finishing up editing their photoshoot and it was almost ready to roll out mid-race, and her interview with the sports magazine had been finalised and was due to be published the day before. But of course, they had their own VIPs coming to Le Mans this year, and she was supposed to be helping Faith film a podcast amid it all.

They were due to have Jennifer Lockhart host a workshop during the UK's October half-term break later in the year. She was using it to test the waters and decide if she wanted her team to be a sponsor and host more frequently. If she did, Girls Off Track would be able to expand beyond the IEC. If they could get Formula Voltz and perhaps one other championship involved, their reach would be astronomical. Even as it stood, they were in a position where they could afford to do pop-ups in different cities across the world.

By the time she was called to board, Lucie felt clearer-headed. The newspaper with Brett's face on it had been folded up and put away, and she had successfully finished her tasks and finalised the schedule for the week. She was ready to tackle Le Mans head on.

Julien had agreed to be more heavily involved in content to take some of the pressure off Garrett in his first race with the team, and so fans hopefully focused more on Julien's growing presence and less on Brett's absence.

As she settled into her economy flight, having agreed with the team that it was silly to pay so much for her to sit in business class for an hour and forty-five minutes, Lucie inwardly rolled her eyes as her seatmate opened a second newspaper, straight onto another article about Brett. Lucie read some of it sneakily, almost laughing out loud at the theories the journalists were coming up with.

They had decided this time that Sienna was pregnant, and Brett was taking a break to raise their baby. None of these journalists were doing research, evidently. Lucie and Brett's sisters had all posted video evidence of him at the farmhouse, and he had hinted at his location, too. It was obvious if they bothered to look. Imagine Sienna on a farm. It was never going to happen.

'This is despicable, isn't it?' the woman next to her muttered in Italian. 'Why can't the tabloids leave the poor man alone? He clearly has something going on, I'm sure speculation is the last thing he needs.'

'They don't care, they just want a pay cheque.'

The woman tutted, outwardly matching the anger Lucie had been feeling since the headline she'd spotted in the departures lounge. 'They should care. Just focus on the sport, I say.'

Lucie silently agreed and spent the duration of the flight stewing over it. What the outside world often failed to understand was how deep an impact articles like this had, not just on the person at the centre of the story, but also on their families. Maggie didn't deserve to see her son being torn apart, his life dissected. Even Sienna, as much as Lucie disliked her, didn't deserve to have the world's media publicly speculating on something as personal as her body and fertility.

'You could at least look happy to see me!' Bea flung herself onto the back seat of the SUV while their driver put her two cases next to Lucie's one.

Her bubbly personality was enough to cheer Lucie up. 'Sorry, hi.'

'I know you usually travel with Brett, and everyone else has a travel buddy. That's why I offered to keep you company,' Bea smiled. 'Plus, when Revolution offers a ride, you know it's going to be decked out with all the best snacks.' She pulled a packet of pretzels from the door pocket in victory, hastily plugging her seatbelt in when their driver returned to the wheel.

Lucie took the pretzel she was offered, savouring the

salt on the tip of her tongue. 'How did we get here, hey?' she teased, referencing a couple of seasons ago when you could cut the tension with a knife any time the two of them were in the same room.

'I had a personality transplant, that's how.'

They spent the drive to Le Mans laughing away as they reminisced about some of the IEC's most scathing behind-the-scenes arguments, fall-outs and frenemy situations. It was just the distraction that they needed before the busy weekend ahead of them.

Stopping briefly at the hotel to drop off their bags and get their room keys, Lucie and Bea went their separate ways once they got to the circuit. Le Mans often felt like the Hollywood of motorsport in the IEC calendar; in the world of motorsport it was only rivalled by Monaco.

It was known to be a hellish twenty-four hours with crashes galore, technical difficulties, challenging team dynamics, a crazy amount of media attention, a higher fan attendance than any other race and a lot more time and money poured into the event. It wasn't just about the racing. There was a drivers' parade in the streets of the city, a funfair, more press, a full week of build-up before the race flag was waved. They had literal royalty here most years, and some of the world's biggest celebrities attended, not just for publicity, but because they had grown up watching Le Mans and developing a love for it that non-racing fans would never grasp. They even had Hollywood actors racing the cars themselves or running teams. Le Mans was different. It was magical.

'Lucie!' Faith's head of blonde hair whipped around

to face her, hitting Julien in the face. He blinked but waved a hello, leaving his wife to abandon their conversation and run into Lucie's arms. Julien often joked that there were three people in the relationship.

'Hello, you.' Lucie squeezed her back. She'd always been a hugger, and thankfully everyone at Revolution matched her energy. 'Ready to crack on? We've got so much to do. First up is the podcast episode.'

'One step ahead of you, I've already got the equipment set up in the drivers' trailer.'

'You're amazing, I hope you realise that.'

Brett was going crazy at the farm. His mum and sisters were gallivanting around the local area, and although he had been busy with restoring Mateo's cars, gardening and cooking with Rosa and sanding the floors, he had spent every spare second glued to his phone. His teammates had, with Jasper's permission, kept him up to date with strategies and statistics in the team group chat, Revolution Royals, and Mateo had happily put the race on the brand-new TV in the living room.

He was kneeling in soil, replanting some of Rosa's flowers, when Gabriel called him. It was the first time any of his bosses had picked up the phone to speak to him. He was grateful for that; some days when the team did choose to get in touch it felt like rubbing salt in the wound. They had stuck to texting every now and then to give him space, so naturally, when *Gabriel Lopez* appeared on his screen in big, white letters, his heart started racing. Why was the CEO of the organisation calling?

'Anderson?' Gabriel yelled over the noise. Did that man ever make use of conference rooms? He seemed to do all his business from cafés, hospitality tents and garages.

'Hey, Gabriel. What can I do for you?'

'What are you doing right now, Anderson?'

Brett frowned, questioning where this was going. 'Just gardening, planting some flowers out the front . . . why?'

'How would you feel if Jasper and I sent a plane out to Florence airport and brought you to Paris for dinner with your team tonight?'

'What?' Brett wondered if he'd heard him incorrectly. After all, it was loud. He could hear mechanics and engineers working away, the sound of engines as multiple cars exited the pits. 'Are you serious?'

Gabriel laughed heartily. 'One hundred per cent! Jasper has had confirmation that you've begun therapy – good on you, by the way – and he wants to make sure you still feel connected to Revolution, that you stay motivated to keep pushing through so you can come back and join us. Like he said, this break from racing isn't supposed to be a punishment! We've certainly missed having you around, Anderson.'

'I'd love to, Gabriel. Thank you.' He swallowed the lump that was forming in his throat.

'Not a problem. Now, Jasper still doesn't want you at the track. He's sticking to his rules. Plus it would cause quite a stir. But he'll give your driver the address of the restaurant, and if you give his last name to the host, they'll seat you. We're not telling the team, either. It's a surprise.'

'Oh, it's definitely a surprise, sir.'

Gabriel gasped suddenly. 'You won't have to miss a therapy session, will you?'

'No,' Brett laughed. 'Had one yesterday. I have three days until my next one.'

'Excellent. Do you need a car to take you to Florence? Sorry, it's all quite last minute. I'm not sure why we didn't think of it before!'

'I think Lucie's dad will drive me if I slip him some euros. He likes having things to do while Rosa is down at the local market.'

'In that case, I'll send through all the information you need. Looking forward to seeing you, Anderson.'

As Brett hung up the phone, he rushed to track down Mateo out by the barns. He was working on his mint-green 1956 Ford Thunderbird, polishing it to perfection. 'Mr Carolan?'

'You all right, Brett?' Mateo stopped what he was doing immediately upon hearing the haste in Brett's voice. 'Has something happened?'

'Um, any chance you could drive me to the airport in Florence, please? The team have invited me to dinner, they're sending a plane.'

Mateo's face lit up. 'That's wonderful! Of course I will. I suggest you change your outfit, though. Not sure muddy knees will convince your boss you've got your shit together.'

'No . . .' He looked down. 'Glad I had my suit

professionally cleaned after that night in Monaco. I knew I'd have a reason to wear it at some point, even if Luce teased me relentlessly for it.'

'Borrow my crocs if you want, that'll make her chuckle.'

After they'd both changed, Brett now feeling much more like his usual self with his work boots left safely in the utility room, the pair set off to Florence, blasting nineties R&B.

Life felt good. Hopeful. For the first time in a long time, he felt motivated to stay healthy and make some changes. Very necessary changes if he didn't want to hit a point of no return. He missed sitting down to dinner with a beer, but he knew that beer always led to whisky or vodka, which was always too much.

Even with the heavy topics he discussed in therapy, he felt clearer-headed. Like he was capable of being so much more than a racing driver.

Why shouldn't he have a happy relationship? Why shouldn't he buy some land and build a house, grow his own food, get a dog. That was what his happy ever after had looked like up until Sienna had broken him. Why was he giving her so much power all these years later? Had she not taken enough from him? He was sick of letting her win. And if he wanted to be the kind of man his dad would be proud of, didn't that mean he shouldn't go through life alone?

It wasn't until he walked into the restaurant a few hours later that it sunk in. He was nervous. The panic attacks of his past had been threatening to make a comeback, but he'd kept them at bay. It was just the night terrors he needed to get under control, and night terrors couldn't haunt him so much in the daytime. But right now? His breathing was off, *he* felt off. He was nervous not only to see his team and crew, but to see Lucie. He hadn't seen her for almost a week, and he knew that there was a strange kind of tension between them. A sexual tension like nothing they'd shared before. He was so worried she would feel as though he was using her, but he didn't want to stop. He just couldn't shake the feeling that his reputation had ruined any shot he had of keeping her.

'No way!' Marco's voice rang out through the restaurant. 'Anderson, what the hell are you doing here, bro?' His teammate's brown eyes went wide as he took in Brett sitting at their table in his fancy linen shirt. He'd sat on the plane and then in the car still as a statue, careful not to crease it. He was hyper-aware of making a good impression today, and purposely hadn't ordered a drink yet so everyone would clearly hear him ask for an iced water.

'Ah! Anderson! You been waiting long?' Jasper was the first to reach him, shaking his hand and making it clear to the rest of the team that he was here by invitation.

'Only twenty minutes or so. Congrats on the great result, guys.' He stood up to greet his team, Garrett Woods included, and gratefully accepted every hug he was offered.

By the time Lucie reached him and threw her arms round his waist, he was fighting the urge to lean down and kiss her right there on the lips in front of the entire restaurant.

The guys had done an excellent job and taken them over the finish line in second place, which was outstanding for a race as gruelling as Le Mans. Lucie and Faith had posted fantastic content, made great progress with Girls Off Track. And Brett? He was *here*. Celebrating with them.

He knew without a shadow of a doubt that he would be back behind that wheel at the very first race next season. He had all the tools he needed to heal, and he was going to make damn sure he didn't let it all go to waste.

26

It had been two weeks since the race at Le Mans, and Lucie had noticed Brett's gradual transition into a ray of human sunshine. He seemed back to his old self. The night terrors had stopped, there had been no tears unless she counted the time he cried at an ad for rescue dogs, and he had upped the ante with flirting again.

But there was a new, emotional layer to their relationship. As he had completed more therapy sessions and had more breakthroughs, he had been much more open with Lucie about his past. Just . . . not about them.

Since the dinner at Le Mans and his family's return to Australia, they had settled back into their daily routine and Brett had completed the living room and the master bedroom. The rough, cracked terracotta walls were now a smooth, bright white, the floorboards had been stripped, sanded down and varnished, and the furniture had been built. Lucie had put down her laptop for a few hours a day and her parents had left them to their own devices, trusting their daughter's interior décor talents despite the fact she had never decorated a room in her life.

Her childhood bedroom back in LA had been plain and boring with a couple of framed posters and some polaroids. That was the extent of her experience. This time around, she'd scoured hundreds of inspiration photos online, relying on Pinterest to make her look like she knew what she was doing. It helped that they wanted a minimal aesthetic. She could work with minimal, but she still wanted to make sure that the farmhouse felt like a home, not like the house they had left behind in the States.

She had ordered a new rug to go under the wooden coffee table, which was a slice of tree trunk from an oak tree Mateo had chopped down at the edge of the property, and today's mission was to find artwork. They were in Italy. It should be easy to find something unique, hopefully directly from an artist's studio.

Lucie headed into the kitchen where Brett and her parents were gathered at the breakfast bar, redesigning the chicken coop for a third time. 'Morning, everyone.'

'Good morning, love. Would you like something to eat? We have croissants. Homemade. Brett helped me whip them up.' Rosa fussed over her, pulling out her chair and pouring her a coffee.

'Thanks, Mum. What are your plans today?'

'Your dad and I are going next door for lunch with Giada and Stefano. We're teaching them English, so we'll be gone all afternoon. They're not exactly, shall we say, easy to teach.'

Lucie laughed, remembering when they had collectively tried to teach Isabella to speak Italian. By that point, they were speaking English at home, and being the youngest, she struggled to keep up when they switched to their parents' native language. 'Well, in that case, Anderson, want to take a road trip? I'm on a mission to find some art for that huge, empty wall in the living room. Need something colourful. Plus, you're already running out of clothes since our last shopping spree, almost all your tops have stains on.'

'Oh, um, I promised I'd prepare the veggies for dinner,' Brett grimaced, looking like he was afraid of getting a telling-off. He was the perfect house guest as always, doing everything he could to help; the result of being raised by a woman like Maggie.

Rosa just tutted at him. 'Nonsense! You're free to go with Lucie. Getting away from the farm for a while will do you the world of good.'

'Thanks, Mama C. You're a star.' He squeezed Rosa's shoulder. 'Eat up, Carolan. We've got a busy day ahead.' He began helping to clear the table, gesturing for Lucie to eat faster.

She rolled her eyes as he whisked the croissants out of reach, handing them to Mateo to package up for later. 'Give me a minute!' she mumbled through a mouthful of pastry.

'You can borrow my work van, if you want,' Mateo suggested.

They met out at the van, both out of their haphazard, paint-covered DIY outfits and in clothing that was more suitable to wear in public. Brett, of course, had broken out the Versace, while Lucie had gone for a lilac floral midi dress she'd not yet had a chance to wear.

'Lilac is your colour, Sunny. Complements your complexion.' He looked her up and down and that warm and fuzzy feeling travelled up her whole body, right up to her cheeks.

'Thank you. Versace is so *your* brand,' she countered to him, knowing it was his most beloved.

'Can I drive?' Brett asked, already reaching out for the keys.

She threw them at him, Revolution Racing keyring smacking him in the chest, grateful not to have to navigate the roads again. They were long, windy, and some weren't even tarmacked. 'If you actually listen to my directions, sure.'

'Are you serious, Sunny?' he scoffed as they clambered into the van. 'Need I remind you of that time we drove from LA to Nashville? Two thousand miles and I can't even count how many times you got us lost. Surprised we didn't get stranded on the side of the road, murdered by some hillbilly.'

'Hey, this is Europe. We're driving for two hours, no freeways. Just country roads. *You* try driving on a cross-country road trip in the US. Oh wait, you never will, because you prefer to sleep, mess around with the radio stations, stuff your face with snacks and whine until we pull over at diners so you can get the all-American experience.'

Brett looked her up and down as he pulled off the dirt track leading from the farm and onto the road, and it made her feel giddy. 'I get the all-American experience every time I get you out of your clothes, Sunny.'

'Oh my God.' She blushed profusely. 'Focus on driving.'

'Kind of hard when the slit in your dress shows off your thigh like that.'

'Anderson, come on. We don't have time for your flirting.'

'Do you even know me at all?' He glanced at her in mock horror. 'I will always squeeze in time for flirting. I'll squeeze in time for anything as long as it's with you.'

It made her uneasy how right he was, as she remembered all the times that statement had rung true. Before every race, he wouldn't get in the car until he'd hugged her. And it was the same each time he got out. He always searched for Lucie first amongst the sea of people, and he clung to her like he'd been afraid he would never see her again.

He always chose her. And she would always choose him, it just wasn't enough to throw away ten years of friendship for a future that would end in tears. She couldn't change who he was fundamentally, and she wouldn't break her own heart trying.

'Left!' Lucie screamed at him as they almost missed their turning, snapping out of her daydream. Not that it was much of a dream. She spent most of her time avoiding the realities of her feelings until rationality took control and brought her back to the cold, hard truth.

'Bloody hell, Sunny! Give a man a heart attack, why don't you!'

'Sorry,' she grimaced. 'Didn't want you to miss it.'

'U-turns exist for people who are friends with people like you.'

There was that word again. *Friends*. It would always apply to them, and it stung.

*

Two hours later, after twenty-six radio station changes, and one stop on the side of the road so Lucie could straddle Brett's lap and kiss the hell out of him to shut him up, they made it to Parma. His hand was still on her leg, approaching dangerous territory as he drove further into the city and his hand travelled further up her thigh.

'Stop it.' She swatted his hand away. 'We're already in a rust bucket of a van which sounds like it's going to fall apart every time you brake, we have enough attention on us without you doing that.'

'People can't *see*, Lucie.'

She gestured at an elderly lady, who was scowling at them through the windscreen as she crossed the road in front of them. 'Why does she look so angry, then?'

'Probably thought, "Oh, it's world-renowned racing driver Brett Anderson, is he about to run me over?" She's too short to see what my hand is doing all the way up here.'

'Your hand,' she removed it completely, 'is going to stay firmly on the steering wheel. Don't you remember the traffic in Milan? Or by the Arc de Triomphe in Paris? It's manic. Europeans have no concern for road safety.'

'I'm about to have no concern for road safety if I don't get to eat something,' he sighed, and Lucie looked away shyly. 'For once, I wasn't being sexual. I meant actual food, Sunny. I'm bloody starving over here. Didn't you hear my stomach grumbling?'

'Not over the noise of Shakira, no.' She frowned at his latest music choice. 'We're supposed to be having a massive dinner later, remember? Mum and Dad are only having a small lunch at Giada and Stefano's. Save space for a barbeque.'

'I'm a growing man, and I worked up quite the appetite this morning.' He referenced their shower antics. 'Besides, I want to try some proper Parmigiano Reggiano.' He pinched his fingers together, mocking every Italian in history.

Lucie laughed at the ridiculous accent he put on. 'That was super stereotypical of you, Anderson. But fine, we'll find food. And then we have six art galleries to go to.'

'Six?!' he choked out. 'I was hoping we'd have time to sunbathe by the pool later, but not if you're dragging me to look at a bunch of paintings *all* day. Should just let me paint something. A watercolour of you, naked. You could pose like Rose in *Titanic*.' He put on a high-pitched voice. '*Paint me like one of your French girls*.'

'I think Kate Winslet would be severely offended if she heard your impression,' she winced. 'Not too sure how my parents would feel about your choice of artwork hanging on their living room wall, either.'

After driving around for twenty minutes, they found a parking space big enough to get the van in and out of, that wasn't too far from the galleries Lucie had already scouted out online.

Lucie usually veered towards a hatred of cities. Not only was the parking a nightmare, but there were too many people. She liked to get away from mass crowds when she wasn't at the track, not be in the middle of them, getting shoved into left, right and centre. What she did love about them was the tourist shops. Her nieces and nephews had huge magnet collections, courtesy of her travels. But those tourist shops also had newspapers outside, and her heart skipped a beat when she spotted one with Brett's face on it, displayed in a rack on the side of the street. To her relief, he failed to notice.

He was too busy on his phone, searching the best places to eat. Looking through Instagram, of course. Because that was what self-titled Foodies did. 'This looks fancy as fuck, let's go here.' He grabbed her hand and pulled her down a side street.

It was cobbled, with the terraced houses towering on either side of them, the sounds of the city quietened by their walls, and it was delightfully empty. Lucie could breathe a sigh of relief to be away from it all.

They walked into the restaurant and Lucie gawked at the interior. It *was* fancy. Not in the nicely decorated, let's-go-here-for-a-special-occasion kind of way, but in the pretentious, the-likes-of-Lucie-Carolan-can't-afford-to-eat-here kind of way. Brett fitted right in wearing his Versace shirt, but her unknown brand dress made her feel nervous, as if she might result in them being turned away by the overly friendly waiter heading towards them.

'Brett Anderson, as I live and breathe!' His accent wasn't Italian. Lucie couldn't place it, but either way, he looked over the moon to see them. 'Come in, please. It is a pleasure to have you and your guest here, sir. My name is Ilyas.'

'Hey, Ilyas.' Brett shook his hand, and he looked like he might faint. 'This is my . . . Lucie.'

Had he been about to introduce her to a total stranger as if they were something? It felt like a slip-up of sorts. She just blinked at them both, like a deer caught in headlights.

'Lucie *Carolan*? You work with Mr Anderson's racing team, no?'

'I – I do! Hello.' Why on God's green earth was she feeling shy all of a sudden. Lucie didn't do shy. It was her job to be bubbly and friendly, but she was thrown off.

'My wife loves your vlogs with Miss Jensen! And that podcast you ladies do! What is it called? *Across Finish*?'

'*Across The Line*.' Brett corrected him.

'Oh, sorry. I got so distracted! Come, sit down.' He led them to a table in the back corner. 'Here are your menus! Can I get you anything to drink? Some wine, perhaps?'

'Just some water, please.' Brett smiled up at him while Lucie shifted nervously, afraid he would somehow forget his problems and order the most expensive wine on offer, as he usually did when they went out to dinner.

Already deciding on what she wanted to eat, Lucie looked around. There was nobody else there, which she would typically take as a bad sign. But then she looked back at the menu and noticed the complete lack of pricing. Ah. That was why Brett had come here. Most people could only afford to eat in a place like this if they sold their organs on the black market.

She had always been intimidated by the way Brett spent money like it grew on trees. She wasn't struggling, and she was lucky enough to be in a position where she could hop on a flight to just about anywhere at the drop of a hat, but almost *all* her money went on travel and accommodation in between races, and she didn't like to splash out.

Lucie often wondered where she would be if she hadn't got so close with Julien, Marco and Brett over the years. Would she have still had friends to travel with? To share her family with? Maybe she'd have gone home to Los Angeles more often. Maybe she'd have had a vibrant dating life, not turned down the offers she'd had throughout her twenties. She knew some of the drivers and mechanics she'd worked alongside for years were put off flirting with her because they'd seen the way she and Brett acted around one another. There was a running joke that they were soulmates. And they were. But Lucie was starting to think she should branch out.

'Do you ever wonder what our lives would be like if we weren't us? If we hadn't joined the motorsport industry?' Brett pondered, looking around eagerly for his food. It had only been five minutes since they'd ordered.

'What do you mean?' she frowned.

'Like, what do you think we'd be doing with ourselves?'

'Hmm. I've never really thought about it because we started out so young. I probably would've ended up reluctantly going to college a year late, after faffing about for a while. Maybe I'd have studied marketing or something.'

'And then you'd have got bored, quit, and gone backpacking,' he added.

She smiled, knowing that was exactly what she

would've done. She had never wanted to stay in the US when she was a teenager. It was why she'd risked it all and taken the job with the catering company. She couldn't bear the thought of being stuck in the LA bubble, and although the motorsport bubble often mixed with the same people, at least it was more exciting, and at least it felt like she was welcome in it. 'What would you have done?'

'That's what scares me, Sunny. I have no idea. There were never any other options for me, it was racing or nothing. It was my goal from such a young age, I never considered a different path. Not even for a second.' He let out a shaky breath. 'It's why I need to get back behind that wheel. I can't fuck up again. I won't. Everything I know, everything I am and everything I love is at stake. If I have to lock myself in a room in between races to avoid temptation, that's what I'll do.' He clenched his jaw. He wasn't telling Lucie; he was telling himself. Reassuring himself. But for the first time, Lucie felt genuinely confident in his words.

'Hey, you're doing good. You've come a long way in a short space of time.' She reached across the table to squeeze his hand.

'Thanks to you essentially kidnapping me and holding me hostage in Capannori, yeah.'

'No, you're the one having therapy and doing the work. I know it's taking a lot out of you, but you're deep into the healing process now, Anderson. That's not to say you won't struggle sometimes in the future, but it takes a lot to get to the stage you're at.'

'Thanks, Sunny. It's a comfort knowing you've got my back, even after the way I've hurt you.' He squeezed her hand back in response.

'That was the alcohol talking, not you. I know you didn't mean it.'

'Add that to the never-ending list of reasons I should never drink again. Dad always told me I had a big personality. He said my aura could fill a room. I don't think I need alcohol to help me be myself, do you? In fact, it would appear it does the opposite.'

As Ilyas appeared with two mouth-watering bowls of Pasta ai Quattro Formaggi, Lucie smiled warmly at the man sitting in front of her. He looked proud of himself for the first time since Revolution Racing had won the championship last season. 'Sounds like Jack was a wise man.'

'Sunny, why did you let me eat so much?' Brett pouted as they entered their third art gallery. The first two had been a bust, but Lucie had been distracted by Brett whinging about being on the verge of a food coma. Between that and him keeping his hand a little too low on her back for her dignity, she'd had a hard time focusing on the task at hand.

She needed a piece of art that was minimal but brightly coloured, and would look good in a black frame. Everything they'd seen so far had been busy, cluttered or muted. Too many landscapes of the Italian countryside. Which made sense for where the farm was located but didn't make sense for her parents' tastes.

304

'You shouldn't have had the tiramisu. I told you there's plenty at home.'

'Yeah, and I paid all that money, and it wasn't a patch on Mama C's.'

'Eyes too big for your stomach, Anderson.'

Lucie came to a stop as they came across a painting. It was an abstract piece, blue hues. It looked like the ocean. It was the opposite of what she was looking for, but it was the right size and shape. More importantly, it reminded her of California. Of summers spent with her siblings at the beach, family volleyball tournaments, working as a lifeguard, sunset picnics on the clifftops. The drive to Monterey, where their family friends had a vacation home. It was perfect, and she was mesmerised.

'Hey, Sunny. They've got an orange version, too.' Brett pointed across the room. 'That would look great in your parents' room,' he noted, and her heart leapt. Just like the blue one reminded her of California, the orange one reminded her of her dad's favourite summer trip. Camping in Virginia, when Lucie had fallen in the river. The painting looked like a campfire, captured with sweeping brush strokes and specks of gold paint.

She checked the price of both. 'Not a chance. This one alone is really pushing the budget.'

Brett picked the painting up and shooed her to the other side of the room, stopping in front of the orange one. 'I'm buying them both.'

'No, you're not.'

'Yes, I am,' he argued.

She knew she wasn't going to win this. It was hopeless

to even try to fight him on it, but Lucie was stubborn as hell. She'd been raised by Rosa Clemente, after all. 'Let me buy one. Mum gave me enough cash for the blue one.'

'It's my thank you to them for letting me stay.'

'You're already thanking them with manual labour and your health.'

'Stop trying to talk me out of it. You know you have no sway here.'

'Ah yes, I forgot. Brett Anderson does what he wants.'

Brett looked at her, that look in his eyes again, a look that promised the whole world, but would he give it to her if she asked? Or would he run? Before she could pluck up the courage to say anything, Brett broke her thought process. 'He does. And what he wants right now is to buy a gift for people he cares about deeply, and then take his sunshine girl home and spend the rest of the afternoon devouring her.' He grinned as he leaned down to plant a kiss on her lips, pulling away smugly and snatching up the second painting to take it to reception. She smiled at his back, hoping they could stay in this dream forever, yet knowing reality would come back to bite them eventually.

27

Brett had raced home, determined not to shirk on his dinner responsibilities for Rosa, and there was a lot he wanted to do before then. Primarily a lot he wanted to do *for* Lucie. They still had four hours until dinner, which was plenty of time. She was in for a treat; she just didn't know it yet. He was thinking an hour by the pool to blend in their T-shirt-line tans that were threatening to develop from days working outside, followed by a shower to cool down. But if he had anything to do with it, they would need a second shower after the first to wash off any trace of their activities.

Maybe a third, if she stayed in his room to hang out and watch an episode of *Narcos*. He wasn't particularly interested in the plot of the show. They had restarted multiple episodes this week, trying and failing to pay attention. He didn't know if that was a sign that the show wasn't all that great, or that he and Lucie were addicted to one another in the kind of way that was going to leave him devastated when it was all over. Probably both.

He should stop. He knew he should stop before he hurt her. Before he inevitably freaked out at the first sign of any kind of commitment. But he'd waited years to be able to touch her again. Spent years reliving that hiking trip. But Brett was starting to realise it wasn't just him. She made the first move sometimes, too. She would look at him with her doe eyes, and he would abandon his task, pick her up and carry her to the nearest surface.

Rosa and Mateo spent so much time next door that it both helped and hindered them. Helped them because they didn't have to keep their newfound intimacy behind closed doors, and hindered them because they weren't getting much work done.

Mateo would sometimes return home and question what they'd been doing all day, but Brett could see that he had worked it out. He had once teased them about setting a date for their wedding, but they'd both stuttered their way through a denial, and he hadn't mentioned it again. Brett knew Mateo didn't want Lucie to be on her own. He wanted his daughter to find someone. And it made sense to everyone except Lucie that that someone should be her best friend.

He wanted so badly to be the right man for her, he just didn't know if he had it in him. Not in the long run. He had thought about it before, about what it would be like to be with her, what their wedding day would look like, and then the reminder of Sienna cheating on him had weaselled its way into his thoughts and fear had got the better of him. Until he could stop running away from his feelings, he had to keep commitment off the cards. Otherwise he would end up leaving Lucie in the dust and shattering their entire world.

'You got visitors, Sunny?' He peered at the dark-grey SUV up ahead, parked on the driveway. It looked out of place next to the vintage pastel paint jobs of Mateo's collection.

'I don't think so.' Lucie shifted uncomfortably in her seat, and it took everything in him not to laugh. She was a terrible fibber.

Abandoning the van on the courtyard, they headed inside with the two paintings, Brett carrying them both because, frankly, they were bigger than Lucie. She wouldn't have managed without tripping over or ramming into the newly painted walls.

They were barely through the front door before Brett heard two additional voices chatting to Lucie's parents. He'd know that weird hybrid Dutch-Belgian accent anywhere. It was Julien. But it wasn't Marco with him. He left the paintings leaning up against the wall and rounded the corner into the kitchen. Jasper.

'Ah! You're home!' His boss came forward first, embracing him enthusiastically before stepping aside to let Julien slap his best friend and teammate on the back.

'Good to see you, Anderson.'

'What the hell are you guys doing here?' Brett was stunned, a huge grin spread across his features as he caught Lucie's eye. 'You knew?'

'Surprise. This is why I got you out of the house today,' she grinned back. 'I mean, obviously I did need the artwork, but it had to be today specifically.'

'Yes, come through to the study!' Jasper herded everyone down the corridor towards Brett and Lucie's bedrooms, and it was at that moment Brett realised he'd left his bedroom door open this morning and Lucie's lingerie was right there. On the floor. In perfect view of anyone passing.

He glanced at Julien, who looked between him and the lingerie and smirked. 'We've already seen it, mate,' he whispered. Great. He was never going to be able to look her parents in the eye again.

'Ta da!' Jasper threw open the door to Mateo's study, revealing a state-of-the-art racing simulation set-up. It was the only thing in the room aside from a treadmill and some weights. All the boxes had been removed, along with the desk where Mateo still did occasional production work on short films, and there was a shelf on the wall above the racing sim containing Brett's trophies and photos of him and the team.

'You guys did this?' He blinked at them all. Between Lucie's pride and Jasper and Julien's sheer joy, he was on the verge of tears.

'We had the delivery arranged for this morning. It arrived about ten minutes after you left, and we followed half an hour later,' Julien said.

Jasper patted his shoulder, his paternal nature coming through as it often did when it came to his drivers. 'It's a gift from the team. We wanted to make sure you know that we're invested in your future with us, Brett. We don't want you thinking we've forgotten about you.'

'But you'd better sit your ass in this seat every day, Anderson. I don't want a shit teammate next year; we've got races to win,' Julien teased, but Brett knew it was a partial threat.

As it should be. Moretz and De Luca shouldn't have

to pick up the slack because Brett hadn't kept up with his training, especially not when his break from racing was *his* problem. He'd already caused enough stress within the team. He'd do anything he could to make his return to the sport easy on everyone.

'Yes, sir.' Brett let a smirk creep onto his face, earning a playful shove from Julien.

'This is the same racing sim we have at HQ, isn't it?' Brett asked, inspecting it closely.

He didn't often go to HQ because each driver had a set-up like this in their own homes. Julien's was in Malmedy, Brett's in Sydney and Marco's in his flat in Monaco. But with Brett being banned from HQ for a while anyway and not planning on leaving Tuscany until he was sure he was on the straight and narrow, this surprise set-up was exactly what he needed.

Jasper nodded excitedly. 'I contacted the company and got you a new one, it's had upgrades so it's even better than the ones we've got at the moment. Sit in it, go on. You and Moretz are the same height so we're pretty sure everything should be in the right position for you.'

Brett lowered himself into the chair and gripped the steering wheel, and immediately felt at ease. At home. 'This is perfect. It feels so much better than my last one.'

'I've been playing around all day, and I think the settings are spot on. They should match what our actual car feels like,' Julien said. 'They're the settings I use, anyway. Oh, and I know you don't usually use a trainer these days, prefer to crack on with things yourself, but my trainer is happy to help you out, get you set up with a programme, if you want. You can do it all online, weekly video calls. We could even train together.'

'Cheers, Moretz. And you, Jasper. I really appreciate it.'

Lucie closed the door on her co-workers, leaving them to play around on the racing sim. It was a serious, strict part of training, but all three of them, their boss especially, were getting carried away with testing how the steering wheel responded. It was the second crash paired with cheers that she took as her cue to make a swift exit and find her parents.

'I can't believe we pulled that off.' She heaved a sigh of relief as she collapsed onto a stool at the breakfast bar, gratefully accepting a glass of water from her mum.

'I can. You're a good girl, Luce,' her dad smiled, but there was a sadness in his eyes that she hadn't seen many times before.

'What's that face for?' she frowned, but he looked nervous. Her mum matched his expression. 'Guys, you can be honest with me.'

'We're just worried about you, that's all. You're putting a lot of your time and energy into work and Brett's recovery. Have you thought about how long you and Brett are going to stay here with us?' Mateo asked.

When Lucie stayed silent, unable to provide an answer, her dad sighed. She didn't think he was disappointed in her as a person, just perhaps wishing his daughter's life looked different right now. They were mid-race season, and that usually meant she and Brett were jetting about all over the place with the team. This was the first year they'd stayed in one place, and although Brett had to work on his sobriety, Lucie shouldn't feel obligated to stick it out with him.

Except she didn't really feel obligated, it just felt like the right thing to do. She wanted to do it. To be here, guiding him and supporting him.

'He's healing, Luce. We sit outside and drink alcohol every evening, and it's like he doesn't even notice. He turned his nose up at the smell of your dad's whisky the other night. But as much as we love him, he has dragged you through hell. That isn't his fault, it's just what happens when someone's mental health deteriorates.'

'Don't you think you two need to sit down and have a conversation about what's going on here? At what point do you go back to your normal lives?'

Lucie just let them speak while she sat there feeling overwhelmed. That trip to Rome had done her so much good in the early stages of this whole debacle, but then Brett had that outburst in Monaco and she immediately dropped everything to be by his side.

Every waking minute was consumed by worry for his mental state, and she had allowed the lines to blur, which was making everything more confusing for *her*. He might be okay with keeping it casual, but Lucie wasn't. She needed space.

Desperate to change the subject, she ignored her parents' firing line. 'Do Julien and Jasper have somewhere to sleep tonight?' They were supposed to have got a hotel in town, but everything had been so rushed and chaotic in the end that she doubted they'd pulled it off.

'Yes. Here. We figured Jasper could take your room, Julien could take the spare and you could just share a room with Brett, since you do that every night anyway.' Mateo held her gaze before smirking. 'You think we didn't know? Lucie, sweetheart, you two couldn't be more obvious if you tried. There are fireworks any time you're in the same room.'

'Dad!' She went beet red.

'Mateo, stop embarrassing her.' Rosa bit her lip, trying not to smile too widely. 'Are you two just, you know, enjoying yourselves? Or is it something more?'

'Now who's embarrassing her?' Mateo retaliated.

'I don't really know what to say, to be honest. He's just . . . it's Brett.' Lucie shrugged.

That wouldn't provide much of an explanation to anyone, but to her parents, who knew them *both* like the backs of their hands, it was all she needed to say.

Lucie and Brett lay in bed that night to the soundtrack of Jasper's snores. They were violent, to say the least. At multiple points, she had debated going in there and suffocating him to get him to stop, but he was still her boss. It wasn't appropriate. In the end, they had decided to turn the TV on to drown him out.

'I can't believe you guys did all that for me,' Brett murmured.

'It wasn't a big deal.' She shrugged one shoulder, the other crushed up against his side.

'Sunny, are you kidding?' He breathed out a laugh. 'My boss and my teammate just travelled from two separate countries to bring a very expensive piece of technology to an alcoholic ex-racing driver.'

She sat bolt upright. 'Don't ever call yourself an ex-racing driver.'

'Well –'

She shushed him by shoving her hand over his mouth. 'Nope! I don't want to hear it. Not until you retire.' She shuffled back down into her favourite spot in his arms, a position she was supposed to be avoiding amongst others, her head resting on his chest while he played with her hair.

'If I was racing a different championship, I could be retiring in . . .' he thought about it for a second, 'ten years? Maybe a few more if I was *really* good.'

'You *are* really good.'

'Yeah, in our championship. They're all different, Sunny,' he laughed, although not in a self-deprecating way. It was true, each championship required different styles of driving and different skillsets. Some drivers were the best in one championship, moved across to another and failed miserably.

'I suppose you're right. But you ended up in the best one, because we've got drivers in their fifties and sixties. I'll probably be booted out before you.'

'You're like Gabriel's adopted child. He would never replace you.'

'Gabriel won't be CEO forever, though. He'll leave one day, and whoever takes his position might want a bunch of teenagers running socials with the way content creation is going.'

Brett kissed the top of her head and she sighed with contentment. 'Can't imagine walking through that paddock without you. If your job's ever at risk, I'll hire you as my personal assistant. You can, like, I don't know, hold my sunglasses and reply to my emails.'

Since the start of their careers, they'd had each other. At the end of every bad day, every good day and everything in between. The only time in ten whole years Lucie and Brett had considered a life where they weren't attached at the hip was when Sienna was in the picture.

To her, a life without Brett was the most terrifying thing in the world. It was the driving force behind her bringing him out here to Tuscany in the first place. Having sex with him daily was never part of the plan, and she knew it couldn't become routine. Brett wasn't going to settle, and it wasn't fair to keep going the way they were going knowing this, and knowing she wanted more. She would end up resenting him, regretting this summer they were spending tangled in bedsheets, and their friendship would never be the same again.

It had to stop. They needed firm boundaries in place, and they needed to learn to stop living in each other's pockets. How was Lucie ever going to get the happy ever after she desired if she couldn't let him go?

28

Brett stood on the driveway, waving goodbye to Jasper, who had sent for a chauffeur to collect him from the farm and take him to the airport. Brett didn't know how he did it. The bloke was constantly travelling around the globe between races for meetings with sponsors, investors and Revolution Racing's team owners. At least when he wasn't travelling for a race, Brett was a free agent. Jasper never stopped.

He was on his way to Hong Kong right now, chartering the team's private jet to secure a new sponsor for the upcoming season. It was part of his grand plan to be able to run a second car. A plan nobody was supposed to know about yet, but Jasper had let it slip last night.

Julien hadn't been ready to go back to Belgium yet, despite Faith and Jasmine being there with Ford. He wanted to spend more time with Brett. They had a busy day ahead before they let themselves back into the office to play with their new toy.

'Are you off somewhere, Luce?' Julien helped Lucie wheel a bicycle out of the barn while Brett watched on.

'Yeah, I just want to go down to the market and get some fruit and veggies, do a bit of shopping.' She smiled appreciatively as he let her take the bike handle, then stretched up to hug Julien. Should Brett hug her too? He mentally scolded himself for having such a ridiculous thought. It would be weirder if he didn't scoop her up into his arms and squeeze her tight.

He wrapped his arms around her. 'Have a good morning, Sunny.' His voice sounded weird. Strained. He hoped he was the only one who noticed.

He was starting to fear they shouldn't have crossed the line. They weren't going to stay in this Tuscany bubble forever, and when they left it, they would go back to their old lives. But what if something changed? What if Brett changed?

'Don't cause too much havoc. And don't let my dad use the heaviest weights during his workout. He can't handle it,' she warned.

Mateo had joined Brett on *one* morning run last week and ended up sitting in the middle of a field, unable to run any further. They'd stayed there for half an hour while Mateo caught his breath and worked up the energy to walk back at a snail's pace. He was naturally lean, and he ate well. He also didn't have a racing car to drive, or intense g-force to contend with. He didn't need to work out every day.

'I am the king of chaos, Sunny,' Brett shrugged. 'But I'll try to behave.'

Julien snorted. 'King of chaos? Sounds like something a character from one of my wife's romance novels would say.' He laughed as they waved Lucie off.

'You know you don't have to say "my wife" every time you talk about her, right? Your wife is Faith. We work together. She's our best friend. We know who she is, ya doughnut.'

'I like saying it.' Julien scowled at him playfully.

'You've been married a while now, Jules.'

'It doesn't get old, Anderson. I would say you'll find out for yourself one day, but you'll be on your deathbed before you get the balls to propose to Luce.'

'What?' Brett snapped, Julien's comment igniting something inside him about a future with Lucie, one he wasn't sure would ever be his.

'What's going on, mate? Because that exchange just now was a bit on the tense side. I've never seen you awkward around Lucie. Not once in ten years.'

'I'm not too sure. It just is what it is. No label, no conversation.' Brett swallowed roughly, looking around in a desperate attempt to find something else to talk about. 'Let's go sort that barn roof out, eh? Should be done mid-afternoon, then you can help me cook dinner for Rosa and Mateo. I'm doing paella.'

Brett and Julien sat on the roof two hours later, each drinking a bottle of water at an alarming speed. It was boiling out there, and although he was Australian and he was used to the heat, he didn't spend any time outside doing manual labour. This was hell.

They'd refused to let Mateo help, because it didn't seem fair to expect a guy in his sixties to climb ladders and fix a dodgy roof when there were two more than capable athletes here to help him out. Instead, he was sunbathing by the pool with fresh homemade lemonade and a fruit platter while Rosa lay next to him, sipping her iced tea and reading a crime thriller Brett had recommended to her.

'Do you still miss your dad?' Brett blurted out and instantly regretted it. Now Julien was going to want to talk about Jack, when Brett had simply wanted an answer to a question that had been on his mind for weeks.

'All the time. And Kailani.' He referred to his late wife. 'But I know they're here with me in every decision I make, everything I accomplish. I'm not religious at all, I just find that believing in that idea makes it easier to cope with the loss.'

Brett sipped the remainder of his water, contemplating, the sun beating down on his face, causing him to squint as he looked up at the blue, cloudless sky. 'Yeah, it's a nice idea, isn't it? That they never really left us.'

'Well, the people we love are a huge part of who we are. They shape us and help us grow when they're here physically, so why can't they do the same when they're gone?' Julien shrugged, as if it was the most obvious thing in the world.

'I'm lucky to have Mateo, I think,' Brett muttered. 'I got pretty upset a few weeks back that I was replacing Dad with him, but spending time with him one-on-one I've just come to appreciate him in such a different light.'

'You know what I appreciate about Mr Carolan? His killer classic car collection.' Julien gestured out over the courtyard, where a few of the cars were parked, sunlight gleaming off the paintwork. 'I'm definitely having a proper collection of my own when I retire.'

'It's impressive, I'll give him that.'

'I thought about getting Jasmine a classic for when she starts driving, but then I think I should be a sensible parent and get her something super safe. Like a Ford. The car is just as reliable as her pet husky.'

'Moretz, come on, mate. The kid's dad is a racing driver. She'd never forgive you if you didn't get her something kind of cool. At least get her a G-Wagon or a new Jeep. Isn't that what all the kids on Oahu are driving?'

He scoffed. 'The rich kids, yeah.'

'And she is . . .'

'Raised to be very down to Earth. She already gets to fly all over the world to attend races, I don't want to push it too far.'

'She also doesn't ask for anything. Ever. I told her to text me a Christmas list last year and she asked me to donate to an animal shelter on Maui. She's a good kid, Jules. One expensive gift isn't going to turn her into a spoiled brat.'

'When are you going to tell Luce you're in love with her?' Julien fired back. He hated it when Brett had valid points, especially when it came to Jasmine. His standard response was to call the other person out. But this time, Brett stared at him like he'd lost his mind.

'I don't know what you're talking about.' Brett's cheeks flushed and he, unfortunately for his dignity, couldn't blame it on the scorching temperature.

'I don't understand it, Anderson.'

Brett finished up his bottle of water and started

climbing down the ladder. If Julien didn't stop talking, he might push him off the roof. 'I still don't know what you're talking about.'

Julien followed him down. 'It's been over two years and I still don't know how it took me months to come to my senses with Faith. One look and I was a goner. You and Lucie are going on ten *years* of stolen glances and chemistry, and now you're sleeping together, and you still won't admit it.'

It felt like the world was closing in on him. Thinking back to his first private interaction with Lucie, on the steps outside his trailer, mid-anxiety attack, Brett came to the hideous conclusion that his teammate might have hit the nail on the head. Unleashed years' worth of pent-up emotion with one sentence.

Maybe it wasn't one look that did it for him. But he couldn't deny that when she'd sat down next to him and pressed play on that song, he'd felt something wash over him. A sense of comfort, belonging. Perhaps, all this time, it had been something else.

Brett hadn't been in love with Sienna. He'd been in love with the idea of her. With Lucie, there was no hidden part of her. He knew her as well as he knew himself, and he wouldn't change one single thing about her. She was perfect as she was. Now and back then.

It was just Brett who was flawed. Brett who had built himself a reputation. Brett who had scarred her with his own troubles, who had been relying on her to pick up the pieces and put him back together again. He hadn't treated her right. He'd been selfish and demanding, he took too much from her without knowing what she needed him to give back. What if his own demons brought Lucie down with him? He didn't need to do that to his ray of sunshine, she didn't deserve the constant worry that was attached to him.

'I'm screwed,' Brett breathed out.

Julien rolled his eyes. 'Of course you're not.' He sat down next to Brett on the dusty ground, neither of them caring about the state their clothes would be in. 'Can I give you some advice, Anderson?'

'Whether I want your advice or not, it never seems to stop you.' Brett tried to laugh so it didn't come out as blunt, but he couldn't manage it.

'I know I don't really talk about Kailani any more, but I'm going to because you need to hear it. I wish I'd told her I loved her more often. I was so focused on my career, on getting into the IEC and securing a drive, that I let our relationship take a back seat. We weren't in a good place when she passed, and I regret it every day. I loved her fiercely, and I felt it in every fibre of my being, I just didn't express it. I often wonder if she spent her final days thinking that I didn't love her, because honestly, I don't think I said it aloud once in the six months before she passed.' Julien shifted uncomfortably, hating emotional talks as much as Brett did. 'I'm a strong believer in saying how you feel. Faith had to really force that side of me to come out, but it did. I can get behind the wheel every race safe in the knowledge that if something were to happen, my wife and daughter know I love them.'

'Okay, but Sunny and I aren't in a relationship.' Brett played with his shoelace, like a child being told off. Julien was in dad mode again.

'You even call her Sunny. You have a nickname for her *nobody* else uses.' Julien laughed at his naïvety. 'Whether you like it or not, from the moment you crossed the line on that hiking trip, things shifted and you two went to a point of no return. Your friendship became more, you were acknowledging that there's something between you. De Luca and I sure as hell never felt that kind of connection with her.'

'Well, no, that's because Marco is scared of women.' Brett breathed a laugh at their teammate's misfortune. 'But I don't know if Lucie will ever trust that I won't hurt her. I've always done what I want, when I want.'

'There is always a period of change and learning when you enter into a relationship, though. It took Faith and me a while to adapt to each other's lifestyles. What exactly will change between you if you tell her how you feel?' Julien challenged.

'She'll realise that life is so much bigger than just being with me.'

29

Brett was stressed. He'd stayed up nearly all night on the racing simulator, refusing to go to bed when Julien had come in at two a.m. and tried to convince him. He needed a therapy session, so he had woken up and immediately contacted his therapist, who had booked him in before Rosa could even get breakfast on the table.

He was starting to love therapy, starting to love the man he was becoming. But what he hadn't told his therapist was the fact he was sleeping with his best friend. Correction: he was making love to his best friend. Because he was in love with her.

'So why do you think you might have kept that a secret? We're honest and open with each other, right?' his therapist, Liz, asked.

'I wasn't ready to talk about it,' he admitted. 'Not only that, but I didn't want to admit to myself that I was falling for someone I can't have.'

'And why can't you have her? Who says you can't?'

'Well . . . nobody, really. Just common sense. History.'

'History?' Liz quizzed, but her facial expression remained neutral.

'My history. I sleep with women like it's a hobby. Lucie doesn't want a guy like that. She's been with guys like that in the past and they've only ever hurt her.'

'Are you still that guy, though? Because having had the pleasure of getting to know you over the last couple of months, I think you have evolved into someone very different. And who's to say you're going to hurt her?'

'Again . . . history.' He rubbed his eyes, wishing he'd saved this for later in the day.

'But that's just it, Brett. It's history. It's not the present, and it doesn't have to be the future. You've been hurt, too. Do you think Lucie is anything like Sienna?'

'No way.' He shook his head.

'Exactly. So I think you've got to give yourself a bit more credit here. The two of you have a very special relationship, and if you've crossed that boundary multiple times then I think it's safe to say there could be more to it. There's no harm in just having the conversation with her. If you're as close as you say, even if she doesn't feel the same way about you, things will likely go back to the way they were before with time, if not immediately. Either way, at least you'll have told your truth.'

'I guess it's just a case of working up the courage.' He tried to push down the fear, but ultimately he knew Liz was right. It was time to talk to Lucie.

'I want you to do something for me. I want you to write letters to your dad, Sienna and Lucie. If you wanted to, you could even read your letter to Lucie aloud. But afterwards, I want you to burn them. Get out everything you need to say, the hurt, anger, guilt and grief. Then let it all go. Can you do that?'

'I'm going to go and do it right now before everyone

wakes up,' he nodded with a hint of enthusiasm. This was good for him. It was a necessary step.

He shut his laptop down and hunted for a pen and paper, ready to pour his heart out to the two people who had broken him, and the one who had put him back together again. He had been giving his past so much power over him, over every decision he made. He'd used it as an excuse time and time again. There had been no personal growth for years, he had just let things pile up until he had become a person he couldn't stand.

This summer, this trip, had changed him. He was ready for his next chapter, and as his pain flowed out onto the page, he could feel a weight lifting from his shoulders. He sat there for two hours, bypassing breakfast and his morning workout, and by the time he finally put down the pen, he'd made a decision. It was time.

'Sunny?' He found Lucie down by the wild horses, feeding them apples from Rosa's garden. She looked radiant in the mid-morning sun, wearing a lime-green dress, her hair in a claw clip and a soft smile on her face as one of the horses nuzzled her hand.

'Oh, morning!' She turned to look at him. 'You're finally awake.'

'I've been awake for hours. I did a therapy session.' He shoved his hands in his pockets.

'How did it go?' She tucked a strand of loose hair behind her ear, now only half-paying attention to the horse. 'Productive?'

'You could say that.'

'I'm really proud of you, Anderson. I mean it.'

'That means the world coming from you, Luce.'

'You want to do something fun today? Go on an adventure somewhere?'

'I, uh . . . maybe,' he stuttered. 'You might not want to.'

'Are you okay?' she frowned, and the reality of what he was about to do dawned on him.

'I love you, Sunny.'

'I know you do. You tell me all the time. And I love you too, Anderson.' She still looked confused, and it pained him more that she wasn't getting it.

'No, Sunny. I'm *in* love with you. I have been in love with you for years now, I was just too blind to realise it and then too scared to tell you.'

'Shit.' She let out a shaky breath and he instantly felt ten times more nauseous than he had since he'd started walking down the hill towards her.

'Right, uh, not the reaction I expected.' He tried to laugh it off.

'Sorry, I just . . . um, I don't really know what to say. You've not exactly exhibited the behaviour of a guy who's in love. What with all the other women and such. And going back to Sienna that time. I'm not sure you actually feel the way you think you do, Brett.'

'Okay. So, that's it then? Cool. Um, I'm gonna get out of your hair.'

'Anderson, please. I didn't mean . . .'

'No, it's fine, Luce. I've done this to myself.'

Brett didn't have it in him to argue. He didn't have it

in him to fight. He'd spent all summer fighting his feelings, his past, his mental health. The fight for Lucie was over. She didn't want him, and he wasn't going to beg her to see him in a different light.

He was already packing his suitcase by the time she reached his bedroom. Their bedroom. The space they'd shared since they'd arrived, her things tossed everywhere. Her bracelet was on his dresser, her sports bra flung over the back of the chair, her hairbrush in his bathroom. Their lives were integrated too deeply, and it was about time he drew a line down the middle. Lucie had made her choice. It was never going to be him.

'Brett?' She stood in the doorway trembling. *Fuck.* He wished he didn't love her so much. So deeply, in so many ways.

He went to her, closing the distance and wrapping her up in a hug so tight it was almost a guarantee that it would be their last. At least for a while. Until they'd had some space and learned to live without each other. 'I need to go back to Sydney.'

'What?!' She pulled back. 'Please, don't go.'

'Lucie, we need to put some distance between us.'

'I don't understand where this is coming from,' she sniffled. 'This whole thing between us was just you using me, wasn't it?'

'Lucie, I never needed you. Not like this. I *wanted* you. That's why I crossed the line, why I risked it all. You're my best friend, Sunny. It was about *you.*'

'So, you weren't using my body as a form of therapy?' She looked up at him with her doe eyes and his heart broke into a million little pieces. How could he let her think that? He was fucked. His reputation was fucked.

'No, Sunny. Absolutely not. Fuck, you're the last person who should be helping me. The guilt of what I've put you through has been eating me alive. You know how hard it is to realise I've hit rock bottom in front of the girl I've been in love with for ten years? I've lost your trust, whether you can admit that to me or not, and I know that despite how much you want to, you'll never see me as someone you can love with your whole heart. I've ruined it, Luce.'

'No, you haven't, this is all my fault, Brett, please,' she pleaded.

'You and I are never going to get any further than this weird limbo we've been in the whole summer. I've got to move on and remember how to be Brett without Lucie.'

'But there's no me without *you*, Brett.'

'That's the whole problem, Sunny. I don't want to go, but I have to. For me, for you, for us.' He watched as her face crumpled.

There was no hiding from it. She wasn't ready to acknowledge the shift in their relationship. She couldn't trust that Brett could keep himself on track and be hers and only hers.

He threw a last couple of things into his case, not caring if he left anything behind. He just needed to get out of here and get on a plane, no matter how much his heart was telling him to stay here with her.

'Brett, you can't do this. We need to figure this out,' she sobbed. 'What about work?'

He took a deep breath, gripping the handle of his suitcase roughly. He didn't want to say the next sentence, but he meant it. With every fibre of his being, he knew this was the truth. 'If moving on from this means driving for a different championship, then so be it.'

30

Lucie was crushed. She was at Bea's apartment in Paris, lounging on the sofa where she'd been for a week straight. The shower was a battle she had yet to face, she'd only changed her pyjamas because Bea told her she was making her perfectly designed interior look shabby, and she had lived off microwave noodles because every time Bea offered her something nutritional for dinner, she wasn't hungry.

Bea had labelled her apartment an 'anti-male zone', which meant even Marco had been banned from visiting. He had just wanted to cheer up his friend and take her mind off things, but woman to woman, Bea could see how much she needed to wallow in self-pity. She had presented her with an open-ended invite, but Lucie knew if she didn't at least try to leave the house in the next few days, she was at risk of overstaying her welcome.

The windows had been opened wide every morning, white tulle curtains flapping in the breeze, but she hadn't had the will to go and stand on the balcony and soak it all in. She loved this city, and she should be appreciating being here without work commitments, but she loved Brett more. She didn't want to be here without him. She wanted to be in Sydney, roller-skating down the promenade without a care in the world.

'Can you respond to some emails for Girls Off Track today? I've got some photos to edit, and I need to do a food shop.' Bea sat down amongst the nest of blankets and turned the TV on.

'Doesn't look like you're that busy,' Lucie scowled, but only because she knew what Bea was doing. She was tricking her. Lucie would never say no to work. No matter how she was feeling, that was something she could always crack on with. Basic human functions? Not doable. Huge work projects, meetings, emails and content edits? Not a problem.

'I like background noise. Come on, there are only six sitting in the inbox. You'll get through them in no time, then I'll give you control of all my streaming platforms.'

'Fine.' She pretended she didn't want to do it, because she didn't want to give Bea the satisfaction of knowing her plan was working.

'Cool. Tomorrow, you can come out and shoot content with me,' Bea grinned.

'What content?' Lucie sighed. Yes, Bea was letting her take it one day at a time, but when she'd been doing nothing for the last six, being forced to commit to something two days in a row felt like a lot. Then again, Lucie didn't *want* to wallow.

She needed to figure out how to move on, but she wanted Brett back. She couldn't have the latter, so her only option was to get over it, get over him. It might take another ten years, but it would happen eventually.

He hadn't texted her, hadn't posted on social media, he hadn't even reached out to his teammates. It was an alien concept for her, not knowing where he was or what he was doing. Had he even gone back to Sydney? Maggie had texted Lucie asking how Brett was doing, which meant his family didn't know he'd left Tuscany. That worried her more than anything. Something like this could tempt him to drink again, and she hated that she could be the cause of a relapse. He'd done so well, and he'd made so much progress.

In the mental state he was in, still trying to overcome his addiction, heal his trauma and secure his return to the team next season, he was never going to look past this. She should've told him she felt the same. Should've just given it a shot.

Hell, he was willing to leave the IEC over this. That's how deeply hurt he was. She had always known she would end up with her heart broken the very first time they slept together in the Alps, but never in a million years did she think Brett would go down with her.

They had been spiralling for two years. The year Faith had joined the organisation, Lucie had seen her relationship with Julien unfold, and she had started to realise that she wanted some of that in her life. She had let Brett up the flirting, started flirting back, and within a couple of months their rendezvous in the Alps had happened and the journey to heartbreak began.

'Luce . . .' Bea was staring at her phone in her hand, white as a ghost. 'You might want to check your news app.'

'Huh?' she mumbled, not really registering Bea's words. She'd had her inbox open in front of her for the last few minutes, untouched, while she'd been mentally tearing herself apart.

'Or search Brett's name, something.' Bea was still reading, and at the mention of his name, something clicked in Lucie's brain.

She scrambled to her internet app and typed in 'Brett Anderson IEC', feeling sick to her stomach while she waited for the results to load. At the very top of the screen, there were a series of headlines. Each of them depicting his drinking problem. His rapidly declining mental health. Some were more brutal than others, but she clicked on one of the worst. The journalist acted like he'd been drink-driving during races, as if the organisation would ever allow that to happen. They had drug testing and breathalysers. There wasn't a chance. Where was *that* in the article?

PR should have been on this. Brett wouldn't have wanted it to get out without an action plan on how to tackle it, which meant either someone within the IEC had broken their NDA and were about to lose their job, or it was someone who had a personal vendetta against him. But it didn't matter who had leaked it, all that mattered was that his secret was out.

'Shit.' Lucie bit her lip, in full panic mode.

'You told Jasper you're not with him any more, right?'

'I did. He made it clear Brett wasn't my responsibility anyway, but I didn't tell him we'd fallen out. He has no idea there's already a risk of him going off the rails, even without this.'

'Do you think you should give him a call? Call it work,

if you want, but . . . you know. You guys at Revolution are a family.'

Lucie scrolled through her contacts until she found Jasper and then hit the call button, suddenly up and alert and pacing the room, her hand dragging through her hair. This was one way to get her out of her cocoon of depression.

'I've seen it, don't worry, PR are on the case.' Jasper didn't sound stressed in the slightest. That was what made him a great team principal; he was calm, level-headed.

'Have you spoken to him?' she asked.

'Yes, an hour ago. He's fine. We're working on a statement which will make it abundantly clear Brett never put himself or anyone else at risk. The drinking was all in his own time, which I have made sure of myself through a lot of in-depth talks with him the last few months.'

Lucie finally stopped pacing and sat on a bar stool. 'Are sponsors freaking out?'

'Yes, but my team are reaching out to them all, explaining all the details.'

'Jasper, what's the plan of attack here? Are we going to be open with the public? Do Faith and I stay silent on social media?'

'Brett wants to be honest. The organisation wants him to be honest. As for Revolution, we'll be standing our ground, supporting him publicly. He still has a spot on the team, Lucie, I meant it when I told him he was welcome back if he stays sober. I've been on the phone non-stop since the story broke. A couple of our big sponsors are happy to weather the storm with us, which is a huge relief. We've worked hard to build connections, and they know Brett well. They've seen his performance and behaviour during race weeks, and they're trusting us and him with our approach to this. They agree that every driver has personal issues away from the sport, and if we handle it well, the damage will be minimal. For now, I want you to keep quiet on socials. Just let the initial reactions wash over.'

Lucie nodded then realised her boss couldn't see her. 'He always said he wanted to be open about it one day, we just didn't expect to lose control of when that happened.'

'I imagine he's feeling quite vulnerable right now. He may be telling me he's okay, but I'm worried. I wonder if someone should go out to Australia and see him. I think I could convince Marco to abandon what he's doing and go, right?' Jasper pondered.

'I, uh . . .' Lucie thought about it for a second, deciding whether she wanted to do what she was about to suggest. Screw it. 'There are some things I need to say to him. I'll go.'

She could practically hear him narrow his eyes. 'Has something happened?'

'We, um, yes? I kind of let him tell me how he feels, and then I just . . . let him go.'

'Lucie!' Jasper gasped. 'He finally told you?'

'What do you mean *finally*? What do you know?'

'You two have been in love for years. I've seen it with my own eyes.'

'Has he told you that?' Lucie flushed.

'No, no. I just knew. You two have something very special, I've been waiting for you to both come to your senses.'

'Hm. Anyway, I'm going to go to Sydney. Today. Well, I'll get there tomorrow. Keep me posted on team business though, please. I know it's nothing to do with me, but Brett . . .'

'Is everything to do with you. You've got it, Carolan. I'll transfer you the cost of the flights. Go take care of our boy.'

Lucie hung up the phone and placed it on the counter, only now looking at Bea's amused expression. 'Did your boss just give you dating advice?'

'I believe he did.'

'Better get you packed!'

Lucie landed at Sydney airport, still very unsure of herself and what she was about to do, or say, to Brett. She'd watched him with countless other girls, hiding the way she felt. If he understood how much that had hurt her, he would understand her hesitation. She needed to explain her side, that she was so scared to let him in all the way, let him know that she loved him too.

It was ten o'clock by the time she got to Brett's apartment, but she'd rung the buzzer eight times until security had informed her he'd been gone all afternoon and evening. Unsure of where to start looking, and being too afraid to call him because she wouldn't know what to say until she saw his face, she headed over to his family home.

'Luce?' Piper answered the door in her pyjamas. 'He's not here.'

'Oh. You've spoken to him, then?' Lucie stared at her feet, unable to look at his twin without feeling immensely guilty for the pain she'd caused him.

'Yeah, he came by for dinner. Surprised us, then told us he'd fucked up.'

'*He* didn't fuck up.'

Piper rolled her eyes. 'You're both ridiculous.'

'Um, do you know where he is?'

'I can track him!' Cleo came running down the hall. 'I told him if he wasn't going to stay with you, so you could keep an eye on him, then he had to download this app. He agreed.'

That made Lucie feel better. If he was going to run riot across the city and drink, he probably wouldn't have let his sisters monitor his every move. 'Can you have a look, please, Cleo? He's not at home.'

'Um . . .' she grimaced. 'Says he's at a club.'

Piper threw her arms up. 'Well, what was the fucking point in you having that app if you don't check it regularly? Come on, Lucie, we're going down there.'

'You might want to change . . .' She looked Piper up and down.

'Don't people wear nightdresses out these days? It's silky, it's leopard print. Cleo, let me borrow your Dr Martens.' Piper held her hand out impatiently while her sister scrambled to find the boots, throwing them at her one at a time as she dug through the cupboard under the stairs.

'Okay, all set?' Lucie asked.

'Cleo, text me the address. I'm taking Mum's car, I'm almost out of petrol. Don't tell her. Or do, I don't really care.' Piper shrugged, keys already in her hand as she herded Lucie back down the garden path.

'Pipes. If he's sober, you're about to witness a grand declaration of love. I know it makes you sick, so if you want to stay outside . . .'

'And what if he's not sober, Lucie?' Piper challenged. 'I'm coming in.'

'Okay. Thank you,' she mumbled, startled when Piper squeezed her arm in reassurance. She was scared for what they were about to find, but knowing that she didn't have to do it alone helped.

'I don't think he's going to be drunk, Luce. I really don't. He went to a bar before, right? Last time you were here, to meet Sienna? He didn't drink then.'

'Yes, but then he got drunk at that event in Monaco, so . . .'

'Doesn't mean anything. He's been around alcohol all summer and he's been fine.'

'But now he's heartbroken.'

'He's also hanging out with his friend Felix tonight. He told us they were watching a film at the cinema, but I guess they've made other plans.'

'Oh. Does this Felix guy know?'

'He went and spoke to him yesterday. He wouldn't let him drink; if he even attempted it, Felix would get him home. Trust me, I know him. He loves my brother as much as we do.'

'What if he's not with Felix?'

'He is.' She gestured at her phone where a text from Felix had just popped up. It read 'Cleo texted me. We're at Vision with the boys. None of us are drinking.'

'Okay, so we don't need to panic.'

'You sure you still want to go? Confess your feelings?' Piper wrinkled her nose in disgust.

'Yep.' Lucie took a deep breath as they turned down the street where the club was located, thankful there was barely a queue. It was a Tuesday night, not exactly the best night for clubbing. Although it was Sydney, full of tourists who wanted to have a night out in Australia's most popular city.

With the car abandoned on the side of the street, the girls hurried to get through security. One glance at Piper's outfit and they smirked, knowing full well that she had thrown her outfit together last minute. Her fluffy socks were peeking out above her boots.

'In you go, ladies. Have a good night.'

'Thank you!' they called out and rushed past the people taking their sweet time, blocking the way to the main room of the club.

With no luck by the first bar, Piper grabbed Lucie by the hand and dragged her through the crowds towards the dance floor. They spotted Felix first, who looked like he'd seen a ghost. But he'd known they were coming. He had told them where they were, so why did he look so surprised? And then Lucie saw him. Them. Brett was in the middle of the dance floor, his tongue down Sienna's throat.

'Fuck,' Piper bit out, tightening her grip on Lucie's hand. One of Brett's friends gave him a shove and Brett pulled away, angering Sienna, who stormed off the dance floor alone.

'Sunny –'

Lucie didn't give him a chance. She was out of there like a shot. Not that she wanted him to relapse, but she couldn't help but wonder if that would have hurt less than seeing him kissing her. Avoiding one girl who had hurt him to run right into the arms of the other. She couldn't tell him how she felt now. She was embarrassed. He might love Lucie, he might be hurt, but he still wasn't over Sienna. He could have chosen *anyone* else.

Sitting down on the pavement, Piper having stayed behind to berate him and Felix and double-check he was drinking soft drinks, Lucie sobbed. There was a growing queue of people now, but she didn't care. She shouldn't have come. She should have let him get things out of his system, given him more time. He had Felix and his family. He didn't need her. Marco could've come, but she'd been too impatient, too focused on what she wanted to say without questioning whether now was the time for Brett to hear it. If he had forgiven her, if he was ready to, wouldn't he have come to her?

'Faith?' Lucie sniffled into the phone.

'Luce? What's happened?'

'Can I come stay with you and Jules in Malmedy?'

Bea's sofa had been replaced with Faith and Julien's. Realising that Lucie was here to stay, Julien was in the process of transforming the office into a guest room so they could have their living room back. They had insisted that she wasn't going back to Italy where she had so many fresh memories of Brett, and she didn't really know where else to go.

Lucie had turned their expensive leather couch into her new and improved depression pit, this time enjoying views of lush, green fields instead of the busy streets of Paris. In her first week here, Jules had gone out and got all her favourite snacks and ingredients to cook her comfort meals, quickly hiding the pistachio cookies when Lucie had burst into tears at the sight of them.

Three months in, and she was finding her feet. She'd been on daily walks and bike rides, regularly had lunch near the waterfalls in Coo, held video meetings poolside. She loved being able to explore Malmedy like it was home and forget that there was hell coming. They had crossed the Silverstone race off their list, and Fuji, and Shanghai.

Girls Off Track had skyrocketed. Their partnership with the Formula Voltz team had been secured, and Jasper had the go-ahead for a second car and was allowing them to advertise the academy and the podcast on its livery next season, for no cost. Everything in Lucie's life was going great, except for her relationship with Brett.

She would be so lost without her friends. Her team. But even as they'd rallied around her, she wondered what the future of this friendship circle would look like. She and Brett had made things monumentally awkward for them, but none of them were going to let him leave Revolution Racing and drive for a different team, or leave the IEC. Lucie wasn't going to be forced to find new friends either, but it was going to be a long time before she and Brett could be in the same room comfortably.

'Your bed is coming today. Tracking just got updated,' Julien shouted across the room from the kitchen. 'Want to help me put it together?'

'Sure. Bet you're itching to get your sofa back, huh?'

'At least you've actually moved from this one,' Julien smirked.

'I was on Bea's for a *week*, Jules. I was hardly going to lay motionless on your sofa and cry for months on end, was I?' She rolled her eyes. 'Also, you chose to buy a stupidly overpriced bed which took eight weeks to arrive and wouldn't let me sleep on the office floor.'

'Only the highest quality for you, Luce,' Julien grinned, biting into an apple as Faith walked in.

'She told you she was happy with an IKEA bed, Jules. You just have expensive taste in furniture.' Faith raised an eyebrow, gesturing around the room. It was immaculate, and he hadn't even hired an interior designer. He hadn't needed to change a thing when they'd started dating and Faith had moved in.

'I'm wearing jeans from a supermarket,' Julien frowned.

'Twenty-euro jeans versus a six-thousand-euro bed frame . . . it's all about balance, huh?'

Julien scoffed and took one of Lucie's favourite chocolate bars out of the cupboard along with a bag of Faith's favourite crisps, backing out of the room. 'I'm going to lay out by the pool and eat these. They're the last of each. Serves you two right for picking on me.'

'It's freezing out there!' Faith yelled as he reached the back door.

'I'm a racing driver, I'm fearless!' he yelled back.

Faith shook her head in amusement. 'He's so embarrassing. Now Jasmine is older, it's like he's made it his mission to crack out every dad joke in the book and make a fool of himself at every given opportunity.'

'He's completely transformed over the last couple of years. I think he just feels more comfortable with where he's at in life, now he has no secrets. You and Jasmine bring out the best in him, make him feel more like himself.'

'Mmhmm,' she murmured, focused on cutting sandwiches for Jasmine, who was upstairs with her tutor. 'It's good to have someone like that.'

Lucie glared her down, half-joking, half-wishing everyone would just shut up trying to convince her to reach out to him. Brett hadn't contacted her. He didn't care. That much had been clear when he hadn't followed her out of the club. 'You got lucky.'

'Love is a choice, Luce. It's not all about luck.'

'Faith.'

'Lucie.'

'He made his choice.'

'Well . . .'

'He did! He kissed her. He fled the country and went straight into the arms of the first woman who broke him.'

'Oh my God. Lucie!' Faith threw her arms out. 'He doesn't know you're in love with him because you let him go without telling him! How can you be mad about it? You two need to sit down and talk this out. Soon.'

Lucie crossed her arms like a petulant child, but only because she knew her best friend was right. 'Well, it won't be next week. That's a work event.'

'A work event where you have to *work* together. You have to film with him, Luce,' she sighed like a disapproving parent.

'You can do the filming,' Lucie suggested. It was the perfect solution. Faith could film and Lucie could sweet-talk sponsors and edit the content.

Faith tutted disapprovingly. 'You're a big girl.'

'A broken-hearted big girl.' She tried to copy the puppy-dog eyes that Marco did when he wanted them to use his ideas for videos.

'Fine, but you must promise me you'll speak to him before Christmas.' Faith pointed at her menacingly. 'It's almost December already, you'd better get it together ASAP. You can't be miserable at Christmas; I won't allow it.'

*

Lucie had known about this event since way before she and Brett had gone their separate ways. It was an annual Christmas fundraiser for the IEC, where all the teams got together and invited their sponsors and partners of the organisation to raise money for charity. She loved it. There was no content schedule although Revolution Racing and the IEC both expected photos and videos to be posted, so it was an opportunity to mingle and enjoy being part of the motorsport world.

But this year would be different. She knew Brett was coming, it was his big test. His welcome back to team duties after months and months away. Marco had come and found her in the hotel and told her his flight had landed, and then he'd sat awkwardly on the edge of the bed while she'd held in her tears and tried not to cry her makeup off.

Tonight was the first time she would have any inter-action with Brett since she saw him in Sydney. She'd spent weeks going back and forth with the idea of reaching out to smooth things over, but it wasn't a conversation to be had over text. She had muted him on social media, so she no longer had to see what he was doing every time she opened the app, but prior to doing that a month ago, she knew he'd just been hanging out with his family every day. There had been no sightings of Sienna, although she couldn't imagine he would want to make that public.

Marco tapped on the bathroom door. 'Lucie? You ready?' he called through.

Having a date to this event wasn't a thing, especially

not for IEC staff, but her team didn't want her walking in alone. Julien and Faith would be arm in arm, and Marco wasn't about to let Lucie go solo and come face to face with Brett without emotional support. Besides, Brett would probably walk in with Elliot from Havelin Racing or Lucas from Talos Sport, all of them, including him, oblivious to the war raging inside her.

'I feel sick, Mars,' Lucie murmured, as he led her to the stairs. The fundraiser was being held in the ballroom of a hotel by Lake Geneva, and it was by far the most beautiful venue she'd ever visited for work.

She should be feeling confident. Her makeup had been salvaged and looked as flawless as it had earlier this afternoon, her hair was in loose waves, and she wore a deep red satin ballgown which accentuated her figure perfectly. Highlighted those curves a certain someone adored. If she homed in on the way her friends had gasped and spun her round, she did feel confident. But it was all torn down the second Brett came to mind.

'Anderson incoming in four, three, two . . .' Marco warned, but no amount of time could have prepared her. Not the months of no contact she'd had, holed up in Belgium. Not the seconds it took them to reach the bottom of the stairs, where Brett stood waiting.

He looked good. Healthy. And Lucie's heart shattered for the millionth time. He didn't need her any more, and while that should be a good thing, it made her feel worse. She wanted him to need her, and it wasn't because of her ego. The look he gave her was no longer one of desire. It was pain. The look of someone who had once known all the right things to say to her, and now couldn't muster up a single word.

Marco simply nodded at him, an indication that they would talk later, and hurried Lucie towards the crowd. But as she took a step past him, the hem of her gown sweeping over his shoes, she was so in her own head, she almost missed it. His hand, brushing ever so slightly against hers. And when she glanced back at him and his brown eyes softened, she knew it had been deliberate.

'Thanks, Mars.' Lucie heaved a sigh of relief when they got to the bar.

'You'll get there.' Marco handed her a double rum and coke.

'Maybe.'

Now seated at the Revolution table waiting for their meal to be served, Lucie could feel his eyes on her. He was unrelenting, but every time she dared to glance in his direction, he looked away. It was awkward. They had never done awkward. They had worked so well as friends because conversation flowed, they could flirt and joke around without consequence, and after the hiking trip they had been able to brush it under the rug. This was new and abnormal, and she didn't know how to approach it. How to approach him. So she wouldn't.

'How's Belgium been treating you?' Brett spoke across the table so out of the blue that she hadn't realised he'd been talking to her. The first words out of his mouth in so long, and they weren't words of anger. It was a start.

'Um, yeah. Good, thanks.' Was that all she could

manage? 'How's Australia?' She didn't want the answer unless Sienna was excluded from the narrative.

'Decent. Been with the fam. Lots of smoothies and cordial.' He looked at his glass, drawing her attention to it. He'd ordered fruit juice, at a Michelin-star-catered five-course meal. It tugged at her heartstrings.

Lucie couldn't give him anything more than a smile as her first course was presented to her, and when she was faced with the food, her appetite vanished along with the strength she had mustered moments ago. She needed to get away from this table. Away from him.

She excused herself and walked as fast as she could to the restrooms in the hotel lobby, only relaxing when she was around the corner and could take a deep breath away from all the prying eyes.

Brett hated this. He just wanted to hold her in his arms and tell her how beautiful she looked, all the things he wanted to do to her. It just wasn't his place any more. Truthfully, it had never been his place. He'd always called her his Lucie, his sunshine girl, but she'd never been his. In his own heart, yes, but not really. He had walked away because she'd hurt him when she hadn't told him she felt the same, and now she seemed to be hurting twice as much as he ever had been. Surely that must mean part of her *did* feel something too?

If Sienna hadn't been at the club the night Lucie came looking for him, they might have stood a chance. He'd have forgiven her in a heartbeat, having realised he had no right to be hurt.

He so badly wanted to prove himself to her. To prove he was so far detached from the person she thought he was, the guy who slept with random women in restrooms and flirted with anyone and everyone. He hadn't been that Brett since the hiking trip. He didn't know why he'd kissed Sienna. She was there and Lucie wasn't. If Lucie had been, it would've been her. If she'd let him.

And now he doubted he would ever get the chance again. He'd been fighting his feelings all evening, desperate to tell her he missed her. Desperate to know if at least *that* feeling was mutual. He had managed a few sentences before she'd walked away, and he felt like an idiot. He should've gone after her. He just didn't know if he was ready. Or her for that matter.

Alcohol hadn't even been a temptation over the last few months. He'd found a genuine love for trying non-alcoholic versions of his favourite beers, and all the different flavoured soft drinks on offer. He didn't want it. He'd been working so hard, doing therapy once a week and doing all the exercises and workshops that had been suggested to him. His racing sim at his apartment had been waiting for him when he got home, updated and ready to go, and he'd thrown himself into it. He'd been rethinking his entire life plan, and he hadn't come up with anything that didn't include Lucie.

'How has she been?' he asked Julien, careful not to be so loud that anyone else heard them. Faith may be one of his closest friends, but he was pretty sure she'd chop off one of his favourite body parts given half the chance.

'Honestly? Pretty decent. She's taken herself off on

353

a few adventures around the area, thrown herself into work, as she does. The crying has died down in front of an audience, but I don't know what she's been like behind closed doors.'

'Do you think I could come and visit soon?' he asked.

Julien nodded, quite enthusiastically all things considered. 'Why don't you come for Christmas? Marco's coming and Lucie is still staying with us, it wouldn't feel right not to have you there.'

'I don't know . . .' He thought about it.

'Faith has it in her head that everything's going to work out, because Christmas is a magical time and all that crap.'

'I'm in,' Brett agreed, hoping he hadn't just committed to making yet another terrible mistake. 'And Jules? Your wife had better be right.'

'It's snowing!' Jasmine screeched from out by the pool, which Julien had reluctantly covered up because Ford kept jumping in. As a husky, he was used to the cold, but Faith and Lucie were tired of having to dry him off. 'Oh, it's so beautiful! I've never seen snow before.'

It was Christmas Eve and Lucie had been sucked into the Jensen-Moretz family traditions as if Julien and Faith were Mr and Mrs Claus themselves. She didn't dare disappear to her room for more than a few minutes of peace for fear of one of them dragging her out of bed like a scene from a horror film, forcing her to participate and find some Christmas spirit.

The truth was, she was struggling to find it within herself this year. She loved Christmas, curling up on the sofa with a blanket and a festive film, decorating the tree, baking tree-shaped cookies and then ruining them with a poor attempt at icing. It was her favourite time of the year, and she always spent it with Brett. He was her partner in crime, indulging in everything she wanted to do even if it meant watching *The Holiday* three days in a row.

She wished she could get excited about him coming to Belgium to spend it with them, but instead she was dreading it. Marco had been tracking Brett's whereabouts and updating her on every step of his journey, so she had plenty of time to prepare, and he'd promised to sit next to her during every meal, so she didn't have to get too close to him. God forbid she had to ask him to pass the mashed potato or cranberry sauce. But Lucie knew now was the time to talk it out. She wasn't going into the new year with this hanging over their heads.

Part of her wished she'd made plans to go back to Tuscany or Los Angeles and be with her family, but she was growing tired of fighting this. They had ten years of friendship behind them, this was surely just a blip. Whether they had feelings or not, their bond was supposed to be unbreakable. She couldn't lose him.

'Lucie, it's time!' Marco came hurtling down the stairs like it was Christmas morning and he'd been told Santa was coming down the chimney. 'He's here.'

Brett pulled up in a black Mercedes G-Wagon, because of *course* he would rent one of the most expensive cars he could find just to drive two hours from the airport. Lucie acted like she hadn't noticed his arrival, in case he looked through the window next to the front door. She didn't want to be caught staring. Or drooling. At him or the car. She made a conscious effort to turn her back and focus on pulling the cookies out of the oven, ignoring the timer and waiting a few extra seconds so she was visibly busy when he walked in.

'Hi, everyone.' At the sound of his voice, Lucie abandoned her plan and turned to him. He looked ten times more uncomfortable than she felt as he stood in the doorway holding three bunches of flowers. All winter

356

bouquets, with cream roses, eucalyptus, fir, cotton and pinecones. They looked exactly like one Lucie had saved to her inspiration board years ago.

'Hey.' She shot him a smile, hoping it would go some way towards dissolving some of the tension. The one he responded with made her feel all warm and fuzzy inside, and she knew it wasn't just Christmas spirit.

'Uncle B!' Jasmine came in from outside with a snowy Ford in tow, both tackling Brett, who was doing his best not to let the flowers get squashed.

'One of these is for you, Jazzy,' he held out a bouquet, 'and one is for Faith.'

Faith wiped her hands on a tea towel and walked towards him, pulling Ford's collar to stop him jumping up. 'Jules, control your dog, please.'

'He's *our* dog, Faith!' Julien took charge of him, nonetheless.

'Where are our flowers, Anderson?' Marco put his hands on his hips.

'Sorry, uh, Luce. These are for you.' He held out the last bouquet, creeping closer to the kitchen where Lucie had stayed rooted to the spot. She removed her oven gloves and rounded the centre island, all her strength diminished as she embraced the moment. She stood on her tiptoes and wrapped her arms around him, in a hug that was so needed, she could've sworn their entire world shifted.

'Thank you, Brett.' She spoke in a hushed tone, and it was only when she spoke that she felt him sigh under her touch before returning the hug, squeezing her tight.

'Get a room,' Julien scoffed. 'Ow! Faith!'

'It's just as well you got here when you did, Anderson.' Faith peered outside. 'The snow is getting heavier; the whole region might be on lockdown soon.'

Jasmine grinned and helped herself to a fresh-out-the-oven cookie. 'That means you all have to stay longer and hang out with your favourite niece.'

'Does it look like I'm going anywhere?' Lucie deadpanned.

'That's true. You're still going to be here when I go to college at this rate.'

'Okay, maybe that's too far.'

'Well, you could,' Julien shrugged. 'I'm building a guest house out the back next year, and I'll probably add an extension to the main house for when Faith and I have more babies.'

'You don't have any babies.' Jasmine rolled her eyes.

He ruffled his daughter's hair playfully which, judging by her dramatic reaction, was the wrong move. 'You'll always be my baby. Even though you're a giant now.'

'If you could have like, six more kids to take some attention off every little thing I do, that would be great. Please. I want siblings.'

'Well . . .' Faith cleared her throat. 'About that.'

'No. Effing. Way.' Jasmine's jaw dropped along with everyone else's. 'Are you really?!'

'Huh?' Marco looked confused.

Faith and Julien shared a smile before he nodded his head and motioned for his wife to speak. 'We're having twins. Due in June.'

'What?!' Lucie rushed to give her best friend a hug, the pair of them squealing and swaying side to side while Jasmine joined in, then Marco, then finally Brett and Julien completed it. 'The first Revolution Racing team babies!'

'This is amazing news, guys! Congratulations. Ford, you're going to be a big brother.' Brett crouched down to cuddle Ford, but all Lucie could focus on was how he looked like he was trying not to cry.

'Wait, what about work?' Marco asked.

'Jules is still going to race, and I'm not going anywhere. We're going to get a nanny and I think my mum might come out for a bit to help. Life doesn't have to stop.' Faith shrugged like it was simple. 'It's happened a little earlier than expected and we obviously weren't planning on twins, but you know, we have a lot of love to give.'

'And a lot of money, thank God, nannies are *so* expensive!'

'Rather you than me.' Marco's eyes went wide.

'Ford!' Brett yelled out as the dog started pulling on the zip of his suitcase. 'Leave. No. Ford, stop. Bad boy.' Ford was in a world of his own, the suitcase scooting around the floor on four wheels with him chasing it.

'Oi!' Julien shouted, and he stopped.

'Seriously? That works?' Lucie laughed.

'I'm going to take my things upstairs and out of the way.' Brett clung to his rescued case and carried it away.

'Which one of you is going to come and make snow angels with me?' Jasmine looked between Marco and her dad.

'Both of us.' Marco grabbed his coat from the banister and shoved Julien through the house. 'Suck it up, Moretz. You're going to spend the next eighteen years running round after two more of her, better start practising again.'

Lucie and Faith soaked in the silence for a moment once they were alone in the kitchen, but Lucie could feel her friend's eyes on her. 'Can I help you?'

'Go up there, Luce. You don't have to have *the* talk, but at least smooth things over. If you don't, you're going to have a long couple of days. It seemed like things were going okay just now.'

'Ugh, do I have to? I just . . . what do I say?'

'You say, "Hey, Brett. Just want to check that you and I are good. Let's have a nice Christmas with our friends." And then you say, "I am deeply in love with you and it's totally okay that you shoved your tongue down your ex's throat." Simple.'

'I am not saying any of that. Well, maybe the first part. Wait, where is he sleeping? There's only one guest room. Mine.' Lucie frowned.

'Yeah . . . about that. We put a blow-up mattress on the floor next to your bed. There's only space for Mars on the sofa. Mars and Brett can always swap, but you know, we thought we should at least try to force you into a conversation. It's our duty as friends and teammates.' Faith shrugged, and then proceeded to hum as she put their flowers in vases, going full florist-mode and ignoring Lucie's look of disgust.

'Snakes, the lot of you,' she sighed and all but stomped

her way up the stairs, seeking out Brett. She entered her bedroom, where she found him gawking at the mattress on the floor. 'I had the same reaction.'

'I can sleep in my car. Put the seats down,' he suggested, looking around like he hoped the ground would swallow him up any moment.

For some reason, that hurt. How had they got to this point? From sharing rooms and beds like it was nothing, to one of them preferring to sleep outside in the dead of winter. She wanted to undo everything. Erase the last two years, start again. But most importantly, she wanted to be in love with a man who was truly ready to give up the lifestyle he had been accustomed to for his entire adult life and choose her. 'No, no need.'

'Try not to snore.' He gave her that soft, shy smile again.

Lucie laughed. 'We both know it's you who sounds like a freight train.'

'Reckon we can sneak some pistachio cookies up here and have a midnight feast?'

'Yeah, I think so,' she agreed, letting the silence wash over them. 'Um . . . Brett, are we good? Can we just . . . get through the next few days? I know it won't be like before, but . . .'

Brett gave her his signature cheeky grin, but it didn't quite meet his eyes. 'We can sure as shit try, Sunny.'

There it was. The nickname was back, and she knew that regardless of how their big talk went, when she finally plucked up the courage to have it, they'd be okay.

*

Christmas Eve brought with it a mad dash to build the gingerbread house they'd collectively forgotten about. They'd spent the better part of the day before building the biggest snowman Belgium had ever seen, having snowball fights and baking an excessive number of cookies. Now, after a sugar crash, everyone was collapsed on the sofa watching *Elf* while Lucie and Brett took charge of salvaging the shambles of a gingerbread house structure.

They'd been getting along so well, if he didn't keep looking at her like he was moments away from kissing her, Lucie might have forgotten that they still had so much to discuss. That she still needed to confess her feelings. But every time she did remember, she struggled to rehearse what to say in her head. *How* to say it.

'Should we cover the roof in sprinkles?' Brett rattled the jar.

'Yeah, but the gold sparkly ones.'

'Ah, of course. I should've known you'd want this thing to look aesthetically pleasing,' he teased. 'What else, black window frames?'

'You know Jasmine is going to plaster this everywhere and give us the credit. I don't want to be associated with something that looks like a six-year-old made it.'

Brett tipped the sprinkles over the top of the house, taking zero care in where they ended up. If it were up to Lucie, she would've used tweezers to strategically place them. She was the reason they'd always won gingerbread house competitions in previous years. 'Ta da.'

He stepped back, looking mighty proud of his handi-work.

'Interesting approach . . .' she laughed when he feigned a pain in his chest. 'It's not looking too bad. We need jelly tots on it.'

'Uh . . .' Brett looked sheepish.

'Oh, for God's sake, you ate them, didn't you?' Lucie narrowed her eyes. 'I take my eyes off you for two min-utes, Anderson . . .' She licked icing off her finger.

'Mm.' He gave her a meaningful look and she felt her cheeks flush.

'Stop flirting! You're putting me off my hot chocolate!' Jasmine shouted from her spot amongst Ford, Marco and a mass of blankets. As soon as she said it, she turned and looked at them in horror. 'Sorry,' she grimaced.

It had been hard not to spill the details of their rela-tionship to Jasmine, since her aunt had been living with them for so long and the first week or so she had been an ugly, crying mess. But everyone was so used to them acting like a lovesick couple, it was no surprise that she had forgotten where they currently stood.

Lucie had been about to brush it off, but Brett's reaction came too quickly. He abandoned the frosting he'd been working on, putting the nozzle down on the counter and taking a hasty step back. 'I'm going to take Ford out for a walk round the property. But before I go, there's something for you upstairs. Top drawer.'

With Ford leaping up to join him, everyone pretended they were still watching the film, while Lucie's eyes darted to the stairs. What was he talking about? She was rifling through the bedside table before she knew it, moving his watches and cables aside in a rush. Then, tucked under a crime novel, she saw an envelope with her name on it. She sat on the bed, trying to prepare herself for whatever was inside, then gently tore it open.

To My Sunshine Girl,

You aren't supposed to be reading this. It was supposed to go up in flames like the other letters I wrote, but I knew it might come in handy. You know I'm no good with emotions. The past year has proved that. But I'm getting better, and more importantly, I'm healing. For myself, my family, my friends, my team. And for you. I don't think there was a single defining moment when I fell for you, Sunny. It was gradual. I fell a little bit harder with every touch, every glance, every laugh, every hug, every kiss. I know you think I'm not the man for you, but I know without a shadow of a doubt that you're the woman for me. And because of that, because I feel it to my core, I want to become that man. I don't want anyone else. I never really did, I used all those women to fill a void, but you were never one of them. You were and are my shining light, my sunshine, on every dark day. I know you wouldn't have crossed a line with me if you didn't feel something for me, whether you knew it straight away or not. That's just not you. And I promise you, I wasn't taking advantage of you. I was being reckless, because I know being with me scares you. Because you think I'm going to screw it up like I screw everything else up. But not this. If you think you might be able to trust that I mean what I say, if you believe in me and in us, please say it. You know you feel it, Sunny. Please. Let me love you.

Yours, Brett

When she finished, she looked up to see Faith standing in the doorway. 'You know, when I met Jules, I didn't know if I was ready. For him, for everything he had to offer. I didn't think our worlds would work as one, but I loved him. I realised very quickly that the universe put us on the same path for a reason. We may have started out on two very different ones, but we were always going to end up together, we just had to be brave and take a giant leap of faith. Now look at us, look at this. You and Brett have something special, Lucie.'

They watched him trek across the field at the bottom of Julien's property with the dog, leaving footprints in the blanket of snow that covered the ground. It was like something out of a film, and the man she loved with all her heart was the star of the show.

'I trust him. I trust him to love me and not fuck it up.'

'Luce, I say this with nothing but love.' Faith gently took the letter from Lucie's hand. 'Stop being an idiot and get out there.'

Lucie was down the stairs and out of the back door in a heartbeat, shoving her feet into Faith's wellington boots and running into the snowfall without a coat. It was just her and her reindeer-print Christmas pyjamas against the world. The closer she got to him, the more she struggled to see. The snow was getting heavier, and she wasn't equipped. She was going to come face to face with him looking like a drowned rat, but if she didn't say it now, the words would never come.

'Brett!' she called.

'Sunny, what the fuck are you doing?'

'Wait for me!' She jumped over the log that was in her way.

'I literally haven't moved.' Brett lifted his arms.

She finally made it to him, teeth chattering as she looked up at him in his bright red Revolution Racing beanie. Her star driver. 'What do you want out of life, Brett?'

'You. Just you.' He brushed her hair behind her ear, the snow melting and making it cling to her forehead. She had always planned on looking absolutely show-stopping when she did this, but to hell with it. This was the real them.

'I know, I know. But I need to know the rest, Anderson. Please.'

'A house, a garden, a vegetable patch. I want to spend my off time between races doing DIY projects and learning to cook, in one place I can call home. Whether it's Italy, America, Australia. I want dogs and chickens. We can discuss babies some other time, but for now? I want goats. And I want to be wherever *we* feel the most at home, Luce. I just want to be with you.'

'I love you. I should have said it in Tuscany. Hell, I should have said it in the Alps that first night. I should have said it when you finally broke up with Sienna, or after your first championship win. Your second. Third. My point is, I've been keeping it to myself for too long, and I'm tired. I'm tired of pretending like my entire world doesn't revolve around you. If I can't have you, I don't want anyone.'

'Fuck me, Sunny,' he laughed in disbelief. 'I love you, too, you wombat.'

'So, you didn't sleep with Sienna that night I came looking for you?'

'No, Lucie. It was never her I wanted.'

'Fuck.' She breathed out a shaky laugh. 'Now I feel even worse.'

'Don't. We were both hurting, we both made mistakes, we were both shit scared of ruining our friendship. But nothing has to change. That's what makes us so perfect. We just *fit*. Nobody on the planet will ever compare to you and the way I feel when I'm with you, and I don't want them to. You're it for me, Sunny. Always have been, always will be.'

'Can I finally kiss you without having my heart ripped out of my chest?' She smiled as his face inched closer and closer to hers.

'Promise me goats and you can have whatever you want.'

'You can have as many goats as we have space for.'

'On our own farm?' he murmured against her lips.

'Mmhmm.' And that was all she managed to get out before his lips were on hers, knocking the wind out of her. It was the best kiss yet. One that held the promises she'd been looking for all this time, a kiss that held their entire future within it.

Ten years. It had seemed like a lifetime while she was living it, but now it was just a drop in the ocean compared to all the years they had ahead of them. She could finally kiss him and touch him without consequences, without worrying that he would never feel the same or she would end up alone, watching him move on with someone who wasn't her. She could watch him get behind the wheel of his beloved racing car and proudly shout from the rooftops that the racing driver the rest of the motorsport world loved was *hers*.

Epilogue

Planning a wedding that the bride didn't know about was either the best idea or worst idea Brett had ever had. His first full season back on track had been smooth sailing, with Lucie holding his hand both physically and emotionally. Sure, he could have done it without her, but now he didn't have to. He would never have to be without her again.

Those few months between leaving Tuscany and seeing her at Christmas had been hell, but they had been a necessary hell. He had learned to live without her, and he'd continued his healing journey, but he would still always be the best version of himself with his sunshine girl by his side. Discovering that she loved him too had felt even better than the day Jasper told him he could come back to the garage three races earlier than planned.

He had grown to love therapy so much that his sessions still hadn't stopped almost two years after he'd started them. Never again would his friends be forced to pick up the pieces, pull him out of a downward spiral. He would never let himself get even close to being in that position. Finally, instead of being in retrograde, he was moving forward.

He had even started campaigning for better, wider

mental health awareness within the motorsport industry, using his own experience as the driving force behind his campaign. He'd been lucky to have the support of his team, and he knew a lot of other teams and sponsors wouldn't have been so open to working with him to turn a negative into a positive.

Today wasn't just about marrying his best friend. In classic Brett Anderson fashion, he had bought their dream home. A farmhouse in Malmedy, right down the road from the Jensen-Moretz property. Lucie had complained so many times over the years about wishing everyone could be in one place, and now they were well on their way. He only hoped Marco and Bea would one day follow suit.

Lucie was clueless. About all of it. They were straight off the back of another Revolution Racing championship win, and she had spent two weeks in London and Berlin with Esme and Bea, hosting the pop-up workshops they'd been planning for Girls Off Track. Faith was here, helping him with interior design in between looking after the twins. He was so proud of Lucie and the hard work she'd put in to securing the future of motorsport, this surprise was the least he could do. It was the bare minimum of what she deserved.

He hadn't got down on one knee and proposed, but she'd known marriage was on the horizon. She'd been sending him photos of rings for months, telling him how she wanted her flowers and what music she wanted to walk down the aisle to. What she didn't know was he had been making notes. She had so much stress on her shoulders, he wanted to take the additional stress of wedding planning away and do this for her. Having said that, he had only decided on a date three weeks ago and now, as she was ten minutes away, *he* was the stressed one.

'Brett, stop panicking,' Rosa patted his arm reassuringly. 'She'll love it.'

'What if she's late? The musician has another event straight after, I only managed to get him on board because I promised to fly him out to a race of his choice next season.' He checked his watch for the third time in ten minutes.

'You left Bea in charge of getting her here. Trust me, she will be on time.' Faith laughed at his furrowed brow. He'd be asking Bea for advice on Botox, at this rate.

'Twins are ready!' Julien walked outside with his youngest daughters, one in each arm, wearing matching pale purple dresses. Lucie's signature colour. There was lavender everywhere, but his favourite part was the arch they would stand under to exchange their vows.

'And Jazzy has the rings?' He whipped his head around until he spotted Jasmine walking out in her lilac satin gown. She was perhaps the most excited out of everyone.

'Yeah, hey, can we take the twins' shoes off? Emmie hates them.'

'Of course. You keep hold of them; I'll do it.'

Brett had been loving staying in permanent uncle-mode since they were born. He was rooting for Faith and Julien to have a boy one day, because he wanted a kid named after him, too. Anderson Mars was a great option to honour both him and Marco, and he'd been vocal about it, which earned him death glares from Faith, who had hated every moment of pregnancy.

Faith and Julien had gifted everyone with Emmeline Lucie and Margot Bea Jensen-Moretz, named after two of the most important women in their lives, and for now, they were enough. Brett and Lucie were warming to the idea of children of their own, although the adoption route was looking like the path they would choose, if they did decide to be parents.

The bonus of Brett and Lucie's new home being on a long gravel road was that it was quiet, and they could hear every time a car turned onto it. So, when they heard Lucie's Jeep coming, he dug deep for his courage and prepared himself for the biggest question of his life.

'Brett, have you got the ring?' Esme whispered.

'Yep.' He nodded and squeezed his hand around the black velvet box.

If he was confident in anything, it was that he'd got this part right. He didn't know much about rings, but it was amethyst and gold and everything she said she wanted. He'd consulted her sisters, her mum and her best friends and between them, they'd had one custom designed for her. This entire wedding was a joint effort.

'It's time, Anderson.' Marco clapped him on the shoulder in the exact same way he did before every race, and Brett stepped forward.

Lucie climbed out of the car, Bea following with a Cheshire-Cat grin on her face, and stopped in her tracks at the sight of Brett standing on the grass. Then she looked up at the house behind him, and all their siblings and closest friends, and burst into tears.

'What are you doing?' she laughed through the waterworks and stepped closer to him.

He opened the ring box, admiring the awe in her expression as she looked between him and the newest addition to her jewellery collection. 'Will you marry me, Sunny?'

'Yes.' Lucie kissed him, not a second of hesitation in her voice.

Brett broke the kiss and whispered, 'Today?'

'What? What do you mean?'

'Marry me. Today. Right here, in our backyard.'

'This is ours?' she gasped, as if the wedding hadn't been enough of a shock.

'Figured we should start married life with a bang,' he shrugged. 'It's fully decorated, too. You've got your flamingo wallpaper in the downstairs bathroom.'

'Brett Anderson, you are insane, and I love you for it.'

'Exactly, so go and get dressed and get your ass back out here. The girls will take care of you.' He placed the ring on her finger. 'Hurry up, the violinist has places to be.' He said the last part quietly, but she ruined it by roaring with laughter.

Lucie walked out of their back door in a short, white satin dress paired with white cowboy boots. It was bordering on cheesy, but it was without a doubt everything she had ever dreamed of. She had never wanted a super serious wedding; she wanted hers to be fun and full of laughter, the kind of wedding where everyone could let loose and half of it couldn't be posted on social media. A classic, backyard country wedding.

The aisle was lined with wooden chairs, all occupied by their nearest and dearest. Even Ford the Husky had a spot, proudly showing off his purple bow tie. Brett had selected part of the property which was dotted with fir trees, and hung strings of polaroids and fairy lights, each photo a black and white print of the two of them over the last twelve years. It was magical. Plucked straight from her inspiration board.

Brett stood waiting under the arch, Jasper with him as their celebrant, and when Lucie's dad took her arm in his, the violinist began playing her favourite country song. She had half-expected Gabriel to be dressed as Elvis, but instead he wore a purple suit and stood next to her mum, bursting with excitement that Lucie's mother was Hollywood B-lister Rosa Clemente.

'You look beautiful, *amore mio*,' Mateo murmured.

'Thanks, Dad. And thank you for making the journey.'

'We'd travel the world for you kids. This is your home now, I'm just glad you found it.'

'Mr C,' Brett grinned when they reached him. 'Luce.'

'I would hand her over to you, Brett, but I think my Lucie has been *your* Lucie for a long time already. There's no passing the baton here. Just take as good care of her as you always have.' Mateo shook Brett's hand and kissed Lucie on the cheek before joining the rest of the Carolan and Anderson clan.

'By the way, if you hear any noises . . . it's the goats.' Brett quickly glanced behind them.

'You got them without me?' Lucie peered over his shoulder and gushed at the six mini goats he had adopted while she'd been away.

'I wanted them to be here to welcome you home.'

'I love them. And you.'

Brett took her hands in his. 'You ready, Sunny?'

'Have been for twelve years, sweetheart.'

And as they exchanged vows full of the promises they'd made over the course of their friendship, both the spoken and unspoken ones, Lucie felt her entire world fall into place, now the proud owner of a gold wedding band that had 'my sunshine girl' engraved on the inside.

It sat beautifully next to her new purple gemstone, symbolising that she may be his sunshine, but Brett Anderson was, and always had been, her rock.

He just wanted a decent book to read ...

Not too much to ask, is it? It was in 1935 when Allen Lane, Managing Director of Bodley Head Publishers, stood on a platform at Exeter railway station looking for something good to read on his journey back to London. His choice was limited to popular magazines and poor-quality paperbacks – the same choice faced every day by the vast majority of readers, few of whom could afford hardbacks. Lane's disappointment and subsequent anger at the range of books generally available led him to found a company – and change the world.

'We believed in the existence in this country of a vast reading public for intelligent books at a low price, and staked everything on it'
Sir Allen Lane, 1902–1970, founder of Penguin Books

The quality paperback had arrived – and not just in bookshops. Lane was adamant that his Penguins should appear in chain stores and tobacconists, and should cost no more than a packet of cigarettes.

Reading habits (and cigarette prices) have changed since 1935, but Penguin still believes in publishing the best books for everybody to enjoy. We still believe that good design costs no more than bad design, and we still believe that quality books published passionately and responsibly make the world a better place.

So wherever you see the little bird – whether it's on a piece of prize-winning literary fiction or a celebrity autobiography, political tour de force or historical masterpiece, a serial-killer thriller, reference book, world classic or a piece of pure escapism – you can bet that it represents the very best that the genre has to offer.

Whatever you like to read – trust Penguin.